THE MIND'S EYE

THE MIND'S EYE

a novel

Alan Krohn

To order additional copies of this book, contact:
Xlibris Corporation
1-888-795-4274
www.Xlibris.com
Orders@Xlibris.com
30051

ACKNOWLEDGEMENTS

I f this tale succeeds, it is because I have managed to depict with some degree of accuracy what happens between a psychoanalyst and a patient. Many people have helped me to understand this complex process. There are my psychoanalytic teachers, most notably Drs Dale Boesky, Alexander Grinstein, Henry Krystal, Ira Miller, Frank Parcells, George Richardson and my own analyst, Dr. Humberto Nagera. As grateful as I am to all of them, I am even more to the patients I have treated.

I would like to thank those who aided me in the writing of this book. Thanks to my girlfriend, Colleen Flynn, for tolerating my self-absorption during its writing and for her critiques along the way, especially her ear for clichés and suggestions on how to correct them. I would like to thank my daughter, Tanya Krohn, who worked energetically and tirelessly over several years on the project. She provided creative advice, stylistic guidance, copy editing, and most of all encouragement, through numerous drafts. Thanks to my son, David Pekarek Krohn, for some key ideas about plot and character.

Readers at various stages constructively criticized drafts of the book: Pam Bowers and Tom Hiller, Kathleen Funkey, Bridgett Karr, Jamie Pekarek Krohn, Daniel and George Kuper, Allie Mackay, Colette Marine, and John and Deborah Silak. Hearing that the story had engaged them was enormously motivating.

I would like to thank my mother, Sylvia Krohn, and my late father, Harry Krohn, who have over the years encouraged my development as a psychoanalyst and as a writer.

When I set myself the task of bringing
to light what human beings keep hidden
within them, . . . I thought the task
was a harder one than it really is. He that has
eyes to see and ears to hear may convince himself
that no mortal can keep a secret. If his lips
are silent, he chatters with his finger-tips;
betrayal oozes out of him at every pore.

Sigmund Freud

I n the dream, the same dream, his only dream, he was the most awake. And alive.

I smell and taste your skin. I am molded to your surface. Every curve and contour of my body finds its perfect correspondence on yours. Heat radiates out of you, mother, and into me. I find firmness, now softness, now the secure hardness of your nipple. My mouth envelops it, you in me, me in you. There is no boundary, no inner me or outer you. Your heat, now liquid, spreads through me, through us. The rhythm of your heart beats into me. On you, in you, of you. I am deeply satisfied.

Suddenly your skin turns cold. Your perfect terrain becomes marblehard and unyielding. Your surface cracks with edges that scratch and cut. Everything is boundary now, all impenetrable. I am filled with pain at the horrific distinction between you and me. You have taken your heat that sustains my life and hidden it somewhere unreachable inside you. I know you are gone, mother, and I am starving for everything.

He struggled to pull the dream into his waking life and hold it there. In the dream he could escape the emotional numbness, the deadness, that had gripped him for years. The struggle always failed as the dream was made only of fragments of smells, sounds, tastes, skin against skin. These wordless, limitless, unfiltered sensations of the earliest months of life were overwhelmingly present in the dream, but upon awakening, slipped away. All gone except for dim mental afterimages that settled in a remote, archaic place in his mind.

The pain gathered in his chest and screamed through his body. He took a handful of drugs, some legal, others not. Until they eased the pain, he lay motionless on the floor, drawing slow, shallow breaths and thinking of the plan. Like the dream, the plan breathed some life into him. He rolled it around in his mind, first seeing it speed from start to finish, then lingering on his favorite parts, trying in his imagination to taste the suffering he would be inflicting. Some he would witness, some he would never live to see. What he lived for now was to finish the plan and carry it out. He was way beyond fear of his inevitable, premature death.

As the light faded in the winter evening, the drugs began to take effect and the pain receded enough for him to struggle to his feet and make his way to his desk. He clicked on the lamp, and the desktop, covered with psychology books, lit up like a stage. When he had settled himself, he looked out at geese and ducks on the far bank of the frozen river and then, beyond it, at a cross country skier gliding on the freshly fallen snow and disappearing into the woods below the huge University Hospital complex. He envied the easy, fluid energy that propelled the skier along.

He had just finished his second careful reading of Freud's *Interpretation of Dreams*, and pushing the book to the edge of his desk stage, he began to write.

CHAPTER ONE

Dr. Ivan Weiss looked down from his seventeenth floor office at students trudging through the snow to their classes. Though it was midwinter in Ann Arbor, when the days are short and everything is indistinguishably gray, he felt generally satisfied with things. He had been promoted a month before to Director of the University of Michigan Psychology Clinic, his book *Early Childhood Loss and the Adult Criminal Mind* had been accepted for publication, and he was looking forward to the most extravagant vacation he and his wife, Dana, had ever taken, a luxury cruise in the eastern Mediterranean and Black Sea. Even the one cloud that had hung over the family for almost a year, his daughter's rape, seemed to be lifting.

He was pleased, too, to be expecting a new patient, Adam Stone, who he hoped would fill a few open hours in his private practice. He liked having some open time, but also was anxious to fill his hours. His friend Jake, another psychoanalyst, had once said to him, "In private practice you're either overworked or you're worried."

A few blocks from his office, the bell tower on central campus sounded quarter past the hour. As the streets below cleared of all but a few stragglers hurrying to their classes, Weiss heard the closing of his waiting room door. Right on time for the first session, a good sign.

From the mild and cautious tone of the new patient's voice on the phone when he had called for an appointment, Weiss had pictured someone small and slight. When he entered the waiting room, he was surprised to be looking up at a tall, slim man with thick dark hair, yet skin so fair as to appear translucent. He seemed to fill up the small waiting room. Just as striking as his height and pale skin were his eyes. They were blue, but so dark that they seemed to be just pupils that had completely dilated, crowding out his irises. And his eyes seemed to have no depth, as if they were painted on his pale face. Despite this, Weiss sensed something inviting and welcoming about him.

Weiss introduced himself and ushered the new patient down the short hallway into the consulting room. The moment the patient crossed the threshold, he stopped and examined his new surroundings. Most patients at this point look around the room, or to Weiss, to decide where to sit. This patient instead walked to the window which ran the length of the room.

"Quite a view," he said, his face almost touching the glass, "like a picture of the world from a satellite. That's a long way down."

During his training one of Weiss' teachers had spent weeks in a seminar analyzing what can be learned from the first moments of contact with a patient. You might think that because the patient doesn't know you, he will be more closed or guarded at first, his teacher had said, but it often works precisely the other way. Being a stranger, you're safer to talk to. Also, the patient doesn't yet know that you will be able to discover some of his more painful secrets.

So what do I know so far, Weiss asked himself, as he motioned the patient to the chair. Rather than simply walking in and sitting down, he first carefully scanned the office. Wary, suspicious. He's no sooner in the office than his focus is outside it, on the view. And the vista looks to him like a picture of the world from a satellite. Is he a man who is trying to get the big picture, to orient himself?

As soon as they were both seated, the patient said, "I'm Adam Stone. I'm sorry, I guess I told you that on the phone." Already apologizing, thought Weiss.

"What I would suggest," Weiss said, in his standard opening of the first interview with a new patient, "is for us to meet for a few sessions. You can tell me what brings you to see me. At the same time you'll have a chance to look me over. Then we can make some decision about what to do. So, why don't you start anywhere . . ." Weiss invited.

The patient fell silent and turned to the window, seemingly searching for something on the horizon. He then fixed his unsettling eyes on Weiss and began.

Though Weiss had done hundreds of evaluations, there was still an excitement in exploring the hidden regions of someone's life, in discovering the most personal, private areas, hidden even from the patient himself. Some of the student therapists he had taught were not excited about this kind of exploration. They might be smart, they might know the theory, but without this curiosity, this professional nosiness, they never went far. You have to be a voyeur at heart, Weiss knew, to be good.

"It's hard to know where to start. I guess my problems, my job problems at least, started a couple of years ago, when I was in Arizona. This was strange, because this was my dream job, assistant to the Director of a major Hopi dig near Winslow."

"You're an archeologist?"

"Sorry, sorry, I'm getting ahead of myself," Apologizing again. "I guess I should back up. I came here this past September from California. I received my Ph.D. in anthropology from UCLA a couple of months before that. My area is Native American archeology. While I was in grad school, I took a leave to work on this dig. It was well funded so we could take our time and do a careful job. There were some very talented and experienced people working on it. Most of all I was excited to be working with the Director, David Lighthorse. He's a senior person, a Hopi himself, highly respected in the archeological community. I really wanted to work with him. It was a great opportunity."

He paused and shifted his body toward the window and seemed again to be searching for something far off. Snow had begun to fall, and the window vibrated from the wind. With the patient's stare off him, Weiss felt more comfortable looking at his new patient. He was dressed in a pinstriped shirt, striped tie, blue blazer, neat black jeans and Nikes, collegiate, but a little dated, more 80's than late 90's. Weiss mused about his age. He could be anywhere from late 20's to mid 30's, but Weiss thought him to be at the younger end of the range.

"As soon as I started on the dig, I began to have disturbing dreams. I'd wake up soaked with sweat, shaking. My jaw would be sore from having clenched my teeth all night."

"It sounds like you were terrified."

"I was."

"Can you tell me one of the dreams?" Weiss asked.

"Sure. This one I remember well . . . I'm climbing up a steep trail. First I'm with a group, I think with people on the dig, but one by one the others get tired and drop away. I feel great that I'm the only one able to continue on. When I get to the end of the trail, I'm on a high mesa looking out at mountains in the distance. The sun has just set. I can't take my eyes off the sky and mountains, you know, the amazing colors you see in the southwest just after the sun goes down."

The patient fell silent, and Weiss thought this was the end of the dream.

"Seems like an inviting scene," said Weiss.

"That's only the first part of the dream. It's the second part that's tough." He cupped one hand in the other on his lap and looked down at both.

"For a little while I feel satisfied, pleased that I've made the climb, enjoying the view. But then everything changes. I've had the same kind of dream so many times that I know in the dream what's coming, and I even try to stop it, but I can't. The scene gets dark, but there are no clouds. Then I see a man. This is the really disturbing part – he has only one arm. Where the other arm should be there are only bloody shreds of flesh hanging. He has a knife, and I know I'm in real danger. He starts to come toward me, and then I wake up, shaken and scared."

"Did you ever have dreams like this before the dig?"

"I think I said I didn't," the patient shot back, with a flash of annoyance at Weiss. He squeezed his eyes closed for a moment and was silent for a while. He again scanned the office.

"You have a nice office here, light, open. I like that plaque, too," the patient said about a bas relief of the Trojan horse on the analyst's desk. He lets me see a hint of anger at me, Weiss thought, and immediately compliments my office and what I have in it, trying to turn the feeling into its opposite. Wondering what Stone might be trying to avoid, Weiss thought of the raw aggression of the man with the bloody, ripped off arm in the patient's dream.

"So, getting back to the problems on the dig. At first I got along very well with David, the Director. He was impressed with some hunches I had about digging sites and some theories I had about some of the finds. I was on my way to becoming his protégé. He made jokes about giving me an Indian name and adopting me. He put me in charge of a team, ahead of others who had been there longer. I know they were jealous. I had never worked so independently before, and I loved it. He let me mark off sections to work, then checked in with me in the middle of the day. We would discuss strategies for unearthing artifacts, and then in the evening we'd go into Winslow or up to Flagstaff, have a drink, and discuss our findings, theories, everything. He told me many times what a promising future I had.

"Then it all changed. Or to put it right, I changed. I became argumentative about everything. It didn't happen all at once. At first, I'd bring up things I disagreed with him about in the spirit of lively academic discussion, playing the devil's advocate. He told me he appreciated that I was so comfortable raising contradictory evidence and putting it on the table. But gradually it got worse. Much worse. Whatever he'd say, I was compelled to shoot down. I just couldn't control myself. And I'd make it personal. Insults seemed to spill out of my mouth, even when I didn't believe them. One day I even found myself talking in an offhand way about removing remains from burial sites, which I knew he was very sensitive about. Then I began to overstep my authority on the dig itself. He would tell me to go to a certain point and report to him before going on. I'd either forget or just ignore what he had said.

"I also began making a lot of mistakes on the site. We were excavating household implements in this thirteenth century pueblo, whole rooms full of them, great finds. These are, of course, extremely fragile. I blundered in, didn't supervise the team well, and one time actually dropped and damaged a cutting tool, probably the best find of that month. He became so furious with me that he dressed me down in front of the team and replaced me on the spot with an obnoxious grad student he knew I hated. I managed to finish out my work there, but by the end I was very close to being fired."

"You seem to realize you were contributing to your problems."

"More than contributing, I was causing them."

"Do you know why you'd do this?"

Adam shrugged at first but then said, "I know I was working hard to provoke him, but I have no idea why."

Weiss collected his impressions as he listened. Stone comes with assets necessary to begin working on his problems: he sees the problems as coming from within himself, can see a pattern in his own behavior, and seems interested in looking at himself. His educational achievements and capacity for introspection both revealed his intelligence. Having worked for a while successfully on the dig indicated his capacity to apply himself to actual challenges in his field. But as ambitious and competent as he seems on the surface, thought Weiss, he seems to have a powerful need to defeat himself, to stop himself dead in his tracks.

His recurrent dream told the same story. He climbs to the top, but then is met by the man with the ripped off arm who is out to knife him. Is he worried that if he goes too far, or gets too good, that someone will maim or kill him?

And what of his relationship with the director of the dig? At first he does well and is being groomed to move up. Then he feels compelled to be hostile to his boss and at the same time hurtful to himself. Does success bring up in him feelings of power, power that contains raw aggression, power he would love to exert over someone? While Weiss considered this, the patient went on.

"There's another reason I came to see you. Women. My relationships never work out."

"What happens?"

"I get quickly involved, feel all this love or lust for the woman, but then things get really bad, really fast." He adjusted his tall frame in the chair and straightened the sleeves of his blazer. "I know when this problem started." He told of a relationship with an intelligent, quirky girl named Carol he had met at a student protest in his sophomore year of college.

"She was rebellious to the core. Whatever was the usual way of doing things, she'd do the opposite. Like once when a couple we knew complained that rain had ruined their plans for a barbecue, Carol looked straight at them and said that rain was absolutely the best thing for a barbecue. 'The wetter, the better.' A week later, it was pouring out, she found me in the library and literally dragged me out, telling me that she was having a barbecue right now. We can't wait, she said, it might stop raining. She'd set a formal table in her backyard, complete with fancy table cloth, silver, and hurricane lamps she'd found somewhere, and six of our friends as guests. She held her wine glass high over her head and made this toast, 'Food courtesy of Carol, drink provided by the gods.' I'd never met anyone like her." He had not smiled so far during the interview, indeed his face had been fixed and rigid, but now something around his eyes relaxed, and Weiss could imagine him smiling. This woman had meant something to him.

"It became a romance," Adam went on, 'romance' striking Weiss as formal and stilted, particularly from a young man. Is this his way of avoiding something painful?

"Being a free spirit had, of course, a big downside. Being with only one man seemed to her a mindlessly conventional thing to do, and she kept bringing up our having an open relationship. She knew I didn't want this, and so she began seeing another guy behind my back." He stopped, tilted his head up, and talked to the ceiling.

"I came over one afternoon, unexpectedly, and found them together. They weren't in bed. If they had been, I'd probably be in even worse shape. But I knew they'd had sex, and she never denied it. I seem drawn to the interesting ones, the ones hard to get, and surprise, surprise, I never get them."

"Maybe not just hard to get, but, like Carol, unattainable."

"Exactly, unattainable, you're right, that's it exactly." He is making quite a show of agreeing with me, thought Weiss.

"So there were others like that?"

"Yeah, I did this in a big way with another woman, and it almost cost me my life. I might be exaggerating, but I don't think so. I'd been working on a summer fellowship in Teotihuacan, about an hour from Mexico City. It was my first dig. I was working under Gon . . . uh . . . a Mexican archeologist."

"You don't want to say his name?"

"I definitely won't tell you his last name, and just then I thought it wasn't such a good idea even to tell you his first."

"Why's that?"

"I'm still scared of him." Stone drew a long, anxious breath. "I wasn't there long when he approached me about smuggling artifacts he'd taken from the site. A dealer in Houston was paying big money for them. We were excavating a palace, so you can imagine the kind of stuff we were finding. He said it was easier for an American than a Mexican to get through. We'd split the money. He assured me he had other Americans doing this over several years and no one had ever gotten caught. He was into this on a pretty big scale. I somehow talked my way out of doing this without alienating him . . . I'm getting to the woman, don't worry." He imagines me as demanding and impatient, thought Weiss.

"Gonzalo, that was his name, had a young wife, Maria. He was middle aged, somewhere in his late fifties, and she was in her thirties. She had a job in Mexico City and would come out to the site on the weekends. He was a coarse and crude guy, and she was really elegant, refined. And beautiful. I was taken with her the moment I met her. Sexuality seemed to seep out of her." As the sky began to clear, sunlight streamed into the office, throwing into relief the patient's angular features and bringing color to his pale skin. Weiss could see how handsome he was and could imagine how attractive he could be to women.

"Not long after we met, she approached me about helping her improve her English. So I tutored her, and it soon developed into an affair. I would meet her during the week at their apartment in Mexico City. I took my time off in the middle of the week which was fine with everybody, because I'd work the weekends when they wanted to be off. He was out of her life during the week, and I was in it. It seemed like the perfect arrangement, and for a while it was. Until he came back into the city unexpectedly, caught us in bed, and was ready to kill me. I mean *really* kill me. As soon as he found us, he ran from the bedroom, and she screamed that he was going for a gun. We ran, half dressed, from the place as he was loading it."

"Why'd you decide, even though he usually didn't come back during the week, to see her in their apartment? And, did you say, their apartment was just an hour's drive from the site?"

"Yeah, about an hour. Good question, very good question, it was really stupid."

"But you're obviously not a stupid man."

"I must have wanted to get caught. I've thought about this and that's the only explanation." What was in it for him, wondered Weiss, to try to get caught? Is this an expression of guilt, a need to be punished, or even killed? Did he want to unconsciously show off to this older man?

"Needless to say, that was it for the job, which was under the circumstances, a very modest loss. I learned later, that Gonzalo had ties to organized crime. He could have easily taken out a contract to have me killed. For all I know he did."

"We've just met, so I don't know what kind of judge of people you are, but don't you think just based on this man's smuggling artifacts on a big scale, you would have had reason to suspect he was involved with organized crime and could be dangerous?"

"I didn't see it at the time." He needed not to see who Gonzalo was and what he was doing. If he had let himself keep his eyes open, he would never have been able to play out this whole, dangerous fantasy, thought Weiss.

"You put yourself at enormous risk, that's very clear, but was it possible she might have left him?"

"No, she was unattainable too. I remember being in bed with her in their apartment in Mexico City just before we made love for the first time. She told me she was crazy about me, but was too scared of her husband to ever leave him. So I knew right off it wasn't going anywhere."

The bell tower sounded the hour, Weiss told the patient they would need to stop, and they arranged a time for the next session.

As Weiss made process notes, a detailed account of what had happened during the session, he thought about the patient's involvements. A triangle and secret liaison in both. He finds Carol with another man, and Gonzalo catches him with Maria.

Triangles, stealing the woman from the older man, battling with the older boss on the dig, it all had an unmistakably oedipal ring to Weiss. Though he had heard intelligent people outside his field mock psychoanalysis for doing nothing but discovering that "you want to have sex with your mother," Weiss took the oedipus complex very seriously.

When the childhood wish to depose and destroy the same sex parent in order to exclusively possess the opposite sex one goes unresolved, it can wreak havoc on people's lives. Weiss had often seen men with oedipal problems believe that all desirable women belong to some powerful father figure who stands in the way and who must be defeated to get to the woman. As the woman unconsciously represents the mother, to be involved with her means breaking the oldest rule, the incest taboo, filling the man with guilt, fear, and self-loathing. Often the relationship then cannot be allowed to flourish or even continue. Weiss had seen the identical struggle in reverse in many women.

Weiss was already optimistic about helping the patient. Stone's problems were oedipal, very treatable by psychoanalysis, and he was self reflective. He was aware that he played a part in his problems and was, beyond that, already working on understanding his tendency to subvert his career and to choose unattainable women.

As he thought about the patient, Weiss was reminded of a time in his early twenties when the only women he found himself interested in were married. A few years later he explored this in his analysis. "The only ones you wanted were already taken," his analyst had observed. "Just like your first love, your mother, the one you wanted most, was the only one you were forbidden to have. This, Dr. Weiss, is the core tragedy for every little boy." A tragedy, he learned later in his analysis, compounded for him by his mother's death and the puzzling circumstances surrounding it. He envisioned his mother's face and a warmth spread through him. Then, thinking of her last day, her face faded and he felt terribly alone. He worked to shake off the awful feeling, as he layered on clothes for his noon run.

CHAPTER TWO

S onya Weiss awoke with the now familiar panic. She was again helpless in his criminal embrace. It was all completely static, like stop action photos of athletes, frozen, quiet. That part completely different from the frenzied speed with which it had actually happened. The rest was exactly the same. The pressure of his arms from behind her, the edge of the knife tugging at the skin of her neck. And then from behind he was suddenly inside her.

She never saw him. He had spoken a few menacing words, but she could let herself remember none of them, only the breathless urgency of his voice. She wondered if she put herself through this panic to try to identify him, as if from her body memories she might be able to find some clues to who he was. Not knowing anything about him, he could be any man. No one was excluded. She felt if she knew anything at all about him, she could be vigilant and careful about certain men and comfortable with the rest. This held the promise of some safety.

She had learned that getting into the routine of her day was the best way to push the memories and panic to the side. They were never really gone, just edged a little over from the center of her life. Get quickly out of bed, turn on the TV, make tea, shower. Just keep moving. As she dried herself after her shower, combed out her hair and put on her makeup, the feelings eased. Just having these feelings intrude was bad enough, but worse was what they had done to her sense of herself. She had always thought of herself as confident, even headstrong, but now she planned things more to maneuver around real or imagined dangers than to go after what she wanted. It felt foreign to see herself as a cautious or fearful person, and she didn't like it. She wanted her old self back.

Home for six months from New York where she had been working as an interior decorator and where she had been raped, she was coming to feel some relief and security being near her parents and back among the familiar surroundings of Ann Arbor. She felt she was beginning to put the rape behind her and was starting to heal. She was comfortable enough to even date again. Thinking about the man she was seeing, Jerry, of his way of making little jokes about himself, calmed her a little.

Though they had been going out for only a month, she felt very secure with him, the first man she had felt that way with since the rape.

As she was drinking her tea and trying to decide what to wear, the phone rang, and she monitored the message on her answering machine. It was the third call in two days from Eric Hanson, who Sonya had had a stormy, month long relationship with six years before. Eric was the son of her father's closest friend, Jake. The moment she heard the insistent, presumptuous tone of his voice, she felt her whole body clench as it had just after the rape. His calls were undoing the fragile sense of security she had been working so hard to build.

"I simply don't understand, Sonya, why you don't return my calls. You're being incredibly rude. You know, Sonya, people do change. I know I have. I'm ready to move to the next level with you, but we have to iron a few things out. I am sure it's a good idea for us to go out. And even if you don't, I do. I know I would be good for you." He talked as if they had just seen each other, as if there was something ongoing between them. I guess, she thought, in his mind, there still is.

Her thoughts returned to the summer before she left for college when she had fallen so hard for him. Good looking, bright, with a rebellious spirit, he seemed to have constructed strong, definite opinions on everything. He was also extremely attentive to her, calling her several times a day and buying her expensive gifts which she found later he was able to afford by selling drugs. Soon his attentiveness revealed itself to be smothering and possessive. He insisted on her reporting to him her every move, where she went, who she talked to. When she angrily refused, he demanded she apologize for being angry and for hurting him by not "sharing" the details of her day with him. When she then told him it was over, he showered her with even more gifts and called constantly. Only when she told him that he was harassing her and threatened to go to the police, did he stop.

She now stood before the mirror in her third outfit, trying to distract herself from the call from Eric. The suit, even with the ruffled blouse, made her look too much like a banker, and the brown, heavy wool dress was even more staid, verging on the somber. Time was running short before her appointment, and her taupe dress, while a little dressy, with a belt and scarf, would have to do. She remembered the woman she worked under in New York telling her that the first sample your client will have of your work is you. Your clothes, their quality and appropriateness, are examples of your work, especially with women clients. Also, she hastened to add before Sonya went out on her first job, when it comes to women, remember, dress as if you were a guest at a wedding, you don't want to outshine the bride or the mothers. If your woman client feels you look too good, she will say, oh, what a nice outfit, but then every design suggestion you make will not be quite right, that's if you even get the job at all.

Not a problem with this outfit, it was professional, but not showy. And anyway the client is a man. The outfit would be perfect with the blue shoes that pick up the very same shade in the scarf, but the Ann Arbor slush had to be considered, and she didn't want to change her footwear at the client's house. She rummaged through her closet until she found her brown equestrian style, lace-up boots, a gift from her mother, put them on, made a final mirror check, grabbed her overcoat, sample books, and briefcase and rushed out.

After months waiting for business, she had a potential client. He had called a few days before, had just relocated to Ann Arbor, and bought a house he wanted decorated. He had explained that he was so caught up with the usual moving in chores, utilities, phone, opening a bank account, that it would have be a few days before they could meet. He was also getting settled in his job and had, in the past few days, "meetings up the wazoo." He was anxious to get the decorating started, he went on, because he's the kind of person who never really feels rooted until he is in a place furnished just right for him. She was pleased that he was so eager and ready.

She drove from her downtown apartment over the Broadway bridge to Wall Street near the river. She thought of the irony that the streets in this area of town were all named sometime in the nineteenth century after streets in downtown New York City, Wall, Broadway, Maiden Lane. Hard to get away from the Big Apple. His house, stucco, neo-classical with small decorative white columns, was across the street from two new University Hospital buildings, the Kellogg Eye Center and Turner Geriatric Center. It seemed an odd location, but the house itself sat in the middle of a large lot with mature trees, oaks or maples, she couldn't tell without the leaves, and somehow stood up well to the imposing University buildings across the street. Though the trim could have used a coat of paint, the outside looked to be in fairly good repair.

He greeted her at the door as she came up the walkway.

"Hi, I'm Nick Streeter," he said in a light and airy voice, "I saw you pull up." He was dressed in khakis and a sweater. He looked familiar. Either he resembled someone she knew, or maybe she had seen him on the street. He offered to make coffee which she declined. I'm nervous enough, she thought.

He showed her around the mostly empty house. A long, narrow living room, a formal dining room with charming built in china cabinets, a nice touch, and a kitchen in terrible condition. Remodeling this has to be high on his list. As she followed him upstairs, to her surprise, his pace slowed, and she thought his breathing sounded labored. When they reached the landing between floors, he stopped for a moment and anticipated her question.

"I have asthma. It's been acting up recently, always does when I'm under stress. The move, new job, guess it's all getting to me." He showed her the three bedrooms, explaining his plan to use the master bedroom as his office, another bedroom as a guest room, and the smallest room, because of its great view of the river, as his bedroom. This room was the only one with much furniture, a neatly made double bed, dresser, bookcases, and a desk under a window looking out on the river, the soccer fields in Fuller Park, and a wooded area beyond it. She admired the view and noticed, as she did so, under some legal pads on the far side of the desk, what looked like the light green covers of books she had seen throughout her childhood: the Standard Edition of Freud's works. Without knowing why she was being surreptitious, she walked around to the other end of the desk, as if she were trying to see more of the view from the window, and nudged the pad aside.

"You curious about my books?" he asked, startling her.

"I'm really sorry, I shouldn't have done that. I saw the book cover, and it looked familiar. My curiosity sometimes has a way of getting the better of me."

"That's alright, don't worry about it. You've read some Freud?"

"A little. My father is a psychoanalyst, and the Standard Edition was like the Bible in our house. When I was little I saw more of these books than I did of my dad." She felt self conscious about the personal turn the conversation had taken. Yet she also felt comfortable with this man. She knew her interest in him was already beyond professional.

"Are you a psychologist?" she asked.

"No. Well, sort of. I don't work with patients. I'm trained as an historian, but my field is the history of child abuse, so I've studied child psychology and theories connected with childhood trauma. My own particular field of interest is the way child abuse was regarded in the late nineteenth century, during the Victorian era." This is not helping, she thought, he's getting even more interesting. She was tempted to ask him more about himself and even had the excuse that getting to know a client well helps you know what kind of world to create in his home.

She compared him to Jerry. She loved the feeling of being protected by Jerry, safe within his strength. She was taken, too, by Jerry's athletic prowess, which reminded her of her awe of high school athletes she had gone out with. They had seemed so refreshingly different from her intellectual family. But they had turned out often to be limited and dull.

She didn't know Jerry that well yet, but she was concerned that he, like the high school jocks, was not interested in anything "deep." Sonya had tried to talk to Jerry about people reinventing themselves as they go through life. She was fascinated by this and wondered if they really become different or are just fooling themselves. Another time she asked him what he thought it would be like to be imprisoned for decades like Nelson Mandela. "Probably lonely," he had said, and she had laughed, but had felt frustrated that he was not very interested in talking further about it. Would anything be worth sacrificing so much for? Was there anything Jerry would do that for? He had certainly done his best to talk about these things, but had not engaged naturally with any of them.

This man, Nick, was different. I've just met him, and already it seems natural to tell him that I'd felt, as a child, pushed aside by my father's career. She caught herself imagining a relationship with him. Cool your jets, Sonya, as her mother would say, you've known him for ten minutes, he's a client, or could be if you don't mess it up with all of this fantasizing. She forced herself to get down to business.

They returned to the living room, and he laid out his vision for his house. As he did, in spite of herself, she listened carefully for any mention of a wife or girlfriend whose input he might want to include in decorating decisions. As they worked together on floor plans for the main floor and went through a few furniture catalogues, to her delight, she didn't hear any.

CHAPTER THREE

U nless they both agreed the streets were treacherously icy, Ivan and Jake Hanson, his psychoanalytic colleague and close friend, set out every noon from the front of Tower Plaza, where both had their private offices, for their daily run. On borderline icy days one would invariably tell the other that this running thing didn't have to be compulsive, that they should do it only if they were enjoying it, and the other would then chide his wimpiness, and they would set off. Though both were private people, they each considered the other to be his closest friend. Being friends for ten years had been a challenge, considering how closely they worked together and how different their temperaments were. Weiss was reserved and contemplative, Jewish, the son of holocaust survivors, while Hanson was at heart an Iowa farm boy, inclined toward action, intolerant of indecisiveness in people. Jake's readiness to take action was in many ways a strength, but when it grew out of impatience, it had led him to be seen as impulsive and had created difficulties for him in his career. Most recently, following the death of the Director of the University Psychology Clinic, where they both worked as teaching faculty, the search committee's concern about Hanson's "unpredictability and tendency to shoot from the hip," as the report had put it, led them unanimously to appoint Weiss Director, in spite of Hanson's obvious talents as a clinician and teacher.

Outside of work they had been through a lot together, mostly crises in Jake's life, his heart attack five years earlier, his stormy marriage and stormier divorce, and his difficulties with his son Eric, who seemed continually to leave disaster in his wake. Eric had become heavily involved with drugs, dropped out of high school, and ended up several times in court.

Eric's interest in Ivan's daughter had tested Ivan's relationship with Jake. Sonya had gone out with Eric for a month just before she left for college. In addition to being concerned about Eric's drug use, Ivan and his wife were deeply troubled by the changes they saw in their daughter. She spoke of Eric with nothing short of awe and at the same time was clearly frightened of him. Ivan's efforts to caution her about Eric were met with adolescent indignation that he would presume to know what kind of man she needed. But only a few weeks later, when Eric began to pressure her to put off college to stay with him, Sonya confided in her mother that she felt like Eric's prisoner. She broke off the relationship the next day. Eric knew Ivan and Dana had been trying to discourage the relationship and so did Jake. Though Ivan had tried to talk with Jake about what had happened, for months Jake put him off with, "It's over, no big deal." Things stayed tense between them. Finally, on one of their runs, Jake had said, "When I first heard from Eric that you and Dana didn't want Sonya to go out with him, I was hopping mad. Give the kid a chance, he's in rehab, don't write him off. What made you think your golden daughter is better than my son. I was really mad. Then I stepped back and asked myself how do I feel about Eric. My answer was, he's my son, I love him, but I don't trust him. He's angry, feels entitled, and rules mean nothing to him." Shortly after, Eric had left town to drift around the country for several years. Jake had told Ivan a few weeks before that Eric had returned to Ann Arbor.

Except during the few steep uphills, they talked during most of their runs. Their conversations were like free association, rambling from one thing to another, the latest news, gossip about this or that colleague, sports, Clinic problems, and especially problems arising in the treatments of their patients. They often spoke about new patients.

They weaved their way through students and headed south on State Street, past Angell Hall with its massive columns, under the bare elm trees, hundreds of crows perched on the high limbs. Sometimes Weiss imagined them to be the souls of professors who had taught in Angell Hall. They ran through the courtyard of the law school, built early in the century to resemble Oxford and Cambridge. The midwinter sun sat so low in the southern sky that the towers and trees, even at midday, cast long shadows on the snow.

"There's all this talk, Jake, about how we're seeing fewer old fashioned neurotic patients these days. At case conferences all we hear about are character disorders, people with no sense of guilt. Or sense of self. People who blame their problems on other people or circumstances."

"You're describing most of my practice," said Jake, thinking but not saying, that the description also fit his son.

"I certainly have patients like that too, but I just saw a man cut from the old mold." Ivan described the interview with Adam Stone.

"Wow, he's already laid out a lot of himself, in what, one session?"

"Yeah, he did tell me a lot. I felt a connection with him right away."

"So how do you see him?" asked Jake. This was the most useful part of their run-talks. In training, which for psychoanalysts can take five to ten years, a student analyst, a "candidate," meets weekly with a supervisor, a clinical teacher, and reviews what happened in the analysis of each training case. They discuss what the patient is unconsciously communicating, the patient's resistances to self observation, transferences to the analyst, interpretations made to the patient, the analyst's feelings toward the patient, everything. One challenge after graduating from this lengthy apprenticeship with its close and careful discussion of cases is to continue the analytic effort independently, to continue to stay attuned to what is going on underneath the surface. Ivan and Jake were, without ever having formally decided to do so, continuing an analytic supervisory process. On their daily runs they not only kept each other physically fit, but professionally fit as well.

"He's a man terrified of the consequences of success, in his work life and also with women," said Weiss. "He engineers things for himself in such a way with women that he's bound to fail with them. He's a guy who's perceptive about people, but he's using this in a self defeating way."

"How so?"

"Well, he understands people, so he picks up pretty accurately from a woman whether she's interested in him exclusively or whether she's attached to another man. Then he chooses to go after the ones who are not interested or not available."

"I see," said Jake, "and the same with his work, he knows just what to do to get the boss to come down on him. So he screws himself up there, too."

"Exactly. With the Director of the dig in Arizona, he started out doing well and then undermined himself."

They ran by the cemetery and turned into the Arboretum, the "Arb" as townies called it, a preserve of woods, hills, and fields running along the Huron River. The snow crunched with their strides as the trail snaked downhill through thick woods toward the river. It started snowing, and when they turned north, cold, biting gusts swept up from the valley. Except for a few students in the distance "traying" down the hills with equipment appropriated from a dorm dining hall, the Arb was unusually quiet, and they ran in silence for a few minutes.

"Does he have insight into any of this?" asked Jake.

"Very much so. As a matter of fact with little help from me, he made pretty insightful observations about his self-sabotaging pattern. It was quite surprising."

"Maybe that's why you felt a connection with him. Insight's vital to our work, but sometimes, Ivan, you overvalue it." I hate hearing this, Weiss thought, but I know it's true. Supervision, even long after training, still stings. "Has he been in any kind of therapy before?"

"I don't know, but I don't think so."

"Do we go for it?" asked Jake about the choice to turn off the easy downhill path and take a steep, rockier uphill one along a stone wall separating the Arb from the adjacent cemetery.

"Sure, we're tough," said Weiss, and they assaulted the hill, panting hard now, no talking. Beyond the pines the path opened onto a peony garden, a few brown stalks poking through the crust of ice and snow. Crossing the garden, they picked up the path, which cut through a woods of tall hardwood trees down to the frozen river.

"I haven't gotten any childhood history yet, but what would you see as the source of his problems?" Ivan asked. They both enjoyed speculating about patients' childhoods from the problems they present as adults.

"I'd guess there was a pretty inflamed relationship with his father. Probably had a father who put him down, maybe physical abuse. The guy's probably terrified of the old man. And of his own rage at him." Ivan told Jake about Stone's dream image of the man with the ripped off arm.

"There it is, pretty graphic, isn't it."

"And all of his self-defeating behavior? What's that about?" asked Ivan.

"Probably another part of the same problem. If he gets the girl or gets the job, he wants to throw those successes in someone's face, to use them as weapons. If he sabotages himself, he disarms himself."

"So if he avoids success in work or in his love life, he's safe. No ammunition, no retaliation. That's how I see him, too."

"Yeah, a really straightforward case, sounds very workable. I'm envious. All these college kids I'm seeing these days seem to be on the brink of psychotic episodes."

They ran along the river and circled the "lower meadow." Ivan loved to run here in the spring when the fruit trees that ringed the meadow were blooming. On this midwinter day the limbs of the trees were barren and bent low under the weight of the snow. They ran single file through the tall grass, crossed the railroad tracks, and picked up a bike path along the river. As he ran, Ivan found himself returning to the beginning of the session with Adam Stone, when the patient had walked to the window and said it was like looking at a picture of the world from a satellite. Somehow, Ivan thought, more was revealed in that comment than in anything else the patient had said. Ivan was about to tell this to Jake, when Jake's beeper went off.

"It's the emergency code for the Clinic. I don't have my cell phone, do you have yours?"

"I hate the thing, never remember to take it. We can probably run to the Clinic as quickly as get to a phone," said Ivan. They turned around and ran the two miles along the river, through the hospital complex and back to central campus on the northeast corner of which, in a converted Victorian house, the Psychology Clinic was located.

The crisis met them the moment they entered the building. A wiry young woman in a short skirt, tights, revealing tank top, military boots, all black, was standing in the middle of the waiting area. She wore white makeup and various lip and nose rings. A small but clearly visible tattoo on her upper arm read "Fuck on or Fuck off." Her eyes were narrowed and fiery. Secretaries, psychology interns, two University security guards and several patients stood awkwardly around her like nervous actors waiting for the curtain to rise. The drama had, in fact, been underway for some time.

A psychology intern, a tall, studious looking young man, was trying to talk to her, as one of the security guards approached her.

"If that fucker touches me, I swear I'll sue all your asses. You get the Director of this shithole out here now!" she said at a volume just below a scream, her arms stiff at her sides, fists clenched, shoulders hunched up, looking like a two year old in midtantrum.

27

"And don't give me this bullshit he's not here. He's here, he's just hiding, sending you jerks out to tell me to get lost. Well, I'm not movin', get it, I'm stayin' right here."

"If you come back in the therapy room, we can sit down and talk about this. I think we can work this out," said the therapist, trying to sound professional and reassuring, his voice quaking.

"You're the last person on earth I'd go into a room with after that pass you made at me. I'll dress any way I like. If it turns you on, deal with it, don't attack me for it!"

"I didn't make a pass at you and wasn't attacking you. I was just trying to help you understand . . . what you might be communicating by how you dress . . ." he said, trailing off, his body curled forward, as if he were trying to make himself as small and inoffensive as possible.

Weiss was reminded of a teacher who had said that treating a reasonably well put together neurotic patient is like peeling an onion. You peel away a layer and the patient cries, you peel another and there are tears again. "But a borderline patient, Ivan, is another matter entirely. Here the mind is like a snake egg, like an egg of a cobra. The shell is transparent and so you see the whole baby snake, it's right there writhing around. So easy to see, so tempting to go after. But when you move in with your interpretation, even a gentle one, a very conservative one, you can nick the shell and the snake jumps out, wild and dangerous."

Weiss sized up the situation. A bright, book smart student therapist finds himself with a borderline patient, much more disturbed than he realized. He thinks her clothing, body piercings, and tattoo have some sexual meaning. Maybe the way she looks has caused her trouble. So the therapist, in the name of bringing warded off feelings into the patient's awareness, points out to her that she is expressing sexual feelings, maybe even toward him. She explodes and shoots back that these feelings are not hers, they're his.

"Ms Reynolds, we can explore all of this if you'd come back in the office," the therapist pleaded, emphasizing the "Ms" to try to mollify her with his political correctness.

"Our relationship is over, finito. Get it? The only person I'm talking to is the Director."

"Well you've got the Director and Assistant Director right here," said Weiss.

"This is going from bad to worse. You guys always dress like that?" she said, staring at Weiss' bony legs in his running tights. "That's a real professional image, it sure inspires confidence."

"We try to promote a kind of laid back atmosphere here," said Jake.

"Real funny," she said, softening a little.

"We were paged while we were out running," said Weiss, explaining their attire to head off her adding it to her list of grievances. "I can see something has really upset you. I think the best thing would be for you to sit down with your therapist and try to sort this out." If possible, Weiss wanted to avoid taking this situation out of the therapist's hands. Working with a crisis like this could be an excellent, though difficult, learning experience.

"That's out of the question, as I said, finito." The therapist looked visibly shaken and crestfallen, his eyes reddening as if he were on the verge of tears.

"A second possibility is to talk with Dr. Hanson and me," said Weiss, including Jake for both clinical and legal reasons. She thought about this, her eyes a little cooler.

"Doctor, we can just remove her," said one of the security guards, impatient with all of this contemplation and talk.

"I think we have this under control," said Weiss. "You can leave."

The guards looked at each other indecisively, and Jake motioned them with a tilt of his head to leave. Jake's size and manner made them feel he was more their kind of guy, no bookish academic, and they left.

"That's the first decent thing that's happened here all day, getting rid of those thugs."

"We're not here to force you or frighten you," said Ivan.

"Don't flatter yourselves, I don't scare so easy . . . alright, so where do we talk?"

Weiss showed her through the secretarial area to his office. Once they were seated, the calm Weiss thought had been achieved, quickly evaporated.

"I'm not going to make any more scenes, and I'll leave under my own power, but unless that jerk is fired, you're gonna be real sorry."

"Maybe we can back off from threats for a moment and try to sort out what happened," said Weiss.

"I come in for some help with these assholes at work who're constantly hitting on me. I try to explain to this sorry excuse of a therapist the suggestive things they say to me, and he starts talking about how I'm dressed, about my tattoo, and then tells me I'm trying to get *him* to hit on me. The guy's nuts. He's a nerd, I don't have the slightest interest in him, and even if he were Harrison Ford, who I *do* think is hot, I don't go around trying to get people to hit on me, most of all my therapist."

Ivan and Jake tried to explain that therapists try to tune in accurately to patients, but that sometimes even the best therapist will be, from time to time, out of sync with a patient.

"I pay him to be right. And he's not the best, he's a student. I'm probably his first case for all I know. I won't pay good money so he can use me as his fuckin' guinea pig. I was used enough by my stepfather and his loser of a son, you know, dirty stuff I won't go into, when I was a kid, and I'm not going to let it happen again." She sucked in one of her cheeks and seemed to be biting down on it to keep something in herself under control.

"Maybe you've just told us something that can help us understand what happened with your therapist," said Hanson. "Let's say that your therapist brought up something that was flat out wrong, barking up the wrong tree. Okay, and let's add to it that his off base remark had to do with sex." She was trying to appear indifferent, looking out the window, then at the ceiling, then examining her cuticles and pressing them back with her fingernail. With all of this posturing, thought Weiss, some of what Jake was saying was probably getting through. "So, your shrink talks sex, he's off base, O.K., but he talks sex. He thinks that's where you're at, that it'd help you for him to talk about this, but he's wrong. Maybe this rings a bell in you. Maybe this reminded you of someone else who was off base with sex? Your stepfather or stepbrother, right? So maybe you carried some of these feelings from the bad old days, which sound pretty terrible, over to your therapist."

She stopped her show of indifference, and they all sat for a while in a tense silence. Ivan and Jake could see that there was a flash of reflectiveness, but like clouds that break open for a moment in a stormy sky and then regather, they both could see in the language of her body, particularly the rigid set of her mouth, that they had lost her.

"You don't get it. I'm not carrying shit over from anywhere. I've just had enough experiences with abusers to know one when I see one, and this guy's getting his kicks by talking dirty to me. He flatters himself that I'm trying to get him to hit on me and then gets off on that."

"I believe he was trying to help you," said Weiss.

"No, he was abusing me," she screamed. "I've been through it before, and I won't again." Though she had been talking mostly to Hanson, she stared now straight at Weiss. "You're going to pay for this! I mean it. I'm going to get to you or . . . someone close to you, I have ways, I know how."

She bolted from the chair, stalked out of the office, bumped her way through people and furniture and slammed the front door to the Clinic, vibrating the glass in the bay windows of the waiting area.

Weiss asked a secretary for the patient's file. He and Jake read it before calling the therapist in. Sara Reynolds, 25, in and out of the University for seven years, chaotic relationships with both men and women. She had reported a history filled with horrendous sexual abuse by her stepfather and stepbrother, along with periods of neglect, both actual and psychological, by a depressed, highly self-centered mother. They called in the intern.

As soon as he sat down, he immediately tried to explain that he was just "interpreting the transference" to the patient, that he saw what she was saying as a communication to him, carried over from some early relationships in her life.

"'To interpret the transference,' as you put it," said Weiss, "requires that the patient has enough basic sense of the actual relationship with you to see that you are there, in reality, for one purpose, to try to help her, even though she *feels* you're not. She has to be able to consider that the feeling she is having toward you now is carried over from somewhere else in her life. This is difficult for any patient, especially at the beginning of a contact with a therapist. For a woman like this, right now it is impossible. It's too soon to know if it would ever be possible."

"But her thoughts about me, the sexual thoughts, seemed to be right there on the surface. They were so obvious in her talking about this guy or that guy making passes at her." Hanson hunched forward toward the intern, appearing to Weiss like a coach ready to explain why a play had gone wrong.

"That's exactly the point. With her coworkers, with you, with everyone, she's always on the verge of feeling that someone around her is going to be assaultive. Everyone is someone from her past. Once she's got that program running, you could be Mother Theresa, and she'd still think you're a rapist."

"So what could I have done to avoid what happened?"

They explained to the intern that with this type of patient the therapist must be very careful to "bring the patient along," to keep the reality of the relationship with the therapist clear to the patient whenever there is any sign that the patient is losing it.

"A better put together patient could say," said Weiss, "I know what I *feel* you are doing, seducing me, rejecting me, making fun of me, whatever, but I know rationally that you're not. That opens the way for the patient and the therapist together to ask why the patient would be feeling these things, why she sees the therapist in the particular distorted way she does."

"Are you saying Ms Reynolds is psychotic?"

"No," continued Weiss, "she's not flagrantly out of touch with reality, but in the therapy situation as you have been conducting it, by not telling her much about what you're doing or who you are, you're inviting her to have these distorted experiences of you. For this kind of patient, these imaginings, these transferences, wash away her sense of the reality of who you are and what you are trying to do."

Jake was growing impatient with the wordiness of Ivan's explanations and could see that the student was not following it.

"Look, you went way too fast and way too deep, especially telling her about her impulses. When you talk to her about her sexual feelings, it's just a fact to her that you're trying to get in her pants. She thinks, you talk sex, that *is* sex. To you you're making fancy interpretations of her impulses, to her it's foreplay, and you're ready to pounce." The intern smiled nervously at these images. Weiss admired and envied Jake's no nonsense directness. This bluntness gets him in trouble with the administration, but it's damn effective with students and probably, when timed right, very powerful with patients he's treating. He probably thinks he's a better teacher and therapist than I am, and maybe he's right.

"O.K. I think I'm starting to get it. But what should I do now?"

"There's nothing really to do," said Ivan. "She might come back, but I doubt it. Make sure you do a detailed write-up of the session you just had with her, spelling out what you said, why you said it, and her reactions. Put a note in, too, about what just happened in the waiting room."

"I'll do that right now," said the intern, still looking very shaken.

"Listen," Jake said, as the intern was getting up to leave, "a case blowing up like this is tough, but we cut our teeth on experiences like this. I'll bet you'll grow as a therapist from it." The intern nodded and left.

"I think he learned something from the experience," Jake said.

"Yes, largely from the way you explained things to him."

"I guess my tell-it-like-it-is style is good for something, even if it's not an appealing quality in a director."

"It's worth a lot," said Weiss, realizing that though they had over the years shared many personal things, they had not spoken before about the choice of Weiss over Hanson for the Director's job.

"Ivan, I'm probably shooting my mouth off again, but I'll say it anyway – don't patronize me." Weiss felt stung by the comment and sensed how deep was Jake's anger and hurt.

CHAPTER FOUR

W eiss ran from the Clinic back to his private office in Tower Plaza, quickly showered, and saw his last three patients of the day. Then he drove to meet his wife at a riding stable west of town. The snow had stopped, and the setting sun dropped below a lid of clouds and shone so brightly that even with his visor down Ivan could barely see the road. The ice crusted fields were glassy and red, and "Go Wolverines!" painted on the sides of several barns along the road were the only indications that he was just minutes from downtown Ann Arbor and not deep in Midwestern farm country. He passed the stable's paddocks along the road, as the sun dropped into silhouetted trees on a distant hill. In the dying light he could see the horses gathered by the paddock gates, as several teenage girls ran back and forth leading them into the barn for the night. Just past the paddocks he turned into the stable's driveway and pulled up next to his wife's pick-up.

Once or twice a week Ivan met Dana at the stable where she showed him the progress she was making with her horses. For a man working all day indoors, immersed in thoughts and words, driving into the country, into this world of farms and horses, even in the worst weather, was deeply refreshing.

He went up to the observation room overlooking the indoor riding arena. A course of jumps was set up and Dana, on her black gelding, Master, was circling at the far end of the arena, preparing to ride the course. Kevin, her coach, was in the middle of the arena shouting to her. "Wake him up, get him listening! Soften your hands."

Though she was wearing riding chaps over jeans and a dusty thermal vest, the tautness and elegance of her body showed through. As she eyed the course, her mental focus seemed to fill the arena. She was riding, as she had explained to Ivan, in a two point position, supporting herself with her knees and thighs, her weight out of the saddle to give the horse freedom to move and jump smoothly. As she widened her circles, she seemed to be floating over the horse.

"O.K., Dana," said Kevin, "shorten your reins a little, more outside leg to keep him from slipping away. Now take him through it."

Before Dana had made horse training and showing the focus of her life, like most casual observers Weiss thought that when a horse jumps an obstacle, the rider simply aims the horse at it and goes along for the ride. He had learned from his wife about the constant communication between the rider and horse. He watched Dana signal the horse through the movement and position of her legs, the shift of her weight and the manipulation of the reins. She had explained that these were not just commands to speed up or slow down, but subtle directions to the horse to lengthen or shorten its stride, to change its gait, and to adjust its balance. He could almost see the other side of the communication, her sensing through her legs, her seat, and her hands the state of the horse's body, how it was moving, what it would do next. As Ivan had come to learn from Dana about this complex interchange, it fascinated him, and he saw similarities to his efforts to understand the subtle, nonverbal communications between himself and his patients.

As Dana broke out of the circle and headed toward the first jump, the horse came to heightened alertness, its head high and cocked slightly to the side, ears pricked up, nostrils wide. They glided through the course, the horse arcing over the jumps, as Dana's body seemed to echo the motion of the horse. She jumped a combination, two jumps close together, and then made a tight turn just below the observation room. She set the horse up for the highest jump which she cleared, the horse's back leg brushing, but not toppling, the rail. She turned right at the far end of the arena, changed the horse's lead leg to balance it, and went over a wide jump to finish the course.

"Good trip, well done," said Kevin, as Dana patted the horse's neck and spoke to it. She continued to canter it around the arena a few times, slowed to a trot, and then walked it over to Kevin.

"That was the best he's done yet. That horse, no, both of you, will go somewhere with a performance like that." Kevin patted her calf as she stood next to him, and she reached down and squeezed his shoulder. Weiss knew the tie between his wife and her trainer was strong. Though Kevin was young enough to be her son, they shared their love of horses and horsemanship and had a mutual respect for the energy each put into their efforts. Though Weiss knew Kevin looked to Dana in many ways as a mother or older sister, having asked her advice about problems with his girlfriend, he still felt jealous.

"Ivan, come down," she called out. Ivan joined them in the arena. "What a ride! Did you see the way he tucked his legs over the jumps, the way he's listening to me now? Kevin thinks I can move up to a new level of competition with this horse."

"It's not just the horse," said Kevin, "it's the two of you as a team. You could shoot for B circuit in the spring."

"You looked terrific, really in command," said Ivan. She hopped down from the horse and kissed Ivan. Kevin offered to cool the horse down and untack him. Dana asked Ivan to take a walk with her. They crossed the snow covered outdoor arena and followed a path through the woods.

"Ivan, I'm so excited about my riding. I love it, and I think I have some talent for it. I've never found both at the same time. Honey, you've been great in supporting this."

"I'm just happy that you've found something you like so much. It's also fair. You had a huge burden raising Sonya when I was in analytic training."

"That's right, you bastard," she said playfully. "Figuring that in, I think I'll buy two or three more horses. Fair's fair." She playfully punched his shoulder. Then she took his hand, and they walked through the quiet of the winter woods back to the stable.

Though Weiss was still worried about how much of his wife's excitement was connected with her feelings about Kevin, he did feel happy and relieved that she had found this avocation which was recently evolving into a real career. For as long as he had known Dana, she had searched, sometimes desperately it seemed, for something around which to organize her life. She had been a modern dancer when they met, began graduate studies in comparative literature, taught gifted students at a private school, and then seemed to have found a more enduring interest in doing advocacy work for adopted children. A child advocacy lawyer she had worked with said that she had both a careful, legal mind and spirit, just the stuff needed to be a good lawyer. He thought she would be an especially good litigator. All that was left was to go to law school. She had applied and was accepted at Georgetown, though not at the University of Michigan. Ivan was willing to move, but to his surprise, she suddenly decided against it. She said she didn't want to disrupt his career or uproot their daughter. Ivan told her he was puzzled by her decision.

"I've been doubting if I really want to be a lawyer," she had said, "I guess I still don't know what I want to do. I'll know it when I find it. It's out there somewhere."

They left her pickup at the stable and drove to a nearby country restaurant, a notch above a greasy spoon.

"I feel this is my day," Dana said, once they were seated. "I rode well, and there's more good news. Sonya has hit it big. A client and a boyfriend!" After graduating from the Rhode Island School of Design with a degree in interior design, Sonya had worked at a prestigious interior decorating firm in New York City for a couple of years. Things were going well for her until the rape. She had tried to regain a sense of safety in New York, but when she found herself struggling to even leave her apartment, she decided to return to Ann Arbor. She had hoped to set herself up independently as a decorator, a hope that had not yet been realized. There had been, during the six months since her return, a few small jobs for Ivan and Dana's friends, but Sonya felt they had contacted her only as favors to her parents. She had worked as a decorator on an hourly basis in a department store, but lost even that job when the furniture area was phased out.

"That's terrific, fill me in."

"We were both in a rush, so I don't know the details. All I know about the client is that he wants her to do a complete redecorating."

"And a boyfriend too?"

"I know a little more about him. He's an engineering student and a musician, interesting combination. She wants us to meet him. She says, 'Mother, I'm not marrying him. Don't push me on this. I like him, but wait a couple days on the wedding invitations.' Do I push her, Ivan?"

"No, you don't. This is an old story with her. When she can't admit she wants something, she makes it our idea. Remember the cheerleader episode?"

Dana, of course, did. Sonya had secretly wanted to be a cheerleader, at a time when all of her friends were hip or punk. To be a cheerleader would have been very uncool. So she told her friends that her mother was pushing her into it. The truth was that both Ivan and Dana thought cheerleading distracted Sonya, already a marginal student, from her studies. Dana also felt that teaching girls that their place was on the sidelines cheering the boys was the height of sexism.

"I do wish she'd finally leave her adolescence behind and take responsibility for her decisions," said Ivan, realizing the moment he said it that he hoped Dana, too, was now finally ending what he saw as her adolescent casting around for an identity. He then thought of the adolescent display he had witnessed at the Clinic. Ivan looked around impatiently for a waitress.

"What's up, Ivan? You seem all of a sudden irritated or something. You like this place *because* the service is slow." He usually did. The small town atmosphere and relaxed attitude was part of the appeal. "This place reminds you," Dana would say, "that all of life isn't broken up into 45 minute chunks, shrink time."

He told her about the incident at the Clinic and realized as he did how rattled he was by it.

"So a spoiled kid mouths off, what's the big deal?"

"It wasn't just what she said. I've had adolescent patients say much worse. And do worse. You remember when I was on the adolescent inpatient service, I'd regularly be dodging various projectiles. This young woman was different. There was a meanness behind her explosiveness. When she said she would get back at me, I don't think it was just an empty threat."

"So what could she do, sue the Clinic, sue you? So what? It'd be a hassle, but you have malpractice insurance, and the Clinic is covered by University insurance, right?"

"Yes, but the Clinic has never been sued. I take over and right away we're in court. It doesn't exactly reflect well on me."

"Is that all that's really bugging you?" She knew her husband liked to be in command of any situation and to be seen as competent and ethical, but she also knew him to be able to confront and tackle problems. She couldn't believe that fear of a lawsuit would rattle him.

"She didn't just threaten the Clinic or me. She said if she couldn't get back at me, she'd get at someone close to me. I thought of you and Sonya."

"Oh, Ivan," said Dana, reaching across the table to stroke his cheek. Her touch, as always, calmed him.

Their usual waitress came, took their order, and then carefully reviewed what they wanted. As she left, Dana rolled her eyes and Ivan laughed, both knowing that there was often a loose connection between the order given and the food that would arrive. Their private joke broke the tension.

"Well, back to the good news," said Dana. "I talked to Terry, the travel agent, and we're confirmed on the cruise, and she's somehow getting us an upgrade to a better cabin, or as she corrected me, 'Suite, it is after all, Dana, a luxury ship.' She makes 'luxury' sound like it's got a hundred syllables."

"Did she arrange the flight to Istanbul?"

"Yep, she's got us on a nonstop Detroit to London, then London to Istanbul. We switch planes in London, but it's all in the same terminal, and our luggage doesn't have to clear customs until we get to Turkey. So, Dr. Weiss, get out that old tux, and we'll see if that sleek runner's bod can slip into it."

They would fly to Istanbul where they would board the ship, cruise to some small ports in Turkey, then on to several Greek islands, back up through the Bosporus into the Black Sea, and finally return to Istanbul. It was to be their dream trip. Not just a vacation, Dana had said, but an adventure.

They drove back to the stable to pick up Dana's truck. They stood for a while in the parking lot in the rural darkness. The sky had begun to clear, and a few stars were out. With her back against his chest, she molded herself into him, and he surrounded her with his arms. It was quiet except for the distant whine of a small plane taking off from the Ann Arbor airport, a few miles away, and the sound of the horses shifting in their stalls. As a car passed, they watched their single shadow cast by its lights appear, orbit around them, and fade away. They stood for a while like this in the country night, feeling each other's warmth against the winter air. She turned around, and they kissed. She traced her finger around the ridges and crevices of his ear, her sign that she wanted to make love.

As Ivan drove home, Dana in front of him in her pickup, he thought about his fear of the Clinic patient, but also of his feelings about Jake's effectiveness with the student therapist. I may be the Director, but in a crisis, I get too wordy, too intellectual. Jake may be envious of me for getting the Director's job, but I envy his ability to be direct. It depressed him to face that he was not perfect at everything. He remembered his worry that he would be rejected for psychoanalytic training because it would be discovered that he had problems, that he was not perfect.

His Cuban born analyst, Dr. Ernesto Sanchez, in his heavy accent, had said, "Dr. Weiss, they are not looking for perfect people. Perfect people don't exist. So when one comes through the door, the Institute would have big questions. So, why do you need to be such a rare bird, Dr. Perfect?" They had gone on to understand some of the roots of his need to be perfect. It had been the most painful part of his analysis.

"Maybe, Dr. Weiss, if you had been the perfect boy, your mother would not have vanished into the grave." One fateful day when he was in the fourth grade, full of enthusiasm about having won the class' "College Bowl," Ivan came home to find the sorrowful face of his father in the circle of relatives. It was the single most important and catastrophic moment of his entire life.

CHAPTER FIVE

"I have some sense now of what brings you to see me," Weiss said to his new patient, Adam Stone, at the beginning of the second session. "Now, why don't you sketch out your past."

"Where to start? I grew up in Detroit. Working class family, only child. My mother is a 50's type housewife. I was very close to her when I was growing up, still am. She always understood me and supported me behind my father's back. I really love her." He hunched forward in the chair in what struck Weiss as a closed and protected posture.

"At the center of my childhood was my father. The man's aim in life was, to put it simply, to break the spirit of everyone around him. He was relentless. He'd dropped out of high school to work at the Ford Rouge Plant. It was a daily insult to him that he was a factory worker. He'd always talk about how he would run things if he were in charge. His whole outlook was that everyone was trying to stop him from doing the great things he was meant to do. He probably felt like nothing. It galled him if anyone felt pride in anything. He could find that one thing that you might really be proud of and go after it. That he was good at. After you'd spent a few minutes with him, you'd feel like nothing yourself."

"You said, 'you' would feel this or that with him."

"'You' is anyone, but I guess I'm not really saying directly that I felt like that. He seemed to know when I was young that I'd go beyond him in school, and in life, and he tried to put me down at every turn. Once when I was about seven, I was really proud of myself for having learned my multiplication tables and getting a perfect score on a test in school. I was sitting at the dinner table bragging about it to my mother." Weiss was reminded of his own mother helping him with his homework. He saw the pleasure in her eyes, when they had learned something together. A feeling of terrible sadness passed through Weiss, as he thought of how she had died.

"My father sat coldly at the table and then after dinner, when she was off doing the dishes, he told me to get down on the floor, face down on the floor. He put his heel on my neck. I still remember the cold, wood floor against my lips, as he pressed my head into it. 'You can learn all you damn well want and show off, but just remember where you are right now,' he said." To learn, to advance himself, must feel to him extremely dangerous, thought Weiss. This is just the history that Jake and I expected.

Adam suddenly lurched awkwardly from his chair, went to the window and began a series of stretches, hunching and relaxing his shoulders, then making a large, slow circling motion with his head, while gripping his neck with his hands.

Though patients in movies often get up from the chair or couch, few of Weiss' patients over the years had done so. His first training case was one of them. The moment after she had lain down for her first psychoanalytic hour, she bolted up and started pacing around the office, talking of quitting the treatment. This doesn't bode well for my career as an analyst, Weiss had thought, first hour with my first patient, and she only stays on the couch for a microsecond.

He came discouraged to his meeting with his supervisor, a senior British analyst, Charles Norcroft, ill with terminal cancer, who was phasing out his own practice. He was Ivan's first supervisor, and Ivan was the old analyst's last supervisee. Before becoming an analyst Norcroft had been a British military physician and served as a front lines medic during the Second World War. He had a no nonsense style and mental toughness Ivan appreciated. While Weiss could still see the British officer in him, he had been impressed with the man's empathy, with his capacity to feel his way into the experience of Weiss' patient, and into Weiss himself, and to communicate his observations with a simple, sometimes disarming directness, all while struggling with his very obvious cancer pain. Even before his illness he had been a laconic man, but now, perhaps to conserve his strength, he was even sparser with his words, sometimes telegraphic. Ivan had never heard the man use a technical term. "If it cannot be said in plain English, it's rubbish," he had said. Weiss sensed an urgency in Norcroft to make sure that his way of doing psychoanalysis would be passed on. He was supportive of Weiss as a young analyst, but he also wanted him to get it right. As Stone stood at the window and continued to stretch, Weiss thought further about what he had learned from Norcroft.

"Weiss," he never called him either Ivan or Dr. Weiss, "you're taking everything so very personally. Forget yourself. Really look at your patient. Her actions reveal her secrets. Watch her. All three of us may learn something."

As he worked on with his patient, Ivan finally did learn something. Whenever she jumped up off the couch and talked of quitting, it always followed recalling her mother trying to coerce her into something. When Weiss pointed this out to her, she responded, "Oh, did I tell you that my mother had this thing about regularity? She'd insist on my reporting to her when I went to the bathroom, and if everything came out alright. If what I said didn't fit with her screwed up ideas about colon hygiene, she'd go for the enema."

"And what would you do?" Weiss had asked.

"I'd get up and run."

"Just like here, off the couch and out of analysis," Weiss had said. The patient stayed, learned about herself, and resolved many of her problems. And Ivan learned what actions in an analytic session can mean.

So what is this new patient trying to tell me or show me with this action, Weiss wondered. He got up, went to the window, and stretched, all immediately after talking of this terrible physical domination by his father. Is he fending off feelings of defeat as he lay helpless under his father's heel? Is he getting up, moving around, and stretching his body, none of which he could do when he was pressed against the floor? This is just an hypothesis, Weiss reminded himself, aware of his tendency, pointed out often to him in training of "running ahead" of his patients. Weiss became anxious when he couldn't discover immediately the meaning of what his patients were telling him or showing him.

Adam combed his fingers through his hair, as he stood at the window. "You can see everything from here." he said. Maybe, thought Weiss, he is saying this is a place where he may be able to see some things not just outside but inside himself.

"But it's all so far away at the same time," Adam said and then returned to his chair.

"My father, as you might expect, was also abusive with my mother. Mostly verbal putdowns, but every so often, when things seemed to have settled down, he would beat her up. My father never wanted anyone to forget that he was in charge, brutally in charge. My mother turned to me. I was her confidante from a pretty early age. After they'd have an argument, she'd come to my room, and I'd comfort her and . . ." He stopped abruptly. He adjusted himself in the chair and then crossed his arms in what struck Weiss as another self protective position. He then trained his unsettling eyes on Weiss. Is he staring me down? Is he literally keeping an eye on me out of some fear of what I might do? Weiss felt again his need to know what the patient was doing, to know it now, to know it with certainty.

"Is there some reason you stopped at that point?" Weiss asked, wondering if Stone needed to avoid thinking or saying more about being his mother's confidante.

"I guess I feel ashamed telling you any more about this right now. I don't really know you yet."

"Right, you don't, and it's unreasonable for either of us to expect you to trust me. You haven't had enough contact with me to know if I'm trustworthy."

The second session had passed quickly. Weiss felt in command of the patient's material, surprisingly so for having seen him for just two sessions.

Weiss told the patient that he would need another session or two before he could make a recommendation. They worked out a time a few days later for their next meeting.

At the end of sessions most patients put on their winter outer clothes in the hallway, once they have left the office, but Adam slowly wrapped his scarf around his neck and pulled on his parka while still in the consulting room. Weiss watched as he then slowly pulled on his gloves, methodically securing each finger in them.

Adam took a few steps toward the door, but then turned back toward the window so deliberately that it seemed as if he had forgotten something and was going back to retrieve it. He stood at the window, his face only inches from it.

"You can almost see the airport," he said, squinting his eyes and moving his head slightly from side to side, as if changing the angle would help him see it better. "Yeah, there's a plane," he said with some excitement. "It's just taken off, flying, I'd say south, heading away." He turned back, with his arm in what looked like an interrupted gesture, as if he were ready to point the plane out to Weiss, but then, for some reason, thought better of it. Instead, he just said, "O.K., I'll see you," and left.

Beginning with this new patient reminded Weiss of why he had become a psychoanalyst, what had drawn him to the work. He loved the exploration of the story behind the story, the hidden, unconscious story, that emerges through what the patient says and does during the session with the analyst. When Weiss began his training, he had no idea that this kind of exploration even existed.

"Weiss," Norcroft had said, after the first week with the "enema patient," "you have a lot to unlearn. You speak of stressors, anxiety, habit patterns. Dry, surface facts. This is of no use. Behavior, not psychology." Weiss' clinical psychology training had been in a program that was heavily behavioral, and his internship had been at a hospital that was stuck in nineteenth century descriptive psychiatry. "Skinner and Pavlov are still whispering in your ear. You need to dismiss them. That is, Weiss, if you want to become a psychoanalyst." Ivan had imagined Norcroft, when he was in the military, weeding out young recruits. Ivan had hoped not to be one of them.

"Maybe watching rats scurrying through mazes is your cup of tea," Norcroft had said, "Or tinkering with EEG patterns in a sleep lab. If that suits you, on with it. But if you choose the Freudian path, you will need an ear for the hidden message, an eye for the covert image. You need to find the secret story, which like a psychological genetic code, determines everything the patient does. Indeed, everything we all are and do. Even you, Weiss. It can guide, even inspire, but also hinder and paralyze. It can drive a person to enormous achievements, or it can bloody destroy his life.

"Analysts and their patients piece these stories together. From an image in a dream or a daydream, a slip of the tongue, or the largest brush strokes of a person's life. Destructive or constructive, or both, there is a beauty to them. And an adventure in the search for them. For the analyst. For the patient. You don't follow, do you? Sounds like some sort of tour of the unconscious, some pointless mental game. It's not." His voice, which had been weak and shaky, now somehow strengthened to emphasize his point. "Discovering the story liberates the patient. He can move outside its confines. He can now write, under the auspices of his own will, a new story."

The supervisor knew his student was still far from understanding most of this. He swiveled his chair around away from Weiss and drank some water, each swallow hollowing out his cheeks and neck and sending some pain up around his eyes. He then let his jaw hang slackly open for a moment in the way very ill people do who are struggling to get enough air, yet lack the energy to draw it. He was working to gather his strength to tell his student about a case, to help him understand.

"Years ago, woman in her late thirties, an automobile company executive began an analysis with me. Bright, attractive, but felt she was nothing. A trail of failed relationships with wealthy, powerful men. She was head over heels about them. And them about her. With each she became quickly disappointed and dropped them. Her friends told her she was just choosy. Reasonable possibility, but in her case, completely off the mark. So what explained this odd conduct? The answer came, Weiss, through how she experienced me.

"At first, I was a sensational analyst, she couldn't say enough about my gifts. I was brilliant, had a marvelous sense of humor, was even good looking – definitely a serious departure from reality. It's delightful, Weiss, to bask in this, just delightful, but it had nothing to do with me. Then suddenly, just as with the men in her life, I disappointed her. 'I'm not changing,' she complained, 'you're not giving me the tools' . . ." Norcroft's body shook with a series of deep, phlegmy coughs. When they subsided, he drank some more water. "That became the refrain, session after session, you have what I need, and you won't give it to me. Then, as I'd expected, she informed me she was leaving analysis. 'So now our little romance, so to speak, is over,' I said. 'Now I'm relegated to the scrap heap of your history.' 'No, no, it's not like that,' she protested, 'it's not like with the men in my life. Absolutely not.' 'Well then, I guess we part company here,' I said and I stood up. 'I want to wish you the very best in your life.' She remained seated. Then for the first time with me she wept. And wept. Then she told me a dream, a recurrent one.

"She's walking alone in a city. She feels good. She looks down to see a young boy walking next to her. A parade comes down the street, and the mayor stops his open car and approaches them. He has something. She's sure it's for her. She reaches her hand out, but the mayor turns to the boy instead, gives him the key to the city, takes him by the hand to his car and shows the boy how to drive it. Can you divine the unconscious story, Weiss?" Ivan couldn't. "Her thoughts about the dream led to the most painful of feelings of being displaced by a younger brother. The father had doted on the boy. He was a star pupil and athlete, popular, a complete disaster for her. Elegant and intelligent as an adult, she had been a most awkward and painfully shy child. An ugly duckling who never thought she'd be a swan. She imagined that her father had somehow given her brother a special something, some male essence, that made him so good at everything, so special, so lovable. She had spent her life looking for some powerful man to give *her* the key to the city and to teach *her* to drive the car. To pass something of himself on to her, to give her his tools, to change her. Give me what you are, and I'll then feel complete. And then you'll love me. She tried this with man after man, was always disappointed, but at every turn resumed her futile quest. Ordinary story, common childhood experiences, put together in her own particular way. Until we analyzed it," Norcroft had said, struggling to lean forward in his chair and making a circle with this trembling hands, "it had a stranglehold on her life."

Years later, as Weiss sat writing notes on the session with Adam Stone, beginning his effort to explore the unconscious life of the new patient, he thought of that first glimpse of the story behind the story. He closed the patient's file and a sadness settled in him, as he thought about the death of his teacher. The vividness of Norcroft's clinical illustrations, his best legacy, stayed with Ivan for the rest of the day.

CHAPTER SIX

H e booked the flight to Nice at the last minute. Full fare, but money was irrelevant now. He never had much of it, but now he felt rich, having more money than time left to spend it. The trip was not even necessary. The nun had said she would mail the letters and documents, but he decided to make the journey to harden his resolve.

Though he often had barely the energy to move, paradoxically it was when he needed to sit for long periods of time that the pain was the hardest to bear. When he changed planes in New York, he took a triple dose of Vicodin to stave off the pain he was sure would build during the eight hour flight. The drug put him in such a deep, dreamless sleep that it seemed to him that the plane had just taken off, when he felt the hand of a flight attendant jostling him awake for landing.

He picked up the rental car, but realized as soon as he drove out of the airport that he was too drugged to make the long trip to the orphanage. He made the short drive into Nice, parked near an outdoor market, and tried to walk off the effects of the drugs. It was morning, and the vendors were setting up in their stalls. He bought a pear and ate it as he walked to the boardwalk along the Mediterranean. He passed a few *patisseries*. She had brought him to Nice on her only visit and bought him a treat, *un pain chocolat*, which became his favorite. He ate it as he held her hand, looking up at her, feeling the soft fabric of her skirt on his cheek, hearing its rustle as she walked.

He could not see her face in any of his memories, but his body seemed to remember her, her hand firmly surrounding his, the feeling of her lifting him up by his underarms to drink from a fountain, her tussling his hair. He remembered, too, her desperate clutching and sudden letting go of him at the end of the visit. He remembered the sounds of sobbing. Her tears? His?

He walked along the boardwalk and then down onto the beach, rolled up his pants, and let the water lap at his toes as he walked. The sand was gritty on his sensitive feet, but the air was warm and gentle and the sea was calm. Though it was still early in the morning, a few people were already settled under umbrellas, and two teenage boys were playing a paddle game in the shallow water, jumping dramatically for the ball and falling with pleasure into the cushioning water.

He passed a group of small children putting the finishing touches on a sand castle, the oldest delicately placing small shells on the tops of spires of sand. The mother of one little boy floated in the water, watching him with obvious love. When he laughed, her eyes lit up; when he became frustrated, this feeling, too, was mirrored in her face. She lived for him. Watching them filled him with the familiar gnawing which he had come to know as the wish to live someone else's life. The wish registered within him only as an ache, a wordless sensation from somewhere deep within his body.

He rolled his pants up further and walked into the sea. He thought of disappearing under the surface and then of sucking in the water with one long, smooth breath. It would be a good place to die. He thought again of her embrace and then of her sudden release. When she had let go, it was as if his skeleton had been torn out of him, leaving him to hold the form of his body by some extreme effort of will. He thought of his dream of her, warm and soothing, then hard and cracked and cold. His stomach felt as if it were filled with broken glass. It would be a waste of his death to die today.

He returned to the market and bought some food for the trip. The effects of the drugs were wearing off now, and he was able to negotiate the heavy, but fast moving, traffic. From Nice he drove west along the Riviera and then at Le Carnet took a series of narrow twisting roads through the hills of eastern Provence to Fayence. He arrived at St. Boniface by midafternoon. This was his first return there, indeed to France, since he left at thirteen, when he was finally adopted by a family in Baltimore. By then the damage had been done.

Though St. Boniface had been officially a school, and some children from the surrounding villages did return home at night, it had been for most of them an orphanage. It had been run by nuns who lived in a nearby convent and monks who lived at the school.

He met the Director, a young nun not much older than himself, at the massive wood door to the school's enclave. He had corresponded with her about receiving the files and letters and had phoned a week before to tell her he was coming. She welcomed him and led him across a tiled courtyard to what the students had called the "chateau" and up a tight circular staircase to her turret office. She motioned him to sit across a heavy farm table she used as a desk.

On the table between them, cradled in textured, yellow paper and a wide crimson ribbon lay the letters in their envelopes, the little elaborate bow on top of the neat stack giving them the appearance of a gift. He slid out one of the envelopes and saw "To my son" and the address of the orphanage written in her delicate, girlish hand, never her name or a return address. A manila file sat beside the letters.

The nun offered to speak English, and though French was for him the language of bleakness, he said French was fine. When he was at St. Boniface, he was determined to speak English as fluently as possible, thinking he would be ready to fit into her life when she came to take him with her. He worked at English more than any other subject, managing by the time he was finally adopted to speak it without even a trace of an accent.

"Would you like to review what you requested?" He thumbed through the file, and counting the letters, determined that they were all there.

"Everything seems to be here, but there is something more I would like," he said, struggling to find the right French verb form. "I want to see the room I lived in."

"I'm sorry. From these records I don't know which room or even which building you were in."

"I'm sure I can find it," he said, his tone now cold as he thought of the room. She saw this turn in him. She leaned forward, adjusted her habit, and seemed to him to be gathering herself together to say something difficult to him. He looked past her out a window at fields dotted with the terra cotta roofs of farmhouses, fanning out from the school. He remembered looking out a similar window in his room on endless, lonely Sunday afternoons.

"I think I have some idea of how hard this is for you to come back here. I know the Church elders would be very unhappy with me for saying this, but I know that this was, during the years you were here, a terrible place for a child to be, especially for those of you who called this home."

"Yes it was awful, Sister, but I never called it home."

He had no intention of revealing any of his history. He just wanted to get the letters and papers and leave, but he felt, in spite of himself, compelled to speak to the nun. He told her that he had thought if he called St. Boniface home, his mother would never come for him. He had worked to make himself into what he imagined she wanted, a good boy, an American boy. Then she would come for him. He had learned all he could about America.

"How did you do that?"

"I read everything I could find about the U.S. I learned about baseball and football, American football, even though I never cared much for sports. And I also tried from her letters, these letters, to find out what life would be like in the United States, what it would be like to be with her there."

"So, she wrote to you often?"

"No, only five times." He felt it tiresome to be explaining this to her. He could tell, too, from her last question that she was trying to put a positive spin on what had been his mother's neglect. "She began writing from the time she left me, when I was a baby. When I was old enough to understand them, the letters were read to me."

"Why did you leave them here?"

"When I left here, I tried to forget her. I tried to kill her off in my mind." He saw the nun shudder when he said "kill." It made him want to say it again, even to lean over the quaint, neat table, with his face close to hers, and yell it in her face. "And with the help of Brother Anthony, I almost succeeded." The sister looked down, her face shielded by the hood of her habit. She knew about Anthony alright.

"I'm sorry," she said in a whisper almost too faint to hear.

"Don't be. He was all I had." She raised her head in surprise.

"He may have fucked me in every conceivable way, but at least there was some caring mixed in." She looked deeply embarrassed. And frightened. You should be, he thought.

"Shall we look for your old room now?" she asked, ready for the conversation to be over and to be safely out of this small room with him. He gathered the letters and the file, and they returned to the courtyard. He led the way to the converted carriage house where he had lived. She explained that it was no longer used to house children, but he was free to go in if he wished. He asked if she could give him some time alone there, and she agreed, relieved to be away from him.

He made his way through the dusty corridor, around old school desks, boxes, and cleaning supplies, the building evidently now used for storage. It was for storage when I was here too, he thought, warehousing children. At the end of the corridor he found the room he had lived in and sat down in the middle of the floor. Though the room was empty now, he remembered it crowded with the small, hard beds. It was late morning, and a shaft of light cut through the room. He remembered days when he would sit for hours here under the weight of overwhelming boredom and watch a shaft of sunlight creep across the stone floor like light marking the time on a sundial. Then the light would inch its way across the geography of the walls' craggy surfaces. He would try to see it actually moving over the features of the stone.

It was out of this utter loneliness that he had turned to Brother Anthony. Anthony was an English teacher, who also served, as some of the monks did, as a "house father." From their first meeting, when the monk tousled the boy's hair, addressed him first in French and then, knowing his mother was American, added "Hey kid!" in English, the boy was immediately drawn to him. He was an American, a graduate of Notre Dame. That would have been enough, but he was also the first person who found the boy in any way special. Anthony spent extra time with him on his studies and helped him with his English. He would say to Anthony, "Tell me how they say it there, in America, not in the books." Anthony gave him American comic books and magazines and told him stories of his own upbringing in Chicago. He also read her letters to him and then later used them to help him learn English.

Anthony was a bridge to her. Anthony would sit close to him on the boy's bed, his hand resting gently on the back of the boy's neck. He would cry as Anthony read her letters. Back then he could still feel. Anthony supported his hopes that she would return for him. "She needs to get her life straightened out before she can welcome you into it," he would say. "She was very young when she had you and needs to complete her education. You wouldn't want her to be unable to feed and shelter the two of you, would you?"

Anthony's stance then changed. "Why are you wasting your time longing for her," he began to say. "She teases you with these letters. She doesn't deserve your love. You mean nothing to her." To be nothing to her was starting to feel to him to be nothing at all. He was overwhelmed by a terrible emptiness. Anthony was there to fill the awful void.

"But you are very special to me," Anthony said. "God works in strange ways, but He always has his divine plan. He has meant for us to be together. We have our special, secret love. But remember, it must be secret. That way no one can take it from us. This secret love is for you. And for me." Over months Anthony promised his devotion and solicited over and over reassurances that their love would be "as secret as silence."

"You remember that anything that is part of our specialness must never be spoken of," Anthony reminded him one dreary, rainy afternoon.

"Yes, Brother Anthony."

"And that the most holy of loves flows both ways?"

"Yes, Brother Anthony."

Anthony folded aside the heavy black cloth of his robe and guided the child's hesitant hand to his penis and then cupped his hand over the child's. He put his monk's hood up and kissed the boy under its shelter. It went from touching and kissing each other, to Anthony taking the boy in the middle of the night to his room and entering the child in every way. Even though there was talk that there were many "special boys," he held tight to the thought that he was the most special. What Anthony did to him felt humiliating at times, physically painful at others, but the attention, the closeness, made it worth it. Later, in bars or in bathhouses, he either searched for Anthonys or for boys who reminded him of himself. There were women, and he was involved with several, but the pain he felt with them was too great.

He was sure in his mind that if she had come for him, he would never have been drawn to Anthony's secret love and never have searched for it with other men. When finally his search ended with AIDS, he didn't blame Anthony or the man who gave it to him, but laid the fault squarely at her door. She had left him in this emotional desert and then teased him with the possibility of her love and a better life.

The trip to France had exhausted him, and he slept again on the entire return flight and felt, for a while, rested when he arrived at Kennedy. When his flight to Detroit was canceled due to equipment difficulties and he could not fly out until the next day, the airline paid for a hotel at the airport. With his supply of pain medication low, he had to reduce his dosages to avoid running out. He considered drinking, but even the thought of alcohol sent waves of nausea through him.

He sat in a hot bath and watched the television reflected in the room's mirror. The movie "Reservoir Dogs" was on, and he watched an undercover cop bleeding to death in a warehouse. He tried to imagine what it would be like to cut his wrists and watch the redness spread through the bath. It relieved him that there was always that one sure escape.

He flew back in the morning and drove directly to Ypsilanti to the clinic where his AIDS was being treated. The technician took blood, and the unkempt young doctor, whose pale skin and acne made him look like a teenager, asked him the same questions as before about his symptoms. The answers were all yes, but worse than last time. The doctor renewed his prescriptions and suggested adding a new drug to the stew. Fine, fine, whatever. The doctor told him to call in a few days to talk about the results of the blood work. He nodded, but had no intention of calling or returning to the clinic, as he had now enough medicine to last through to the end of the plan.

He stopped in the rest room, vomited, and staggered out to his car. He had planned to go to the police station to file the complaint, but was too exhausted. It could wait a few days, and anyway, he wanted to make sure he was at his best when he went. He started the engine, locked the doors, and turned the heat up high. As he drifted toward sleep, he mouthed the words to describe the dream he was falling into. I smell and taste your skin . . . The rhythm of your heart beats into me . . . On you, in you, of you . . .

CHAPTER SEVEN

"Dr. Weiss, can I talk to you a minute?" asked Mary, Ivan's Clinic secretary, poking her head into the basement meeting room where he was teaching a seminar. Ivan stepped out into the hall. "I wouldn't have interrupted you while you're teaching, but I think this is important."

"That's alright. What's up?"

"The father of a patient is on the phone, and he's hopping mad. I told him you were in an important meeting and would call him back, but that just set him off even more. He said, 'Just get him. Nothing's more important, lady, than talking to me!'"

"Do we know which patient his daughter is?"

"Actually, I think it's his stepdaughter. His name is Samuel Dexter. His stepdaughter was the young woman who made such a scene the other day, Sara Reynolds. Dr. Weiss, he sounds really creepy."

She feels that way for some very good reasons, thought Weiss. Even on the phone, he was ready, it seemed, to force himself on the secretary, on the Clinic, just like he probably forced himself on his stepdaughter. Mary went back up to her desk and transferred the call downstairs.

"This is Dr. Weiss, what can I do for you?"

"You know what the hell you can do for me! Sara told me about the pass that shrink made at her." The pot calling the kettle black? You can't be sure, Weiss reminded himself, if what she had said about her stepfather's abuse was true, but from what she had enacted with her therapist, he was fairly certain it was. Samuel Dexter is trying to make his crime ours.

"Mr. Dexter, I think you understand I can't discuss your daughter's treatment without her permission . . ."

"Right, hide behind all that confidentiality bullshit."

"I have no desire to hide behind anything. I'm simply telling you that I'm not at liberty to tell you anything about her psychotherapy here. What I can tell you is that the Associate Director and I met with your daughter in an effort to sort this out, and that I have also met with the therapist. I can tell you with absolute certainty that no one did anything sexually inappropriate with your stepdaughter."

"I'm not satisfied. That's the bottom line. Someone will pay for this." He hung up. Threats from him, just like from her. Did he level these kinds of threats at her? Very likely and likely, too, she repeats these scenes by putting herself in his position and threatening other people. All the while she goes on feeling terrorized by him. I can see why. As threatened and assaulted as he had felt by Sara Reynolds, Ivan felt even more so by her stepfather.

Weiss felt annoyed that this problem was not going away. I must have been so caught up in my fantasies of the power and prestige of being Director, he thought, that I'm surprised and annoyed that these problems are coming up at all. I can't just sit back in my nice office and be the Director. I actually have to do the job.

After the seminar it was with relief that he left for the calm and control of his private practice. Generally reflective patients, no administrative hassles, no students, a respite.

His first patient, Jane O'Brien, a concert pianist and music professor, was an obsessive compulsive woman in her early forties, pinched, mousy, asexual, her life plagued by a paralyzing inability to make decisions. Every choice, no matter how minor, she felt might be potentially catastrophic. She would ruminate on conversations she had with people, dwelling on how a particular word or nuance had affected them, imagining them as being either stricken by what she had said or powerfully helped by it. I know what I can do to people, she would say in session after session, and if something terrible happens to any of them, it will be my fault.

A key event in her childhood was her psychotic mother asking the patient to make a fateful decision. When the patient was eight, her mother told her that the "voices" were saying that the patient's father was trying to poison the family. It seemed hard for the patient to imagine this was true. Her father had always seemed to her loving and gentle. Should I leave him, her mother asked her? She remembered wanting to tell her mother that her father would never hurt anyone. But the patient had seen how wild her mother would get if anyone tried to talk her out of her delusions. Going along with the delusions kept the mother calm and seemed worth the high cost of losing her beloved father. She told her mother she should leave him. The mother did, and tragically, the father died of pneumonia four months later. A deadly choice. Anyone she came near, anyone she had contact with, she felt unconsciously, was in jeopardy. All choices were dangerous.

They were making some progress with these anxieties, freeing the patient to take some small steps out of her isolated, protected world. She spent the session talking about a new professor of music who had shown some interest in her. She told Weiss she was surprised that she wanted him to ask her out. She still worried that she could somehow hurt him, but the feeling was not as strong as usual. The patient was pleased with this change, and Weiss was too.

His next patient was Jennifer Andrews, a blonde, statuesque woman of 29, always overdressed, with more makeup than she needed. She was a pathologically jealous woman with powerful needs to be admired. Whenever she became involved with a man, she would quickly become obsessed with thoughts that he was secretly interested in another woman. Her life was dedicated to a quest to win the excited attention of every man who had even a moment's contact with her. She was preoccupied with her appearance and spent hours choosing her clothes. Behind her ferocious wish to be admired was an unconscious feeling of being totally unlovable. In her analysis, which mirrored her life, she ruminated about what Weiss thought of her. She would look for any sign of his "real feelings" behind what she felt was his infuriating analytic "mask." She would spend whole sessions describing in detail her fantasies of seducing him.

"Just tell me what you think of me and we can get beyond this." The "this," he would tell her, is exactly the problem that had brought her to psychotherapy. She had for many weeks returned to thinking how she compared to other women patients she had seen coming and going from Weiss' office. "Don't you ever treat any ugly women?" she would ask and then proceed to demean other female patients' taste in clothes or point up their body imperfections. Lately, since seeing Weiss and his daughter on the street, her jealousy had focused on Sonya.

"Who is she, your young lover?" she taunted, Weiss sensing her jealousy intensifying and that she was ready to up the ante with him.

"You clearly think she is." Weiss noticed that she looked different today and then realized she had a new hairstyle. It was very similar to Sonya's.

"You clearly think she is," she said, mocking Weiss. "What do I have to do to get to you?"

"Is that your goal, to get to me?" She rolled her eyes and ignored the question.

"I don't know if I ever told you about Jim, my ex-boyfriend. Also ex-con. I've been telling him how I try to get you to drop that psychoanalyst crap. He gets a real kick out of it. He's rooting for me to seduce you, giving me ideas on how to do it."

"So what if you did seduce me? What would that get you?"

"You. I'd get you. Isn't that obvious?" Today, even more than before, she was determined not to step back and look at what she was doing or wishing.

"Let me try to put into words what I think is happening in your therapy. There is something very troubling from your past that you're playing out with me. In any therapy reliving the past has to happen, but then the next vital step is to try to understand it. You're dead set against doing that. So our work for you has come down to getting me to have sex with you. You seem to think that would accomplish something, maybe help you feel better or get better."

"So, Jim had this idea," she said, continuing to ignore what Weiss was saying. He's just the guy to come up with this, extortion is his specialty. That's what they locked him up for the first time. Second time was for dealing drugs, though he took so much of the stuff I was surprised he had anything left to deal."

"You seem to have sort of seduced him into your therapy."

"Yeah, I guess I have, that's kind of funny. It's the only way I'll seduce him now."

"What do you mean?"

"Well, he denies it, but I think the guy's got AIDS. He was good in bed, but even I'm not dumb enough to risk that." She had talked of Jim before, and Weiss had tried to explore, with no success, why she had chosen to be with such an obviously dangerous, psychopathic man.

"Jim's idea, this is really good, inspired, is that I can force you to have sex with me by threatening to sue you for trying to rape me. Get it? See, if you don't have sex with me, I'll claim you tried to rape me, and if you do have sex with me, then I won't sue you. I think it's terrific." She described, as she had before, her fantasy of taking off her clothes, undressing Weiss, and each saying sexy and admiring things about the other's body. Having sex was thrown in at the end of the fantasy as an afterthought. The mutual admiring, not the sex, it was clear to Weiss, was what she desired.

Weiss was beginning to realize how much he had underestimated the strength of this woman's needs and how completely they could overrun any respect for the professional boundaries between them. Weiss tried to stem the patient's slide into action and manipulation by speaking strongly to the underlying wishes which were fueling them.

"You want to seduce me to prove to yourself that you are a desirable woman . . . maybe to quiet a feeling that you're not."

"Who knows," she said, and Weiss saw all of the drama and posturing suddenly cease and her face go slack, as if she had, just for a moment, looked inside and glimpsed her own insecurity.

"Oh, by the way, Jim had some other extortion ideas."

"Oh?"

"I'll just save those for another time," she said, trying, it seemed to Ivan, to restore a feeling of control by intimidating him again.

With fifteen minutes left in the session she got up and walked out. Ivan wondered if he had underestimated the level of Jennifer Andrews' pathology in the same way as the Clinic intern had with his patient. His mind drifted to what other extortion the patient's ex-con boyfriend had in mind and how likely it was for her to try to carry it out. He was upset with himself that he had missed this more severe level of disturbance in her.

During the session with Jennifer Andrews, the respite and comfort of his private practice had slipped away. He spent a few minutes trying to settle himself down before his last patient of the day, Adam Stone. Weiss had been looking forward to seeing him. Is it just the fascination with a new person, new history, new story, he wondered? Certainly after a patient like Jennifer Andrews, a self observant patient like Stone was a welcome change.

When they were seated, Weiss asked if he had any reflections on the sessions so far. The patient was quiet and seemed tense.

"Before I get to that, I want to apologize for how I've been with you."

"Oh, how was that?"

"I've been very difficult. You ask me questions to try to help me, and I snap at you. I also wasn't being cooperative when I wouldn't talk much about being my mother's confidante." Weiss had certainly picked this up, but was struck by how excessively guilty the patient seemed to feel. Perhaps he is trying to tell me about guilt over something else he thought or wanted to say. Does he want to challenge me and then feel anxious about the consequences? Certainly with the kind of father he described, it would be very risky to confront or challenge. Better to be very careful with such a father. Better yet, be apologetic and show how hard you are trying to be good and polite. Just as he's being with me.

"And in the first meeting, I was trying to be so macho. I should be trying to get help here, but I just spent the time bragging."

"In what way were you bragging or macho?"

"Talking about the women I've had."

"You were telling me of some difficulties you've had in letting yourself find women who are available. To do that, it would seem, you have to tell me about your experiences with women."

"I don't know, I was just parading my exploits with women in front of you."

"Alright, let's say you were not just telling me of your struggles with women, but at the same time trying to show off or brag. So what? Why would that be such a problem for you?"

Clearly the patient was beginning to enact something with Weiss. He felt Weiss would be put off by his being "difficult" and what he considered his bragging about women. Transference, carrying over an experience of someone from the past to the analyst, was beginning to happen. But it concerned Weiss that this was happening so quickly and so early in the relationship. Weiss reminded himself that he had seen early, intense transferences in patients who had been subjected to severe, repeated trauma. Stone's experience of his father standing over him, the father's foot on his neck, would certainly qualify as traumatic. And such events rarely occur just once.

"It's inconceivable to me that you'd just stand by and accept me showing off. I felt you'd be dead set against it."

"Seems like you see me as calling the shots here, and as ready to judge you, criticize you, and tell you how to behave. In particular, you seem very worried about my reaction to your presenting yourself as a man, and as a man who has had relationships with women," Weiss said, offering his first interpretation of something in their relationship to see how the patient would be able to work with it.

"I guess I do. That's interesting. Maybe I see you like my father."

"How so?"

"He couldn't handle it when I would go out with girls or when girls showed an interest in me. When I was in seventh grade I received anonymous notes from a girl, telling me how cute she thought I was. I knew who it was, one of her friends told me. I told my parents about it, and my father said, 'She must have you mixed up with someone else, she couldn't be interested in a nerd like you.'"

Weiss continued to be impressed with Stone's ability to reflect on his own thoughts and reach insights. In particular, he was most excited by the patient's capacity to do this "in the transference," being able to see his experience of Weiss as directly influenced by his feelings about someone else in his early life, right now his father. Weiss found a beauty in the way a past relationship comes to life in the patient's experience of the analyst. Even after many years as an analyst, there was still a thrill for him in analyzing the ways the past comes alive in the present.

The bells in the tower sounded the quarter hour. "What's that?" asked Stone, going to the window.

"The bells from Burton Tower. You haven't heard them before?"

"Well, I guess I must have, but I never paid much attention to them." He stood at the window almost in a trance, scanning the horizon and then looking down at the streets below. "Where are all the people, the students?" he asked, almost inaudibly.

"You seem drawn to the view," Weiss said.

"There's a lot to see, but today I can't find anyone down there." Now during class time there were, of course, fewer people on the street than when Adam had arrived on the hour. The street was, however, far from empty.

"The airport seems quiet today, too, no planes." He returned to his chair. They sat looking at each other. Weiss had never been naturally comfortable sitting with someone in silence, but he had come to understand how important it is for an analyst to tolerate it. Adam again scanned the office, looking from time to time out the window and then resting the gaze of his large, flat eyes on Weiss. Silences with patients have their own individual qualities. With Weiss' discomfort with silence and love of words, he had trouble trusting what he could learn from these quiet, wordless periods. He had colleagues who were much better working in these nonverbal realms. He tried to sense what kind of silence this was. Definitely not the intimate silence of old friends or lovers. Not an angry silence either, or a withholding one, these he could pretty easily recognize. No, this was of another type, but what he could not yet say. The phrase "empty silence" crossed his mind.

"I had a dream last night. Should I tell it to you? Would that be helpful?" So careful, obsequious, thought Weiss.

"Of course. If we decide to work together, dreams can be very useful." Later in the work, thought Weiss, we will work on why he needs my permission. "Please . . ." said Weiss, with an inviting sweep of his hand.

"I'm on the dig in Arizona . . . it was so vivid, it's as if it really happened . . . I'm with someone, a man I'm pretty sure, and we're looking for artifacts of a lost civilization. We come upon a box, and the man I'm with can't decide whether to open it. I say, sure, go ahead, and when he does, a grotesque creature leaps out. It's a huge cat, like a tiger, but with rodent teeth. It has talons so long that they curl under its paws. As it leaps out, I see that a kite is tied to its tail. It circles around the box for a while, and then it comes for me, you know, comes at me. It gets closer, and then as it slides onto me, I can feel its fur against my face and its tremendous weight crushing down on me. I'm looking up at its belly. Part of it is smooth, and there are tattoos on it."

A rich dream. For some analysts, the dream is just one of many ways the unconscious can express itself. For Weiss the dream had a special place among a patient's communications. The dream for Weiss, like Freud, was the "royal road to the unconscious." Not the only road, but definitely the "royal" one. To analyze a dream held for Weiss the same satisfaction as discovering the full richness of a poem by unearthing the thread of symbols within it. Dreams, his own and his patients', were for Weiss personal poems, written by the unconscious mind, and he loved analyzing them. Dreams were Weiss' forte.

"Do you have any ideas about your dream?" asked Weiss, again testing the self-reflective waters.

"Yeah, I thought about it just after I woke up. The most important part of the dream seems to be the box and opening it. I think it's about coming here and looking into myself. It seems dangerous to open the box. I even feel a little scared telling you about it now."

"Scared of what?"

"Well, that there's something in me I don't want to open up."

"Yet in the dream you tell the man to open the box."

"I was just thinking maybe the dream has things switched around, so that I'm not me in the dream, I'm the other man, the man who is unsure about opening the box." Very possible, thought Weiss, who was playing around with the same understanding, the use of reversal, common in dreams. Stone says open the box, but that hides his worry by placing the struggle about opening it in the other man. Weiss was struck by the patient's natural capacity to think psychologically.

"That's an interesting possibility," said Weiss. "Then who might you be in the dream?"

"Well, that's kind of your job to help me open things up, so maybe I'm you in the dream. I'm saying what you would – 'Open it.'"

"That, too, is interesting. What about the creature in the box?"

"As I said, just scary things, thoughts, feelings." He paused and closed his eyes. Unlike the previous silence, this interruption felt definitely like one of withholding, of resistance.

"Are you holding something back?" Adam's eyes remained closed, and he brought his hand up slowly to cover his face. It was clear to Weiss how much the patient was struggling with himself.

"There are some thoughts about the dream I don't want to get into." Weiss considered his next move. It would probably be best to let this be for now. This patient looks as if he's already engaged in an analytic process. There will be time later to get into this secret. Yet Weiss did not or could not heed his own advice.

Weiss sensed something in this dream that was dark and unsettling; he needed to know what it was. He forged ahead.

"When you can't speak freely here, it's very important, really vital, to explore whatever is getting in the way."

"I told you I was worried about how you'd react to what I said last time. Well, I'm much more worried about what you'll think of me when I tell you more about this dream. It has to do with something I haven't told you about myself. Once you find out about it, you won't want to continue with me."

"Why not?"

"Because of . . . your background."

"My background?"

"I gather from your name that you're Jewish. Are you?"

Weiss was instantly thrown off balance. Though not an observant Jew, and married to an equally nonpracticing Protestant woman, he still felt Jewish. It was a feeling evoked every time he looked in a mirror and saw his Semitic features, deep set brown eyes and dark, kinky hair. It was also a feeling that overcame him every time he went to New York to visit his invalid father, a survivor of the Nazi death camp at Treblinka. As he thought about what this patient was saying, Weiss saw his own father's eyes, looking out from within his withered face, eyes filled with overwhelming sadness. Weiss intuitively knew that his thoughts about his father had some connection to what this patient was going to tell him. He needed first to explain to the patient why he was not going to answer questions about himself.

"I'm not going to tell you if I'm Jewish or not. If we work together it will be to your advantage that I remain somewhat opaque. But it's clear that you feel that I won't be able to remain helpfully neutral in my response to what you are trying to say." Weiss could hear in his own wordiness a signal of his own anxiety. He worked to manage it. "I can tell you that I will try my best to listen, to understand, and I have no intention of pulling away or rejecting you."

"O.K. I'll try to talk, try to tell you the dream." Weiss felt relieved that he had fielded his own strong emotions so he could reassure the patient. This seemed to be clearing the way for the patient to continue to work with his dream.

"I said there were tattoos on the creature's belly. One was a star, a six-sided star, a Jewish star." He paused again. "I can't talk about this when we're sitting face to face. Maybe I should lie on the couch, maybe that would make it easier."

Before Weiss could respond, the patient crossed the room and lay down on the couch. It was unusual for a patient to use the couch before the evaluation interviews were over, before actually starting analysis, and Weiss would have liked to explore with him further why he decided to do this. But the patient did it, and Weiss certainly was not going to order him to return to the chair.

Adam twisted around on the couch and tried different positions for his hands, placing them first at his sides and then behind his head. He seemed to be trying without much success to get comfortable. The head of the couch was a few feet from Weiss' chair, and he could hear the patient's breathing. It was slow and deliberate, but not a relaxed breathing. It was tense, from high in his chest.

"There are some more things in this dream, you've probably picked them up already, about Jews." He glanced over his shoulder, trying to see Weiss. "It feels really odd lying here. I thought it would be easier, but I feel instead like you're not there." A visible shudder passed through Adam's body. It seemed to Ivan the strongest reaction he had seen in a patient, as if he were on the edge of a panic. "Are you there, Dr. Weiss? I know you are, but . . ."

"I'm here, I'm here." said Weiss.

"O.K., so getting back to . . . I can't do this lying down right now. I thought, I don't know, but I feel at loose ends or something . . . so I think I'll just sit up again." He went back to the chair and seemed quickly composed. Weiss wondered why the patient had been unable to stay on the couch and thought about his anxious question, "Are you there, Dr. Weiss?" The patient seemed to Weiss at that moment to have felt terrifyingly alone.

"So, let me go on. There are more things in the dream about Jews. There's the kite. When I think of kite, I think 'kike.' I'm sorry to say this, I really feel bad about it. But I'm going to be honest. There's another tattoo on the creature's body, a swastika." Weiss' whole body clenched. "O.K., so this is what I don't want to tell you about myself. Since I was a teenager I've had this obsession with the Third Reich. I collect Nazi memorabilia and read everything I can get my hands on about Hitler. The whole thing holds this incredible allure for me. I'm even fascinated by the concentration camps."

This was Weiss' Achilles heel. He felt himself stiffen and tried to keep his reaction from showing. He wished the patient were still lying on the couch with Weiss out of the patient's view. Memories of the hours spent listening to his father talk about being in the camp surged through him. His father had said, "Your mother is too weak of spirit to talk about those times," but he had needed to tell someone. Weiss remembered being simultaneously fascinated and frightened by what his father had told him.

Seymour Weiss survived by being a barber. The women being led to the gas chambers at Treblinka were told they were being given a haircut before being deloused. The barbers, who were Jews, cut the hair of these women, knowing of course, that they were going immediately to their deaths. Any barber who revealed to the women that they were going to be put to death would himself be tortured and killed. So day after day in the camp, Seymour Weiss kept the secret and tried for years in his talks with his son, Ivan realized later, to expiate himself. Ivan felt caught in a terrible struggle about what his father had done. Should his father have revealed to the women what was going to happen? Was his father, as he claimed, humane by having these women's last minutes of life be calm ones by allowing them to believe they were being prepared to be workers at the camp? Was he just trying to survive himself? Was that not the most selfish thing he could do? Was it not natural to feel that way? The questions went on and on.

"Your father was your first patient," Weiss' analyst had observed to him. "A little boy's shoulders are not big enough to carry such a heavy load." Ivan had developed a way to protect himself from feelings about what his father was telling him about the camp. He would stop hearing. He would try to listen or at least appear to be, but in his mind what his father was saying would fragment into a swirl of words and phrases. Whenever his analyst would bring up any troubling feelings about these conversations with his father, Weiss would stop hearing him in exactly the same way.

The problem also showed itself in Weiss' work with his patients. At the beginning of his career, whenever patients brought up antisemitic feelings, the Nazis or the holocaust, Weiss found himself tuning out, just as he had done with his father. As he was able to reexperience this pattern in his own analysis, he came to listen better to his patients' communications in this area, but the problem was far from resolved.

Now as Adam talked, Weiss reminded himself that he was no longer a little boy being overwhelmed by a father's pain. Listening and trying to understand this material was going to be, however, a major challenge. Over the years Weiss had seen several patients whose hostile feelings toward people in their lives, past or present, had been directed at Weiss in antisemitic form. One man had the recurring thought, whenever Ivan gave him a bill, that "you're a penny pinching Jew." It soon became apparent that the man was enraged at his Methodist father who had abandoned the family and given neither love nor money to them. The patient clearly had some antisemitic feelings, as everyone has prejudices, but the hostility was at its root not toward Jews but toward his father.

In the analyses of many other patients, antisemitic feelings would come up from time to time. Adam Stone was different. The Third Reich and holocaust fascinated him. They were parts of an obsession and understanding its source might be central to his analysis. If this turned out to be true, Weiss wondered if he would be able to hear him and stay with him emotionally, both crucial to helping the patient.

He then shifted his focus, putting himself in Adam's place, and a question occurred to him. "I can see how hard this was to tell me, but let me lay something out for you to consider. As you said, you inferred from my name that I might be Jewish. Why, if the Nazis and the holocaust are so fascinating to you, would you choose to see an analyst you thought was a Jew?" As soon as he posed the question, Weiss was pretty sure he knew the answer.

"I don't know offhand, but I just thought about what I did with Lighthorse, the Director of the dig in Arizona. I went out of my way to provoke him. I'd say things to him that I knew would insult him. I just couldn't control it. Maybe I want to set this up again, you know, pick someone who'd be offended by what I have to say. Then I could fight with him, challenge him."

"Him?" Weiss asked.

"You."

This was exactly what Weiss was thinking. He is setting up a battle with me in an effort to rework the relationship with his father. His hatred of his father and his wishes to turn the tables on him are being expressed by choosing me, a Jewish analyst, and then torturing me with his thoughts about the holocaust. He does with me what he always wanted to do to his father.

Though this was certainly a difficult area for the patient to talk about and for the analyst to hear, Weiss still felt a satisfaction in understanding the unfolding of this pattern, this transference. And unlike his previous patient, Jennifer Andrews, whose sole aim was to act on her wishes to seduce and extort, Stone seemed very willing to look at his actions and find meaning in them. As the hour drew to a close, he felt this patient's analysis was already underway. Weiss was coming to feel that Adam Stone was an ideal psychoanalytic patient.

CHAPTER EIGHT

"**I**van, this guy's too good to be true," said Jake, interrupting Weiss' narration of the third session with Stone. They were midway through their downtown running route.

"It's true, his material is clear, and he is enacting his struggles with me early, but haven't you seen this in patients with a history of severe abuse? They have such a strong need to repeat the traumatizing scenes. They're never very far from them."

They interrupted their conversation, as they slowed to maneuver around pedestrians on Main Street. The street was lined with restaurants, galleries, and shops that had helped reverse the neighborhood's deterioration and made it, especially in the warmer weather, a thriving, lively place. Even on a winter day, many people were walking, and a skateboarder was out practicing stunts. There was at all times of the year the palpable energy of a street that had fought its way back.

"I've seen that, too," said Jake, when the pedestrian traffic had thinned, "but I don't think that fits this guy. Ivan, you're sharp, you pick up unconscious themes better than most analysts I know, so I'm not surprised that right off the bat you come up with a complete picture of his psychodynamics. But his material still strikes me as *too* clear. It's laid out for the picking. He plays out a transference. You ask him to look at it. He does. Then he interprets pretty subtle things about himself. And all in the first three sessions, for Christ's sake. There's no resistance, or at least it's not obvious. Maybe he's leaving out some of his feelings. Maybe there's some bigger secret or symptom he's not told you about. I don't know. It's just too easy.

"The Nazi stuff, for example. He chooses a Jewish analyst, you point this out to him, and then, like a well trained dog, he comes so quickly to the realization that he needs to challenge and fight with you. If he understands things so easily, what's he there for?"

He wanted to think that Jake was talking out of envy, but he knew well his own need to be right and his sensitivity to criticism. He sensed in himself a wish to have Adam Stone be a great patient and for himself to be a great analyst.

The sun came out for the first time that day, as they ran south on Main out of the downtown area and turned into a neighborhood near the Michigan Stadium, where

Ivan and Dana had lived as graduate students. They passed the brick house, with the huge shaggy pine overhanging it, that they had rented. Their fatherly landlord had invited them to park cars on the lawn during football games, as the landlord and his own wife had done when they were students living in the house. Ivan and Dana had done this and used the money to make it to the next fellowship check. Sometimes after the lawn was full, they would go to the game themselves.

He remembered, on one of those fall days, returning home after an Ohio State-Michigan game and conceiving Sonya. Weiss had been immersed in his dissertation research, with a part-time, low paying internship, and Dana was teaching dance at a poorly run studio that paid her very little. It had seemed to Weiss no time to have a child, but Dana was insistent, at times desperate, to have one. Though as a psychologist in training, he had worked with some child patients, he had not been drawn to have children himself. From the moment Sonya was born, his feelings changed. He didn't know that he could love another person so completely, so unambivalently, at times so overwhelmingly, as he did his daughter. He loved being with her through all of the twists and turns of her childhood, loved providing every opportunity for her to develop her skills and pursue her interests, and loved her love of him. He had missed her terribly during the recent years when she had been away at college and then in New York. Though she had returned defeated, unable to master her feelings about the rape, he was still delighted that she had come home.

Weiss realized that he would rather think about Sonya coming home, even if the reason for her return was a terrible one, than to think about what Jake was telling him. And Jake had more to say.

"Ivan, you've been a great help to me, through the rough times during my divorce, through my son's problems. And my troubles with our so called colleagues. You've told me things about myself I didn't want to hear. Well, I want to do the same for you, but I know you get rattled when anyone suggests you're anything less than a perfect analyst." They turned east at the football stadium, onto Stadium Boulevard, ran over a bridge as a freight train clattered underneath, and headed north into Burns Park, a neighborhood of stately, traditional homes and streets canopied by mature trees, the part of town popular with academics, where they both lived. As they turned north, a bitter wind met them, and they ran for a while without talking.

"You know me well, Jake," said Ivan, when the wind subsided, "but don't tiptoe around my neurosis, not that you tiptoe around much."

"No, tiptoeing's not my strong suit. I see how you work with this guy. Probably the way you work with other patients. It has its strengths and weaknesses. Strengths are obvious. You want to know the weaknesses?"

"I'm ready," said Weiss, as the wind whipped up again. "Why don't we stop at my house and warm up while we talk." They stopped at Ivan's house. No one was home, and they sat in the living room which looked out through a bay window onto the street. Ivan brought glasses of water for them.

"Ivan, you have an amazing mind, you're so good at tracking the way symbols play themselves out in patients' thoughts. You listen so well to the words, but at times, you get lost in them, seduced by them. Sometimes you miss the forest for the trees.

"You miss what's not in words, what's in the air with the patient. It's like the smell of the patient, the atmosphere he brings in with him. It also involves the whole countertransference area, what you feel about the patient, what the patient brings out in you."

Ivan knew that Jake was right. One of his teachers had called it tunnel vision, another told him, "I know you're smart, you know you're smart, even the patient probably knows it, so stop being so smart and just listen!"

"Thanks for telling me this. It's an old blind spot. I wish I didn't still have it."

"We all have our blind spots, Ivan. Mine are pretty glaring, like my irritation with my patients' resistances. I know I need to explore their avoidances and interpret them at the right time, but I find myself trying to break them of their resistances like getting a horse not to kick. Your blind spots are more subtle."

Weiss thought about his sessions with Adam and resolved to try to broaden his own vision. Maybe Jake was right that things are too clear, unfolding too much according to plan and that I can't see it, because of how I'm listening or not listening to him. I'm just tuning into his words. But what do I feel when I'm with him, what comes up in me, if I just let loose inside, if I dip deeper into my experience of him?

His thoughts were interrupted by seeing someone pull up to the curb in front of his house. The glare of the bright sunlight reflecting off the snow made it difficult to see who it was. He went to the window, looked out, and thought he saw his wife's pickup pull away.

"Was that Dana?" he asked, half to himself.

"Come again?"

"Nothing," said Weiss, still at the window, trying to recall what he had just seen. Was that her truck? The silhouette of someone in the passenger seat flashed through his mind. Was there someone with her?

"By the way, did you hear there's going to be a race this Sunday?" asked Jake. "It's the first time they're having it. I think it's called the Frozen Foot Run, for real die hards like us. You interested?"

"Sure, sure," Weiss said absently, watching the vehicle disappear around the corner at the end of the block.

"Ivan?"

"Sure, that's great. Dana is a . . . is going down to Ohio for a riding clinic, so I'm free all day." Was that her, he continued to wonder.

"Good." Jake finished his water. "Speaking of frozen feet, ready to set out across the tundra? I've got a patient in half an hour."

They ran back to Tower Plaza, Weiss changed in his private office and returned to the Clinic. He checked his e-mail, nothing important, and then his voicemail. "Just a reminder, Dad, Gratzi's tonight to meet Jerry. See ya." Good thing she reminded him, he hadn't put it in his schedule. Then Dana. "Ivan, Kevin wants to work with me on some things with my new horse. He's giving lessons all afternoon and anyway, he wants to wait until the arena is free, which is not until the early evening. So, this is getting a little long winded. Bottom line, I'll be a little late for the dinner with Sonya and Jerry. Tell them I'm sorry. I'll get there about 8:30. Sorry. Thanks. Bye." She sounded rushed, pressured.

He settled back in his swivel chair and tried to stop the direction he knew his thoughts were going. They were sliding down to a place they had been before. She's with Kevin, their interest in horses is a strong bond, as is their student-teacher bond. Is that all there is between them? Of course. But Dana is such a passionate person. Can she be attached to Kevin without giving everything of herself to him? He then thought about seeing her stopping at the house and then speeding away. Was she speeding? Was it even her? Was she with Kevin? He felt himself getting swamped by these concerns, these old, very familiar worries.

During the early years of their marriage, Weiss' obsession with Dana being with other men was the problem that had led him to seek psychoanalysis for himself. He had just received his Ph.D. and been chosen over many applicants for a faculty position in the Psychiatry Department at Michigan, but he had become so preoccupied with thoughts of his wife cheating on him that he was losing his ability to focus on his patients, his students, or the professional writing he was supposed to be doing to get tenure. He was floundering. He would call Dana during the day under the pretense that he missed her and wanted to hear her voice, trying to force an intimate, caring tone. The real reason was to keep track of her, to quiet what had become to him near certainties that she was off with another man. It progressed to the point that he was driving home in the middle of the day to see if her car was there. When he found himself surreptitiously following her, he became concerned about himself. When it went beyond even that to being on the verge of calling a private detective, concern about himself turned to alarm, and he asked a colleague for the name of a psychoanalyst.

Unlike many psychoanalysts who enter psychoanalysis as a required part of their training, Weiss had begun his own analysis before he had even thought of applying to the Institute. He had started because he had some big problems, and he knew it. He loved Dana but could sense his love for her souring into paranoia. These problems were not totally resolved, but he had learned a great deal about their sources and had relived in his analysis some of the experiences that lay behind this terrible symptom.

"You feel your rages and your sexual excitements drove your mother into her grave," his analyst had said. "Maybe a perfect boy, a totally nice, sanitized boy could have kept her alive. So here you are now, married to a woman who turns you on, who enrages you, too. You are not a perfect, sanitized man. No, you are man full of impulses toward her. You put the face of your mother on your wife and are convinced that your passion and your anger will drive her away too. Any woman you are close enough to love and to hate, you feel in your gut you will lose." Here I am again. The thoughts of Dana and Kevin being involved together are gaining ground in my mind. Now I understand these thoughts, now I can analyze them, as I have analyzed them before. Hopefully I can keep them from taking over.

He rocked his chair back, closed his eyes and saw his mother's face the morning of her last day, looking over her shoulder at him, as he left for school, the corners of her eyes creased by her smile. It was this same look in Dana's eyes that first drew Ivan to her. He felt tears well up and blotted them dry. You don't have to lose everyone you love, he whispered to himself.

The tower bells, signaling the hour, interrupted his unsettling thoughts. He struggled to turn his focus to the seminar he was about to teach, one in his area of special interest, for which he was gaining a national reputation, the role of early childhood neglect and abandonment on the formation of the criminal mind. As he walked downstairs, he thought, years ago my paranoia threatened my career and my sanity. I must somehow prevent that from happening again.

CHAPTER NINE

S onya and her new boyfriend, Jerry, were already seated in a booth at Gratzi, when Ivan arrived. Jerry was a square built young man with an open, ruddy, boyish face. He looked like a slightly older version of two football player boyfriends Sonya had dated in high school. The speed with which the young man was on his feet and extending his hand to Weiss revealed how eager he was to please. Ivan cautioned himself not to stereotype him, but he had trouble overcoming a feeling that Sonya deserved better. Ivan explained that Dana would be late, and they ordered drinks. After a few minutes of small talk about the restaurant and the weather, Sonya set out on her mission to have her father like Jerry.

"Dad, you know before Jerry got into football in high school, he was a sprinter. I've told him about your passion for running."

"Sonya said you run in races. What's your distance?"

Weiss explained that he didn't have a favorite distance, but seemed to be most competitive in the 5K.

"If you're good at the 5K, you might try some even shorter distances for speed, if they have such races for . . . um, older, I mean . . . senior . . ."

"They call it masters runners," Weiss helped out.

"Right, masters." Jerry then launched into his opinions about athletics as a good preparation for competition in the business world.

"Is business what you are interested in?" asked Weiss.

"Didn't I tell you, Dad, maybe I told Mom, that Jerry's studying engineering, in a really interesting area. He's studying to be an acoustical engineer, he wants to design concert halls. He's also a violinist, and his teachers told him he was really talented, good enough to perform professionally." Listen, Dad, she really wanted to say, he's not some dolt engineer or dumb football player, he's interested in the arts. Sonya knew she was working hard to have her father approve of Jerry. She wondered, for a moment, if she was also trying to convince herself.

They talked about Jerry's decision to become an acoustical engineer, how he found the endless practice hours necessary to become a performing violinist tedious and lonely, and how he was now combining his longstanding interest in mechanical things with his love of music. He talked of his fascination with the acoustical problems at Lincoln Center's concert hall, and how the problems were finally resolved.

Ivan was coming to feel he had misjudged Jerry, but still had trouble seeing him with Sonya. She seemed to be promoting him, but not really involved with him. Ivan reminded himself that after New York it might be a while before his daughter could be involved with any man.

As Jerry extolled the acoustics of the University's Hill Auditorium, Ivan noticed it was after nine and began checking the door for Dana. Everything with horses seemed to take longer than planned, "stable time," he called it. Cooling the horses out, dealing with endless equine injuries, always something. Even though he had come to expect such things, he was nevertheless annoyed that Dana was late. They ordered appetizers and another round of drinks.

At about 9:30 Dana rushed in, gave Ivan a peck on the cheek, squeezed Sonya's shoulder, and apologized to everyone. Sonya introduced Jerry and her mother to each other, Jerry again jumping to his feet, shaking her hand and pulling out a chair for her. Seems like a young bank president, thought Dana. But kind of charming and caring just the same.

After the waitress took their dinner orders, Jerry asked Dana about her riding. She talked briefly about how she became involved in it when she won a free riding lesson at a raffle and from then on was hooked. Jerry talked about trail riding he had done out west the previous summer.

"How did things go with Kevin and the new horse?" asked Ivan.

"Oh . . . yes," said Dana, seeming to Ivan momentarily puzzled by his question. "Kevin set up a jumping chute to help me work with the horse. Things went fine." It surprised Ivan that Dana, who took any opportunity to talk about her work with horses, was saying so little. It took Sonya to draw her out.

"Jumping chute?" Sonya asked.

Dana described a jumping chute, barriers set up to create a kind of alley ending at the jump. If the horse is urged forward, it cannot go around the obstacle. She explained that this frees the rider to do such exercises as jumping without holding the reins, or jumping with her eyes closed.

"Mother, why do you want to jump with your eyes closed?" asked Sonya, some alarm in her voice.

"To teach me to rely on all the cues, mainly the physical ones, from the horse. When your eyes are closed, you learn to listen better to the horse's body, what it feels like as it moves, as it readies and takes the jump. Kevin, that's my trainer, Jerry, thinks I've improved a lot, but that I'm not quite in tune with the movement of the horse as it starts to jump. I'm behind the horse, behind its motion." Dana, it seemed to Ivan, was now speaking with her usual enthusiasm about riding.

"So with your eyes closed you learn to anticipate the moment it's ready to jump?" Jerry asked.

"Right, that's it."

"Sounds very demanding and athletic."

"It surprises a lot of people that riding is athletic," said Dana.

"Jerry's been very involved in athletics," said Sonya. "We were talking about running before you got here."

"What sports are you involved in?" asked Dana. Jerry jumped on the question.

"Football. In high school, it was my life. I was almost at the level to play for Michigan, but not quite. It was a big disappointment. I still play intramural football. There I'm great. Big fish in a small pond."

The food arrived, and the conversation moved to Jerry's childhood growing up in the Upper Peninsula of Michigan. His father was a car dealer, the only Ford dealer for 100 miles, his mother an elementary school teacher. He talked of going, when he was young, with his father to dealers' meetings in Dearborn, near Detroit, and how overwhelmed he had at first been by being in a city. On one of these trips, they visited the University of Michigan, and Jerry decided that he would do whatever he could to go to college there. Ann Arbor had seemed to him even then to have the advantages of a city, but still close enough to farm country that it reminded him of home.

As he talked about how close he still felt to his family, his father in particular, and of how torn he was between making a career for himself in some urban area and going back to a rural life of the Upper Peninsula, Ivan sensed a depth to this young man. Is he good enough for Sonya? Maybe no one is good enough for my little girl.

When coffee was served, Dana asked Sonya how things had gone with her new client.

"It was just a first meeting, things went alright," said Sonya, hoping her understated tone would keep her attraction to her new client from showing.

"Is it a big job?" asked Ivan.

"I think it might be. The place has a lot of potential. It's one of those turn of the century neo-classical style houses, large rooms, high ceilings, all kinds of neat stuff you can't pay to have built now, like carved cornices over the doors, built in corner display cabinets, things like that. With some work it could be really striking and at the same time subtle. It depends on what he wants to do."

"How can you tell what someone wants?" asked Jerry. "If I bought a house and needed to decorate it, I wouldn't know where to start to tell a decorator what I want."

"Even though you might not be able to put it into words," said Sonya, "you have your tastes. You know when you walk into a room if you love it or hate it, or somewhere in between. There's inside everyone an environment they'd be most comfortable in."

"Sonya and I have talked about how what she does and what I do are in some ways similar," said Ivan. "Clients come to her looking to construct their surroundings or to change them, but they can't say, don't really know, what the new environment should look like. She tries to sense by getting to know them what that world looks like. Patients come to me wanting the same thing, to become something they sense they can be and want me to help them find, but without knowing yet what that new self is."

"Like the sculptor trying to find the statue hidden in the uncut stone," offered Jerry.

Sonya, Ivan, and Dana were all impressed by Jerry's comment. They had all underestimated him, and each at that moment knew it. Sonya looked at Jerry with a smile more inviting that at any time since they met. Being smart and insightful, Jerry was discovering, were the most respected qualities in the Weiss family.

CHAPTER TEN

"**D**etective Farley, I hate to disturb you during your lunch, and I know it's not procedure to do so . . ."

"Don't sweat it, Marge, what's up?"

"Well there's a man down here who demands to see someone right now. He won't even sit down and fill out the complaint sheet. Detective Vernon is supposed to be on duty, but I can't locate him, and his backup is out on a call or something and won't answer my page."

"It's alright, Marge, send him up."

John Farley wrapped up the sandwich he had just started, swept the crumbs off the desk, and tightened his tie. He was, after a few months in the department, far from comfortable with its stiffness and formality. Like Marge everyone was always falling over themselves to apologize for anything that wasn't "procedure," every belch or fart had to be logged, people sat in front of their computers all day, political correctness reigned supreme, and no one would call him John.

"Everyone seems to have a police manual stuck up their ass," he had said to his wife, whose idea it had been to move. It bothered him, too, that everyone, the people he worked with, along with the perps and the citizens, were constantly claiming they were being mistreated. It seemed to John like whining. Most of all, no one he was working with seemed to like what they were doing.

He had left, a few months before, the only department he had served in, in Brownsville, Texas. He had risen through the ranks, to Chief Detective, supervising a department of ten, and was ready, at the time they decided to move, to run for Sheriff of the County. Though John loved his job in Brownsville, he and his wife, Cheryl, had never felt fully part of the community and each had come to feel personally limited living there. They had talked often of leaving, so when Cheryl decided to go back to school and was accepted, to her surprise, to Michigan's School of Social Work, they decided to move.

Ann Arbor had been their dream location. Cheryl, who had grown up in Ohio, looked forward to the change of seasons she had so much missed. They were both drawn to Ann Arbor as a culturally richer, more diverse community. They both loved ethnic restaurants and music of all kinds, and Cheryl loved to go to museums and art galleries. All of this they were pleased to have found in Ann Arbor.

There was also, at least so far, a serious disappointment. They were finding it difficult to meet people. They discovered Ann Arbor to be composed of many small, insulated communities, and the people hard to get to know. Cheryl, who loved to cook and entertain, had looked forward to intimate dinner parties with interesting conversation. So far there were no couples she and John knew well enough, or liked well enough, to invite. They were coming to regret the move.

Marge showed the man into Farley's office and handed the detective the blank complaint form. Late twenties, handsome, but with a sour look on his face. Maybe he's been in Ann Arbor too long.

"What can I do for you?"

"The first thing you can do is improve your Department's responsiveness to someone coming in with a complaint. I had to wait altogether too long and then was told some clerk would talk to me. I know my way around police departments, and I know how things should be handled."

"O.K., we screwed up, now what can I do for you?"

Farley could see that his reaction had surprised the guy, who was itching for a fight.

"Well, O.K., I'm glad you said that, so I'll go on. Something dangerous is going on that I want to report. I want it investigated. I'm frightened." Farley had seen many frightened people, from wives terrified of abusive or homicidal husbands, to men with huge gambling debts. He had seen fear in underworld types with contracts out on them and the fear in people whose houses have just been robbed. He knew what fear smelled like, and he didn't smell it here. At least, not yet.

"Tell me about it."

"I'm being harassed, and I think I'm also being stalked. The harassment I'm certain about."

"So how did this all start?"

"I came to Ann Arbor last July to join the Psychology Department. The phone calls started about a month ago. So far that's what it's mostly been. I'd get messages on my machine, saying things like, 'Ann Arbor seems to be a pretty nice place, but don't be so sure,' and 'You think you've made it. You haven't. There's only room for one of us.' I got a few anonymous e-mails that said the same things. He phoned me only when I wasn't home. He seemed to know just when I wouldn't be there, even leaving messages on the only evening I'm out teaching. I wondered, of course, if my house was being watched.

"Things went on this way for about three weeks, and then about two weeks ago the calls got more menacing. He said things like 'Watch your back' and 'You're up to no good and someone has to stop you.' I got sick of this and thought that if he's leaving messages when I'm not there, maybe he doesn't want to talk to me, and maybe if I talked to him he'd get scared off. So I broke my routine and stayed home to be there if he called."

Alarms from the Fire Department, which faced Farley's office, sounded, and they both looked out the window to see the doors swing open and the trucks roar out, sirens wailing. Farley thought of times early in his career, when he would go on police backup to fire calls in Brownsville. He had always been torn between the excitement and action of being out on the front lines, making quick decisions, decisions that meant something, and the quieter life of detective work, interviewing victims, suspects, and witnesses. Right now he wished he were out on a fire call. This man spoke well, was obviously intelligent, and his story hung together, but there was something odd about it. Is it, Farley wondered, that I still don't sense in him the fear he's talking about? Or is there something else?

"So did he call the day you stayed home?"

"Yes. I could hear his surprise that I'd answered, and then he said that he was going to make life a living hell for me. I asked who he was. Of course, he didn't say. I asked why was he harassing me. I asked him if I knew him, if maybe we could discuss this, maybe there'd been some misunderstanding. I tried to be reasonable, but it was no use. He just said, 'There's room for only one of us,' and hung up."

"I assume you tried Caller ID?"

"Of course, and *69, but he blocks them."

"You know, with harassment, the victim often knows the harasser. Do you have any idea who this is?"

"I don't, I really have no idea."

Farley thought back to what the harasser had said, that there was "only room for one of us."

"Is there someone competing with you over something?"

"I can't think of anyone." It seemed to Farley that the answer came too quickly. Why doesn't he give himself any time to run through the people in his life who might have such feelings toward him?

"Why don't you take a minute to think about it."

"You think I haven't asked myself this question? Of course I have, many times. I think about it all the time. There's no one I come up with."

"O.K., O.K., but I have to tell you, in these cases it's usually a lead from the victim that gives us somewhere to start."

The firehouse doors rumbled to a close, and the sound of the fire truck sirens dissolved into the routine sounds of the street. Farley swiveled his chair around, as he thought about what else to say, and saw children lined up and ready to file into the Children's Museum next to the firehouse. He heard his own stomach growl, felt the interview going nowhere, and wanted to finish his lunch.

"You said you started last July in the Psychology Department. Is there anyone there who might not want a new guy coming in?"

"I don't think so. That would be more likely if I were in some important position. I'm not." He paused and looked up at the ceiling. "Unless, of course, that person was not seeing things rationally. Which would fit with the way he sounds. He sounds nuts."

"What's your specialty?"

"I study the psychology of habitual law breakers, criminal psychology." This interested Farley who in Texas had taken courses toward a masters in criminology. The courses in forensic psychology had always fascinated him. It struck him as slightly odd that a man studying criminal personality had just called the harasser "nuts."

"Do you think it's possible that one of the criminals you've studied could be doing this?" The young man seemed surprised by the question.

"Well, I guess that's possible, I'd have to think about it."

"Yeah, you might want to do that." Farley thought of some criminals he'd known who wouldn't take to someone knowing too much about them or to being treated like guinea pigs in some prof's research.

As the detective continued to ask him more questions, waves of fatigue washed through the young man and were so distracting that he was barely able to even hear the questions. He had not expected the interview to go on so long. Maybe, he thought, he should have waited even longer after returning from France. Jetlag would be a problem for anyone, but his AIDS symptoms were making it a hundred times worse. Making this harassment complaint sound totally credible was a key part of the plan. His fatigue was making it hard to get words out, and he was worried he was not convincing. The danger had to be considered absolutely real.

As the detective made some notes, the young man marshaled strength from somewhere inside himself. He's listening, he's asking questions. That's a good sign. If he realized this was all a web of lies, he'd have found some polite way to get rid of me, or worse, accuse me of making a false complaint. No sign of any of this. Just the fact that I'm still here talking, with him taking notes, tells me it's going fine, but I'm so exhausted. Just hold on a little longer . . .

As Farley looked up from his pad, he saw the young man begin to slump to the side, as the arm he had been leaning on suddenly buckled. The man's face turned ashen, and he began to fall forward out of the chair.

"Are you all right?" Farley asked, coming quickly from around his desk to help.

"I'm fine," he said, brushing the offer of help aside, clutching the arm of the chair to right himself. "I didn't realize how exhausted I was. I've lost a lot of sleep over this."

"Sure you're alright?"

"Yeah, I'm O.K. now." He worked to pull himself up in the chair and find some strength in his voice. "But some water would be great."

The moment he heard the door close behind the detective, he reached into his left pants pocket, the one where he kept the uppers, fished out a couple of pills and, aware of the possibility of surveillance cameras, palmed them into his mouth during a fake cough. My stomach is empty, they should get into my system quickly. I can make it through this.

Farley returned with the water and sat back down.

"You sure you're alright?" asked the detective, as the man closed his eyes and drank down the water in long, slow swallows.

"Yeah, I'm O.K. now."

"Well, I'm really not sure there's much I can do for you. These are anonymous calls, probably crank calls, and the caller hasn't made any specific threats against you."

"Someone is threatening my life, and you're calling them crank calls!" the young man said, summoning all the energy he could to sound irate. "I know what a crank call is, and this isn't one. This guy apparently knows me and has got some vendetta with me."

"This may not be much of a reassurance to you, but people who harass like this, by phone, usually aren't dangerous. They choose this kind of crime, because they're fearful, introverted types. They can threaten only over the phone, anonymously, rather than in person. This guy could be the exception and be a real threat to you. I don't know. The main thing is that I can't do much more with what you've got." The young man felt a desire to take this further, to demand a court ordered wire tap. He felt the urge to push just to see if he could get it. But this helpful cop might actually get one, and that would mean more investigation than his story could take. He needed to keep his eye on the goal and not be distracted by the temptation to manipulate the detective.

"So I just wait until it gets worse, until he comes after me?"

"The long and short of it is, that's right, but if and when he takes that step, we're here and we'll help. Now if you'll fill out the complaint form and drop it off with the desk sergeant downstairs, we'll have all the information at the ready." Farley rose from his chair.

"O.K." he said, took the form, and left. Downstairs he filled it out using an alias. Weeks earlier, in a letter posing as a prospective student, he had requested and received from the Psychology Department a set of bios of the faculty and their research interests. From it he had chosen the perfect alias, Joseph Benedict, a young assistant professor with a research interest in criminal personality. He handed the desk sergeant the form and left the station, relieved that it was only a few minutes now until he could get to his car and collapse.

Farley unwrapped his sandwich and wondered why a young man, even having missed some sleep, would almost pass out? As he gazed out of the window and ate, he had the uneasy feeling that he had been duped.

CHAPTER ELEVEN

S onya had raced around all morning picking out last minute sample books to show Nick Streeter. After months of trying to fill her time, she was now getting so busy that she was barely able to make it on time for her appointment with him. Just as she was leaving her apartment, she took a call from another new client, an older man whose wife had just died, who felt the need to describe to Sonya in excruciating detail his house and the plans he and his late wife had to redecorate it. He told her he had to get started on it right away. She felt impatient with him and wanted to tell him to mourn his wife. He could redecorate his house just the way the two of them had planned, but when he finished he wouldn't find his wife there.

She twisted the rearview mirror to check her makeup and clothes. Different outfit, of course, from the first visit, sweater, a little on the tight side, shorter skirt, sexier to be sure. Still professional, she reassured herself.

He met her before she rang the bell. Had he seen her primping in the car? The moment of worry and embarrassment gave way to feeling pleased that he wanted to look at her. Maybe he had been watching expectantly for her to arrive. Since the rape, the interest of men made her instantly anxious. The image of the taut forearm pressed against her remained stubbornly fixed in her mind, reinforcing the simple, brutal fact that most men could overpower her. Since the rape, this knowledge hung in the air, whenever she was alone with a man. I feel only a little edgy about him looking at me, but not panicked, she thought. Maybe that's a step forward.

He showed her into the living room. An antique silver tea pot was on the sideboard, and she smelled coffee brewing.

"Would you like some coffee or tea? I also have some sweet rolls from a place I discovered over the bridge," he said, pointing in the direction. He's gone to some trouble for me. She was pleased.

"Tea would be great. You seem to be finding your way around Ann Arbor."

"Yeah, I guess I am. It's been easy. Must be midwestern friendliness. You ask people for directions, and they're eager to help. At the same time there's a sophistication here. Yesterday I walked up to Main and poked around some of the art galleries. I found this market area and a bakery called, I think, Fatboys?" She laughed.

"Doughboys, but your name for it is better, you certainly can quickly turn into a fatboy, or fatgirl, if you make that a regular stop. The market area, it's called Kerrytown, has really shaped up. My parents still remember when it was considered the 'bad' part of town. Personally I think it's getting a little too chic. I liked it better when it still had some of the old warehouse feel. It seemed more like the real world. The prices have become unreal, too. Be careful, the delicatessen and the fish market are wildly overpriced." Not a good business move, she thought, to plant the idea of overpricing, when I haven't talked money with him yet. For some reason this is of no concern to me, she thought. There is something so familiar and easy about him, I feel I can say anything I want to him.

"You should go down there on Saturday mornings in the spring, if it ever comes. The farmers bring in produce, there's all sorts of fruits and vegetables and great flowers, picked the same day." She loved the flowers spilling out into the aisles and the little jars of homemade jam. Saturday morning trips to the Farmers Market were a family tradition. One of her earliest memories was of riding on her father's shoulders, as they walked through the market, her mother handing a few flowers of a bouquet up to her. She remembered how funny it was, as she rode along, to see the tops of peoples' heads.

She was surprised when these memories suddenly gave way to an image of strolling through the market with her arm locked in a man's, her head bobbing every so often to the side to feel his shoulder and then looking up to see this man, Nick, who was now pouring her tea. Why don't I see Jerry in this scene?

"Sounds like the place to be on a Saturday around here."

"It is," she said, their eyes meeting for an uncomfortable moment, as he passed her the tea.

They talked about his ideas for the house. He wanted the decorating to enhance the traditional style of the house, but wanted the look to have an "edge" by adding some more modern touches.

"I've seen houses of this vintage made too quaint for my taste," he said. "I don't want to feel I'm living in a country B&B, no matter how charming." He offered her a sweet roll. "Don't get me wrong, I like B&Bs, and with the right person they can be great, but I don't want to live full time in one." She felt the urge to put the decorating task aside and ask him what B&Bs he had been to, where he had traveled, and most of all, if there were a "right person" in his life now.

She overcame her urge, accepted the sweet roll, and discussed with him how these days there are many ways of decorating along the lines he was suggesting. She pulled an Architectural Digest from her briefcase and showed him an article illustrating the transformation of a neo-classical house like his in Connecticut. It had been nicely restored and decorated mostly in a traditional style, accented by a few Asian pieces and a colorful rug with a geometric design. The effect was definitely not cute. He looked very carefully at the article, while she sipped her tea.

"This is exactly what I'm looking to do. These rooms are open and inviting. I don't like the feeling in an old house decorated in an ultra modern trendy way. I find that jarring. But I also find traditional Victorian rooms with all that overstuffed furniture oppressive."

"You seem to know your way around decorating."

"Not really, but I do know some about Victorian style. I think I told you I've done research on child abuse during that era. I've also done some work on Victorian women and hysteria."

She found herself again wanting to put discussion of his decorating needs aside and talk about his research. She imagined how easy it would be to discuss it together. She was again comparing him with Jerry. She often found with Jerry he didn't quite understand what she meant. If she made a joke, she had to explain it before he would laugh, which he sometimes would just to be polite. The problem ran the other way, too. He would tell her a story about his childhood up north, and she wouldn't get the point before he explained things about farming and rural life. This had frustrated her, and they had talked about it. He acknowledged that they were from different backgrounds and that if they were going to have a relationship, they would have to "build bridges." Whenever they had done so, it had strengthened their relationship. It did, however, take work. Talking with Nick seemed, in contrast, so effortless. Maybe he's from the same kind of background as me, though I don't know the first thing about him.

She showed him a preliminary sketch of her suggestions for the living room and then found places she had marked in catalogs and sample books to show him various furniture and wallpaper possibilities. She suggested they go through the house to show him her ideas for the other rooms. They went first through a small room just off the front entry hall, probably originally a bedroom, which could be made into either a library or office, or possibly a guest room. In an old fashioned gentlemanly way, he gestured for her to precede him up the stairs.

Before she was through offering her suggestions about the second bedroom, he said that they would need to continue the planning another day, hopefully soon, even tomorrow, if she had time, but that he needed to be somewhere.

"I'm really excited about these ideas, but I guess I didn't think you would have worked them out already in such detail, so I didn't set aside enough time for our meeting," he said. She glanced down at her watch. She had been there an hour.

"I guess I had worked up more than I thought," she said.

"No, it's my fault. I should have arranged for more time." Though an hour was the usual length of a meeting with a client at this stage, she felt hurt that he had not set more time aside. I'm taking this very personally. It doesn't take a genius, she thought, to figure out why – I want it to be personal, very personal.

"No problem. I'll leave the sketches and sample books. Look the stuff over, and we'll get together soon."

He helped her on with her coat. She smelled his cologne, subtle, not too sweet.

CHAPTER TWELVE

I van awoke at eight to the phone ringing. Who's calling so early on a Saturday morning? He reached for the portable phone on the stand by his bed, but Dana had already come around to his side, answered it, and left the room. He sat up and heard her padding down the stairs and then quietly close a door. He lay back down for a few minutes and then got up and began to read through the paper he was to deliver at the Psychoanalytic Institute that afternoon, a psychoanalytic study of Charles Manson.

This was something new for Weiss; he had never tried to do a psychological study of someone he had never met. He had, in fact, written critiques of other researchers who played fast and loose with a few facts about historical or current figures and then indulged in wild speculation about their subjects. However Charles Manson was too tempting a subject for Weiss, who had tried in his research and writing to show a connection between the trauma of early life abandonment and the development of criminal personality. Here was a real life example, and one whose fame might draw wider attention to the dangers of early childhood abuse and neglect.

He read through the paper, taking the same critical approach he would with someone else's work. It is certainly somewhat speculative, but at the same time, there is a lot of well confirmed data about Manson's early life and adult personality from credible sources. He crossed the room to get a pen to make notes, when Dana returned looking shaken.

"That was Kevin from the stable. Master, my gelding, is collicking. The vet's already there. I've gotta go." Dana had explained before to Ivan that colic, which is annoying and frustrating for human infants and their parents, is potentially fatal in horses.

"What are you doing today?" she asked distractedly, as she dressed. He was surprised she had not remembered he was giving the paper, as she had seemed particularly interested in the subject and had talked of going to hear him deliver it.

"I'm giving my Manson paper this afternoon."

"It's today, damn, I totally forgot. I wanted to hear it, too. Well, maybe if this colic gets taken care of, I'll ride in with you or go myself." He knew this was unlikely. Her horses had collicked a few times before, and he remembered her being out there for hours, once all night.

"It's at 2:00 at the Institute, right?"

"Right."

"I'll see how it goes. So, I'm going to take off," she said, pulling some jeans from the dresser.

"The horse can't wait for, maybe, twenty minutes or so?" he asked, with his eyes inviting her to come back to bed. "You said the vet's already there. What more can you do?" She stood for a moment with the jeans in her hand and then dropped them and crawled in close to Ivan, molding herself to him. Though she was a tall woman, when she was worried or felt insecure, she could make herself, as she did now, very small against him. He felt a shudder move through her and looked down to see her eyes tearing up. He knew all she wanted was to be held.

"You're really worried about the horse."

"Yeah, I guess so," she said, holding him tight. He brushed a tear from her cheek and kissed her. She began to pull away.

"I know you're worried, but the last thing the vet needs is a nervous mother looking over his shoulder."

"Right, but I've got to be there. You remember how I was when Sonya had even a sniffle." He, of course, remembered. She had been the most protective mother Ivan could imagine, at times overprotective. Ivan had worried that Sonya would become a hypochondriac or overly cautious. As Sonya moved through her adolescence, Ivan had come to realize that Sonya's personality had been influenced by her mother's overprotectiveness, but in a different way than he had anticipated. Maybe to break free from her mother, Sonya became a risk taker. Ivan had even wondered if not being concerned enough about her own safety had played some part in her getting attacked.

"You're a dedicated mother, Dana, to children, to horses. I know you've gotta go. I hope your horse is alright."

"Good luck with your paper."

After she left, he went downstairs and fixed himself breakfast. While he ate, he made some last minute changes to his paper. He practiced reading it aloud a few times, working on his delivery. He then went for a run. When he returned, Dana was not yet back. She had been gone almost three hours. He reminded himself how long these colic episodes took to resolve. Just as he was about to step into the shower, the phone rang.

"Dr. Weiss?"

"Yes."

"Terry from the Cruise Center. Is Dana there?"

"No, Terry, she's not."

"Do you know when I can catch her?"

"I don't. She had a problem with her horse and went out to the stable. I don't know how long she'll be out there, could be some time. I can leave a message here for her to call you."

"Well, O.K., but it's got to be by five. We close then, and she's got to get me the deposit today."

"Hmm, that's odd, I thought she sent you the deposit a week ago."

"She said she would. We got the flights worked out, great fares, and I told her I needed the deposit to hold your reservations for the cruise. Your wife said fine, and that she'd be down the next day to drop off a check, or she'd call and put it on a credit card. I've been calling her and leaving messages all week with no luck." Ivan was puzzled. Dana was so excited about the cruise, that it was hard to imagine her not returning the travel agent's calls.

"I don't know what to say, Terry, I didn't know anything about the deposit. Monday's too late to get it to you?"

"Yes, well at least for this booking. The Eastern Mediterranean is a really hot destination right now, maybe because the peace talks are going well, I don't know. You should know that if we rebook it, I won't be able to get you as good a deal. If you guys still want to go, I can put the deposit on your Visa right now." Ivan disliked making decisions under pressure. They often turned out to be poor ones. Being an analyst was, in this respect, well suited to him. Seeing patients four or five times a week, over a number of years, there was time for things to unfold, for themes to become clear in his mind. The reality of the world outside the analytic consulting room did not usually afford this luxury to contemplate choices.

This seemed like a simple decision. Put it on the credit card. But why had Dana not done that and not even called Terry back? Did she get a better deal with another agent? Is she bargaining for a better price? Possible, but that wasn't Dana's style. Or, was she having second thoughts about going on the cruise, the cruise she had been pushing them to take for years?

"Terry, frankly I don't know why she hasn't called you back. I'll try to reach her at the stable. You say you need to know by five. Either she or I will get back to you by then."

"O.K., Dr. Weiss."

He showered, dressed, and reviewed the paper one last time.

When Ivan grabbed his overcoat on his way out, he was surprised to see Dana's heavy rubber farm boots, the ones she always wore at the stable, on the floor of the closet. Maybe, he thought, she has another pair out there.

It was 12:45 now, ample time to get to the Institute in Farmington Hills by 2:00. I'll call Dana on my cell phone on the way and then call Terry.

He felt edgy and rushed, not how he wanted to feel before giving a paper at the Institute. He had spent time in his analysis trying to separate his experience of the Institute and its members from his unconscious fantasies about them. He still felt defensive around his colleagues, as if they were always ready to criticize him for being less than perfect. Sometimes at the height of his irrationalities, he feared he would be thrown out of the Institute. He came to understand that he lived with an unconscious dread that it would be discovered that these faults, these flaws, had been the cause of his mother's death. Though his analytic work had made this fantasy less powerful, on a day such as this, it could again take hold of Weiss.

Driving faster than his usual conservative, cruise controlled 64 mph, he tried to reach Dana at the stable, but received only the recording. He tried again and when the recording started, he slammed the phone down on the carseat. If she were in the arena, she wouldn't hear the phone, but a colicking horse would be in its stall within easy earshot of the phone. He saw in his mind her barn boots in the closet. Where was she? Maybe she's on her way home, maybe even home by now. He suddenly had to know. He turned around and sped home. She was not there. He then drove toward the stable, driving now dangerously fast, running a couple of lights, and skidding on the slippery country roads. When he was halfway there, he glanced at the dashboard clock and was shocked that it was already 1:30. He turned around again and headed for the Institute. He then called his daughter.

"Hi, Dad, I was just about to call you guys. I met with the client I told you about, and we're going ahead with the decorating. He seems ready to do a pretty complete job! He said . . ."

"That's terrific," Ivan said, cutting his daughter off. "Listen, Sonya, have you talked to your mother today?"

"No. Why? Are you alright, Dad?"

"I'm fine, just a little keyed up about a paper I'm delivering today." He explained the cruise deposit problem, and Sonya expressed her surprise that her mother had not made the deposit.

"All she's been talking about lately is the cruise," she said, "that is when she's not talking about her horses."

"I don't understand it either. I need you to do me a favor. I'm on my way to the Institute to give the paper. Could you swing by the stable, and if she's there, have her call me on my cell phone?"

"Sure, Dad, I'll head out there right now."

"Thanks, Sonya, I really appreciate it. Take care." Sonya had not hung up, and there was a pause at the other end of the line.

"Sonya?"

"Yeah, Dad . . . Listen, I'd like to talk to you about something I'm a little confused about. Could we get together for lunch sometime in the next couple of days?"

"Sure, sweetheart, I have a break on Monday around two. Why don't we meet for lunch at the Thai restaurant near Kerrytown."

"That'd be great."

Just as he pushed "end" on the phone, and exited the expressway, the phone rang. It was Kathy, the administrative assistant at the Institute.

"Dr. Weiss? I just wanted to make sure everything was O.K. and that you were on your way." Weiss glanced down at the dashboard clock. 2:10. "You're always so punctual, always early, so I just . . ."

"I'm heading up Middlebelt right now, two minutes away." He sped up, while trying to collect his thoughts about his presentation. He pulled into the Institute lot, and though he was late, sat for a moment in his car and took a few deep breaths to try to calm down.

There was a large audience for the paper, some who respected Weiss' work, but more who were drawn by the infamous subject, Manson. There were many faces unfamiliar to Ivan. After he was introduced, he looked out over the audience and began.

"We are all born to be Mansons. Every one of us. We all come into this world with limitless desires for every kind of pleasure and every kind of cruelty. We all dream in the most secret recesses of ourselves of having every need met and of destroying anyone who stands in our way. We all have a taste for sadism and murder. We also all long to have the blind, unconditional love of others and have them completely under our control." He paused, took a drink of water, and was pleased that the audience was becoming uncomfortable. He wanted their attention and was getting it.

"So what stops you and you and me," Weiss asked, making individual eye contact with people in the audience, "from murdering? The answer is that most of us have a barrier that protects us from these primitive desires. You are probably thinking, sure, rules, laws, morals, in our lingo, the superego, the conscience, stops us. Yes and no. It plays a part, but it's not the essence. What stops each of us from being a Charles Manson is that we come to know, not just intellectually, but know in the depth of our beings, that when I hurt you, that you, just like me, will feel pain. If I take from you, you will feel loss. If I murder you, I know you will lose what I, too, value. Life. It is this basic sense that other people are living, breathing human beings that feel pain and pleasure, just as we do, that helps us keep these deeply selfish, homicidal wishes in check. And where does that sense of others as truly alive come from? Very simply from a secure, uninterrupted, reliable bond with one person, usually the mother, in the first two years of life. It develops only during that one critical period. If it fails to develop then, it simply never will." Weiss then went on to explore the fateful, massive disruptions in Manson's ties with people in his early life which then led him to become, as an adult, a man who could only be described as evil.

Lawrence Block, a senior analyst, gave a prepared response in which he praised the paper, saying Weiss' work was a model of what psychoanalysis beyond the consulting room could be, and that it applied beautifully the findings of child psychoanalysis to the most serious disturbances in adults.

Questions and comments were then invited from the audience. Several concerned the details of the murders, which seemed to Weiss irrelevant to the main point of his paper. He tried to direct the discussion back to the themes he had presented. A bright student of Weiss' asked the excellent question whether the disruption in the early mother-child bond by itself was enough to produce a criminal mind such as Manson's. Aren't there many people who have had this type of disruption? Why don't they all turn out to be like Manson? Weiss responded that this was a very important question. The timing of these mother-child disruptions, a low or high threshold in the child for being overwhelmed or traumatized by loss, and other factors we don't understand make one person with early childhood loss become an unhappy adult and another a murderer.

Gerald Goldberg, who could always be relied on to say something overtly or subtly cutting, began with some flowery praise for the paper, which made Ivan suspicious about what was coming next. He then asked about the ethics of doing a psychological study about a living person.

"I doubt," he pompously said, surpressing a cruel, little smile that began to form at the corners of his mouth, "that you have there at the podium a signed 'release of information' form signed by Mr. Manson."

"He's faxing it to me," said Weiss, "it should be here any minute." The audience broke into laughter.

A few more questions were raised, one about the differences between a man like Manson and Jeffrey Dahmer, and another about how a person with such a basic incapacity to make contact with the world or people was able to gain the blind trust of the women who followed him and murdered on his command. The discussion ended with a comment by Philip Hillock, an analyst who had always remained peripheral to the functioning of the Institute, but whose clinical sensitivity Weiss had always respected. He would never be considered for a leadership position at the Institute, but his practice was filled with spouses and adult children of its faculty. He was one of the most skilled analysts Ivan knew.

"Very nice paper, Ivan," said Hillock, whose blue blazer, nautical tie, and tasseled loafers would be perfect at an old money country club in Connecticut. "Manson has always intrigued me. You emphasize his connection or lack of it with the object world, the world of people. I've been interested in what kind of sense of self such a person has. Years ago when I read about the murders, I remember thinking about his name. It's an alias you know, he made it up. Manson, the son of a man. It's the expression of some basic wish. The name cries out, 'I am the son of a man, I am the son of someone.' Very poignant, very sad, too." Definitely, thought Weiss, the best comment of the afternoon. Edward Bolin, the moderator, called the meeting to a close.

Weiss checked his watch, already 4:15, and remembered he needed to reach Dana and call the travel agent. He tried politely, but briefly, to respond to comments of a small group of people who had gathered around him at the podium and then walked quickly out of the building to his car. He saw Jake going to his. He hadn't noticed him at the meeting.

"Jake, how's it going? I didn't know you'd be coming in. We could have ridden together."

"I didn't know until the last minute I'd be able to get away. I got held up talking to Eric. I think I told you he's back in Ann Arbor for a while."

"Yeah. How's he doing?"

"Hard to say. He's got a part time job at a bookstore. He seems a little more settled, or maybe I just want to think so. We can talk a little better now, but he's still always so hyper, so much on the edge."

"I hope things go well for him."

"We'll see." Ivan thought he heard Jake sigh. "That was a real fine paper."

"Thanks, Jake."

"Larry Block isn't too free with kudos, and praise from Phil Hillock, at least in my book, counts for a lot too. I heard Larry say that you're training analyst material." Ivan hoped to become a training analyst, which would allow him to supervise student analysts on their cases and to conduct their personal analyses.

Ivan sensed there was something odd about their conversation and then realized that they were standing far apart from each other.

"You want to go for a run later?" asked Ivan.

"Naw, I've got a bunch of stuff to take care of. Gotta take off." Jake shot a look at Ivan that scared him. There was something that Ivan labeled to himself as "wild" in Jake at that moment. Jake also looked a little disheveled, as if he had dressed absentmindedly. Jake walked quickly to his car, spun the wheels on the icy pavement as he backed it up, and then again as he drove off. Jake's envy goes on, thought Ivan. The general response to the paper and the training analysts' comments were just adding fuel to the fire. But maybe he's just caught up in worries about his son. Weiss wanted to talk to his friend, but he also needed to get the cruise problem settled before the travel agency closed.

The look in Jake's eyes stayed with him as he sat in his car in the Institute parking lot and dialed his office answering machine. No message from Dana, one from Sonya. He could hear the sound of horses in the background.

"Hi, Dad, I'm out at the stable. Couldn't get you on your cell phone, so I'm leaving the message here. Mom's not out here. I guess she and the vet must've already left. Sorry I couldn't find her. Looking forward to having lunch with you." It was 4:45. He called Terry and told her to put the deposit on their credit card.

It puzzled him that Dana was not at the stable when Sonya got there. Sonya must have gone out there shortly after Ivan had talked to her. So Dana was not at the stable and not at home. So where had she been? And had she left the stable alone? He saw her in his mind getting into her truck with Kevin. They drive around on the country roads, talking about her horse's close call. He saw them drive into town to Ivan and Dana's house and go up to the bedroom. Kevin is worried about getting caught, but Dana tells him this is the ideal time, because her husband, at this very moment, is delivering a paper at a professional meeting. Weiss felt himself descending into a deep, painful, obsessive rumination. Is this why she didn't follow through with the travel arrangements? Does she want to stay here close to Kevin? Wasn't that Dana and Kevin who drove away when Jake and I stopped at my house? He was being engulfed by the paranoia that had brought him to his own analysis years before. If he didn't get a hold of himself, he knew he would be paralyzed.

He had to talk to Dana about where she had gone, but he knew that if he failed to sort out his jealousy himself, nothing she could tell him would dislodge the obsession. He would need to revisit the old demons that had, years before, given rise to his paranoia.

He was startled by a tap on his window. He rolled down the fogged window to see a young woman, whose name escaped him, who had been a psychological intern at the Clinic.

"Hi, Dr. Weiss, I don't know if you remember me, Jill Sanborn, I was a student at the Clinic a few years ago."

"Sure."

"That was such an interesting paper. I have a job now working with delinquent kids at a detention center, so I was thinking a lot about some of my cases there. I found what you said real helpful." She stood by the car, the wind whipping snow into her face and turning her fur hood white. Weiss was ready for her to turn and go to her car, but she seemed to have something more to say.

"The wind's pretty bad, why don't you get in," he said.

She came around, brushed the snow off her coat and got in the car.

"When I was at the Clinic, I was painfully shy and could never get up the nerve to talk to you. I wanted to tell you what a great teacher you were." She pulled her hood back and released her thick blond hair. "Dr. Weiss there's something more." Ivan thought of Dana being off with Kevin. He imagined Jill telling him that when she was an intern she had a crush on him, still was attracted to him, and wanted to have an affair. As he thought about Dana, he saw himself going off through the winter afternoon to a motel with this young woman and having sex. As he thought this, she was still struggling to talk.

"I'm still very shy with you. You always seem so much in command of yourself." Little did she know how little in command of himself he felt at that very moment. He knew his need to be perfect made him often come across that way to people, no matter what was going on inside. "I just wanted to know, if . . . you'd take a look at something I wrote, a little paper on one of my cases." She looked up at him, and he could see in her fearful, pleading eyes her deep sense of inadequacy. He was both disappointed and relieved that this was all she wanted from him.

"Sure, I'd be delighted to take a look at what you wrote."

"You would? Thanks a lot, I'd really appreciate it . . . Well, O.K., thanks again." She hesitated for a moment, and Weiss wondered if she had wanted more or wanted him to ask her for more.

"Well, I'll see ya," she said, as she opened the door.

"Goodbye, Jill."

He pulled out of the now empty parking lot, found some classical music on the radio, and as the darkness of the evening seemed to surround the car and press in on him, drove back to Ann Arbor.

When Ivan returned home, Dana was in the kitchen making dinner. NPR was on the radio, the counters were a clutter of bowls, tomato sauce was everywhere, and the smell of garlic, basil, and olive oil filled the air. Even before he turned the corner of the L-shaped kitchen and saw his wife in her Italian flag apron he had bought her in Little Italy in New York, the familiarity of it all calmed and reassured him.

"How'd the paper go?" she asked, turning the flame down under a pan of sauce ready to bubble over the sides. She seemed happy when he told her it had gone well.

"Smells good," he said, coming up and wrapping his arms around her waist from behind.

"My usual throw in everything Italian extravaganza."

"Did you get my messages, honey, about Terry and the cruise deposit?" Did he feel her body tense when he asked her this?

"No, I just came right from the car and started cooking." He told her about Terry's call, sending Sonya out to the barn, and the deadline for the cruise deposit. Dana turned down the flame and fiddled with the sauce, carefully guiding the edges into the middle. Ivan tried to read the expression on her face reflected in the window.

"So why didn't you get her the deposit?"

"I guess, Ivan, I've wondered if this is the best time to be away. Sonya seems to need us around, you're getting settled in the Directorship. And I'm in a place right now where I don't want to be away either."

"Why?"

"I'm finally reaching a new level with my riding. I don't want to interrupt it."

"To tell you the truth, I'm really baffled, Dana. You've been so excited about the cruise."

"I know, I know I have. And in a way I still am." She rummaged through a cabinet, pulled out some more spices, and added them to the sauce, the mood she had been in now slipping. She stirred distractedly, as they both looked out the window at the bird feeder in the neighbor's frozen yard. A cardinal was feeding, and a couple of squirrels were darting around after the fallen seeds. A few cars crunched over the snow covered street, and a report on daily life in Jerusalem began on "All Things Considered."

"I don't think you understand, Ivan, what my riding means to me. You've got your career. You're respected, successful. I'll bet you automatically think that everyone has a direction or a mission in life. But lots of us don't. Other than being a mother, which has been great, I've never really found a career I love. Well now I have my equestrian life, the horses, the training, the shows. This could be it for me. Right now I'm still an amateur. It's a glorified hobby. You know, the psychoanalyst supporting his wife's dilettantish interest in horses."

"I don't feel at all that way about what you're doing."

"I guess you don't, but I do, and it's sort of true, or at least has been. But now I'm on the verge of it being something more, something professional. I've gotten to the point that I can see myself being a trainer. I could compete at a much higher level. And teach more than beginners." Ivan knew this was all true, but he felt this wasn't the whole story.

"Alright, I understand, Dana. So what should we do, cancel it? I've put the deposit down."

"Let's just see, Ivan. If we lose the deposit, we lose it. Maybe my feelings will change as it gets closer. I'm sorry, honey, this has been a real special dream trip for both of us. We've really built it up. Hell, for all we know we'll get on board and both be seasick."

The water for the pasta came to a boil, and she dropped the fettucine in. A cloud of steam billowed up over her face, and she turned away from Ivan, wiping her face with her sleeve. Still turned away, she wiped her face again. This time, he thought, to clear away some tears.

CHAPTER THIRTEEN

I van met his daughter at a small Thai restaurant where he often went for lunch. He chatted regularly with the waitresses, who called him "the crazy person doctor" and joked that each should see him as a patient. He had told them he had a daughter in New York, and they often asked him how she was doing. They were very pleased, when he introduced her to them, several shaking her hand and bowing.

"You're quite a local celebrity," Sonya said once they sat down. "This was a great idea. I haven't even thought of having Thai food since I left New York. I used to eat it all the time. I think I've tried to forget everything I used to do there."

Ivan had over the months gently invited Sonya to talk to him about the rape, but all she would say was, "I've got to sort things out myself before I can talk to anyone." She had not been so laconic immediately after it happened. In a series of frantic calls from New York, she was in tears over night terrors and nightmares. She had a few panic attacks, the most serious of which happened when she met with an executive who was interested in her redecorating his company's office suite. It was the biggest job she had been considered for. The moment the meeting began, her heart had started racing and pounding. Her hands were shaking and sweating so badly that she could barely make notes. She gave some excuse for cutting the meeting short and left, breaking into a run as soon as she left his office. Too anxious to wait for the elevator, she ran down fifteen flights of stairs and was gasping for breath by the time she reached the street. Later she realized that the executive's voice had sounded like the rapist's.

Ivan had offered to find her a good analyst in New York and help pay for the treatment. Sonya said that she had always planned to go into analysis in order to better understand herself, but that if she went now, she would feel that the rapist had forced her into it, and that she would again be his victim. Ivan had tried to explain that these feelings that he still had control over her were the very ones that she needed to understand and would be explored with a good therapist. Still, no.

Maybe, Weiss thought, she is ready now.

"It's tough to try to erase those years in New York," said Ivan.

"That's exactly what I've been trying to do. There were lots of really good times in New York, too. But when I try to think of anything that happened there, my mind seems to slide to the rape."

"I know this feels like something out of your control, Sonya, and right now it is, but if you can get of hold of why your mind keeps going back to the rape, then it won't need to anymore."

"I've read about post traumatic stress disorder. Isn't that what I have?"

"You can call it that, but that's just a label, sweetheart. It doesn't explain why the thoughts are there, what their function is." It seemed to Weiss that he was explaining this more and more these days, to students, in his writing, to new patients, now even to his daughter. Psychology and psychiatry were returning to a 19th century approach to mental illness. Just label symptoms and behavior to create the illusion that something has been explained.

"I know, Dad, you think analysis is the answer. I am still thinking about it."

"Well, I'm glad of that."

"But all of this wasn't why I wanted to have lunch with you."

"Before you say anything, let me say, Sonya, that I feel I misjudged, really prejudged, Jerry. I had some stereotypes about him, but when I met him I found an altogether different young man than I had constructed in my mind. It really was unfair to him and you."

"That's alright, Dad, after some of the losers I chose in high school, I'm not surprised you expected him to be another one." The waitress, a tiny middle aged Thai woman, took their orders and then shyly complimented Sonya's hair, "so curly and thick and shiny." Sonya thanked her. When straight hair was in, her hair never seemed to be right, but now thank goodness, curly hair was back in style, and she loved it.

"You're right, Jerry's different from those high school guys, definitely brighter, more caring. And the biggest difference from those jocks I'd chase after in high school is that Jerry likes me. He's pursuing me."

"And how do you feel about him?"

"That's a problem. I definitely do like him, but I feel I have to work at it. We're from really different backgrounds and somehow don't click right away about things. He and I joke that we're like anthropologists doing cross cultural field work with each other. That has been kind of fun, too, you know finding out about the differences, but I wonder if we're trying too hard. I think about you and Mom and how you look at things in the same way. You have the same sense of humor, sometimes weird to me, but you share it. I don't feel that with Jerry."

"You're talking as if you have to make some final, lifelong decision about him."

"I know. I guess I'm getting more lonely and less scared of men and really want to be with someone. Jerry seems in many ways non-threatening. Non-threatening doesn't really go far enough. I feel he'd protect me and fight for me." She also found Jerry attractive and sexy, but felt embarrassed saying this to her father.

The food came, and they began to eat. Sonya asked her father about his new position at the Clinic, and he talked about how it was already more demanding than he had thought it would be. He then asked her about how her work was going. She told him she was pleased that she was finally getting some clients and then talked enthusiastically about the work with Nick Streeter.

"I'm really into this new project. I think I told you a little about it. It's for the young professor. The house is one of those neo-classical houses, great potential. It's been fun working with him. He has a really good style sense. Amazing. And, not to brag, but often very much like my own. It's exciting."

"Sounds like a very gratifying project, one that is going to really use your talents."

"I think so. Oh, you might be interested in this. He's a psychohistorian. I think that's what it's called. He had all of those familiar books, you know the ones I'd call the 'green books' when I was little . . ."

"Freud's works."

"Yeah, the Freud books." She looked away, her enthusiasm faded, and her eyes narrowed.

"What is it, Sonya?"

"You know I really hated those books. I could never say that. You were always off in your study with them."

"I know."

"You were like in love with those books."

"That's very true, I was in love with them a lot of the time. And even when I wasn't, I still had to read a couple hundred pages a week during psychoanalytic training."

"Right, psychoanalytic training, the Institute. Sacred, everything took a back seat to all that," said Sonya, her tone changing from light and chiding to serious and angry. Weiss wanted to tell her how sorry he was that psychoanalytic training had robbed her of the kind of attention she clearly had needed from him, to explain to her how much time the training demanded, on top of holding down his hospital job, publishing to get tenure, and building a private practice to finance it all. He stopped himself, knowing she needed just to tell him what she was telling him, without his trying to explain himself, defend himself, or apologize.

"You always talk about the importance of childhood, but how about mine!" she said. "I'm sorry, Dad, that's not fair. You were there, we did a lot together, but I guess I felt pushed aside by your training. I never told you this, but that green party dress that I loved so much when I was little reminded me of those book covers." This saddened Ivan.

"Maybe a green dress could draw your father away from those damn green books."

"Seeing those books really triggered a lot." Tears were welling up in her eyes. "I want you to know you were a good dad." She reached across the table, squeezed his hand, and they sat quietly for a moment.

"So," she continued, blotting tears from her eyes, "he had the books, and I told him what you do."

"Did he say what he was studying?"

"Something about child abuse in the nineteenth century. Oh, yeah, also Victorian hysteria. We were talking about Victorian furniture, that's how his field came up."

"Sounds like you really enjoy working with him." Sonya fell silent, put her chopsticks down, and sipped some tea.

"He's really easy to work with. I felt immediately comfortable with him. We were able to ease so quickly into a conversation, and things just flowed."

She looked out the window, and he followed her eyes. A boy and several girls from Community High, a small, artsy high school near Kerrytown, were running and sliding down the icy parts of the sidewalk. The boy fell, the girls pulled him up, carefully brushed him off, and then pushed him into a snowbank. The girls all laughed, and he chased them back towards the school. Ivan saw a smile on his daughter's face. High school had been, in many ways, her happiest time.

"That was funny. They were so careful and serious about brushing him off, and then he's up to his ass in the snow. I think of being silly like that with someone. With a guy. Just having some simple fun. Someone I can click with." She took a few halfhearted bites of rice.

"And you hope to have this with Jerry?"

"I hope so, but I don't think so. The reason, Dad, I wanted to have lunch with you is because I might be falling for this guy I'm doing the decorating for, this guy Nick."

"Sonya . . ."

"Don't say it, I barely know him. That's right. And I'm not jumping into anything, at least I don't think I am." Her doubt worried her father. "I just feel this deep connection with him. It's almost eerie the way we see the world, like through the same eyes."

"It's fine to listen to your heart, Sonya, but try to listen to your head at the same time. I know that's not always easy."

"I hear you, Dad." He was far from sure she really had. "Just to reassure you that I have my head on somewhat straight, I did make one good decision about a man."

"What was that?"

"Eric Hanson called me the other day to go out, and I politely but firmly told him no." Not wanting to worry her father, she left out that Eric had then left many messages on her answering machine.

"You're right, good decision, he's still a very troubled young man."

The waitress brought the check. A small child of about four peeked around from behind her skirt.

"Don't be shy, come out and say hello," the waitress said. She explained that she had told her daughter that Dr. Weiss was here with his daughter, and that the little girl had said, "Why is she so big?" and wanted to meet her.

"I was a girl, just like you once," said Sonya to the girl, who ventured a slight way out, "and every year I got bigger and bigger."

"She think all daughters are little like her," said her mother, laughing.

"Well, it's very nice to meet you," said Sonya, extending her hand to the girl, who smiled, but quickly returned to the safety of her mother's skirts.

"Very shy child," said the waitress.

"Lots of kids are shy," said Ivan. "It's still a pretty big confusing world for kids at that age."

He paid the check and walked out arm in arm with his daughter into the winter afternoon. As it had turned sunny, he refused her offer to drive him back to the Clinic, preferring instead to walk. They hugged, and Ivan felt himself not wanting to let her go.

He walked by the Fire Department and City Hall and then along Huron Street where the traffic was slowed by a truck spraying salt on the street. When he reached Huron and State, a corner he passed all the time, he was surprised that he was thinking about one of the first patients he had treated, a young woman who had lived in a co-op house he could see from that corner. He shuddered to himself at the thought of how young and immature he was when he took his first job here. Twenty four, fresh out of graduate school, he found an "indispensable" hospital job to keep his draft deferment. She was the first patient he tried to treat in psychoanalytic psychotherapy. He had been so uncomfortable with himself, so at sea about being a therapist, that he conducted a rigid caricature of psychotherapy, often remaining silent, emotionally restrained, and cold.

The patient, Bernice Folson, at the time in her late twenties, repeatedly chose men who were abusive to her. Though she was in many areas a good judge of character, someone her friends sought out for relationship advice, she was unable to use this capacity in choosing men for herself. She would be blind to obvious indications in men she dated that they were going to be at the least verbally degrading to her and often violent. On one occasion, she chose a man who became so enraged that, in a fit of wild, possessive jealousy, he threatened her with a knife. Her history had been unusual, because she did not have the highly abusive background often seen in women who make these poor choices in men.

Now he understood why he was thinking about her. There was little that was traumatic in her childhood, but there had been a key incident in her young adulthood which had led her to choose dangerous men. When she was a freshman at Michigan, she had been raped. He hoped his own daughter, still psychologically reeling from the rape in New York, was not needing to unconsciously repeat and rework her experience by choosing a violent man. Unless Ivan's sense of Jerry was very much off the mark, he was not such a man. But what about this man Nick? And Eric Hanson. He was reassured that Sonya was not interested in Eric, but still worried that down the road, in her risk taking way, she might get involved with him. She's a grown woman, he tried to tell himself, she can take care of herself. He thought about the little girl at the restaurant finding safety and security close to her mother. It is so much easier, Ivan thought, to protect them when they are young.

CHAPTER FOURTEEN

After he took his evening AIDS drugs, he opened the manila envelope and pulled out the file. Though the information in it was much more important than the letters, he set the file aside and carefully, almost lovingly, slid the bundle of letters from the envelope. They looked to him so appealing, and innocent, in their heavy, richly textured paper, tied with the crimson ribbon.

Though it made sense to just read through, or even skim, all of the letters, he wanted to space out his reading of them, saving the last ones to read as the plan was being carried out. They will help me keep my focus, he thought, keep my resolve.

He pulled the end of the ribbon, and the bundle fell open, the letters arraying themselves like cards ready to be dealt. Though the letters were old, the envelopes were only slightly yellowed. Each envelope had in French the date, and even the time of day it was received, and the signature of the monk who had received it. They seemed, he thought, to have taken much better care of the mail than of the children. He could see compulsive Brother James, who was always complaining that the children were "wickedly wasteful" with the paper napkins, bent over a ledger recording useless information about the incoming mail.

Seeing the envelopes, each with an American stamp, none, of course, with her name or return address, he remembered a time when he had felt something, a dim memory of anticipation, of hope.

He still had something inside him, like feelings, but really only the shell of them, just a pressure or tension that moved through his body, something that no words could describe, closer to pain or fever or illness. It was like he had gone emotionally blind. All that was left was a sensation that there was a hole in the middle of his body, a silent, dead, empty cavern that oddly left space for nothing else.

Since realizing how close he was to death and then devising his plan, he sensed a change. When he thought of what he was going to make all of them go through, he was beginning to feel again. Daydreams of their suffering were thawing him out.

He pulled the oldest letter from its envelope and smelled it. He hoped it would smell of her but only the musty air of St. Boniface rose from the dry paper. He cleared all of his books and papers from the desk and stacked them on the floor, and, ceremoniously, unfolded the letter and laid it on the desk.

August 10, 1970
Dear Son (I never gave you a name),

It's really silly to write to you, you're only a baby, but the people at the orphanage (they call it something else, but I know that's what it is) said someone will read the letters I am sending you when you're old enough to understand them.

I'm on the plane, sitting between my parents. We've just had a huge argument about my writing this letter. They want what they call the "ordeal" to be behind us. They looked relieved when we got on the plane, but when I started the letter to you, they went nuts. "You've put us through hell with this. We've aged ten years in the last one because of you," on and on, they just completely lost it. You get the idea. Well, you don't, but when you're older you will.

I'm supposed to go back to high school now like nothing's happened. Just be a happy-go-lucky kid, go to proms, think about college and my rosy future.

Of course the fight on the plane was nothing compared to what happened when I told them I was pregnant. They went absolutely wild. "You've got to get an abortion, you're too young." I probably shouldn't say this to you, but maybe I should have gotten an abortion. But I wanted you. I wanted to try somehow to be a mother to you. They threatened they wouldn't pay for college, and then they tried bribing me with promises of cars and clothes. It was all so pathetic. It showed how little they really know me. I think they don't have a clue as to who I am, not a clue. I think sometimes I got pregnant just to wake them up.

They tried everything, even going to a French lawyer to see if they could declare me insane and have the abortion done against my will, you know, like, she's too nuts to have a kid. That was just going a little too far for my mother, who nixed that idea. By the time they had worn me down and I agreed to an abortion, a doctor said that I was too far along to have one safely.

They were so embarrassed that their social set would find out I was "in trouble," as they called it, that they put me in a French school for unwed mothers and told their friends I was studying abroad. So we agreed that I'd stay in France during my pregnancy, have you in France and then bring you back to the States, and you'd be adopted there. Quickly, before their friends found out. They said finding good parents for a healthy, white baby would be easy.

My father's job was over, so he went back to the States, and my mother stayed in France with me. He traveled back and forth often and would tell me about all the plans for getting a nice home for the baby. But I see now that they were all lies. They wanted the "ordeal" left behind in France right from the start and never planned to bring you to the U.S. You've been with me for the last three months, longer than anyone thought. I can still feel you, just yesterday, snuggled against me.

The day after I had you, and it was a difficult birth, and I was in no shape to listen to anything or decide anything, my father gave me all this crap about legal difficulties with the French and American governments, and that if I didn't sign these papers that he dropped in front of me, right on my hospital bed, you'd end up in really bad place, a "state home" he called it, and not in a better one, run by the Church. The difference between these places, he kept repeating, is night and day, so you've got to sign.

So I did. Why does he have to go to an orphanage at all? Why can't he be adopted in the U.S. like we talked about? He will, he will. They'll just keep him at the church home temporarily. The Church has all kinds of contacts. He'll be in a good home before long.

The deal I made with my parents is I get to write to you but I won't tell you my name or where we live. I don't like it, but I had to agree or they'd do who knows what. Chain me to my bed probably.

So, drink your milk and do what babies do. I hope you'll be with really, really great parents soon.

Mom

He slipped the letter, like a delicate artifact, back into its envelope. He remembered this letter being read to him when he was six, after he was returned to the orphanage, following two years with these "great parents." They turned out to be an old, grim, foster couple on a dairy farm north of Lyon. The father, a squat, taciturn Englishman, who looked like Popeye, had stayed in France after he had fought there during the War and married a French farm girl, whose family had sheltered him when he had been wounded. His only interest in taking in the foster children, they had four or five at any one time, was for the government stipend and the free labor they provided. The foster mother was a quiet, fearful woman who took the children in to show God how much she was suffering and sacrificing for Him. He could not remember the entire time he was there, from four to six, ever being held or touched by either of them, except, of course, when he was beaten by the father for misbehaving.

Two days after his sixth birthday, he found his foster mother dead in a pool of fresh milk by an overturned pail. The very next day he and the others were dispersed to various orphanages. He was sent back to St. Boniface. At the farm he had gotten close to an older "sister" who tried to mother him, but he never saw her or any of the others again.

When he returned to the orphanage, the monks and nuns seemed to blame him for the placement not working out, as if the foster mother's heart attack and the foster father's decision to get rid of all of the kids were somehow his fault. The only one who saw things as they had really happened, the only one who cared for him, was Brother Anthony. He had loved Brother Anthony, but later came to see the hidden costs of his love. He never knew if Anthony really cared for him or only needed him to satisfy the monk's warped, pedophilic interests. He did know that what started with Anthony ended with the fateful man from whom he received the virus, and that the virus is all he felt he had ever received from anyone.

He put the letter back with the others, retied the bundle, and opened the file. All the information he wanted was there: his medical records, before and after the foster home, report cards, a note from Brother Anthony about his great potential, and most importantly the name of his mother. The name he had wondered about and guessed at whenever he received one of her letters, the name he had always hoped in the next letter she would reveal. In those days he still had something in himself that could be called hope.

The name in the file was not a surprise. He had already received the report from a search service he had hired to find her. The file was just the confirmation he needed. He didn't want to waste his life, or his one and only death, on the wrong people.

He put the letters and file under his bed, stared vacantly out the window, and then set to work on his harasser's note. When he finished it, he called the Detective and identified himself.

"This is Joseph Benedict, you remember, the guy who's being harassed?"

"Sure."

"This nut is moving to a new level. He just left a note on my door. Want to hear it?"

"Go ahead."

"'I will not tolerate your being here. I am the expert, and you are nothing. If you know what's good for you, you will find a position somewhere else. I've studied criminals, and I know how to do some serious damage. This is not a personal thing. I'm just not going to sit by while some asshole takes over my territory. This may not sound sane to you, and you would be right. I am not a sane man.' It just astounds me that anyone would get so hot over me being here. But then again he's saying he's not sane. That scares me even more." Farley still couldn't hear the fear.

"Alright, I still can't do much more for you right now, but why don't you bring the note down to the station, and I'll have one of our lab guys take a look at it."

Farley hung up and swiveled around a few times in his chair. He called the University operator who connected him with the Chairman of the Psychology Department.

"John Farley from the Police Department. Do you have a Joseph Benedict in your Department?"

"Yes, we do. Is there a problem?"

"No, just collecting some routine background information connected with a case."

"Is Joe in some kind of difficulty?" The Chairman sounded to Farley like the nosy type who might get a kick if his young colleague were in some trouble.

"No, he's not in any difficulty or trouble. I just need to confirm that he's in your Department and a couple other things. His specialty is criminal personality. Is that right?"

"Yes, he's into a lot of areas, but that's one of them."

"One more thing. Is there anyone else in your Department or the University who does research in that same area?"

"As a matter of fact, there is. I just heard him deliver a paper at the Psychoanalytic Institute."

"Who is that?"

"The new Director of the University Psychology Clinic, Dr. Weiss, Ivan Weiss."

*   *   *

Sonya and Jerry met late in the afternoon in Gallup park and cross country skied. She was pleased that they shared this activity. There was a stark beauty to the snowswept shores of the Huron River. Wooden footbridges crossed back and forth over the river, and a path snaked through the woods and then followed the river east under an expressway toward Ypsilanti.

As he skied ahead of her, she enjoyed looking at his broad shoulders, their strength, grace, and power. After the rape, being close to a man, especially a strong one, brought up fears of him using his strength against her. Now with Jerry, for the first time since the rape, she felt his power was on her side, that it would keep her safe. She was back in touch with her attraction to strength in a man, especially physical strength, and that it turned her on. As they skied, she found herself striding in unison with him, wishing their understanding of each other had that same natural rhythm.

She thought again about Nick and that instant connection she had felt with him. Am I attracted to him sexually? She wasn't sure. Maybe it's a minor part. Instead it's the feeling of a shared outlook.

When the path broadened, she skied up next to Jerry and playfully bumped into him. He play acted that she had thrown him off balance, flailing around, crossing his skis, and falling down. She burst out laughing. I guess we do share a sense of humor, even if it is a totally different one than with Nick. But am I trying to talk myself into liking Jerry? She felt confused again. Maybe this is the time to get from my father the name of a therapist.

The horizon glowed red with sunset. As they reached Jerry's car, a snow squall of large feathery flakes began. Two small children were pleading with their parents to let them stay longer so they could continue their snowball fight. The parents finally packed the children into the car and drove off, leaving Sonya and Jerry, and a few geese, alone in the parking lot. The squall turned into a more serious snowfall, covering the roads and muffling the sounds of the cars. It was very quiet, as they took off their skis. Jerry told Sonya that he had enjoyed the afternoon so much and then added, a little awkwardly, that he really liked her. I like being with you, too, she said, but wondering again to herself, how much, and in what ways.

They drove downtown, had dinner at an Italian restaurant, and then Jerry drove her home. She could tell he wanted her to invite him in, but she told him she needed to get up early for an appointment the next day, and he left. She set her skis down by the outside door of her apartment building and fumbled for her keys with her fingers still numb from the skiing. Got to get some better gloves, she thought. Just as she unlocked the outer door and was trying to wrestle her skis through it, she felt someone holding the door open from the inside.

"Nick," she said, self conscious that in her surprise at seeing him she had used his first name. "What are you . . ."

"I just came by to leave some flowers for you. I was up at the market, saw the flowers there and, you've been so helpful, I don't know many people here yet, so I just wanted to say thank you." What a sweet thing to do, she thought, but felt at the same time a little uncomfortable that he'd come to her apartment. How did he know where she lived? Had she told him? There was no local address on her business cards which she had made up before she came back to town, and, after the rape, she felt more secure having an unlisted number and address. And how had he gotten in the outer door? He must have rung other apartments until someone buzzed him in. That sounds a little sneaky, but then again she had done this in New York herself. You're getting yourself all worked up and scared, she chastised herself. It's flowers, it's a nice surprise. Can't you just take it as that? Any surprise from a guy, even from a guy I like, and I'm instantly in defense mode, ready to be attacked. That rapist is still fucking with my mind.

Though she could feel her heart racing as she thought about the rape, she tried to calm herself and invited him in.

"No, I can't stay right now," he said, "and anyway I didn't mean to impose on your time. I just wanted to leave the flowers for you." God, he's so tuned in. That is exactly what I needed him to do, to bring flowers, but then to give me room. Her heart slowed, and she smiled at him.

"That was really nice of you, really nice. Thanks." She carried her skis to the elevator, rode it up to the third floor to her apartment, where she found a spring bouquet propped against her door with a note saying simply, "From Nick. Thanks."

Though she had spent much of the day with Jerry, as she snipped the stems of the flowers and arranged them in her favorite vase, she thought only of Nick.

CHAPTER FIFTEEN

Ivan woke early Sunday morning to the high whine of Dana's truck wheels spinning on the frozen driveway. He went to the window and saw her shifting back and forth, gears gnashing, trying to rock the truck out, but managing only to dig deeper ruts in the snow and ice. Through the truck window, he saw her slam her hand down on the steering wheel. She was going to meet Kevin at the stable, pick up the horses and trailer them to an indoor horse show in northern Ohio. He got dressed and went out to help her.

"I knew we should have gotten the four wheel drive, damn it." This was obviously meant for Ivan, who did not want Dana to shovel the driveway, refused to hire a plowing service, but then put off doing it himself. This was a long standing winter problem between them, but today, it seemed to Ivan, Dana was excessively angry. These days every feeling in her seems up a notch or two.

He spread the melting salt on the driveway, shoveled behind the rear wheels, and pushed her out. She stopped at the end of the driveway.

"See you, Ivan. What are you doing today?" she asked, the question an afterthought.

"Remember, I'm doing that Frozen Foot Run up at Whitmore Lake."

"Oh, did you tell me about that?" He knew he had and felt angry that her mind these days was rarely on him.

"You going with Jake?"

"I think so. We'd planned to. Things are still a little tense between us." Like they are with us, too, he thought, but didn't want to open this up now.

"What a bad time this has been for him. All the problems his son's had and you getting the Director's job. Poor guy." She tossed her head and brushed her long hair back, as if she were, at the same time, brushing aside some thought.

"I should get going," she said. He reached in the window and squeezed her hand. She gave a perfunctory squeeze and smile back.

"Good luck at the show."

"You, too," and she backed onto the street and drove off.

Weiss went back into the house, ate his usual prerace half bagel and changed into his running gear. He called Jake to see if he wanted to ride up together, but reached only his answering machine.

He drove out of Burns Park to Hill Street, lined with fraternities and sororities, and down Main. Sunday morning anywhere is usually a quiet time, but in a college town in the winter, it is especially so. Except for a few ambitious students heading for the University libraries, some street people rummaging for Saturday night returnables in the trash cans, and a few people on their way to church, the streets were empty. As he drove through the quiet street, dusted with snow, he tried with difficulty to conjure up the scene of the street in summer when it is alive with street corner musicians, rollerbladers, bicyclists, and people enjoying the long Michigan evenings in sidewalk cafes.

He thought of sitting with Dana outside the Half Moon Grill, planning the cruise, and then he cast his thoughts further back. To taking Sonya to ballet lessons at the dance school, to the surprise fortieth birthday party Dana had thrown for him at Gratzi, and to buying their first washing machine at an old Sears store, long since closed. But these thoughts were all fleeting, pushed aside by his sense of the street as empty and grim. He knew that at other times this quiet Sunday street would feel peaceful, but today the scene filled him only with coldness and emptiness. He felt Dana was slipping away. As he drove slowly through this late January Sunday morning, he felt suspended between memories of the fall and summer and what seemed like an endless chain of days until the spring thaw and the summer that lay beyond it.

He headed north on the expressway to Whitmore Lake, one of many small lake towns that dot the landscape north and west of Detroit. Ivan checked the map on the race brochure and easily found the high school where registration was taking place. He looked around for Jake, but he wasn't there, at least not yet. Typically, Weiss, rulebound, was early, and Jake, if he were coming, would push the limits and get places just in time or late.

Except for a short section along the lake, the course ran north up one expressway service drive, crossed the expressway, and ran south down the other. It was a dull and boring course, but straight and flat. A midwinter race on a course good for setting personal records, this was a race for die hard runners.

The runners, mostly men in their late 30's to mid 50's were stretching and running in place in the halls of the school. A few struck up conversations with Weiss, the sole purpose of which he soon realized was to find out if he was competing in their age range, if he was one of the enemy. These guys were a very competitive bunch.

Beginning to lose the sensation in his toes as he stood in the cold wind at the starting line, Ivan was relieved to hear the starting gun. The course began on the town's main street, which ran by bait stores, still open for ice fishing, lots filled with boats in bright blue shrink wrap, cottages boarded up for the winter, several massive, expensive houses that seemed to be made half of glass, and a few ramshackle motels with various letters missing from their signs. The town, like many in the area, was in transition from a summer cottage community to a year-round suburb.

At the first mile marker of the 5K, 3.1 mile, race, he checked his running watch. 6:45. Not bad. Ivan liked warm or hot weather, even when it was combined with the midsummer Michigan humidity, but he ran best in the cold. The course turned west toward the expressway, and then onto the service drive. While the main street was closed for the race, the service drive was still open to traffic, the course now following the shoulder and marked off by cones. Then over the expressway to the service drive on the other side. Second mile marker, watch check. 13:46. Second mile in 7:01. Slowing down a little, but considering the headwind from the north during the past mile, still running strong. Heading south now, wind's at my back, maybe I can make up some time.

Though the semis and double trailer trucks roared and rattled by on the expressway, he was barely aware of the noise, absorbed in the rhythm of his own breathing and monitoring the state of his body. He was trying to stay at the edge, pushing hard, but not so hard that he would trigger a familiar pain in his side that had on some runs slowed him to a walk.

He wished Dana could see him. She had come to some of his first races, and he remembered her near the finish line cheering him on. He wanted her with him. He ached for her to be there.

Then he saw her truck. It was on the other side of the expressway, turning onto the service drive he had run north on for the first half of the race. About a hundred yards away. Not close enough to be sure if it was hers. A moment after he saw the truck, it seemed to speed up, turned onto the northbound expressway ramp, and was quickly out of sight.

Was that her? His guts churned with the same doubts and questions he had when he was with Jake and thought he saw her pull away from their house. What was she doing here? And why would she be going north? None of her horse activities were up there. She had a college friend they had visited many years before in Flint, but other than her, they knew no one up there. And most important of all, the horse show she was going to was south, near Toledo.

He ran the rest of the course back into Whitmore Lake, distracted, preoccupied, confused. I wanted to see her badly enough that I just imagined I saw her truck. Then an image of her being with another man crept into his awareness, and he felt hurt, angry and humiliated. Then he felt frightened for her. Maybe she's in some kind of trouble. All of these feelings whirled within him and then seemed to meld into a huge, indefinable fear.

Adrenaline pumped through him, and he ran faster than he ever had. If he had checked the clock at the finish line, he would have seen that he had run in an impressive time, but of course he didn't even notice it and ran right from the finish line to his car, sped north on the expressway in what he knew was a wild, futile effort to find her.

As he drove, he thought that seeing her twice in these same unexpected ways in the space of a few days meant one of a several things. It was just a coincidence, each time having a reasonable explanation, it had not been her either time, or she was hiding something from him. A last possibility, Ivan considered with a shudder, was that he was once more completely in the grip of his paranoia.

CHAPTER SIXTEEN

He felt more energetic today than he had in weeks. A few months before, he had talked a doctor into prescribing Ritalin, and in the last few days he had taken double doses of it, along with some amphetamines he had bought on the street. Though he had tried this combination before, it had never had much of an effect. Now it did. Maybe getting on with the plan is revving me up, he thought. The sense of energy in his body, a buzzing in his muscles and bones, did not alter the total inner emotional deadness, the state of inner anesthesia. But the energy he felt in his body encouraged him that today he would be able to set up the room where he would hold her. As he thought of this, he gazed out at a leafless, winter tree, a skeleton tree. His eyes suddenly locked into sharp focus on it, and he traced a thin black line around each limb and branch of the tree. It looked like a tree he had once seen in a Van Gogh painting, the trunk and limbs gnarled and twisted and encased in a black border. Maybe I've taken too many drugs, he thought, but then again maybe I'm just hyperalert. And alert is what I need to be.

He rented a van and drove to the futon store. After a chatty new age co-ed tried to sell him a lot of extra crap she insisted he must have for his "apartment," he bought a bottom of the line futon and a small bedside table and loaded them in the van. To avoid drawing suspicion he bought the rest of what he needed at different stores on the way: a hardware store on the outskirts of Ann Arbor, a Wal-Mart in Ypsilanti, and a boat supply store in Belleville. When he had the space heater, portable generator, gasoline cans, folding chairs, card table, lamps, extension cords, blankets, camp stove, portable john, and of course, chain and locks, packed in the van, he got on the expressway. The handcuffs he already had, having ordered them online from a paramilitary website. Though he wouldn't need it for a few days yet, he stopped in Dearborn and bought a cell phone. As he was walking back to the van, a small oriental rug in a store window caught his eye. Though it made no sense to buy it, he did anyway. He returned to the expressway once more and headed for downtown Detroit.

This was his fourth trip. He had picked the place and had begun to set it up.

Finding just the right place had been the trickiest part of the plan. It had to be isolated, easy to get in and out of, where no one would hear her, and within easy driving distance to Ann Arbor. An abandoned cabin or rented farm seemed like obvious and logical choices, and easier ones to set up, but they held no appeal for him. No, from the beginning of the plan, he had a picture of another kind of place.

The place certainly could not be in Ann Arbor. Living in Ann Arbor had been a jarring experience. All those bright eyed kids living the collegiate life, heading off into promising futures. It sickened him. Nothing about the town connected with anything inside him.

He had worked hard to find a place which, like him, was in decline. A place dying, but not yet dead. A place with some slim hope. Most important, the place had to distance her from those she loved and them from her. There had to be a cold, vacant space between them. Unbridgeable. Maybe permanent. The place he had chosen was perfect.

Though it was the middle of the day, the streets seemed deserted. He drove by block after block of boarded up stores and vacant lots covered with dirty snow. As he approached the alley, his alley, behind the abandoned building, he slowed and checked for cars and people. In his rearview mirror he saw a few cars a block or so behind. Pretty far back, but he wasn't taking any chances, so he drove around the block. Second time still some traffic. On the third pass, as he turned the corner, the street was empty. He accelerated to the alley entrance, slowed, checked around one more time, and turned sharply into it, the van slipping on an icy patch and then jolting as a tire caught the far curb. At the end of the alley, past a crumbling loading dock, he parked the van behind a rusted out dumpster. The dumpster was just where he wanted it. Most of this was planning, but some was luck. He had rarely felt himself to be a lucky man.

The rest was simple, like running tech during his days in the theater. He had rehearsed it all. Just follow the plan and stay backstage, out of sight. He turned off the engine, opened the window, and listened. When he was sure no one was around, he got out and checked the piece of tape he had placed between the outside of the door and its doorjamb. The tape was undisturbed. No one had come or gone. As the door could be unlocked only from the inside, he had to get in through a high window. He pulled the van flush with the building, climbed onto the roof of the van and pushed open the small window.

Before he climbed through it, he found himself looking up the alley toward the street. The alley was littered with a slushy mess of cans, newspapers, broken glass, chunks of asphalt and snow. Even in the middle of the day, it was dark and bleak. But he found himself looking beyond the alley and the street, looking up at the tall, distant building, its curved, mirrored skin reflecting the sun and billowy clouds. In some way he could not explain to himself, this distant view was part of what made this just the perfect place to bring her, to hold her.

He pulled himself back to the task at hand. Straddling the window sill, he turned on his flashlight and scanned the area inside. Holding onto the sill, he lowered himself inside and then dropped the last couple of feet to the floor. He unlocked the door, which was a few yards from the van, but still hidden by the dumpster.

His energy still holding, he hauled the equipment through the bowels of the building to a storage room. He had chosen the room, because it was easily accessible to the outer door, but still far enough into the interior of the building that with the door closed he was sure no sound could be heard from outside the building. The room was windowless and, though there was no heat in the building, the temperature of the room today was surprisingly comfortable, ten or fifteen degrees warmer than the outside. He was pleased with this, for he wanted to use the electric heater and the gas generator that powered it as little as possible, to prevent the noise or fumes from attracting attention. Three trips to the van and everything was in.

The challenge had been to find a way of exhausting the fumes from the gas generator, without putting it outside where it would certainly be heard. The problem engaged him. The whole process of setting up the room brought back his days in the theater, mostly in New York, building scenery and doing whatever tech work was needed, electric, sound. Setting the stage, creating the backdrop, working out lighting sequences, with all the works kept secret from the audience, but at the same time creating a world, a fake world, for them. Actors, directors, and other techies would talk about connecting with the audience or entertaining them, but for him it was always about manipulation, creating a false front to draw them in. Come into my house, and I will draw you into my illusion. Come into my world, and I will jerk you around and make a fool of you. Sometimes he would think of it as raping the audience.

His set building began when he returned to the orphanage, after the disastrous stay at the farm. He found a bag of old, broken dollhouse furniture. He remembered setting up little rooms with the miniature furniture in an orange crate. He remembered, in the only distant way he could, the days when he must have loved doing it. He remembered the scenes he had constructed being so inviting that he had wished he could make himself small and sit in the tiny chairs or curl up in the little bed beside the delicate match stick bedside table.

He thought of this, as he carried the generator up a short flight of stairs and then up a frozen escalator to a cavernous space. Display cases were scattered around, some tipped over, most with their glass broken, all covered with dust and a chaos of spider webs. Cardboard boxes and rusted hangers littered the floor. A mezzanine overlooked the main floor, its elaborate, black ironwork railings in perfect condition. High windows bathed the room in what struck him as old fashioned light of the kind he had tried to create on stage.

He ran the heavy duty extension cord from the generator down to the storage room, made another trip up with the gas can and filled the generator. With a couple of pulls the generator sputtered and then whirred to life. The hardware clerk had said the generator was quiet, and it lived up to his promise. By the time he reached the bottom of the escalator, its sound had faded to a hum. Standing inside the outer door of the building, he could not hear it at all. He returned to the storage room, hooked up the space heater, set up the card table, and covered it with a table cloth. He plugged the lamps into the extension cord and spent some time deciding just where he wanted them. He arranged two folding director's chairs and even laid down the oriental rug that had caught his eye.

He unrolled the futon, flopped down on it, and fell immediately asleep. When he awoke, it was late afternoon. His clothes were damp with sweat. He thought he was in the kind of fever he had early in his illness, but then realized that the space heater had overheated the room. He went upstairs, turned off the generator and returned to the van. As he drove back to Ann Arbor, he thought how smoothly it had all gone. As he pictured the room, he felt drawn to it. It was just like the miniature rooms of his childhood.

He picked up some Chinese food, went back to his house, and wolfed it down. He was starved. As a reward for completing this part of his plan, he read her second letter.

February 8, 1971
Dear Son,

I know it's been a while, and I'm sorry about that. I guess you are nine months old now. I feel sorry for leaving you.

I've left one world, your world, and rejoined mine. I'm back at school, and it's a little awkward, but no big deal. Kids ask me where I went, what happened, and I just say it was a tough year, my parents sent me to a school in Europe, and I'd rather not talk about it. Except for that, I'm doing really well. I've dived into things here. Whatever there is to do, I do. It keeps my mind off things. I volunteer for everything. I'm busy every minute. I'm on the field hockey team and am going to try out for the volleyball team. The school has a real good team, and it's going to be hard to get on it, but I've been practicing and I'm really dead set on making it. It feels better to be doing all this stuff. I don't get distracted by any bummer thoughts. I don't lie awake anymore worrying about you. I just force my thoughts to be about happy things and it's working. Maybe my parents were right about my needing to put things behind me.

I want you to know, though, that I haven't forgotten you. I really, really will make sure everything turns out good for you. I don't know how I'll do it, but I will. I promise.

Winter break is coming up and my parents and I are going to Florida. I've never been there and I'm looking forward to flying out of winter. It'll be great.

My parents don't know this, but I'm going to write another letter to St. Boniface, to whoever runs the place, to find out if they've found a family for you. I hope they have.

When I started this letter I felt so glad to be back in my world here, to be a pretty normal teenager, but now, when I think about you, I feel sad. Maybe I should have stayed with you.

Your mother

He slipped the letter back into the envelope, found its place in the stack with the others, and retied the bundle with the ribbon. He dragged himself to the bathroom where he took his evening medications and collapsed on his bed, falling first into a deep and dreamless sleep. Then towards morning he was in the dream of her body, the wordless dream of navigating over her skin, her heat spreading through him, as he finds her nipple and molds his mouth in perfect unity around it. All pain, all need, all frustration dissolves as the milk heats him from the inside, just as her skin warms him from the outside. Then inevitably, her body grows suddenly horrifically cold and sucks the last bit of warmth and life from him.

CHAPTER SEVENTEEN

W eiss found his first analytic hours on Mondays difficult. Freud had described patients' analytic material on Mondays as the "Monday crust." Material that had been rich and available the previous week was now, with the weekend interval, again repressed. There was, Weiss thought, a Monday crust in analysts too. It took him a while on Mondays to listen beyond the surface communications of the patient, to find his way back to the unconscious currents.

Beyond his usual Monday crust, Ivan was distracted today by his concerns about Dana. He had not asked her if she had been in Whitmore Lake, thinking he would seem paranoid. He was thinking, too, about how strangely unenthused she had been about the horse show, though she said she had done well. He was disappointed when she responded with a vacant laugh to his playfully coming into their bedroom wearing only a race ribbon. She did seem more positive about the cruise, saying she felt herself being more "ready" for it, but then puzzling Ivan when she said she was trying to "get past a few things." Is one of them your affair with Kevin? An ache filled his body, as he imagined the two of them together.

By midmorning when his third patient, Leonard Malick, a surgeon, arrived, Weiss had managed to push his concerns about Dana to the side and was engaged in his work. He was breaking new ground with this patient, a man who could sometimes be the picture of an authoritative doctor, and at other times an inhibited frightened man who let his colleagues and his wife mercilessly boss him around. Weiss and the patient were coming to understand that when the patient felt in command and successful in his work he became, for as yet unknown reasons, anxious. Being successful included doing "big cases," which he often backed away from, even though he was perfectly capable of doing them well.

This turned out to be a watershed session. He reported a dream in which he was surrounded by men who were ready to attack him with machetes. He followed this by saying he felt scared about coming to the session today. Weiss invited him as always to say whatever would come to mind about the dream and about his fear coming to the session.

"I feel here today more like a patient than ever before."

"What kind of patient?" Weiss asked on a hunch.

"A medical patient." After a long pause and some deep breaths to try to clear his anxiety, he went on. "I always think of myself as a doctor here, I hold onto that, like we're two doctors, instead of that here you're the doctor, and I'm the patient . . . . I don't know if I ever told you that I made sure to choose a psychoanalyst who wasn't an M.D." Weiss, trained first as a clinical psychologist, had a Ph.D.

"No," Weiss said, "but you are telling me now. So you've tried not to feel like a medical patient by choosing a Ph.D. analyst, but you're feeling like one anyway. It's making you, for some reason, very anxious." After another long pause and more nervous sighs, the patient looked back over his shoulder at Weiss.

"I'm remembering now that when I was a child, I was terrified of doctors. Absolutely terrified. And here I'm a doctor now myself." He gave a forced, coughlike laugh. "When I was five, I had a tonsillectomy. To get me to go quietly to the hospital, my parents tricked me by saying the doctor was just going to look at my sore throat. Right! The big lie. Then when I was about eight, I had this botched foot operation. So I had to have another operation a couple of months later. Those bastards butchered me!"

"I'm thinking of the men with machetes in your dream," said Weiss. "You felt those doctors when you were a kid weren't doing surgery on you, they were hacking you with machetes. Maybe you feel an echo of that in your fear of me today. You looked back at me just now to see if I had my machete out." The patient laughed and was obviously relieved.

"I guess this could have something to do with my anxiety doing big cases. Maybe, when I do them, when I have the scalpel, I'm the guy with the machete."

Weiss and the patient knew they had understood something important.

The next patient was Jennifer Andrews, the patient with strong needs in the transference, and in her life, to be admired and loved, the patient whose ex-con former boyfriend was helping her force Weiss to have sex with her. She was dressed today even more seductively than usual.

After the previous session Weiss had reviewed her history and worked to refocus his understanding of what she was doing with him. Sexually abused as a child, she was now turning the tables, trying in her adult life to control and overwhelm Weiss and others with her sexuality. Yet Weiss could hear in this a cry for a closeness from much earlier in her childhood, a hunger to be fed and protected by her mother. The psychologically fatal fact of this patient's early life was that her uncle who molested her was the only person who showed any consistent interest in her. She had turned to him to meet needs her mother could not. In her mind emotional intimacy always required surrendering to someone else's sexual needs.

She began as she often did by slowly and coyly taking off her coat, her scarf, and her sweater, as if she were doing a striptease, and then arranging herself seductively in the chair. She wore today even darker lipstick, tighter jeans, and a skimpier top than usual, and Weiss had been able to smell her perfume before he had opened the waiting room door. She looked over at the couch across the room.

"You've never suggested I lie on the couch. You probably don't want me to, because it would turn you on so much that you'd jump my bones. What would you do if I just decided one day to lie down? Or get undressed?"

In spite of her overly dramatic posturing, she was still very attractive and had been able easily to draw men into intense, brief affairs and then drop them. It sounded to Weiss like the men ended up feeling, not surprisingly, abused themselves. Just as he had felt during the previous session when she had talked of suing him if he refused to have sex with her. As he felt now in response to her aggressive seductiveness.

Ivan could imagine how easy it would be for a therapist to get sexually involved with a patient like this. He knew therapists who had, with disastrous consequences for the patient and for their own careers. Weiss had felt the pull from her and from other patients with similar dynamics before, but had never succumbed. Though the seductive energy from a patient like this could be enormous and the analyst's own wish to be the object of such a patient's attraction could be equally strong, Weiss reminded himself of what he very well knew – that the psychoanalytic or psychotherapy situation invites wishes and longings for unmet or overmet needs from important people from the patient's past. Though the analyst might want to flatter himself into thinking he is irresistible to the patient, in fact the feelings toward him are almost all carried over from other people.

Though he felt himself getting aroused by her talking about him jumping her bones, Weiss could see clearly today through her behavior to the ten year old, excited and terrified when her uncle responded to her sexually, and to the five year old parading around, hoping someone would notice her, and behind it all, to the baby, longing for contact, wanting to be noticed, held, and cuddled.

He reminded himself that she might be pushed by emotional pressures of childhood, but she was in reality an adult with the capacity to do some very adult damage. If she felt spurned and hurt enough by his refusal to respond to her advances, Weiss was increasingly concerned about her potential to hurt him back. He thought of Glenn Close's character in "Fatal Attraction" and shuddered.

"So you have a daughter in town, I see." She waited for his reaction. He worked hard to contain and conceal what he was feeling. Ann Arbor being a small town, an analyst's private life never remained completely private. "You're not going to tell me, but I know you do. I saw an ad in the *Observer* for her decorating business. I'm sure it's her. That's probably who that young thing was I saw you with." She continued to look at him expectantly.

"You're looking to me for something right now. What is it?"

"I want you to stop being such a stone. Can't I ever get you riled up, for Christ's sake."

"You feel if you're just yourself, I'll be as unresponsive to you as a stone. So you have to be challenging. And intrusive. Who am I in all this? Is there someone you once tried to reach, who felt to you cold as a stone?" She seemed on the verge of remembering something and letting difficult feelings surface. She had once before in the treatment let herself get in touch with her feelings of inadequacy and loneliness, after which she propelled herself into a spree of promiscuity.

Weiss knew that seeing Sonya's ad and realizing the woman she had seen him with was his daughter were both terrifically wounding to the patient. In all of the patient's fantasies about Weiss, she never imagined any other woman in his life. She needed to imagine he was there only for her. The fantasies were constructed in this way to fend off a deeper sense that she meant absolutely nothing to him. Or to anyone.

Weiss could see she was beginning to seethe. For her to be able to sit with these feelings of rage, to tolerate them, would be for her an enormous accomplishment. Ivan found she was not yet at that point. He realized as he had in the previous session that he had been overestimating the strength of her inner controls.

"Ivan fucking Weiss, you and your special daughter can just get fucked." When she thinks of me and my daughter, Weiss observed to himself, she peppers her language with "fuck." He heard the echoes of the sexual abuse by her uncle.

She then grabbed her clothes in a lump and stalked out, her coat sleeve knocking the tissue box to the floor. A few moments later she returned, poked her head in and said, "Oh, and, you looked pretty good at the race yesterday," and slammed the door hard.

So she knows my daughter is in town and either happened to be at the race or, more likely, followed me there. He felt her invading his life. This is how, he realized, she must have felt during the many times she was molested. The transference, Weiss would often tell his students, is not just the patient unconsciously experiencing you, the therapist, as some important figure from their past. Often things emerge reversed, with the patient unconsciously playing the part of someone from the past, while putting you in their own childhood position. This time around I will do to you what was done to me. This seemed very likely what Jennifer Andrews was doing with him.

The patient's seductiveness toward Weiss, her rage at him, and her intrusiveness into his life all presented therapeutic challenges, but her effort to force herself into his daughter's life was much more troubling for Weiss. Though this patient, as far as he knew, had no history of physically attacking anyone, Weiss was shocked by how little guilt there had been in the previous session around her former boyfriend's thoughts of extortion.

As he reviewed his notes on the previous session and wrote notes on today's, he realized there was something more he needed to face about Jennifer Andrews. Not only did she show no guilt over her thoughts about extorting sex from Weiss, she was clearly excited by them.

He reviewed his notes on his last patient of the day, Adam Stone. Though he took notes on every hour with all of his patients, he always took particularly detailed ones on the first several sessions with a new patient.

Transference heating up early. Wish to show off to his father by trying
to surpass me, other older men; fear of retaliation for this, and self generated

punishment for this. The wish to surpass is followed by need to apologize for imagined insults directed toward me.

Dream of the grotesque tiger with rodent teeth. Insight gained about fear of looking at dangerous thoughts or feelings in himself. His worry about my reaction (anger, rage, murderous retaliation against him?) to his interest in Nazi memorabilia. (My worries too about my reactions to this.) His choice of a Jewish analyst is an oedipal challenge, just like his need to be challenging with the Director of the dig. He is at war with his father, a guerrilla war. Maybe he replays this so that this time around he can be in the power position – he will be the Nazi, I will be the weak one, the weak Jew. He will have his shoe on my neck.

The therapeutic alliance with this patient feels already strong. He shows remarkable insight for someone so early in treatment.

Ivan free associated to himself about the patient. The Nazi material, he thought, makes me uncomfortable. Why can't he play out his oedipal struggles in some other way? But there was, nevertheless, a beauty to the unfolding of this patient's material. He always loved building with a patient, from the patient's own thoughts and feelings and actions, a picture of the patient's inner life. It was like a duet, or making love.

The patient was late for his appointment. As Weiss waited, he wondered why? He had seen countless meanings of patients' latenesses, from unexpressed hostility, to a need to avoid painful thoughts, to avoiding the experience of waiting passively in the waiting room. Weiss reminded himself that he would need to know where the patient was psychologically today to even begin to know why he was late.

"Sorry for being late," said the patient, ten minutes late, as he took off his parka and sat down. "The Department Chairman called me in to talk about some harebrained idea he has about a course I'm teaching. I couldn't get myself to interrupt him to say I had an appointment I needed to get to." Weiss considered how the patient was beginning the session. He starts right out with a little battle with the Chairman, the authority, the father substitute, and then must give in to him, at his own expense, missing some of his session.

"You felt you needed to submit to his needs, while you put yours aside."

"Yes, that's right, but I was also not submitting to *your* needs," he added, his provocative tone unmistakable.

"How so?"

"You want to start the session, but you can't do that without me."

Dominate or submit, or do both at once, that's the pattern.

"So you obey, you submit to him, and at the same time make me submit to your lateness." The patient did not respond to Weiss' comment, but looked at the couch. Weiss remembered the near panic the patient had felt on the couch. Does lying on the couch mean to him submitting?

"I had a dream that might be important. I think it has something to do with you."
While he was talking, he had been scanning the office, but now he fell silent and
fixed his eyes on Weiss. As his gaze stayed locked on the analyst, to his own surprise,
Weiss felt a stirring within himself. Before this man's eyes had seemed to him flat, but
now there was something liquid and sensual about them. A fantasy crept into Weiss'
awareness. He imagined himself walking across the room and extending his hand
to Stone who takes it, as if he were accepting an invitation to dance. Then, they are
standing face to face, and Weiss strokes Stone's face and runs his fingers through the
patient's hair.

The feelings did not alarm Weiss. Though Freud considered human beings to be
underlyingly bisexual, in talking to male colleagues, Weiss had found some of them
deeply uncomfortable with their own sexual feelings toward their own male analysts
or toward male patients. During their own analyses several had confided in him that
discovering homosexual feelings in themselves had been nothing short of personal
crises for them.

The most severe and tragic example of this was that of a young, talented
psychiatrist who began psychoanalytic training at the same time Weiss did. Late one
night during the second year of their training, Weiss received a panicked phone call
from him about what "my so-called analyst wants to do with me. He's constantly
making suggestive remarks. I think he's trying to change me in some weird way, or
seduce me." Weiss encouraged him to step back and examine how he was experiencing
his analyst, but to no avail. He precipitously quit his analysis, dropped out of
psychoanalytic training, had a succession of short affairs to prove his heterosexuality,
and then became a lifelong critic of psychoanalysis. Though Weiss had some rough
and painful times in his own analysis, confronting homosexual feelings had not been
for him especially difficult. When an analyst is comfortable with such feelings, he can
hear them in his patients.

Ivan was intrigued by the emergence of his fantasy. And by its vividness and
strength. Maybe I'm feeling this simply because he's offering me what I love to work
with most, a dream.

"In the dream I'm at a lecture. The speaker is someone famous, a man, older,
and I'm expecting a lot. I've heard about him and think he'll be great. He comes in
from the side, like from the wing of a stage, and he climbs up on a high platform. The
podium, I realize, is way up, and he's climbing up some kind of flimsy scaffolding.
When he gets up there, I'm surprised that he's quite short, and the lectern is so high
he can barely see over it. The audience starts to chuckle, but I don't. Then someone
gets him a stool or box to stand on, and everyone gets serious again. He begins to
talk, and it sounds very learned, but then I look at him, now clearly, and I see he's got
stains on his shirt, his tie is really mismatched with his suit, he doesn't have shoes on,
and his hair is going every which way. You know, his hair was kind of like a clown's.
I hadn't thought of that until now. The whole audience seems to be noticing all of
this just as I am, and there's a lot of whispering and muttering about it. I'm trying to

listen to what the lecturer is saying. It sounds important, and I'm trying to get people to listen to him. I feel I'm on his side, that I'm the only one, and I feel sorry for him. I want to help him."

Once again the oedipal story. In the dream he puts the speaker high up, both by reputation, and literally by putting the man on a high platform. Is he putting him on a "pedestal" and then knocking him off? He doesn't knock him off physically in the dream, but he does mock him by making him short with funny, stained clothes and no shoes. He starts as a famous man and soon ends up a clown. Then the dreamer feels frightened or guilty about what he knows he's doing in the dream and comes to the rescue of the lecturer.

"You told me one association to your dream, that the man looked like a clown. What other thoughts come to mind about the dream?" The patient said nothing for a while, turning his head slowly back and forth, as if he were trying to stretch the muscles in his neck. He then brought his hands up and cradled his neck and head.

"This is a little hard to say, because it has to do with you, with your life outside of here." He now leaned far forward in the chair, pulled at his collar and ran his fingers sensuously through his hair. Weiss felt again drawn to him. "I think the man giving the lecture was you."

He now sat up abruptly and looked directly at Weiss, as if searching for some reaction to what he had just said. "I saw a notice in my department that you were giving a lecture at the Psychoanalytic Institute on Charles Manson." Weiss was startled. Though the new President of the Institute was intent on building bridges between the Institute and the various academic communities in the area, Weiss was surprised that a notice of his talk had been sent as far afield as the Anthropology Department. He suddenly felt the distance between himself and the patient had shortened and wanted to move his chair back. He felt something vaguely threatening about the patient knowing about his giving his paper.

"So I think the lecturer in the dream is you. The part of the dream I think about most is that I'm trying to help you. I'm on your side. The others are making fun of you, and I'm thinking, stop, he has some important things to say." Weiss was not surprised that his patient had fastened onto this part of his dream, for this portion constituted the defense: See, I'm the good guy, I'm helping you. The others mock you, but I don't. This all seemed to fend off the wish in the dream: to mock the lecturer, Weiss in the transference, but probably on the unconscious level the patient's father.

"Yes, I can see that in the dream you're on the lecturer's side, on my side, but you have to remember that the whole dream is yours. Even the part where the lecturer is portrayed as a clown and the audience laughs. It's all yours." The patient smiled.

"That's interesting and clever, very clever," nodding in agreement, it seemed to Weiss too much so, making a great show of complimenting Weiss' comment.

"So you make me the fool in the dream for some reason and now tell me how clever I am."

"I guess I can't say again that's clever of you." He smiled and shifted in his chair. "So you're saying that at some level I want to make you look like a clown, to look foolish . . . That may be. I guess my need to fight and challenge rides again. You know, I did it in the meeting I just had with the Chairman. It's got to do with the Nazi stuff. He's Jewish, and really lets people know it. He's much closer to the Jews on the faculty." He paused, cleared his throat, and sat in a tense silence. Weiss asked why he had stopped.

"I know I'm supposed to say everything I think, but I guess I don't want to . . . Alright, I thought about the Chairman and the other Jews as, 'kikes in the ghetto.'" Weiss saw an old faded photograph his father had shown him of Ivan's grandfather standing by a pushcart in a ghetto in Poland. He felt his stomach twist up, and he wanted to yell at the patient to shut his filthy mouth. He felt his brow knot and jaw clench, but the patient seemed not to notice.

"I thought about how cliquish they are, how much they stick to themselves, always feeling like such special people." Weiss squirmed in his chair. "Sorry to say all this," the patient said, sounding to Weiss like an afterthought.

"I know I should just say things as they occur to me, just as I'm thinking them. That's the most useful thing to do, right?"

"Yes, it is," said Weiss, though he wanted the patient to put all of this Nazi crap away and never to bring it up again. Why can't he play out his competitive, patricidal wishes in some other form, for instance by mocking Weiss for being shorter, or older, or dumber. Weiss knew that his feelings were stemming from his own issues. The patient needs to play out his struggles in his own particular way. I want him to be my perfect patient, my ideal boy, which includes his having the kind of conflicts I decide he should have.

Weiss then glimpsed something in himself he would reflect on further after the session, an emotional tempo of the session that could reveal something about the patient or himself, or both. In each session Weiss felt the patient at first to be so promising, his material so consistent, so intriguing, and the patient's communications to be like pieces of a well fitting puzzle. Then Weiss was suddenly let down and disappointed by the patient. He found himself thinking of Dana's rhythm as she rode a jumping course, the signals that passed back and forth between horse and rider. Then he thought of the times when it all went suddenly wrong, when the horse refused to jump or spooked at something, and Dana was thrown. He had seen her take a few falls, fortunately none serious. I'm being thrown by the patient. My hopes are high. Then he puts me off, he disappoints me. Realizing this, Ivan could listen somewhat better.

"The Chairman seems to have, I'll just say it, a little kike club. I see club spelled with a 'k,' then I think of the KKK. I'm awful, aren't I? He'll sometimes use Jewish words in faculty meetings. Some of them are common now, and I understand them, but often I have no idea what he's saying and have to ask. Makes it real obvious that I'm not in the club, that I'm an . . . outsider." Struggling to listen past the antisemitic material, Weiss could hear something raw and emotionally immediate when the patient called himself an "outsider." It seemed to Ivan to be the most important thing he had said so far in the session.

"During the meeting, after we talked about how my courses are going, we somehow got on the topic of the holocaust . . . you can imagine, one of his favorite subjects. He talked like he was an expert, about different camps, the dates they were liberated and such. I corrected him right and left. That wouldn't have been so bad, but then I felt compelled to tell him about my Nazi memorabilia collection. When I told him, the blood drained from his face." Weiss hoped the blood was not draining from his.

"The Chairman tried to discuss my interests like a good anthropologist, saying that what I collect are just like any other archeological artifacts. But I know he didn't believe a word he was saying. He was offended, insulted, and began to think of me as the enemy. But you know what I was thinking? Just try to fire me or refuse me tenure over this, you fucker. I'd love it. You push me out, force me out, and I'll point the finger at you. Just try it."

Weiss thought of the many nasty tenure struggles he had heard about over the years from colleagues and patients. When Weiss thought of Adam Stone seeking tenure, a vivid image occurred to him of his patient balanced on the edge of a cliff, his back to the precipice with the Chairman standing in front of him. Stone has been refused tenure, and he is shouting at the Chairman, "Kike, kike, dirty Jew!" The Chairman struggles with himself, but then pushes Stone off the cliff to his death. Police swarm around the Chairman and arrest him.

Does this man, Weiss wondered, know just what to do to get under people's skin, especially those in authority, until they can't control themselves and attack him? Then, from his position of the victim, he accuses his attacker and brings him down.

The patient's dream of the lecture came back to Weiss' mind, and he was impressed at its clarity and the facility with which the patient was working to understand it. He remembered again Jake's caution about this patient.

"Let me share with you an impression I have about our work so far," Weiss began. "Whatever you bring up, events of your life, dreams, reactions to me, with everything really, you have such an immediate and quick ability to reflect on them, to come to insights about them. Understanding and insight, those are, of course, our best tools here, but it's the way you work with things, I'm wondering about. They seem all sewed up. Your dream today, for example, was so incredibly clear and straightforward. No loose ends. It's as if you're going down a road, looking only straight ahead. There can be some very interesting things on the side or even off the road." Stone was listening very closely. "You don't seem to have let yourself play around with anything in the dream that's not connected with its main story."

"Like what?"

"One thing might be the setting of the dream."

Stone shifted in his chair, unsettled. "The setting? Well, I didn't think . . . I didn't think that was important." Good. Weiss felt he had been right.

"About the setting, O.K., I'll tell you every detail I can remember," Stone shot back defensively. The patient's eyes narrowed to a squint, as he thought.

The bell tower rung the three quarter hour. A child's cry could be heard from a neighboring apartment. A door slammed down the hall. The sky which had been gray and leaden all day now began to clear, letting through brief flashes of sunlight.

"The lecture in the dream doesn't take place indoors. It's instead on something floating, like a large raft or the deck of a freighter or oil tanker. Better yet, a barge. It's a huge, flat expanse, and I'm at the back of it. Even before the people start to make fun of the speaker, I look around and see that I'm very far back, in the last row, at the very edge. Oh, yes, I'm remembering now, I'm so far back that I feel the back legs of my chair beginning to slip off the edge." He paused.

"Is there more?"

"Yeah, I'm wondering if I fall off will I be able to swim. The water is rough, and I know somehow that there are strong currents. I'm right in the middle of this water, the same distance to each shore. I see huge silos, like farm silos, several of them, different sizes. They're new and very shiny. I'm drawn to them. They're right in front of me, I'm looking at them dead on. Beyond them it all looks different. Bleak. It's as if I'm really high up, and I can see over them, and everything beyond looks dark and grim. I seem to be flying over all of that now, miles of streets, but they're all deserted, everyone has gone."

The dream sent a chill through Weiss, and he could feel within himself his own resistance to going further with it. He felt relieved that they had run out of time.

"We'll have to stop here today."

The patient got up, put on his coat, and at the door, turned back to Weiss.

"We didn't get to this, but I've just met a new woman." Stone seemed to be scanning Weiss' face for some response to his announcement.

"You seem to be looking to me for some reaction to what you've just told me." The patient just continued to stare and then, with no further word, walked out.

He brings this up at the end of the session, when he's on his feet, coat on, ready to leave. Ready to run? Is he again seeing me as his father? With a father who would tell his son no girl could possibly be interested in him and who would stand with his foot on his son's neck, Weiss could easily imagine how frightening it would be to reveal to an older man his interest in a woman. Again, a squarely oedipal conflict.

Weiss could feel himself want to see Stone's struggles as oedipal, but the chill he felt listening to the bleak dream image of miles of deserted streets suggested struggles around profound loss and separation, conflicts arising during the first fifteen months of life, long before the beginning of the oedipal phase at three and a half. He wondered if he wanted to avoid in himself feelings that would be stirred up by these more archaic struggles over loss.

"Patient and analyst can collude to avoid," Norcroft, his supervisor and mentor, in his spare way, had said. "Patient speaks of a matter that makes analyst uneasy.

Analyst sends subtle messages to patient not to tread on ground painful to analyst. The process becomes useless.

"A tourist and a traveler. Familiar with the distinction, Weiss? Probably not," the old analyst had said without waiting for a reply. "The tourist doesn't remain anywhere long, sees the standard sights, never learns how or where the people live. A traveler explores, has no timetable, goes off the beaten track, immerses himself in the peoples' lives. Risky, even dangerous to be a traveler, but if you have a taste for it, much more rewarding. In some analyses the analyst and patient are tourists. They see the standard intrapsychic sights – unconscious fantasies, wishes, reconstructions of childhood experiences – but the work has a stock, tinny quality. All canned, stagnant. The analyst retreats to routinized interpretations, mantras the patient and analyst repeat. Both avoid what you call in this country, the real stuff. Nothing changes. An analyst who is a traveler, now that is a true analyst! Off the beaten path, way off, in the underbrush."

Weiss had the increasing sense that he was caught in a struggle between his defensive need to be a tourist and his adventurous desire to be a traveler with this patient. What scares me, he wondered, about going into that underbrush. What scares me about Adam Stone's secrets?

CHAPTER EIGHTEEN

The flashing light on Sonya's answering machine signaled two messages, and she knew before she pressed the play button that they were from Jerry and Nick. She looked at the skis still leaning against the door where she had left them after her outing with Jerry and then at the flowers from Nick, now fully open and very appealing. She played the messages from the two men, each asking her to call back. She somehow knew both men wanted to ask her out. She picked up the phone and started to punch in Nick's numbers, but stopped before the last one, cautioning herself to slow down, not to act impulsively. She put the phone back in its cradle.

She then did what she had so enjoyed in the past, but which she had not felt comfortable enough to do since the rape, she drew herself a bath. For someone who always felt in a mad rush to move on to the next thing in life, lying in a bath, the water almost too hot to take, forced her to slow down. Since the rape, even with her bathroom door locked and the double dead bolt locks on her apartment door set, the anticipation of the languid pleasure of taking a bath had been pushed aside by feelings of vulnerability. She had needed to be on the alert, ready to defend herself, ready to run. She had taken a karate course while she was still in New York and had learned moves to defend herself, but all the moves started with her standing up. What about if you're lying down? There were no special moves to protect yourself while you're in your bed, or in a bath. I should have asked about that. Even just taking her clothes off had been a trial for her at first, but had now become tolerable. Her need to stay hyperalert after the attack had made even listening to music in her apartment frightening, for she worried that she would not hear an intruder trying to break in.

Today she still felt a little anxious, but something had shifted enough in her that she put on her favorite Enya song, poured in some lavender bath oil, and eased herself into the bath, her body relaxing against the warmth of the scented water. She was pleased she could do this and put Jerry and Nick aside. She became absorbed for the first time in months in a book, reading having been also difficult for her.

When the disk changed and some music by Sade came on, she put her book down, lay back and thought about Jerry's back, broad and strong, as she skied behind him. She felt a stirring that had been shut away since the attack. She had felt at moments since the attack some sexual reawakenings, but the moment they emerged, disconnected memory fragments of the attack, like shards of broken glass, flew into her mind. The sexual feelings would be instantly hidden away.

But today, as she lay in the bath, her mind passed quickly over the rape and settled comfortably on Jerry. Though they saw the world in such different ways, sometimes jarringly different, she felt at the same time a bedrock security with him. She was also very attracted to him. She let her hands move to and linger over abandoned areas of her body. She thought of this as opening a vacation cottage which had been closed up for the winter, dusting things off, opening the windows, all in anticipation of the new season. She cupped her breasts, squeezed her nipples gently, and listened to her breathing quicken. Then imagining her hands were Jerry's, she found just the right pressure on her clitoris and came, still with some caution and restraint, but came. After, she relaxed in a way she had not for a very long time.

She dried her hair and called Jerry back. He was excited, he told her, that a friend had given him tickets for this Friday to the Guarneri String Quartet.

"They play these old instruments. The sound is incredible. I don't know if this is the kind of music you like. I guess I don't know yet what kind of music you like, but . . . would you go with me?"

They were face to face again with another difference. With music so important to him and his career, he had tried to get a sense of her preferences, but wanting to avoid pointing up yet another difference between them, she had answered evasively that she liked all kinds of music. With the exception of Debussy or other light classical music, which in the right mood she could work herself up into enjoying, she found classical music dull. String quartet music, in particular, seemed formal and stiff. She reminded herself that she had really heard little of it and had not heard any in a long time.

"Sure, I'm game. Classical music isn't my favorite, but I haven't really heard much of it." Talking about classical music, so soon after feeling so sexual, with Jerry as her fantasy, struck her as funny, and she laughed.

"What's so funny?"

"Just a little private joke. I'll tell you about it sometime." When we know each other a lot better, she thought.

"I'm glad you're willing to give this classical stuff a try. Next time we do something, you choose."

"It's a deal," she said. He was quiet for a moment. He then cleared his throat in a nervous, self-conscious way.

"Speaking of music, when I think about us, I think of the song that goes, 'You say tomatoes, I say tomotoes, you say potatoes, I say pototoes . . . let's call the whole thing off,' but then at the end of the song, they don't call it off. I know we're different, but I feel something for you beyond all the differences." She was pleased he sensed the differences and was willing to discuss them. She wondered though what the "something beyond" was from her side. "I'm not trying to force you to tell me what you feel about me, but I can tell our differences have been on your mind, too."

"They have. I'm glad you're aware of this. But our differences aren't the only problem. Since the attack I've been confused about my feelings toward any man."

"I understand." And she knew he did. In spite of the many differences between them, when she had first told him about the rape, he seemed to have an immediate appreciation of how cautious she would need to be with him.

"I didn't mean for this to get so heavy," she said.

"That's alright. So I'll pick you up at five. I'm really glad we're doing this," said Jerry, with a boyish enthusiasm that Sonya found very appealing.

Just as she hung up the phone, it rang.

"Hi," she said, with some exuberance in her voice, thinking it was Jerry calling back about the arrangements.

"Sonya?" She felt startled it wasn't Jerry and then realized it was Nick.

"Yes," she said a little formally, embarrassed about the excited "Hi" meant for Jerry.

"This is Nick. I had a new idea for how to do the living room that I want to run by you." He described a plan to set the main pieces of furniture on a diagonal, papering one of the walls, and using a screen to provide a boundary between the entrance area and the living room. He went on the tell her where he would position the furniture, lamps, rugs, and plants.

As she talked on the portable phone, she pulled on her bathrobe, went to her desk and looked at her working sketch for his living room. What he was describing so matched what she was going to advise him to do, even down to the one papered wall and screen, that she was for a moment speechless. Had he seen these recent sketches or notes? Not possible. She had done them only last night. Had she seen something he had drawn or had they talked about any of these specific ideas before? She was sure not.

"So, what do you think? . . . You there?"

"Yes, yes. I think those are really great ideas. They are along the lines of what I was going to recommend you do with that room. Maybe you should go into the business yourself. I'm not sure you even need me." The moment this was out, she regretted saying it. It sounded self demeaning and unprofessional.

"These ideas grew out of what we talked about. I think they're just extensions of your ideas," he said. She knew this was not true, but appreciated that he was rescuing her. She also continued to wonder how their plans could be so alike. This is just what I like about him so much. We think alike, our aesthetic sense is the same. His tastes are my tastes, my humor is his. Looking at him is like looking in a mirror.

"There is something else I want to ask you. There's an exhibition of Art Deco furniture at the Detroit Institute of Arts. I thought you might want to go." He hesitated. "To go with me." She had heard about this special exhibit and wanted to see it. It was probably the only thing that had ever come to the DIA that she wanted to see. Unlike the concert she was going to with Jerry, she wouldn't have to try to like this event. Nick knew just what she wanted.

"Nick, let me think about this," she said, proud that she was not letting herself be swept away by her impulse to say yes. "I know I'd love that exhibit, but we have, you know, a professional, a business relationship, and it could get complicated if I go on a . . . I guess it would be a date, a date with you."

"I understand."

"Let me think about it, Nick. O.K.?"

"Sure. Anyway, let's set up a time to talk about these decorating ideas." She thought he would be more disappointed at her not accepting his museum date. He moved so easily back to business. Maybe he's just patient. That's a nice quality. But she was still so confused about her feelings about him, about Jerry, about men altogether.

She checked her appointment book and arranged to meet with him Friday afternoon at three. Ample time to go over the plans and then to get ready for Jerry to pick her up at five for their date that evening. She then saw the two men in her mind, standing side by side. She walked around them, inspected them, as if she were trying to make the best shopping decision. In her fantasy, she then kissed each and compared them.

She got dressed and was ready to leave when the phone rang again. This time she decided to monitor the call on her machine.

"I know you said no to going out. I think I deserve an explanation. You gotta tell me why. Call me." She was stunned. Nick had seemed so calm when they talked. Did I even say I definitely wouldn't go out with him? Then she realized the voice, sluggish and slurred, wasn't Nick's. It was Eric Hanson's, and the message was a command. She wondered if he were back on drugs. She had no intention of calling him back. This decision was easy.

*   *   *

May 4, 1974
Dear Son,

The sisters have written to me that parents have been found to adopt you. I'm so excited! A farm family, with lots of kids, in a beautiful area of France (though they felt it would be best not to tell me where). I feel sad that I won't know where you'll be, but I'm so happy that you'll finally have a home, a good home. Home. It sounds so much better than orphanage.

I've been accepted to college and will start in September. I don't know yet what I want to take or major in, but I'm really glad to be setting sail into my adult life. You've found parents and are probably glad to be going to them, and I can't wait to get away from mine.

In my mind's eye I see you going down a long straight road with plane trees neatly pruned on both sides the way I remember them in France, and you're riding down this road in a nice car, like a little gentleman, and a farm woman with a warm smile is standing in front of the farmhouse waiting for you.

When they hear you coming, the other kids come spilling out of the house, and the father, who has been in the fields, climbs down from his tractor and comes to meet you. They all welcome you. They all want you. They are ready to love you.

That's how I see it, that's how I want it to be. I know it sounds rosy and corny, but you deserve better than you've had. This is the last you will hear from me.

Have a great life,

Your mother

As he read this, he sensed strongly, but fleetingly, the hope he remembered having on his way to the farm. He felt it now only as if someone had drawn his intestines into a knot and was pulling hard on both ends.

The farm in her "mind's eye" was a fairy tale, and she was wrong, too, about his never hearing from her again. He did, of course, hear from her again, and now many years later, she had heard from him. Now the tables were turned. The thought of her suffering through what he had suffered stirred him further into life.

The torturing loneliness at the orphanage followed by the excited anticipation of going to the farm and back to loneliness again were now all locked in his body's cycle from pain to its sweet subsiding and back to pain again. This was the only topography on the otherwise deserted plain of his inner life.

He had learned ways to set the pleasure-pain pendulum in motion. Heroin had worked best. He had been a serious addict for a year. The rocketing euphoria and then the descent into desperate cravings were the most powerful of these body rhythms. However, on heroin he had been barely able to function and had been on the verge of losing his theater job. He had seen down the road turning to crime to support his habit. He had enough will to survive to get into a rehab program and break his habit.

When he worked in the theater, either as an actor or techie, the tension around a performance could stimulate him out of his numbness. As the curtain would rise, he felt something wake up inside himself, something start to thaw out.

The anticipation and danger of quick, late night encounters with men or women had, for periods of time, also brought him a little to life. Especially when he picked up men in bars or had an anonymous fuck in a bathhouse, worried every instant about HIV, he felt himself shocked into life.

The plan he was now carrying out grew out of this same need. It was like the theater again, setting up the room, inventing and reinventing himself in the various roles he was playing, lying to everyone, about everything. And in its completion the plan held for him the excited anticipation of murderous sex followed by his own death. No play, not even the best hit of heroin, could come close to that finale.

CHAPTER NINETEEN

"**D**r. Weiss, the Dean of Students has called twice and wants you to call him right back. I told him you weren't here, and that I tried to reach you at home and at your private office, but he was still very irritated that I couldn't get in touch with you. I think I did all I could." It was only nine in the morning and already the Dean was trying to reach him.

"You did fine, Mary, I'll call him right now."

"Oh, also, a Detective Farley from the Police Department called." He poured himself some coffee. Though just brewed, it already tasted to him sludgy and bitter. Probably less the coffee and more my mood, he thought. He settled himself at his desk and called the Dean back.

"Ivan," the Dean's loud and formal voice boomed through the phone, "an irate young woman, Sara Reynolds, with all manner of body piercings and an offensive tattoo, and her little fireplug of a stepfather have just been here leveling scandalous accusations against her therapist, you, the Clinic, and the University. I think I was thrown to the dogs, too. It seems this is the age of the consumer complaint. These two got here at some God awful hour of the morning. They were camped out in front of my office when I got here at eight."

Within the limits of confidentiality Weiss reviewed the situation for the Dean. He could talk about his own experiences with the patient as he was not treating her, or supervising her treatment, but could not discuss anything that she had said to her therapist. Without therapy material, Weiss was unable to explain that this woman's history of sexual abuse led her to imagine others were ready to abuse her again. He could not share with the Dean some crucial information – that this stepfather, who was supporting her complaint that she had been harassed, had very likely abused her himself.

"I don't have to tell you, Ivan, we're in an incredibly litigious climate right now, and sexual harassment is the hot button for the politically correct. You probably should contact the University attorney and just run the situation by him. Between you and me, I think the Admissions Department was completely out to lunch when it allowed a nut like this to slip through. Ivan, I thought they were going to physically attack me. First time I appreciated the gigantic desks they give administrators. I'm also concerned about how a situation like this could get twisted around if the *Daily* got hold of it."

Ivan would have liked to be able to reassure the Dean that everything was getting resolved, but felt in the long run he should be candid.

"George, I appreciate all of these concerns, and I wish I could tell you everything is under control, but frankly it's not."

"Well, by God, get it under control! Tell me what you've done so far."

"I met with her, I've talked with her stepfather by phone. I thought I might be getting through to her, but then she suddenly closed off and went on this rampage."

"Look Ivan, these two are, to my layman's eye, unbalanced, but I've got to tell you she was pretty convincing about the intern abusing her. Did he make suggestive remarks or make a pass at her?"

"No, of course not. He just didn't understand that you don't get into certain areas early in a therapy with a woman like this. He's a very responsible, bookish kind of student, not at all as she's described him to you, I'm sure."

"He sounded like a serial rapist."

"He's not."

"Ivan, I don't know. I want to support you and the Clinic, but I have a responsibility to these two, weird as they are." Ivan heard the Dean let out a despairing sigh. "Why was such an inexperienced intern assigned to her?"

"George, for half of our interns this is a first clinical internship, so we always have some less experienced people. But they are intensively supervised and we do our best to assign difficult cases to more advanced interns." Ivan felt like he was sinking. He had not reviewed how disturbed the patient appeared during the evaluation or how the assignment to the particular intern had been made. Fortunately the Dean let this drop. He moved on to something even more worrisome to Ivan.

"Ivan, I should also let you know they made some vague threats toward you and your family. I told them this has no place in our discussion, and I wouldn't tolerate it. Are either one of them capable of doing anything violent?"

"I don't know. As for her, if she ever returns to the Clinic, her aggressive potential could be further evaluated, but until then I don't think we can assume these threats are only talk." Weiss considered what he could say next. "You saw yourself how impulsive and threatening they can be, but I can't, for reasons of confidentiality, say more." Weiss thought, of course, that a man who can trample on sexual rules and taboos with his stepdaughter was certainly capable of ignoring limits in the aggressive area as well.

"If you would like, I can have the campus police keep a watch on the Clinic for a while. I've never needed to do this, to use them to protect a faculty member from a student, or I guess here a patient, but I'm certainly ready to do it. Shouldn't we call the police about this too?"

"Thanks, George, but let's hold off on both right now," Weiss imagining some of the more anxious and phobic patients having to pass through a gauntlet of University security guards when they came to the Clinic. He also doubted that extra security at the Clinic would protect his family.

"Alright, Ivan, but I'm not just worried about you and your family. I've got the University to consider, too, and I don't want another incident over there. That's an order, Dr. Weiss," said the Dean half joking, but only half.

"Right, George." He hung up and went downstairs to teach a seminar.

This was a continuous case seminar where a student presents weekly the ongoing treatment of a long term case. The case was one of special interest to Weiss, and he hoped it would distract him from his worries about Dana and the problems with Sara Reynolds and her stepfather. Ivan had a remarkable capacity to keep even large personal concerns compartmentalized in his mind.

The treatment being presented was of a young man who had spent his early life in a series of foster homes. Though he was now a successful businessman, Weiss was trying to show the students how the early disruptions in the patient's relationship with his mother and later foster mothers had left an indelible mark on his capacity to form and maintain relationships. Though he appeared to have ties to people, such as a girlfriend and other friends, he remained within himself profoundly cut off from everyone and lived with a bedrock sense that no one could be trusted. Weiss used examples from the way the patient behaved with his therapist to show the thin, two dimensional experience he had of other people. The overwhelming sense of loss caused by these early abandonments had been too great for the small child's emerging personality to handle. In the face of these feelings, he had developed the capacity to numb all of his feelings, to make himself feel dead.

As Weiss spoke, thoughts about himself intruded. To be cut off like this man, to be numb, seemed far better right now than the mounting anxiety about Dana. He wished he, too, could eradicate all of his feelings. Though he knew he did not live with this patient's lifelong, profound sense that no one could be trusted, he felt his trust in Dana severely challenged. He was dimly aware of how little it took for his trust, especially of a woman, to begin to crumble.

"The patient feels just like you described," said the student. "Yesterday he said he felt as if he were going through the motions of life, like a robot. He often says he feels dead inside."

The group then discussed, at Weiss' suggestion, how the patient with such profound losses and inner feeling of emptiness could achieve so much in his life, at least from an external point of view, while other people with similar early experiences, Charles Manson, for example, would become psychopathic and homicidal.

After the seminar he went back up to his office, returned several other calls, and then called the detective, who was out. He sipped his coffee which had gotten, if that was possible, worse as it cooled. He swiveled around to face an antique mirror, a gift from his wife, and the tiny Buddhas he had collected years before that stood next to it. He caught sight of his knotted brow in the mirror and tried without success to relax it. Have I always looked that worried?

He reviewed his face. Semitic features, lean compact face. Dark eyes, deep set and sloping down at their outer edges, seeming to rest on his cheeks. Eyes that many patients saw as soft and sympathetic. Thick lips that Dana called sensuous the first time they made love. And an angular jaw that gave strength to his face. Though his hairline had receded and his hair had thinned, it was still dark. He usually looked younger than his 46 years, but as he looked at himself today, in the dim light of this overcast morning, with all of his features drawn taut by inner strain, he could imagine his face streaked with wrinkles, his skin thin over his bones, his face carved into hollows, and his eyes sunk even deeper into their sockets. He could see himself vividly as an old man. While he had known for days that he was in the midst of tremendous inner conflict, today he could see it written on his face.

He tried to think through what was pressing in on him. Dana was, for some reason, pulling away from him, being the Clinic Director was already presenting a clinical, and perhaps, legal crisis, and he was worried about Sonya, so much so that he had called the Chairman of the History Department, an acquaintance of an acquaintance, to check up on her new love interest. Using the pretext that the Psychoanalytic Institute might be interested in Dr. Streeter giving a seminar on psychohistory, Weiss asked the Chairman what kind of teacher he was and what he was like to work with. His fears were allayed as the Chairman talked of what a reliable man Nick Streeter was, how much students liked him and how much his colleagues on the faculty respected him for his psychohistorical work on the Victorian era. He sounded like a man who would treat Weiss' daughter well.

He leaned back in his chair, closed his eyes and tried to associate to the problems at hand. I feel Dana is unhappy about something and has gone off with another man. I feel Sonya is in danger. They are both troubled now. He felt like he was being thrown back into the worst time of his life, the time of his mother's death. The troubled woman becomes the endangered woman. Life and death. This time around I'll save the woman. I'll keep her with me, it won't happen again. But what did happen to my mother? Did I make her unhappy? Mother goes away from a bad boy. How can I separate my childhood fantasies of what I did to her, from reality, when I don't even know what the reality was. Was the reality unknown to everyone? Is it still a carefully protected family secret?

"Single car accident," he would hear, repeated in hushed tones. The realities: she was driving fast, which she always did, then veered off the road into a bridge support. Middle of the day, summer, fine weather. No skid marks. What did skid marks have to do with it? As a child he didn't understand this part and was too frightened to ask. Later he understood.

His father had laughed when a blood alcohol test was suggested. He knew she never drank. In the end he agreed to the alcohol test and an autopsy, although he called both violations. No alcohol in her blood and the autopsy revealed nothing.

Maybe she fell asleep or got distracted. Or had a stroke or seizure. Her father had died young of a stroke, and a cousin had temporal lobe epilepsy. The accident having happened before the days of seat belts, the damage to her head and brain from the crash impact had been so terrible that it had been impossible to determine if she had a stroke or a seizure.

Or maybe overtaken by some private demon that day, she had deliberately turned the wheel of the Buick and pressed to the floor that delicate foot Ivan had watched with little boy fascination slip into her shoe.

"So you felt, Dr. Weiss," his analyst had said, "bad things you did, making mistakes, whining, crying, had somehow been too much for her. You imagined she collapsed under the weight of your badness. In your mind, you murdered her. You are still trying to figure out the evil inside you, the evil that made her die." Over several years, as his analysis unfolded, he came to discover that he felt unconsciously that his just dessert for this "crime" was to never have a woman stay with him, but instead to lose her, over and over.

*   *   *

Dana Weiss stood in the cold aisleway of the stable, Master, her big gray gelding, next to her in crossties. She was warming the bit under her arm, the reins over her shoulder. As on most afternoons at the stable, she was alone. A few horses rustled in their stalls, the rest turned out in the paddock for the day. One horse whinnied every so often, waited, and then was answered by another outside. She had curried and brushed her horse and was now picking his feet. As she held his foot up and cleaned the bottom of his hoof, he shifted his weight toward her, and she was reminded of the massiveness of these animals. Yet she was so comfortable with them, safe with them. They were often much easier for her than people.

She positioned the saddle pad, slung the saddle up onto the high back of the horse, fastened the girth, and slipped on the bridle. Rather than taking the horse into the indoor arena, as she always did in the winter, she led him out the back of the stable and mounted him. The horse registered through his body the change in the routine and the unfamiliar area. He lifted and turned his head, pricked up his ears, and took little, nervous, stamping steps on the hard, frozen ground. By letting him have a look around and talking to him, she calmed him and eased him away from the barn and onto a trail.

Dana had taken this trail during the summer on her other horse and had promised herself she would try it in the winter, but never had. Today was somehow the day. When the trail opened onto a field of deep, powdery snow, she asked for a canter, and the horse moved forward around the edge of the field, sending up little puffs of snow with each of his long strides. The sun was low and weak in the late afternoon sky, the thin clouds near it a pale pink. She sat deep in the saddle and could feel the softness of the cushioning snow through the horse's body.

She picked up the pace. At the end of the field she turned, the horse's rear legs slipping a little, and cut diagonally across it. As the horse accommodated to the deep snow, she did figure eights, serpentines, and circles. She rode the horse hard, feeling the heat rising through his body into hers and smelling his sweat. She brought him back to a walk, picked up the trail on the far side of the field, and passed through a windbreak of trees into another clearing.

For the first time since her life had started to unravel several weeks before, she felt back to herself, back to something she deeply loved, the harmony with the horse, the pleasure of sharing his power, and the ease and grace of his motion. Everything else in her life had begun to feel like it was spinning wildly out of control.

Just three weeks before, her life seemed finally to be settling into place. She was sure that she had discovered, after many false starts, something she was both good at and loved, and her daughter seemed to be healing emotionally from her terrible experience in New York.

Two days before, Kevin had given Dana a huge vote of confidence. He had asked her in the spring to show one of his horses, because he felt her skills were better suited to this horse than his were. She loved Kevin for all he had taught her, for his confidence in her. For many things, in many ways. Riding through these snowy fields, she was tasting the life that Kevin had opened to her.

She walked the horse to the center of the field, signaled him again to canter and rode him in a spiral pattern, starting with tight circles and widening to larger ones. As she came out of her circles and rode the edge of the field, she spotted a downed tree. She had jumped with this horse higher than this before, but the conditions had been very different. It had been in familiar arenas with good footing over obstacles the horse had seen before. Here she was in foot deep snow, not only slippery, but hiding potentially dangerous holes on both sides of the downed tree. Though Master had settled down some, the surroundings were still strange to him, and he became skittish, switching his leads, moving sideways, and shying. She knew it was dangerous and foolish to try this jump, but all the reasons not to attempt it made her want to do it all the more. If I can do this, she thought, I can do anything. If I can do this, I can put my life back together. It will be a test, the outcome an omen. Another thought then passed through her mind, that if she failed, maybe she'd be knocked unconscious, freeze to death right here, and be free of it all.

She circled the horse about fifty yards from the downed tree, turned him toward it, and rode strongly forward. As she approached it, she collected the horse, pushing him on with her legs, holding him back with her hands, compressing his energy, like a spring ready to be released. She softened her hands, and the horse lengthened his stride and picked up speed. He saw the jump, lifted his head, flared his nostrils and shot out spurts of breath like dragon fire. As she approached the tree, she saw in the distance lights from farmhouses. Cozy, secure. Not cold and risky. She lifted out of the saddle, freeing the horse to jump. He hesitated, shortened his strides, but with a firm leg she urged him forward. She adjusted his stride for a good take off point and asked for power. Clouds of fine snow, kicked up with each stride, surrounded them. Foolish to do this, but here we go.

A few strides before the tree the horse started to lose traction, his front legs splaying out to the sides. He managed to regain his balance just before he left the ground, rounding his body almost perfectly over the tree, and landed softly on the other side. She galloped him to the end of the field, slowed him to a trot, then a walk. She patted his neck in thanks.

As she walked the horse back in the fast darkening evening, she thought of the possibilities for her life. It was all promising. Very promising. But now the promise was in doubt. She imagined Ivan reading the note she had just left for him and thought of the worry it would certainly stir in him. She untacked the horse, put him back in his stall, changed her clothes, and drove to Metro for her flight to New York.

CHAPTER TWENTY

A s Sonya walked to her car in the parking lot adjacent to her apartment house, a car on the street honked insistently until she turned toward it. A young woman was in the passenger seat, and a man with a wide, puffy face in the driver's seat was leaning across her and shouting out the open window.

"If they try to mess with my daughter again, I'll mess with you!" The man and the woman both glared at her for what felt to Sonya to be an interminable moment. "Get it? I can play this game too!"

The young woman said nothing, but her face expressed what Sonya herself at that moment felt – terrified. As the man slid back over the woman into the darkness of the car, the woman leaned forward in her seat, and the light from the street lamp glinted off the rings that hung from her nose and lip. The car pulled away. Who was messing with his daughter? Was that her in the car? Maybe they have me confused with someone else. She felt shaken. Just as I'm going to Nick's house, which is challenging enough with all the feelings I have for him, this happens. I don't need this, I just don't need this.

Distracted by what had happened, Sonya spent longer at the paint store than she had planned and slid to a stop in front of Nick's house late. She felt resolved about her decision not to date him, but wondered if she would feel so firm and clear about it when she actually walked through his door.

She rummaged around the back seat for her fabric sample books, furniture catalogues, and the paint charts she had just picked up. She was about to open the car door, but decided, even though she was late, to sit a minute and collect herself. A jogger went past and then a young couple walking toward the hospital, the woman's long overcoat open, showing her white medical coat and a stethoscope hanging from its pocket. He also looked like a medical student or resident. His arm was protectively around her shoulder. Sonya imagined their life. They kiss goodbye at the hospital and go off to different departments. They meet at the end of the day, share experiences, cook a quick dinner, study late, and then drop exhausted into bed. They wake in the night, make love, and fall asleep in each other's arms. She turned around in her seat to watch their easy gait, as they passed over the bridge to the hospital and out of sight. No one shouts things at them or attacks them. They live a nice, peaceful life.

She wanted to tell Nick about the man shouting at her. She felt he would understand. As much as she wanted to tell him, she knew she needed to mark off better boundaries in their relationship, not dissolve them by bringing up her personal fears. Things were already complicated enough with him. She was determined to keep her personal life to herself.

As she made her way up the walk, she rehearsed what she was going to say. He opened the door as soon as she knocked.

"Sonya, come in," his voice more excited than she had heard it before. An undercurrent in it, too. Strained, pressured, like someone who is trying to appear to be having a good time when it's obvious they're not. He showed her into the living room where she laid out her catalogues and sketches. She wanted to get the personal matter settled first.

"The usual?" he asked, meaning the camomile tea she had before.

"That would be great." He went over to the sideboard, poured her tea, and set it down by her. Her carefully rehearsed speech about why she wanted to keep things platonic and professional between them had flown from her mind. She blew on the tea, which didn't need it, and sipped it for a few moments, trying to regroup.

"Nick, first we need to talk about your wanting to go out with me." He tilted his head back, and with his hand slowly followed the contour of his chin down to his neck. She knew he was listening attentively to her. This made him even more attractive. "I feel a kind of connection with you that I can't explain, like we're on the same wavelength." I wanted to tell him why I won't go out with him, and I'm telling him why I do! Get a grip, Sonya. "Let me just say it. I've been going out with someone. I don't know how serious it is, but I guess I want to see where it goes, so I'm not going to date anyone else right now."

"I understand, Sonya. No problem. But if you find yourself available in the future, maybe you'll let me know?"

"Sure," she responded, a bit too eagerly.

"So where are we with the decorating?" Just like when I told him I wasn't sure about going out, now when I say no, he again takes it so easily. Did he really want to go out with me? Maybe he just wanted to have a fling. Or maybe he just wanted to have someone to go with him to the museum. That last possibility disappointed her most of all. It's selfish, she thought, but I wanted him to be really hurt by my saying no to him.

"Well, I've thought about what you told me about the living room," she said, unrolling her sketch and placing paint chips, carpet samples, and furniture catalogues around it. She opened a catalogue to a couch she was certain would make an ideal focal point for the room.

She was pleased with how she had arrayed everything around her sketch, some of the catalogues sitting precariously over the edges of his coffee table. The opened catalogues, paint and carpet samples struck her like the rim of a wheel with her sketches the hub in the center. Her approach to decorating consultation was that everything should be presented together. She had seen other designers show a client how a paint choice matches a furniture fabric, or how a carpet sample goes with a wallpaper, but not how it all goes together. She wanted the client to see everything at once. It could make for some clumsiness in arranging samples and catalogues, and some clients could at first feel overwhelmed, but in the end she felt it made for the best presentation.

"More tea?"

"Yes, that would be nice."

He filled her cup and then put his sketches in the middle of the wheel next to hers. The wheel now had two hubs which somehow unsettled her.

His sketch was exactly as he had described it on the phone, almost identical to hers. Her eyes passed between the two drawings, identifying the similarities and differences. She found a few differences, but then a moment later lost them. Her mind seemed somehow sluggish.

The sketches now seemed to be fluttering as if a breeze was lifting and then settling them back on the table. His sketch seemed to lift off the table and descend slowly onto hers. And then there were not just two sketches but a stack of them, like cards, yes, she thought for a moment with a comforting sense of recognition, playing cards, that's what they are. The deck somehow cut itself, and the cards began to shuffle, as if by invisible hands. She was fascinated by how the cards wove themselves together during the snap of the shuffle. She then became concerned about her sketch. Where was it? It had become a card lost in the deck, but she would find it later. The cards shuffled themselves over and over, the sound seeming like a whispering of words she could not quite make out.

She reached for her tea, which she was sure she had set on one of the furniture catalogues, but the ring of catalogues seemed now to be a huge lazy susan revolving, like one she remembered at a Chinese restaurant. She spotted her cup, reached for it, but it eluded her grasp, circling around to the far side. She worried someone would take it before it returned to her. She now watched it approaching her, picked it up, and sipped it. The tea seemed for a moment to help her focus, but a second later the lazy susan changed into a roulette wheel and was spinning faster than ever. She tried to center herself by concentrating on the warmth of the tea as it went down, but she was then distracted by its taste. Was this the same tea he had served her before? There's some taste, an undertaste, or is it an overtaste? No, that's overtone, but that's sound.

She had suddenly an overpowering urge to lie down and looked around for something to collapse on. Everything looked washed out, like an overexposed photograph. She strained to open her eyes, to find something to orient herself. She searched for the window, but saw now that the room was defined not by walls and windows but by doors. Doors of all kinds, a few feet apart, some ornate and large, others small and plain. Then, as if someone had thrown a switch, they all opened at once, and people she struggled to recognize came into the room.

Where's Nick? People are coming in from everywhere. One looked like the man in the car. She saw him leading Nick away. The young woman with him then came toward her. The woman had rings everywhere, pierced through her nose and ears, lips and eyebrows. Her face was barely visible beneath the jewelry.

Sonya now felt hands cupped under her elbows guiding her. Hands from behind, unknown hands. Are these the New York hands? No, she was certain these were not those hands. These were angular, with more bone and sinew. She tried to connect these hands with a face and then saw the challenge as a puzzle with sets of hands in one column and faces in another, the object being to draw lines to match up the face with the hands. She saw Jerry's face, then Nick's, then the puffy glaring face of the man in the car. And then a commanding message rang in her mind, "Call me." Eric Hanson. She tried in vain to see his hands. She could barely bring up an image of his face.

One of her arms, then the other, she felt being pushed through a sleeve, like a small child being dressed, buttoned, ready to go out. Why can't I do this myself? Then a door closing, another door. Slap of cold air. Car door, yielding soft seat. Finally down, lying down. The shake and hum of the motor vibrated through her, and she felt the reassuring, cradling pressure of the seat against her body.

CHAPTER TWENTY ONE

Ivan had called Dana several times during the late afternoon to ask if she wanted to meet for dinner. He wanted to go to the Earle, in the basement of the old Earle Hotel. With dark brick walls, candles, and soft jazz piano, it had a big city feel that Weiss from time to time craved. He felt comfortably anonymous there. He left messages at home and at the stable. When there was no response, he went home, thoughts of her leaving him for Kevin filling his mind. Very much out of character, he poured himself some Scotch and drank it down fast. The way he threw his head back reminded him of how his father would take his medicinal jigger of shnapps, set on his bedroom dresser every morning by his mother. His father had told him that it was in the morning that his memories of the camp were the most vivid. He thought of all the pain his father would try to wash away with that morning drink. And his own pain now. He could feel Dana slipping away.

He checked his home answering machine, where there were no messages and then called into his office machine. The first message was from Jennifer Andrews, the patient who had bolted from the office a few days before over feelings about Weiss' daughter.

"You know, Dr. Weiss, I have enough problems without you throwing yourself and your daughter in my face. I don't think it's too much to ask that I not constantly see you escorting her around town. A Thai restaurant ring a bell? You just don't respect boundaries. I'm quitting my treatment." There was a pause, and he heard her turn away from the phone and say "Yeah, I'll say that, that's good," to someone with her. "But this isn't the end of our relationship, you never know where I'll show up. Or, if not me, a helpful friend."

If he were not so caught up in fear and worry over Dana, he would have tried to work on the meaning of the patient's behavior and plan a strategy to help her back into psychotherapy. But right now, his thoughts were much more selfish. He felt both relief that she had left treatment and concern that she might begin stalking him. She had probably been at the race in Whitmore Lake and followed him to meet Sonya at the restaurant. He worried that the "helpful friend" was her former boyfriend, the ex-con.

He listened to the next messages, one from a patient about rescheduling an appointment, another from a colleague asking for a copy of the Manson paper, and last Terry, the travel agent, saying that the cruise documents should arrive early next week and reminding them to make sure their passports were current. He thought they were, but wasn't sure.

Though it was far from certain that they would even go on the cruise, he turned his attention to the passports, half aware that this seemed a more manageable problem. Limited, simple to remedy. Just renew them if they are expired. He knew that even up to the last minute there were expediters who can do this quickly, because he and Dana had done this years before when they needed to go on short notice to Israel for the funeral of one of Ivan's uncles. Under the pressure of his anxiety, he felt his thoughts darting off into details of how to get the passports renewed.

He rummaged through the "important drawer" in the kitchen pantry, through copies of birth certificates, marriage license, his professional license, coupons and various warranties, most for appliances they no longer owned. The rummaging became a frenetic rifling. He tossed things haphazardly onto the counter, until he found their passports. He brought them to the kitchen table where there was more light. On the table he saw a note written in Dana's flowing hand. Graceful she is in all ways, he thought. He put the passports aside and read the note.

Dear Ivan,

I know I've been acting strangely lately. This is going to be stranger yet. I'm sorry about this, Ivan, I really am, but I need to be away for awhile. I'm alright, but there are some things I need to take care of.

I wish you could help me with this, and if I were braver somehow I would let you, but I can't. I wish I could, but I can't.

Dana

P.S. Don't try to find me, it will make things worse.

Not "Love, Dana," just her name. Things worse? What things? He read the note over and over, compulsively, as if its secrets would somehow jump out from between the lines. He saw her with Kevin. She's gone off to have a fling with him. Ivan was now certain he had lost her. He thought of the last day with his mother, turning back to see her through the kitchen window.

He thought beyond losing Dana to a life without her. He thought of waking up in their bed and turning to her to find only the emptiness she would leave behind. He imagined the world without her drained of color. He thought of himself as barely alive.

Then he thought of losing her in another way. Maybe the "things" concerned her health. Tests she needs to get, biopsies, cancer. Two people he knew had just gone through this. Diane, Dana's closest friend in Ann Arbor, waited anxiously for weeks as she went through test after test, ending in relief that nothing was seriously wrong. The other, a patient of Weiss', developed a cough, then shoulder pains. The doctor told him, after a scan, that this was an "easy" diagnosis, lung cancer. Aggressive, rampaging cancer, the man died within three months of the diagnosis. But why would she not let him help her with something like this?

No, she wasn't ill. She had been competing in horse shows almost every weekend, had begun working out, and seemed to have inexhaustible energy. No, that wasn't it. She was physically fine.

The simple, inescapable fact, the hard edged piece of reality, was that she was involved with another man. The only question was who she was with, but he was almost certain it was Kevin. After she had ridden well, Kevin had patted her thigh with the familiarity of a lover. Weiss had seen it. It was Kevin. No question. He poured himself another Scotch.

His mind was now flooded with Dana and Kevin. The images he had tried to drive out or to keep vague and indistinct became overwhelmingly vivid. Everything was clear. Their bodies, the setting of their lovemaking. After their working with her new horse, they put him away and go to Kevin's apartment at the stable. They slowly peel off each other's clothes. He gives her a massage which Ivan knew she loved. His hands wander to her breasts and beyond. He kisses her all over, and they make love. Ivan could think of nothing else.

He thought of how, years before, at his most paranoid, he had furtively followed Dana. This time around there'd be no snooping around after her or endless ruminations about whether his suspicions were true. This time he'd behave differently. He'd confront them and fight for her and take her home.

He splashed cold water on his face to try to sober up enough to drive, pulled on his coat, and headed for the stable. The rural road that was usually so quiet and comforting when he would drive out to see Dana in the early evenings was now a tunnel of stark glare from his headlights, with the trees a tangle of bony prominences crowding in on him. The fields were dark wastelands.

Mud splashed up as he drove fast into the stable parking lot. He went straight to Kevin's apartment off the observation room and knocked on the door. No answer. He imagined them in Kevin's bed, frozen with fear that he'd shown up, lying as quietly as possible, holding their breath.

He tried the door and found it open. He walked through a combination kitchen and living area with a television and some shabby furniture and then barged into the bedroom to find clothes, magazines, and horse tack of all kinds spilling off the unmade bed onto the floor. No one was there.

He walked back through the observation room and down the stairs into the empty arena. From the stall area off the arena he could hear Kevin's voice, talking in a whisper. He walked slowly and quietly across the arena and into the dimly lit aisleway that ran between the rows of stalls, the horses pawing and shifting.

"It's alright, Baby, just calm down." Kevin's voice was coming from the end of the barn, but, in the low light, Ivan could not see him in the aisleway.

"It'll be fine, just fine." Ivan heard him say from within one of the stalls.

As Ivan approached the open door of the last stall, he saw in his mind Dana standing with her back against the rough wall. Kevin is clearing tears from her cheeks, as she tells him that she's leaving Ivan to be with him. Ivan listened for her voice or the little gasps she would take between sobs when she cried.

When he thought he could hear her, he went cold and numb. He had no feelings now, but his body had a life of its own. He entered the stall and saw Kevin's back in the stall's dusty darkness. When he heard Kevin start to speak softly again, Ivan grabbed him from behind to pull him away from her.

"You son of a bitch, you . . ." yelled Weiss.

Kevin fell into the straw and then grabbed Ivan's leg, pulling him down. The horse that Kevin had been trying to calm reared up and let out a terrified call that was answered by another horse at the other end of the barn and then by several more. Kevin brought Ivan down, straddled him, and was ready to pound him in the face. When he recognized Ivan, he stopped just before landing the blow.

"Dr. Weiss, is that you?" he gasped, unable to believe his eyes. "What the hell are you doing?"

Though he could see that Kevin had been trying to calm an agitated horse and that Dana was not there, Ivan was so caught up in his paranoia, that reality made no difference. Dana was having an affair with Kevin. He was sure of it.

"Look you bastard," yelled Ivan, his arms pinned under the young man's knees, "I'm no fool, I can see what's happening. You and Dana, I have eyes."

"What the hell are you talking about? Doc, you're off your rocker, totally off!" As their voices grew louder and more strident, the horse became even more agitated, stamping, breathing fast, and shifting from side to side in the corner of the stall. "Easy, easy," said Kevin in a gentle voice.

"At the drop of a hat, she runs to you." Ivan shouted, the accusations coming in a flood. "Colicky horse, extra lessons, that show last weekend. And don't think I didn't see the two of you in her truck. Going who knows where!"

"Well, I don't know where," Kevin shouted back, "I don't think I've ever been in her truck. And what the hell show are you talking about? We didn't go to no show. I haven't seen your wife in weeks!"

CHAPTER TWENTY TWO

I t was seven by the time Ivan left the stable, his back and shoulder aching from the scuffle with Kevin. When Ivan had calmed down, Kevin had let him up and explained that Dana was a talented horsewoman, he enjoyed working with her, but there was absolutely nothing more between them. Ivan wanted to believe him.

As he drove, he tried to remember the last time he had physically fought with someone. He had restrained a couple of adolescents when he had worked on the inpatient service, but the last real fight had been in high school when a cruel and antisemitic kid had taunted him with, "Everyone knows your mother offed herself." Ivan, who was shorter and slighter than this boy, had beaten him almost unconscious.

From his cell phone, he called in for messages from his answering machine. After the electronic voice said, "You have one message," he could almost hear Dana's voice, he wished for it so much, saying everything's been cleared up, all was a misunderstanding, sorry to worry you, everything's fine, honey. The message wasn't from her.

"Doc, things have gotten real bad," the voice was a man's, gravely, deep. "I can't take it anymore. I had a gun to my head just now, but . . . well, no guts to pull the trigger. Not now. Maybe later. You gotta see me. I'm coming to your office right now." Click, and the electronic voice, "End of messages."

Ivan was confused and alarmed. He didn't recognize the voice. Which patient was this? He had one who, at the beginning of his treatment, was seriously suicidal, but in Weiss' judgment was not now. It had been a long time since he had heard this patient's voice on the phone, so he couldn't be sure, but he didn't think it was him. The "Doc" also puzzled him. It was too informal for most, if not all, of his patients. The only person in any area of his life who addressed him that way was Kevin. He had just seen him, but the message could have been left earlier. But the voice didn't sound like Kevin's either. He wondered if the patient had mixed him up with an emergency room doctor, Larry Weiss. This had happened a few times over the years. In any case, though he had no idea who this patient was, there was no question, he had to go straight to his office to meet him. Anything less would be professionally irresponsible.

He pulled out of the stable parking lot and headed back into town. As he went over in his mind the other male patients in his practice, he barely noticed passing a car parked on the shoulder of the road. Just as he was about to make a right turn onto Scio Church Road, he happened to glance in his rearview mirror to see the lights of the car turn on as it left the shoulder and pulled on to the road. After Ivan made the turn, he sped up and then looked again in his mirror to see the car make the same turn and follow him. Or was it the same car, he wondered? Yes, definitely. The car was at least a couple of hundred yards behind. When Weiss slowed, the other car slowed too. I'm being followed. He reminded himself that his sense of reality might be slipping, it had just slipped in a big way with Kevin. Someone might be following me, but it might also just be my imagination. A few moments later, when he turned onto Seventh and drove past the high school, the traffic thickened. Ivan tried to pick the car out, but his rearview mirror was now filled with headlights.

Students were flooding back to central campus after the Friday evening basketball game. There was so much traffic that he had to park in a structure almost four blocks away. He nodded to the doorman and took the elevator up to his office. As soon as he left the elevator and turned down the hall to his office, he saw blue footprints, dark and congested near his office door and then fading as they came toward him. The carpet in front of his door was soaked with blue paint, and the walls of the corridor were splattered too. The smell of the fresh paint hung in the air. The job had been done fast, impulsively. The message on the door communicated the rage expressed by the whole scene: "Keep Your Quacks Hands Off My Daughter." There was no patient there.

Whose hands? He saw in his mind the Clinic patient raging at her therapist, and behind this, raging at the real abuser. You violated your stepdaughter, thought Ivan, just like you violated my door. It made it even more understandable to Weiss how the stepdaughter of such a man would experience even the mistimed interpretation of an inexperienced therapist as if it were a violation of the worst kind.

He unlocked the door, smearing the still wet paint on his hands and sleeves, and flipped on the light. He was so sure that the aim was to send him a message and not to burglarize that he had to remind himself to check the office to see if anything had been taken. Nothing disturbed. No paint inside. Everything was in its place. Almost certainly the work of the Clinic patient's stepfather, but he never got past the door. At least one boundary remained intact.

He was just about to call to report the vandalism, when the phone rang.

"Dr. Weiss?" the anxious voice said, before Ivan could even say hello.

"Yes."

"This is Jerry . . . you know, Sonya's, uh . . . friend, we met . . ." Weiss could hear a nervous breathlessness in his voice.

"Of course, Jerry. Are you alright?"

"Not really. Calling you seems like a kind an immature thing to do. To call a girl's father when she stands him up. Maybe that's all that's happened. If it is, I feel really dumb calling you."

"What's happened?"

"Maybe I'm overreacting, but I'm worried about Sonya." Ivan heard Jerry turn away from the phone to clear his throat.

"Worried about what?"

"Sonya was supposed to meet me outside her apartment house at 5:30 this afternoon. We were going to a concert in Detroit. I waited, buzzed her apartment, tried calling her on the phone. No luck."

Ivan was not certain she had not stood him up. When she was a teenager, she would announce that she had "blown off" this guy or that. Ivan could also imagine Sonya, in her continuing reactions to the rape, going into a phobic panic and just fleeing from a date. But the blue paint still dripping from his office door gave him pause.

"Dr. Weiss, I know you're thinking she just stood me up, and maybe she did, but the weird part is that she called me a few hours earlier to tell me she'd be a half hour late. She said she hadn't scheduled enough time to meet with this new client. She said she was so glad she reached me. She even added that she was worried I'd show up and she'd not be there. I'm not a psychologist, but why would she make sure to call me if she were ready to stand me up. It sounded like she was definitely going to be there. What do you think, Dr. Weiss?" Ivan thought of the note on the door – "Keep Your Quacks Hands Off My Daughter." Eye for an eye, daughter for a stepdaughter?

"There's probably a simple explanation for this, Jerry," said Ivan, trying to sound reassuring, "but I'll see if I can reach her. Did she say anything about the client she was meeting with?"

"Yeah, a guy she's been talking about a lot, the one she mentioned at the dinner at Gratzi's. He's redoing an old house he's just bought. I don't think she told me his name, or maybe I just don't remember it. Do you know who he is?"

"I think I do. Let me try to reach him. Just sit tight, I'll call you as soon as I get in touch with her." Weiss had tried to sound sure and confident talking to Jerry, while he saw Sonya, like Dana, slipping away.

He tried to call the doorman to report the vandalism. When he found the line busy, he took the elevator down to the lobby. The doorman was on the phone, apparently talking to his girlfriend. Weiss gave him a look that ended his conversation. He reported the vandalism to the doorman, who said he would call the police. Weiss asked him if he had seen anyone suspicious come in in the last hour. He checked his log.

"Oh, yeah, well, I don't know if he was suspicious, but a delivery man, a short stocky guy, I think he had on a Fed Ex uniform, came with a delivery, a pretty large package, for Dr. Lawrence. He said he called the doctor a few minutes before, so I buzzed him in, and he went up. Seemed alright. We let delivery people in all the time." Generally safe building, safe city, lax security. Weiss tried to recall the Dean's description of the Clinic patient's stepfather. Something like stocky. Oh, yeah, a little fireplug. Ivan had imagined him like a boxer or street fighter.

"Did you see him leave?"

"Now that you ask, no, I didn't. But you know we're a lot more interested in who comes in, Doctor, than who leaves."

"I understand, but you didn't see this guy wearing a uniform leave?"

"I don't think I did. I guess that's strange." Right, just a little strange, a delivery man comes and doesn't leave.

"Yes it is. If you see him leaving, tell the police about that, too."

"O.K., Doc." I guess more people than I realize, call me "Doc," thought Ivan.

Before returning to his office, on a hunch, Ivan checked the trash room at the end of the hall. The Fed Ex uniform, covered with blue paint, was stuffed in a corner behind bags of trash. He went back to his office and called Sonya.

Reaching only her answering machine, Ivan drove to her apartment. Her car was not in its space. Using his emergency key, he went into her apartment, no one there. Everything pointed to her being ready to go out with Jerry. As usual before anything important, she had left notes for herself around her apartment. "Remember the beaded purse – in hall closet." "Wear orange scarf, not green one." Clothes were neatly arranged on her bed with a note on them: "Jerry at 5:00" No question, she was ready for this date. At least when she left her house she was. He reminded himself that gripped by panic and anxiety, she might have felt the only thing she could do was to run. He thought, too, that if she had been with this client, Nick Streeter, she may simply have been swept away by feelings when she was with him and, on the spur of the moment, decided to stand Jerry up.

A sick feeling welled up in Ivan. Dana drifting away. Maybe Sonya too. The feeling was familiar. And old.

He felt the summer heat as he made his way through the cars parked helter skelter. He burst through the door to see the circle closed around his father, the circle that held the emptiness. He felt, as he had then, faint, and sat down on his daughter's couch. He brought his head down to his knees and was reminded of his father that day, bent over, cradling his head.

Weiss tried to stem his mounting anxiety. All that has happened with Sonya, he reminded himself, is that she didn't meet Jerry. The simplest explanation, one he worked with everyday, was that this was a psychologically motivated forgetting, a parapraxis, a slip of the mind. After the assault in New York, she is underlyingly terrified of men, so she arranges to meet Jerry, but is so frightened that she unconsciously avoids being with him by forgetting to meet him. A total plausible, psychologically sound explanation. Ivan remembered, too, how erratic she had been during her high school years.

Ivan was looking for the simplest, most innocuous explanation. She went to the appointment with the new client, Nick Streeter, wanted to spend time with him, and deliberately or unconsciously stood Jerry up.

So just call Nick, Weiss resolved. He may, in any case, have been the last person to see her. He found a phone book and Nick Streeter's number in it. With so many people, it seemed to Ivan, with unlisted numbers, he felt lucky to find it so easily. He punched in the numbers and reached a voicemail.

"This is Nick Streeter, not here, leave a message." The voice was curt, even a little rude, and also sounded older than Weiss had expected, not old or even middle aged, but the voice of someone in his late thirties or even early forties, much older than Sonya. He also had some kind of accent, southern, or Texas. It surprised him that Sonya had not said anything about him being older or from the South. It seemed to Ivan that she would have mentioned that. But maybe neither were important to her.

As he was getting up off the couch to leave, he felt, wedged between the cushions of the sofa, Sonya's address book. The book was so much Sonya, her father thought. It was covered with a rich, colorful African print cloth, probably made it herself. The cover to the touch was soft and sensual. He thumbed quickly through it. Mostly friends from New York, only one of whom he knew. Jerry was there, as was Weiss' own office address and phone number under D for Dad. He smiled. Streeter's listing was there, address, phone, followed by: Client (maybe more!). He wasn't sure what use it would be to him, and he felt intrusive about doing it, but he took the book with him.

He made the short drive home. He was vigilant, scanning all the way. Watching for someone following him and looking for Dana's truck at the same time. He found his house empty. Empty apartment, empty house. Unnatural emptiness everywhere.

He wandered aimlessly around the house, half expecting, with each door he opened, to find Dana and Sonya, coffee mugs in hand, leaning toward each other, locked in what Sonya called one of their "female bonding," mother-daughter talks.

When he went up to the bedroom, he was suddenly overtaken by fatigue. It was as if the anxious energy that had been driving him for hours had run out. He felt an overpowering wish to escape in the most elemental way, by sleeping. He lay down, but just as he felt himself drifting off, he was startled awake by the doorbell. He sat up, tried to clear his head and walked quickly to the front door. No one was there, but someone was pulling away fast, lights off, from the curb in front of his house. Taped to the door was an envelope.

Weiss took the envelope and went into the small library off the living room. He sat with it sealed in front of him. He wanted to leave it sealed forever. *Everything I do just plunges me into ever more terrible possibilities.* He hoped magically, that if he left the envelope sealed, he could just stop everything, could prevent the next, even worse, thing from happening.

He remembered reading a case of a catatonic woman who had the delusion that she was sitting on the moon, looking back at the earth, and that the tiniest movement of her body would destroy the earth and everyone on it. If, however, she remained catatonically still, then she could prevent this world holocaust. He empathized at that moment with what enormous power and control over the whole world, along with terrifying responsibility, this woman must have felt she had. At that moment, Ivan Weiss ached to have that kind of control over the cascade of confusing, frightening events in his life. *I'll take the responsibility, if I could somehow have the power.*

He swiveled his desk chair around to the window and watched a couple arriving at a party across the street, arm in arm, the woman's laughter inaudible through the closed windows, but very visible in the language of her body. *Whether I sit immobile here or move or shout,* he thought, *everything out there will go on just the same.*

CHAPTER TWENTY THREE

O nce he had half led, half dragged her from the van into the room, he laid her on the futon, and handcuffed her to a chain he had looped around a heavy pipe that ran along the wall. He sat transfixed for a few moments watching her in her deep, drugged sleep. He climbed the stairs and escalator, filled the tank, and started the generator. When he returned to the room, he turned on the space heater, which warmed the room quickly. As he watched her heavy, slow breathing, he read the last two letters.

April 8, 1976
Dear Son,

I just heard the terrible news. Or at least I've pieced it together the best I can from what the sister at St. Boniface told me in our part French, part English conversation over the bad phone connection. If I understood her right, your foster mother died somehow, and the family was split up. It sounded like things weren't working out very well there anyway. The sister said you're supposed to be back at the orphanage in a couple of days.

You are not going to stay there long. I'm coming for you. I'm going to do what I should have done from the beginning. I'm going to take you with me and be your mother. I don't know how I'll do it, but I'm coming for you. I promise, I promise.

Your mother

And she came. She drove with him through the countryside in a big comfortable car she had rented, telling him in her broken French how sorry she was for leaving him. Though he spoke English by that time far better than she spoke French, he was so wary and closed with her that he could not tell her he spoke English at all. He sat pressed against the car door, tracing with his fingernail the ridges in the fabric of the seat, looking furtively up at her and seeing a tear slide down her cheek, fall on her white blouse and spread like a little star. Is she crying for me? If there are tears enough, he thought, she will take me with her.

She said she wanted to show him the sea, and they drove to Nice. By the time they arrived there, when she held out her hand, he cautiously took it. Her hand was firm, but the skin soft and warm, and she held his hand gently. The hands that usually had held his were rough and old. They grabbed or punished or molested. Her hand was there to protect. He remembered all of this now detached, like someone else's story. There were no feelings left about any of it.

Just before she left, she had searched for the French word for "soon" to tell him when she would come back for him, *"le moi prochain,"* or *"plus tard."* He didn't understand why, but the nuns and brothers explained that she needed to get some papers, some permission to take him to the U.S., that she had given him up and so, even though he was her child and had given birth to him, she would have to adopt him. He realized that the word she had been searching for was *bientôt.* He could hear in his mind the English word, "soon." As he lay in bed, he whispered the word over and over, and it sounded after a while like a breeze blowing, or a song. He decided then to work even harder to learn English, and to learn it well, to be ready for her when she came for him.

He took the young woman's uncuffed hand and examined her fingers as she slept. They were long and elegant, like the fingers of a much taller woman. Fingers like his mother's. Like the fingers that had penned the letters. She stirred for a moment and squeezed his hand suddenly, startling him, leaving him for a moment confused about who was holding his hand. As she held it, his own hand seemed to him very small in hers.

He pulled the last letter from its envelope. This had come months later, long after he had given up comforting himself to sleep with "soon." It had come so long after, that he had by that time learned from Brother Anthony enough English to read the entire letter himself. He pulled it from its envelope, and though the room was heated only by the electric heater, his face felt on fire. He thought of having acted once in a Japanese play, and that shame was depicted by a red face. The skin of his face felt like it was pulled impossibly tight over the bones underneath, and as if the bones were glowing red like the coils on an electric stove, ready to burn through his thin, fragile skin. He thought of running out into the street and slapping handfuls of snow on his face to put out the fire.

Everyone knew she was supposed to come for him, they all knew of her promise, but many of the older kids told him she would never come. They never do. You're just a loser like the rest of us.

November 20, 1976
Dear Son,

I could tell you that I'm not coming for you because I couldn't get the right papers to adopt you, but I'm going to tell this to you straight. At least I've always been honest with you. Unreliable, yes, but honest.

I'm breaking my promise. I'm not coming for you. I met a man, in fact, shortly after I visited you. I probably shouldn't go into this, but I need to explain myself, to defend myself.

I can't bring you into my life with him. If I were a stronger person, maybe I could, but I just can't. He's a kind, gentle man, who loves me and I love him. He's accepting in just about all ways. Except one. And it's because of this one thing I can't come for you. I'm terrified that he will find out about you. Maybe someday I'll tell you why.

I'm sorry, sorry, sorry. I'll try somehow to live with this. I don't know if I can.

Your mother

His watch beeped, signaling that it was time for his medicines. He used the times during the day he took his medicines to review the status of his body. Today it felt as good as it ever did. Maybe that snot nosed doctor was right that the new combination of drugs would make a difference. The state of his body would be vital to carrying out the next step of his plan. He could imagine it with the vividness of an hallucination. From the moment he learned he was HIV positive, he was determined to use it as a weapon. Power flowing from his own defeat. The evil gift. What goes around comes around, mother. He took his medications and then folded the last letter and slid it into the ribboned packet with the others. He put some food and water on the table by the futon and returned to Ann Arbor.

The first thing he did when he returned to his house was to collect all evidence of her visit, the catalogues, sketches, fabric samples, even her tea cup, and stuffed them in a garbage bag. After taking her car keys from her purse, he threw it in the bag too. He looked out through the small windows beside the front door for the street to empty. When it did, he hauled the bag across the street to a dumpster behind an apartment building and heaved it in. He then moved her car several blocks away. He returned to the house and called Farley, ready to ask if he had made any progress on the harassment complaint. Farley was not there, but it was enough to leave his name on the detective's voicemail. At this point, he wanted only to remind Farley of his case so when the time came, the detective wouldn't hesitate with the question, "Who?" or "What case?" He wanted the detective to take action immediately, ideally to come to the tower himself. Another beautifully worked out piece of theater. Though he had been an actor and a techie, he could now appreciate a new facet of the theater, the thrill of being a director. The numbness which he constantly lived with was being eclipsed by a sense of control and power he was already having over the actors he was moving about on his stage. Imagining them under his complete domination was, to his surprise, even arousing him sexually.

*   *   *

She felt herself to be deep under the ocean, the pressure of miles of water above her. Though it seemed strange to her, she could somehow breathe. She looked up and saw the water rippling over her, as if she were looking down on it from above. The rays of the sun shimmered turquoise, like she had seen in the Caribbean, a color she had been drawn to in many of her decorating schemes.

She needed to get to the surface. Not a desperate need, definitely not an emergency, but she knew she had to figure out a way to do it. The water seemed to get thinner and thinner. How marvelous, she thought, the water is turning into air, like magic.

There was a phone in front of her. Has it been there all along? I need to call Jerry. If I can get through to him, then I'll get to the surface. She suddenly remembered their date. Did I stand him up? What happened? Maybe we went out already. Maybe weeks ago. If I can get to the surface, I know everything will be a lot clearer. She tried to reach for the phone, but something was stopping her hand. She tried again and felt a heavy bracelet on her wrist. I hate bracelets, she thought, they jangle and get in the way when I'm trying to sketch. Why would I be wearing one?

The beautiful turquoise glow was beginning to fade, and everything was turning gray and drab. She smelled a faint odor of smoke, like the smell of a camp stove, and her body felt suddenly cold. She reached once more for the phone, exerting herself this time, and pain shot up through her wrist into her arm, and she awoke. She looked at her stubborn hand and saw one end of a handcuff on her wrist. The other end was locked to a chain around a pipe that ran along the cracked, cement wall next to her.

She scanned the room with the precision of a designer's eye. About 15' by 10', no windows, a card table across the room by the door, director's chairs on either side of it, a standing lamp to her left, and a small oriental rug in the middle of the room. A bedside table with scallop edged top was within her reach. On the table, along with a small glass lamp, was a pitcher of juice, a glass, and a plate of bread, fruit and nuts. Her eye was drawn to how things were arranged in the room. There was a balance, a symmetry to it all, and a good use of the limited space. If I were to set up a room with just the minimal necessities, this is exactly how I'd do it. If I were to set up a room to hold someone I had kidnapped this is how it would look.

Kidnapped. Yes, she thought, with no feeling, or more accurately with so much feeling that she needed to turn away from it. I've been kidnapped. She began to feel panic welling up in her and thought about a conversation she had with her father about how people in concentration camps, like Grandpa was in, focus only on what they can control and review in their minds who they are and what they did before the terrible things started. I guess that's what I'm doing. I'm a designer, so I'm caught up in the design of the room.

She thought about her father's close friend, Eric's father, Jake, who told her that during his heart attack, he just kept analyzing his own reactions to it, so he wouldn't think he might really die. She remembered, too, Jake saying that he kept from being totally overwhelmed by thinking about all the people who were important to him. I guess I'm doing that by thinking about Jake, Grandpa, and my father.

She saw Jake lying on a stretcher and then pictures of people, barely more than skin and bones, in the concentration camps. They are all just waiting. They can't do anything. Passive, helpless. Hopeless. She stood up and rattled the chain on the pipe, just to hear the sound, just to know she could do something, could make the noise. Then she began to scream, to yell for help. She yelled, then listened for some response, and then shouted out again. All she heard was the distant growl of traffic, deaf to her cries.

*   *   *

Ivan opened the envelope. The note was hand-written in neat block letters.

> I HAVE SONYA. DO NOT GO TO THE POLICE OR TELL
> ANYONE OF HER DISAPPEARANCE OR YOU WILL
> NEVER SEE HER AGAIN. GO ABOUT YOUR NORMAL
> ROUTINE AND YOU WILL SOON LEARN WHO I AM.
> NOW LET ME SAY THIS AGAIN, DO NOT TELL ANYONE OF
> THIS! NOW ALL YOU CAN DO IS WAIT. AND WAIT.

The blood seemed to stop in his veins, and he could feel his breathing become shallow and fast. His head started to swim, and he remembered once hyperventilating to the point that he had fainted. Tingling around the lips, numb fingers, what were the other symptoms? He remembered then that you're supposed to blow into a paper bag. He stumbled dizzily to the kitchen, and rifled through cabinets until he found a bag of dried beans. He tried to dump the beans in the sink, but he was so dizzy that most of them spilled on the counter, bounced around, and rolled onto the floor. He sunk to the floor, blew into the bag, and felt, for a moment, his head clear.

Then he passed out. He was unconscious for less than a minute. When he came to, he was looking at the door of the refrigerator. He remembered the only other time he had fainted – the day his mother died.

He saw himself running home from school, brimming over with the news that he had won the class "College Bowl," feeling he could barely wait to tell the most important person in the world to him, his mother, the news. Not his father, only her. He burst through the door to find his aunt Miriam, the Golds, concentration camp survivor friends of his parents, and several policemen, circled like football players in a huddle around his father, who sat in a chair in the middle of them, his elbows sunk deep into his legs, his face held in his trembling hands. Two more policemen were standing off to the side talking to his uncle.

When they saw him come in, whispers, like a hissing, filled the room. "Does he know?" "Did someone tell him?" "No, he was at school." The circle broke open, and his father lifted his tear streaked face and looked at him with his impossibly sad eyes. He motioned his son to come to him. As he walked toward his father and became aware, for the first time fully aware, of the absence of his mother, he felt as if he were drowning and started to gasp frantically for air. His head felt light, like when he had a fever, and then just as his father reached out his hand and began to speak, things went splotchy, then dark, his legs buckled, and he collapsed. Sonya. Oh, my God. Is she dead too?

Though he was still weak from having fainted, one thing was completely clear to Weiss: any law enforcement person would advise going to the police no matter what a kidnap note said, but Ivan was absolutely sure he would not. He was caught up by a deep, and very old, distrust of the police. His father's and his own. He would follow the note exactly. But he had to do something, to take some action. As an analyst he was well able to tolerate being passive, waiting often weeks or months for themes to become clear enough to interpret to the patient. But never in treating any patient was there so much at stake. He saw Sonya in his mind held by some psychopath, in fear for her life. This was all terrifyingly different.

He thought about the note and struggled to reconcile in his mind the impulsiveness of the message on his private office door and the more deliberate, sadistic tone of the kidnap note. He had seen patients who were out of control of themselves at one moment and well oriented the next. Some borderline patients, in particular, could maintain their emotional equilibrium as long as their needs were being perfectly met, but then launch into a vitriolic rage as soon as they experienced the slightest ripple of disappointment or frustration.

I must follow my routine, he thought, but at the same time, do all I can to rescue my daughter and find my wife. He was terrified he would never see either of them again.

I've got to find out more about the stepfather of the Clinic patient. He couldn't remember her name, but he could find that at the Clinic. As Director of the Clinic, would going there, even late in the evening, be within my normal routine? Sure.

As he drove by Tower Plaza on the way to the Clinic, two policemen, probably there to investigate the vandalism, were leaving the building. He wanted desperately to stop his car, grab one of them and scream, "My daughter's been kidnapped, you've got to find her! Please help me!" This was the first test of his resolve not to go to the police. He avoided eye contact with the policemen as he drove by, as if in some irrational way this would be proof to someone, even the kidnapper himself, that he was living up to the letter of the kidnapper's demand. "See, see, I have not made contact with the police. See, even better, I haven't looked at them." He then thought maybe the kidnapper was watching him at that very moment, peering through the blinds of a window in Maynard House, across the street. Just as he looked up at the apartment building, he saw a window go dark. Was there someone moving in the darkened window? He craned his head out the car window and kept looking up until he was jolted, when he hit the car in front of him, which had stopped at a red light on State. A young man wearing a Michigan jacket with a bright yellow M on the back jumped out of his car, swearing, and looked at his rear bumper. Weiss got out of his car and approached the man.

"Why the hell don't you watch where you're going," the young man exclaimed, not even looking up at Weiss, intent on examining his bumper for damage. The car was a new BMW. "This is my father's car. Damn it! I had to talk him into lending it to me, and you plow into it. Christ, almighty!"

"I was distracted by something," said Weiss. "I'm sorry, it was totally my fault."

"Just get my old man to believe that." Cars were backed up behind them in the narrow street. Horns began to honk, and Weiss saw the two policemen, who he had just seen leaving Tower Plaza, coming toward them. The young man looked up and saw them too. Though this had nothing to do with the kidnapping, crazed images crowded into Ivan's mind of the kidnapper looking down from Maynard House, seeing him talking to the police, and then murdering Sonya. His panic mounted.

His panic was taking a new form. It wasn't just the familiar tightness in his chest or the cold sweat, it was more. The panic was eroding the barrier between past and present, so that old scenes like short, vivid film clips flashed in his mind. First he remembered a scene and then, losing his grip on the present, he was in it. The panic as the policemen threaded their way through the traffic sent him back into the past.

"A couple of policemen came to school today." A shadow passed over his father's face. "They told us how to call the police if there's an emergency, like a robbery or if someone's hurt." His father turned away, sat silently, and then turned back to his son. "Ivan, Ivan, you have a lot to learn."

"Seymour, stop it!" his mother said.

"Ivan, the police are not always . . ."

"Seymour, just stop it. It's different here. You know it is, that's why we came here." She turned to her son. "Ivan, your father and I lived in a place, in Europe, in a different time, a different world entirely. Your father doesn't understand this. There was a bad government there. It persecuted the Jews. The police were part of that bad government. They were its agents. They were not our friends. They were the enemy, and we avoided them at all costs."

The policemen, enormous in their heavy winter coats, were less than ten cars behind them. They walked with a professional, military deliberateness. Unstoppable. With their faces lost in the shadows of their visors and their hats and uniforms indistinguishable from their bodies, they looked like some malevolent combination of human and machine.

Weiss felt trapped. He had to get away.

Fortunately so did the young man.

"Look, I didn't exactly tell my old man I was taking his car. If there's some police shit about this accident . . ." He quickly looked again at the bumper. "It's dark, but I think it's alright. Let's just forget it." With the police now only a few car lengths behind them, they both jumped into their cars and quickly drove off.

CHAPTER TWENTY FOUR

W eiss drove around to try to calm down, but was still shaken, as much by the sudden darkened window in Maynard House, as by the accident. Behind it all was his fear for his daughter. The words of the kidnapper's note repeated in his mind, each time growing louder, until they boomed in his head.

He managed to get himself to the Clinic. When he got there a few minutes before ten, he was surprised to find the Clinic receptionist still there and to hear voices from the basement staff room. He then remembered Jake was teaching a seminar on therapeutic crises that evening. He remembered, too, that in response to interns' requests for more time to see patients, the Clinic had added later evening hours. At least the Clinic patient census was up. That was all he could think of that was going well.

Too distracted to even say hello to Cyndi, the evening receptionist, he went straight to the file room next to his office. He struggled to remember the patient's name. He knew he had read it in the file after the waiting room incident, and he thought the Dean had used it when he had called Weiss about his confrontation with her and her stepfather. Weiss usually had an excellent memory, an asset for an analyst who must remember countless details about many patients. Right now it was failing him.

He asked Cyndi to bring him the schedule for the intern who had been treating the young woman. While he waited, he pulled the kidnapper's note from his portfolio and laid it on the desk, hoping magically that it would say something different, that it was not a kidnap note, that he had been in the throes of some delusion and just imagined it was.

The receptionist brought in the intern's schedule. He was treating five patients. Three men, two women. He pulled the file of the first woman: Hispanic, 49 years old, mother of two teen age children. He flipped past the three men. He pulled the file on the second woman, Sara Reynolds, White, 24. Yes, that was her. He looked at the face sheet. Under parents: John and Phyllis Reynolds, (John deceased), 84 Laurel Pl., Flint, Michigan; Samuel Dexter, stepfather, 17 Portage Rd, Port Austin, Michigan. Ivan remembered staying with Dana at an inn in Port Austin after bike riding along Lake Huron. Though easy driving distance from Ann Arbor, the area was in a different universe, rural, conservative, Michigan Militia turf. He saw Sonya held in a deserted farmhouse at the mercy of this child molester. He turned to the end of the file to see if there had been any further contact with the Clinic. Nothing. The last note was a very detailed account by the intern of the episode in the Clinic waiting area. Ivan had told him to document it well for legal reasons, and this studious intern had certainly taken the job seriously, with five pages of description of the incident.

"Dr. Weiss," he turned to see Cyndi at his open office door. "Dr. Hanson's seminar is going to break up in about five minutes, and he said I could leave a few minutes after, so if it's alright with you . . ."

"Just go, Cyndi," Ivan said with a harshness she had never heard in him before. Just go, he thought, just like all the women go.

"I'm sorry, Dr. Weiss, I can stay if . . ."

"Sorry, Cyndi, I've got a lot on my mind. Go whenever you like, I'll lock up."

He could hear the students coming up the narrow stairway from the basement and could hear Jake's strong voice, as he animatedly discussed a point with a student.

Things had continued to be strained with Jake. Whenever Ivan asked him to go for a run, Jake claimed to be "up to my ass" in work. It was the first time in years that they had missed almost a week of running together. In Clinic staff meetings, anything Ivan brought up Jake immediately contradicted. Jake seemed to be seething underneath. Ivan wondered if something were going on with Jake's son. Maybe that's why he's been so distant. Could be, thought Ivan, but he felt himself to be the target of Jake's envy fueled anger.

He missed Jake and longed to tell him about the crises that had descended and engulfed Ivan's life, but was filled with doubt about trusting him. Ivan realized at that moment that he trusted no one.

Ivan heard Jake's voice move toward the front door and then the rattle of hangers and shuffle of clothes, as Jake and the students readied to leave. Weiss was about to go out and tell Jake he wanted to talk with him when his eyes fell again on the note. "Wait" the note repeated. Does Jake feel he's had to wait before he can really shine? Ivan thought about Jake's stony silence after Ivan was appointed Director and then of the look in Jake's eyes in the Institute parking lot after the Manson paper. Something desperate, crazed in that look.

Ready a moment before to stop his friend, to pull him into his office and tell him everything, Ivan now instead settled back in his chair and heard Jake's and the students' voices silenced with the closing of the heavy front door. The Clinic was now quiet, and a feeling of terrible coldness ran through Weiss' body. He set the alarm, locked the front door, and drove home.

As he drove, the kidnapper's note continued to repeat itself in Ivan's mind. He imagined Samuel Dexter writing it. A powerful desire welled up in Ivan to drive to Dexter's house and threaten him somehow, with a gun or a knife. He thought where could he get a gun and then tried to remember if he'd ever even held a gun, much less loaded or fired one. He had been good at archery in camp as a kid. He thought of going to a Meijer's at midnight, buying archery equipment and then going to Dexter's door and threatening him. The image of ringing the doorbell and then fumbling with his new bow and arrows when the man opened the door was so absurd if he were not so close to his emotional breaking point, he would have found it funny. He put confronting Dexter on the back burner. Anyway, Dexter would be a fool to take her to his own house.

Abandoning the plan to go to Port Austin, he tried to reconstruct what had happened before she disappeared. She saw Nick Streeter and then was supposed to meet Jerry. Was there someone else she saw or somewhere else she went after she met with Streeter? Jerry had said she made their meeting time later because she might be at Streeter's longer, but maybe she got through earlier and went somewhere else. And where was she before she went to Streeter's? I don't even know that she got to Streeter's. Can I even trust what Jerry said? Maybe even he . . .

Ivan moved quickly through the empty house. He felt if he slowed down he would be engulfed by its silence. Everywhere he turned there were reminders of Dana. Her scarf on the chair, one of her many hairbrushes on the bathroom counter, her riding magazines everywhere. And in the air of their bedroom, the remnants of her perfume and, behind that, the scent of her body. These reminders now stirred less in him than they might have a few hours before, for he was starting to feel he had already lost her. Dana had left a note. Had left it herself. She was operating under her own volition. It meant to him that she was probably in less danger than Sonya, but at the same time she was choosing to be away from him, maybe permanently.

He had to reach Dana, not to get her back, but rather to get her to help him in searching for Sonya. Dana's deep and intuitive sense of people and situations would help find their daughter. He imagined Dana just crisply saying, here's who's taken her, it's so obvious, and here's where she is. What are we waiting for, Ivan, let's go get her and bring her home.

He called the stable again and reached only the machine. He then called Dana's two closest friends to ask if they had seen her, telling them that he and his wife had gotten their signals crossed and he needed to find her. Though he tried to affect a matter-of-fact air, they both asked if everything was alright, and Ivan tried to assure them that this was just a mix-up in communication and, yes, everything was fine.

For the time being he would have to search for Sonya alone. He felt overwhelmed by the challenge. Where to start, where to look? Then he remembered another search.

Years before, at the beginning of his career, he and other staff members had searched the grounds of a mental hospital for a suicidal boy Ivan had been treating there. The police had been called when the boy ran off, but Ivan and several of the ward staff couldn't wait. They fanned out over the two hundred acres of the hospital grounds. Walking and running, Weiss all the while called out to the boy. He finally found the patient, huddled against a tree, shaking, a kitchen knife clotted with blood and earth lying next to him. Blood from the wound on his forearm, fortunately not life threatening, had dripped down his wrist and collected in a crimson pool in his palm. I'll find her the same way. Not by phone or car, but just by covering the ground, searching the territory. Go where she goes, be where she's been.

He would run. That would keep him close to the ground. It was also active and, he hoped, would quiet his mounting panic. And he might find her.

He planned a night route that would pass everywhere in town he could think she might be. First her apartment again, and then to Nick Streeter's. He looked him up in Sonya's address book. He thumbed through it again. He came across Jake's son, Eric. It was an old address, his father's address. The whole listing was crossed out. He got Eric's address from Directory Assistance and added it to the list. His insides churning with anxiety, he had the patience only to change into his running shoes, pull on a wool watch cap, and grab his gloves. Skipping his usual stretching routine, he took off.

He first ran back to Sonya's apartment. As he was unlocking the door, he heard a man and woman talking. She's back, everything's fine. The note had been just some cruel harassment by a disgruntled patient. But when he opened the door, everything was quiet inside. He could still hear the voices from the apartment across the hall. He checked the apartment, empty, nothing changed. He left and ran around the streets neighboring her house, looking for her car. He then ran north on Main, through downtown, still alive with activity, people leaving restaurants after dinner, trickling in and out of stores that were near closing time. He usually enjoyed the bustle of downtown, but tonight the people were just interfering with him reaching his next destination.

After being caught behind a group of older people, walking slowly and taking up the entire sidewalk, he ran fast to try to beat the light, but stopped when it changed. As he ran in place at the corner, his eye was caught by the "Wait" sign. Wait. That's what the note had said. And repeated.

When the light changed, he took off again. He passed the bank, crossed the street and ran past the courthouse. He ran through Farmers Market, the outdoor market area empty in midwinter. As he ran over the Broadway bridge which spanned both the railroad tracks and the river, he looked down at the old ornate, stone railroad station, retired from service many years before and transformed into the Gandy Dancer restaurant. A stretch limousine, unusual for Ann Arbor, waited at the curb, its windows reflecting the gas lamps in front of the restaurant. He remembered taking Dana there when she was pregnant to celebrate the end of her morning sickness and the beginning of a voracious appetite that lasted until Sonya was born.

He turned on Wall Street and found Streeter's house. The house was much as Sonya had described it, though it looked, even in the dark, to be in more need of repair than she had said. Maybe she was seeing beyond what it looks like to what it could be. Maybe it just needs a good coat of paint.

The house was dark. Ivan rang the bell, and when no one came, he knocked loudly on the door. After the first knock, he thought he heard a sound from within the house.

The creaking of a floor or a bed? He went around the back of the house, the crusty snow breaking noisily under his feet and the powdery snow underneath collecting and melting in his running shoes. He stopped and listened again. Now silence, except for the frozen, bare trees around him groaning in the wind. He peered in several windows. Except for a few pieces of second hand furniture and boxes scattered around, the rooms were empty. He pressed his ear against the cold glass of the window. Now total silence. Standing in the snow, with his shoes and socks wet, his toes were stinging with cold. Short of heading home, he knew he could warm them by running again. Nothing more to be found here, he headed for Eric Hanson's apartment about a mile away, up the steep Broadway hill and out Plymouth Road.

Eric lived in a fairly nice townhouse across Plymouth from the University's North Campus. Maybe with his bookstore job and sharing the place with a roommate, he could afford this. Or, more likely, Jake was paying the rent. Ivan rang the bell.

While he waited, he tried to remember the last time he had seen Eric. It seemed like two years before, but might well have been more. After Jake's divorce Eric fell apart. Though always an isolated, insecure boy, following the divorce he seemed to feel everyone owed him, especially his father. He became demanding, feeling he deserved to be compensated for something. For the divorce? It was never clear to Weiss. Eric ended up in court, first for stealing, then for drug possession, and finally for stalking a girlfriend after she had broken up with him. Rules and laws seemed to mean nothing to him. He felt he had been in some way so deprived that he now deserved to do anything he pleased.

Jake would talk with Ivan about Eric's current problems, but would say almost nothing about his son's childhood. Jake alluded to a major dislocation in Eric's early life, being sent off to a boarding school at an early age, but said little more about it. It was obvious to Ivan how guilty Jake felt about whatever had happened in Eric's early life.

After Eric had somehow talked his way out of the stalking charge and left town, Jake had little contact with him. When he managed to stick with a drug rehab program long enough to stay clean for a few weeks, he would call his father. Then he would turn to drugs again, and there would be no contact for many months. The only area that had seemed to hold any promise for Eric was the theater. He had talent as an actor and had also done some sound and lighting work. He had stayed clean long enough to act in a small, short run, San Francisco production of, fittingly, *No Exit*, which his father had come out to see. The day after the last performance he was back on drugs. Whenever Ivan heard about Eric's life, he felt relieved that years before Sonya had ended her relationship with him.

Weiss rang again. When the door opened, even before he saw Eric, Ivan was met with the acrid, sweet smell of pot. Ivan was shocked at Eric's appearance. When Ivan had last seen him, he had looked like a younger and larger version of Jake. Before he had left Ann Arbor, through all of his problems, he had retained his robust, boy next door look and manner. He was now a shadow of his former self. He had lost a great deal of weight, and his skin, even in the dim light of the doorway, was sallow and unhealthy. There were deep hollows in his cheeks, and his hair had thinned. His eyes, which seemed to be sinking into the dark rings under them, were glassy, while the stare he fixed on Weiss was intense and urgent. He moved slowly, but his speech was rapid and pressured. Ivan was sure that if he had not known this was Eric Hanson, he never would have recognized him.

"Well, Dr. Weiss, Dr. Weiss, or do I call you Ivan now?" he said, hard for Ivan to hear over the cacophony of the stereo and TV, both too loud. "I'm an adult now, or presumably so, presumed so, supposed to be. Adult to adult. Man to man. Equal to equal. Right?" Weiss tried to break into this, but Eric talked over him. "How nice to see you, though I can't say I can see you too well out here in the dark. But to see is not just to look. I am seeing you. You are here. Not like a sea, an ocean, that's different. But we're not seeing each other. Are we?"

The most recent drug rehab that Jake had told Ivan about had obviously failed. Eric was back on something and likely, Ivan thought, more than marijuana, speed probably, maybe cocaine. Unless he was in a manic episode, which would be almost as bad, but at least treatable with medication. He might be suffering with a combination of the two. Ivan finally managed to interrupt the flood of disorganized words and ideas.

"Eric, it's nice to see you, too. Can I come in?" Without saying anything, Eric turned away and with a limp sweep of his arm gestured Ivan to follow. The apartment was overheated, which was to Ivan welcome, as his feet were beginning to go numb. Eric walked vacantly down a short hallway into the kitchen, his gait labored, pushed aside a pile of dirty dishes in the sink, ran the tap for a long time, and then filled a glass. He seemed now oblivious to Ivan's presence.

"Eric, I need to ask you something. Come here and sit down a minute." Ivan guided Eric to a stool at the kitchen counter. Eric calmed at Ivan's touch and seemed aware again of his being there. Ivan considered what he would say next. The note had said not to tell anyone of her disappearance, but to simply ask a question seemed different.

"Eric, Sonya and I were supposed to meet earlier this evening," he lied. "We must've gotten our signals crossed, because she didn't show up. I thought as I was running by, I'd stop off and ask if you'd seen her today." Ivan's question seemed to snap Eric out of his stupor.

"She has no use for me. I've called her. She doesn't call me back. No mixed signals there. Signal clear. I've been through a whole hell of a lot, and I deserve better. You better goddamn believe it!" His eyes were now riveted on Weiss. Everyone still owes him, thought Ivan.

Eric's breathing became raspy, and he drank the water slowly, his Adam's apple protruding from his thin neck, rising and falling with what looked to Weiss like pain at each swallow.

"Are you high, Eric?" Ivan asked.

"Of course, Dr. Weiss, and, uh . . ." He held the glass of water up, turned it, looking at it from different angles, as if searching for something in it.

"Is there something more, Eric?"

"I'm sick. Little Eric is a sick boy. His mommy forgot to give him his meds."

"Meds for what?"

"Just a touch of Hep."

"Hep?"

"Hepatitis."

"Sorry to hear about that, Eric."

"Everyone's sorry. Sorrys are cheap. Sorrys are worthless."

Ivan asked to use the bathroom. Eric nodded in its direction and then walked back into the living room and sank into a dilapidated chair in front of a snowy image of sports on the TV screen. When Weiss reached the bathroom door, he looked back to see Eric's feet sticking haphazardly out from the chair. Ivan quickly checked the bathroom, filthy, but nothing out of the ordinary. He then closed the door loudly, from the outside. He went through the two bedrooms. Eric's bedroom was strewn with clothes, old newspapers, half eaten food and in the corner, on a crate, drug paraphernalia, including syringes, a small bag of either cocaine or heroine, and an elastic band. He was mainlining something.

He looked in the closet and under the bed. He kicked aside the debris of a life in decline, looking for anything of Sonya's. After checking to make sure Eric was still immobile in his chair, Ivan searched the other bedroom, empty except for some clothes, books, and luggage.

When Ivan returned to the living room, he found Eric still in the chair falling into a drugged stupor. He looked exhausted. Concerned that he might have overdosed, Weiss shook him.

"Alright Dr. Weiss, she's not, not, alright, alright, here . . ." he said, startled and confused. He struggled to get upright from his reclined position, his arms flailing for the chair arms, his eyes wide and bulging, looking to Ivan terrified.

"Take it easy, Eric, take it easy." It took a few minutes for Eric to settle down. "O.K., Eric, I'm going now." He fixed on Ivan with an intense stare from within his exhausted, depleted eyes. He then stood up and rather formally shook Ivan's hand. Though Eric seemed stiff and odd as he did this, Ivan was surprised at how oriented he suddenly seemed to be. Though Ivan knew that some drugs, such as amphetamines, can have the dual effects of hyperalertness at one moment and disorientation at the next, he still wondered how high Eric actually was. At one moment he seemed too high to function at all, no less kidnap anyone; then at the next he appeared clear and focused, more than enough in touch with reality and in control of himself to be an effective predator.

CHAPTER TWENTY FIVE

O ut in the winter night, Weiss imagined going back to his house. In his mind, it appeared like a huge cavern, ready to swallow him. He could not face it. He left Eric's apartment, crossed Plymouth and ran through North Campus, by the Music School and Aerospace Laboratories. Like Central Campus, North Campus had its own plaza with a bell tower, this one sleek, severe, and modern. As Weiss ran through the plaza, it seemed like a surreal landscape. He ran by the V.A. Hospital, crossed Fuller Road, and struggled through a field, his feet sinking into the snow and the long, thick grass under it, to the railroad tracks. He ran up an embankment to the tracks and ran between the rails.

As he ran, he heard in the distance an approaching train sound its horn. The light on the train's engine began as a dim flicker, and then as the train came out of its curve and headed toward him, it grew to a single, bright unrelenting eye. Like a cyclops, he thought, with its eye on fire. He could hear the clatter of the train on the tracks.

He approached a trestle over the river. It was only wide enough for the one track that passed over it. There were high chain link fences on both sides, probably to prevent kids from jumping into the river. In spite of his awareness of the train coming toward him, now close enough for him to see the lighted windows of passenger cars strung out like an illuminated tail behind the engine, Ivan started over the trestle. He could feel the railbed and ties vibrating under his feet.

Halfway across, Ivan could see the faint lights behind the engineers' windows, sitting like a single eyebrow over the cycloptic eye speeding towards him. He knew he was at the point of no return. Keep running over the trestle toward the train, and he might make it. Stop, and it would surely be over. To stop held for him the promise of enormous relief. Stop and be instantly free of the problems that were engulfing him. He could pass into a simple, free nothingness. Its allure slowed his pace.

Then the gate to the past again suddenly opened, and he saw her. Not in the kitchen window lovingly sending him off to school or welcoming him back home. No, she was in her car. Alone. The scene washed white by a summer sun. "No skid marks." He was in her mind, looking out through the two paned windshield of her car.

This is where she was. Faced with this same horrific choice. To live or to die. Living with whatever were her demons or escaping them. Choosing the sweet nothingness of that ferociously glowing eye racing toward him. The sound of the train whistle as it approached the overpass exploded through the night air and the unrelenting, tempting eye bore down on him. He made his choice.

He sprinted toward the train as fast as he had ever run. As it thundered by, so close he could smell the oil of its pistons, he just made it across the trestle and jumped off the tracks. He rolled down an embankment. The pain of the stones of the railbed which cut through his clothes and raked his skin, along with the cold of the wet snow at the bottom of the embankment, were exhilarating sensations that told him he was alive.

Huge snowflakes were thickly falling. He looked up at the sky and let the flakes settle and melt on his face. They reminded him of a winter scene in a children's book he had read years before to Sonya. Flakes so big they must be make-believe. If only this were all make-believe. He lay for a few minutes and when the snow slowed, he picked himself up and ran on.

A bright red almost full moon appeared on the horizon, shining like a warning he thought, and then disappeared behind the fast moving clouds. He remembered just a few days before looking up at the stars, as he and Dana embraced outside the stable. It seemed to have been in another life. "At this moment they are somewhere," he said in a quiet voice.

He ran into a thick wood in the Arb, the light of the rising moon filtering through the trees, helping him to follow the path. He ran back over the river on a wooden footbridge, passed a flock of sleeping geese, their heads nestled into their own backs. Between a stand of pines and the tracks he followed a path where he had often seen rabbits. He had told his daughter that when she had children, he would take them there to see the rabbits. He had not thought much about being a grandfather, but this particular picture of showing his grandchildren the rabbits was very vivid and appealing.

He ran up the steep Arb hill, through the tallest trees in the preserve, their high limbs catching the strongest wind, creaking, and dropping powdery snow. He ran out through the stone pillared entrance to the Arb, cut over to South University, where a few students were still celebrating what Weiss could tell was Michigan's victory over Notre Dame in basketball. It was 1:00 a.m. when he got back to his house. Though he was consumed with worry over Sonya, he was now exhausted enough to sleep.

He immediately descended into a dream. He is in the ornate lobby of the Waldorf Astoria Hotel in New York, where the winter meetings of the American Psychoanalytic Association were always held. He's given the job of putting on a play there and is holding auditions. He's sitting in a director's chair and holding a megaphone, like an early Hollywood mogul. Actors are milling around, waiting for him to tell them what to do.

He scans the actors and calls to one in the far corner of the room to come toward him. The actor is a large man dressed in a suit, but Weiss can see what look like denim overalls showing under his suit jacket. The actor walks to an open area in the middle of the lobby and tries to make a fearsome grimace, baring his teeth, squinting his eyes, just like Weiss once saw in a Japanese Kabuki play. Weiss laughs at the actor's effort and sends him away.

He scans the room again and beckons another actor to come forward, a small stocky man, who tries to make the same kind of frightening grimace. Ivan does not laugh this time, but still feels that the act is not completely convincing. He might cast him, but probably not. As he sends this second actor away, the actor calls Weiss a son of a bitch and stalks off.

He invites another actor onto the stage. This one announces that he will first sing two Beatles' songs. He clears his throat and sings "Lucy in the Sky with Diamonds." Then he sings "Help," but for some reason as he sings he says "Helps." When he finishes, he goes off, sinks into a large chair and looks over his shoulder at Weiss. Even though he has made no grimace, he is much more frightening than the other two. He is so far the most likely to get the part. In the dream Ivan finds himself hoping that the play will never be performed.

Then without calling on them, a man and two women appear before him, and the man announces that he's going to do a dramatic reading of Freud's works. The women stand at his side. Weiss drops the megaphone and bolts from the chair, knocking it over. This act fills him with fear. As he is about to say something to these actors, a curtain comes down from somewhere in front of them, a curtain covered with eyes. Sets of eyes. A sea of eyes which at first he thinks are painted on the curtain, but then realizes are somehow real, disembodied sets of eyes, looking around, blinking, even winking. The eyes, he now notices, are all exactly the same and are all very familiar to him. As he tries to place them, the man who had been with the two women comes out from behind the curtain and holds something up. The stage is almost completely dark now, and Weiss can't make out what it is. He calls for a spotlight to be trained on the actor, and after the spot makes a few passes by him, it settles for a moment on his raised hand, and Weiss can see he is holding up a book with a large, gray, steel cover and heavy metal hinges where the binding should be. Then the stage goes dark.

He woke up in a sweat, his jaw tight, and his hands clenched into fists. He knew he needed immediately to analyze his dream. Knowing that his mind was his only professional tool, to keep his analytic skills honed, Weiss analyzed himself regularly. Sensing that the dream was trying to tell him something about the crisis he was in, he knew that analysis of it, tonight not for professional reasons at all, was vital. Though it seemed almost impossible to distract himself from the wracking worry about his daughter and wife, he sensed that saving his daughter and finding his wife would involve a journey into himself.

He went downstairs, lay on the sofa in his living room, and began to free associate to the dream. He lay for a while in silence, listening to the winter quiet, broken at moments by gusts of wind rattling the shutters. Then he began to speak.

"I'm a director in the dream. Director. Director of the Clinic. Proud of that. A director directs. A director is in control, exactly what I'm not right now. Probably my wish. To be in control. That much fits. Actors. People seeming to be what they are not. I'm being fooled. My old paranoid worries. Then the actors themselves. They're trying to be scary. Scary. I'm trying to pick the scariest of all, the one just right for the part. So I'm asking, who should I fear? Yes, that's it, who's dangerous, who's the one who has Sonya? I'm asking that in the dream. Follow this. The first actor looks formal, professional on the outside, but he's a hayseed underneath. He's big, an oaf, a farmer. I can almost see the straw sticking out of this mouth, smell the mud on his rubber boots. Do I know someone like this? An image of the Great Plains passes through my mind, Iowa, Nebraska. It's Jake, of course. In auditioning him I'm asking, does he look scary? Out of his envy would he do something to me? Would he kidnap my daughter? No. As much as he tries, he can't look frightening or dangerous."

"What about the second actor in the dream? There's not much about him, less to identify him, few details. I can't really see him in the dream, no visual cues. Maybe this is someone I've never had visual cues for, someone I've never seen. He's a hot head. Dexter, the Clinic patient's stepfather, it's obviously him. I've only spoken to him on the phone, never seen him. The Dean described him as small and stocky. A little fireplug, that's what he called him. He's scary, might get the part, but he's not completely convincing.

"Then the third guy, the one who sings. The songs must be important. 'Lucy in the Sky with Diamonds.' Beatles, I've always liked them. What about that song. People used to say it was really about LSD, Lucy, Sky, Diamonds. So drugs, drug use. Someone on drugs. Then the way he sunk into the chair. Something familiar about that. That's just the way Eric Hanson was sitting, while he was watching TV, deep in his chair, legs sticking out as if they were an extension of the furniture.

"The last part of the dream. The man and the two women and the eyes. The women standing with him are obviously my wife and daughter. He's got Sonya. Do I think he has Dana, too? Who is he? Is he one of the other three? Maybe I have cast one of them, and now he reappears? I don't know. Does the image in the dream bring anyone to mind? He's indistinct in the dream. He looks standard, ordinary, generic, could be anybody.

"Then there's the curtain and the eyes on it. The eyes are the most disturbing part. I feel my stomach knot up just imagining them. Eyes, eyes. My eyes. My wish to look, to know, to see who this is. That feels sort of right, but the eyes don't look like mine at all. I'm missing something. Many eyes. Play around with another dream disguise, reversal. Many eyes means no eyes, blind. I do feel blind. I can't see, and then the curtain hides the man altogether. I want a thousand eyes, but I have none. Why does this still not feel right?

"The book, the metal book. It's solid, metal. Is it locked? Is the secret in there? Try reversing it again. O.K. Not heavy, light. Not hard, but soft. It's flat, dull gray. Battleship gray. Battleship, battle. I'm in a battle now. So again, opposite of gray. Is there an opposite? No, but maybe some reversal of dull. Dull to . . . colorful. Sonya's address book. Disguise a soft, colorful, cloth covered book as a gray, metal one. But the metal still is important not just as a disguise. It also leads to thoughts of something being locked, impenetrable."

He got up from the couch, feeling light headed. He could not remember when he had eaten last and knew he needed to eat. Though he had no appetite, he forced himself to drink some orange juice and eat a bagel. As he ate, he once again opened Sonya's address book. He found Jerry's listing. Could he be the fourth man in the dream? He tried to imagine him kidnapping Sonya. He certainly was large and powerful enough to do it, but Weiss couldn't see it. There was a caring, empathic quality about him. He would never do anything so deliberately cruel and destructive. But could he be such a good actor to have feigned his concern and anxiety about Sonya? Psychopaths, he reminded himself, can be amazing actors. The dream was filled with actors. Of all the actors, one is putting on a terrific performance.

He closed Sonya's address book, and then set it on its binding to see where it would fall open. It opened to the page with Streeter's listing. He read the listing again carefully:

Nick Streeter
Client (maybe more!)
220 Wall St.
734 555 8507

He looked at it again. Something seemed wrong with it. Then he thought of the book in the dream. The cover was large, much larger than Sonya's little address book. A reversal again? Maybe not. Is this simultaneously another book? Another book with addresses, but with a larger cover? A telephone directory? Yes, the image in the dream was both Sonya's address book and a telephone book, a condensation of the two. He remembered looking up Streeter's number in the Ann Arbor phone book at Sonya's apartment. He found a phone book and looked up Streeter.

Streeter, Nicholas, 2412 Baldwin St., Ann Arbor, 48104, 734 555 6428

He opened Sonya's address book one more time to make sure. The addresses were different, so were the phone numbers. At first Ivan thought this could be easily explained. After all, Sonya was doing a complete decorating job on a house he had recently moved into. He might have moved from the Baldwin address to the one on Wall. But why move from Baldwin Street in Burns Park, such a nice neighborhood, to Wall Street. Properties along Wall Street were being gradually bought up by the

University. It was a street far along in its transition from a residential street to one with large University Hospital annex buildings and parking lots. Also, there was at the corner a Detroit Edison yard which generated traffic and noise around the clock. The previous fall Ivan had given a series of lectures to psychiatric residents at one of these University buildings on Wall and could barely hear the students' questions over the noise of the double trailer rigs coming and going under the second floor window.

If you owned a house here, Ivan thought, you might hold it until the University bought it or rent it out to medical students or medical residents. But it would be very strange to sell a house in Burns Park, a beautiful area with ever increasing house values and buy a house on Wall Street. In a pinch you might rent here, but not buy. Though maybe like some recently divorced friends Ivan knew, he wasn't thinking straight. Just as he thought Sonya would have told him that the man was older or from the South, he thought she would have mentioned that he was recently separated or divorced. But maybe not.

He was ready to pick up the phone and call the Chairman of the History Department to ask where Streeter lived or if he had moved, when he glanced over at the clock and realized it was only five in the morning. He slumped into his favorite chair and watched through the window the first hints of the morning light. As he moved toward sleep, his mind returned to the dream, to the second song the character he knew now to be Eric had sung. "Help." Help, I need somebody, he heard the Beatles crooning. Eric needs help. And needs it badly. But he sang, "Helps" in the dream, not "Help." Help, need, assistance, aid. Make it plural. Needs, assistances, is that even a word? Aid, aids, AIDS. He saw Eric's gaunt face and debilitated body. Drugs or hepatitis could explain it, but it might be something even worse. I'm saying in my dream, Ivan thought, just before he drifted off, that Eric Hanson has AIDS.

CHAPTER TWENTY SIX

S he had eaten the bread, fruit, and nuts. She knew now she had been drugged and suspected that the orange juice had been spiked. Although her mouth was parched from thirst, she left it untouched. She thought at first that she could not move from the futon. Now, as the effects of the drug were wearing off, she realized that she could slide the chain her handcuff was attached to along the pipe. In the corner of the room, where the pipe disappeared into the wall, was a portable john. Though it was awkward with one hand fastened to the pipe, she managed to use it.

As the effects of the drug faded, she was not only more alert to her surroundings, but also more clearly aware that she had been kidnapped. Yet she was not panicked. The drug must have dulled my feelings, like a tranquilizer, she thought. I'm frightened, but not terrified. I've been kidnapped by some lunatic, I'm locked to this pipe, alone, who knows where, yet I don't feel overwhelmed with fear. After what happened in New York, I thought if something like that ever happened again, I'd go totally crazy or even die. And it has, and I'm somehow alright. At least for now.

So where am I? She looked around the room again. The arrangement of the objects was strangely comforting. The bedside table and futon on her side of the room nicely balanced the table and standing lamp on the other, and the diagonal placement of the small oriental rug softened the boxy feel of the small room. Everything seemed somehow just right. I've got to get serious, she told herself, about figuring out where I am and escaping. Forget the stupid aesthetics. A windowless room, probably a basement or ground floor room. An abandoned building. A warehouse or old school building or office building. She listened for sounds outside, but the whir of some kind of motor on the floor above her masked all other sounds.

Now that she was fully awake, she tried to reconstruct what had happened. She remembered going to Nick's house, laying out her materials, drinking the tea, looking at the sketch he had made and comparing it to hers. Then everything had started to swim around. Drinking more tea. It must have been the tea. Unless something happened after all that. She remembered all the doors and the people coming through them. Maybe they came in and robbed us, maybe Nick is also being held somewhere, hurt, or even dead. She remembered, too, Eric Hanson's voice. He was certainly angry at her refusing to go out with him and crazy enough to get back at her by doing something like this. Of all the men she knew, he was by far the most frightening of all.

She got up and walked back and forth the length of the room, the chain scraping loudly as it slid along the pipe. She began to wonder what else might have happened to her while she was unconscious. She thought of all the news about the date rape drug. Was I raped? She put her hand down reflexively and protectively over her genitals, but had the strong sense that nothing had been done to her. Her blouse was tucked just the way she liked it, and the tip of her belt was still slipped back under the belt itself, the way she had seen in a fashion magazine and since then had always worn it. A rapist would not have gone to the trouble of redoing it just so. She knew no one had tampered with her clothes. She knew she had been, so far, safe within them.

She had a dim memory of someone holding her hand, examining it, like a palm reader, except instead of examining the lines on her palm, he had run his hands along her fingers, as if he were studying them. She couldn't see in her mind who this was. Nick? The man she had seen in the car with the young woman? Eric Hanson? Or one of the other nameless people who had come through the doors? She didn't know. She had the sense this had taken place here, but she was far from certain.

Just as her walking took her to the end of the pipe near the door, the whirring above her abruptly stopped, the light from the lamp flickered, and then a moment later she was plunged into total darkness. She carefully made her way back to the futon. What if I trip, she thought, and break my wrist or my leg and then go into shock. This stirred in her the fear that no one would ever find her. She felt with her hand for the little table by the futon and then found it with her foot. She stepped around it and carefully settled herself down on the futon.

Though she was blind, with the whirring stopped, she could now hear beyond the room. A weird bargain, lose my sight, gain my hearing. She was sure she would much prefer to see, but immediately took the opportunity to listen for sounds from outside the building. The sounds were so faint that her own breathing covered them. She held her breath and listened, turning her head at different angles to pick up anything she could. She heard the heavy rhythm of a truck changing gears, then the growl of a bus pulling away, and a siren, this much clearer, and from time to time, car horns. She knew from the horns that she was not in Ann Arbor. It had struck her, when she had first returned from New York, how rarely anyone used their horns in Ann Arbor. In New York, and in other big cities she had visited, the moment a traffic light changed, the insistent honking would begin. I'm definitely in a city larger than Ann Arbor.

She thought of the possibilities. The most obvious, of course, was Detroit, an easy hour drive from Ann Arbor. But Toledo, to the south, was just as close. Was Toledo big enough to be a car honking place? She didn't know. She remembered being there only twice, both times when she was a child, on school trips to the Toledo Zoo. Could be Flint, but these noises, faint as they were, sounded more like a bigger city. Yet the sounds were definitely different from the constant din of New York traffic.

She realized that she was assuming it was daytime. The traffic noises were sparse for a city during the day, but it could be the middle of the night. She had no idea what time it was. But what about the bus sound. Buses don't run in the middle of the night. Or do they? She thought of the auto plants, the River Rouge Plant in particular, that operate around the clock. So maybe buses do run all night to accommodate night shifts.

She felt her mind spinning with this question of time. It really makes no difference. I'm just trying to get my bearings. Alright. All I know is that I'm in a city. Some city. She realized she had been thinking only of cities near Ann Arbor. But I have no idea how long I've been drugged, she thought. It could have been hours, even days, since I remember being led to a car. I could be anywhere. A vast map opened in her mind, and she felt terrified. All I really know is that I'm alone. Alone, manacled, kidnapped.

Kidnapped. Why? My father makes a good living, but my parents are far from super wealthy. She thought of the fancy cruise they were ready to go on, and how it had taken some serious budgeting to afford it. Her mother had never earned much. Quite the opposite, she had been a drain on the family's finances. Anyway, there were far wealthier people in Ann Arbor, people outside the academic community, automobile executives, real estate developers. One of her high school friends lived in what seemed to Sonya a mansion in Barton Hills, with a live-in housekeeper, a cook and several gardeners. Ann Arbor was filled with much better targets for a kidnapping.

The room was growing colder. With the generator out of gas, along with the lights going out, the electric space heater had stopped. She began to shiver and felt for something to wrap around herself. Was there a blanket on the futon? I must have not been as attuned to the decorating as I thought. She reached as far as she could and found a wool blanket at the end of the futon. The blanket was awfully thin, but better than nothing. She extended herself as far as her manacled arm would permit and felt around with her feet. She located the standing lamp, then the card table leg, and then what she was looking for, the small oriental rug, the one she thought was so nicely placed. She gripped it with her feet and pulled it to her. It was comfortingly thick. She pulled it and the blanket around her like shawls.

For a while she felt a little warmer, but then the room grew colder yet, and the shivers returned. She knew she was also becoming dehydrated. She felt for the juice in front of her. Maybe it's not drugged, she argued to herself, and drank it. She lay down and pulled the blanket and rug more tightly around herself. With the room growing colder, every time she moved her arm, the now icy steel of the cuff stung her wrist. In the absolute pitch blackness of the windowless room, she managed finally to ignore the pain and sleep.

*   *   *

Weiss awoke to the ping of sleet against the living room bay window. A moment later the phone rang.

"Dr. Weiss, this is Laura at the Clinic. The students have been waiting here for your continuous case seminar. Has it been canceled?" Weiss checked his watch. 9:30. Seminar scheduled from 9 to 10:30. Just cancel it. No, the note said stick to the schedule. He felt an odd security in adhering religiously to the directions of the kidnapper's note. The note was the only sure, real, concrete connection to his daughter. It was also an unchanging point of reference in his fragmenting life.

He knew he could get to the Clinic in 15 minutes. They'll still have half the seminar, 45 minutes. That's about the limit of my concentration now anyway, he thought.

"Tell them I'm running late and will be there in ten minutes." He threw on some slacks and a sweater, drove too fast to the Clinic, and ran down the stairs to the basement conference room.

He apologized to the students for being late. They were looking at him strangely, and he realized his hair was uncombed and he had forgotten to shave. He could not remember the last time he had shaved. He wondered, too, if the emotional toll of the last few days showed on his face. Very likely, he thought. He asked the student to begin his presentation of the most recent sessions with his patient, the businessman who had learned to numb himself against all emotions.

Ivan barely heard a word of the presentation. A comment here or there that connected with his crisis filtered through. When the student described some of his patient's fantasies as "homicidal," the word reverberated in Weiss' mind.

Homicidal. He thought about a couple of homicidal patients he had treated early in his career. Like many therapists starting out, he needed patients and accepted ones who were impulsive, suicidal, or even homicidal. The therapy with these patients rarely could be contained within the confines of the consulting room. He realized that he had not given any thought to the possibility that a patient he had treated in the past might be the kidnapper.

He thought of one of these patients, a brilliant mathematics professor. He was so frightened of his own rageful feelings, he could never admit them to himself. Instead he would see other people as enraged at him, as persecuting him. During these paranoid episodes he needed either to flee or go on the offensive.

The most frightening moment in the man's therapy, one of the most terrifying moments in Weiss' life, was when this patient, in the middle of a session, opened his briefcase, from which he often drew notes to compulsively control the session, and instead drew a gun. Weiss realized too late that the patient had done with him what he had done with others. He had projected his murderous wishes onto Weiss and developed the delusion that Weiss was out to kill him. The gun, he had announced to Weiss, was just there to protect himself.

"I'm just going to be listening very carefully to what you say and if there's anything suspicious, I'm ready to do whatever is necessary to protect myself," the patient had said. Weiss had managed gently to invite him to consider how he had reached the conclusion that Weiss was now his enemy. He managed to raise enough doubt in the patient's mind about his delusion that he put the gun away. He had averted, for the time being, a catastrophe, but the man's delusions never really disappeared. The treatment ended when, having become convinced that the local police were after him, he left the state. Weiss had no idea where he went or where he was now. Though it had been many years since he had last seen him, Weiss reminded himself that the unconscious mind is timeless. He could imagine the patient still constructing the idea that Weiss was out to ruin his life and again going on the attack to protect himself. Reviewing patients he had treated in the past seemed an overwhelming task. It would be useless anyway. All I can do is wait. And the waiting was driving him crazy.

"So, Dr. Weiss, was that a good point in the session to make the interpretation?" Weiss had been so mired in his own preoccupations that he had no idea what interpretation the therapist had made. He was not the kind of person to try to fake it, so he said he had gotten distracted and asked the therapist to go over the portion of the session when he had made the interpretation. Though it took tremendous effort, Ivan managed to concentrate on the material and to make some comments about it.

After the seminar, he found two notes in his mailbox, both concerning the vandalism of his private office, one from the business office of Tower Plaza and the other from the Ann Arbor Police. Of course he would return neither of the messages. No contact with the police, the note had said, so no contact would there be. He crumpled the note slips and tossed them in the waste basket as he left the Clinic.

When he arrived at his private office, two maintenance men had just finished removing the paint from the door and were packing up. The hallway smelled of paint thinner.

"Some of those people you see are pretty nutso," said the younger of the men, with a snide, superior twist to his mouth. Weiss found the remark offensive and ignored it.

"Thanks for cleaning it up."

"Next time," the same man said, "you might suggest the nut use a water based paint, this was a dog to clean up." Though Weiss felt tempted to smack the arrogant smirk off the man's face, he just unlocked his door and went into his office.

He reviewed the recent notes on the patients he was due to see that day. No matter what was pressing in on Weiss, and there was now more than at any time in his adult life, he needed to continue to analyze his patients. That was what the note instructed, and he owed it to his patients. He remembered hearing a talk by a famous Los Angeles analyst, who had the even more famous Marilyn Monroe in treatment when she committed suicide. He described the importance to him and to his other patients, on the day she killed herself, that he continue his work. Beyond that, Weiss knew that his own doggedness, his unrelenting need to push forward no matter what, would leave him with no choice but to work on. This quality had served him well in graduate school, in psychoanalytic training, and through the struggles in his own analysis. Dana had often felt herself lazy in comparison. "Doggedness, Ivan, describes you so well. You're like a dog that has the cuff of someone's pants in its teeth and just won't let go." She admired this quality, envied it, and, at times, could be infuriated by it. But his doggedness was now fraying. He struggled to read the notes and to remember what was going on in each patient's analysis.

As he struggled to listen to his patients through the afternoon, he kept his eye on the red light of his answering machine which stayed resolutely unblinking. Maybe the kidnapper would slip a note under his door or leave one in the waiting room. His ears were tuned to any sounds between the usual 45 minute entries and exits of each patient. Nothing.

His first patient was Norma Weinstein, a slight, pale woman, whose serious expression and hair pulled back in a tight bun, made her look older than her 32 years. She was the most obsessional woman he had in treatment. She looked nervously at Weiss as he escorted her from the waiting room. As soon as she lay down on the couch, she said, "What's happened to you? Something's not right." She sat up on the couch and seemed to be searching Weiss' face. "I've upset you somehow, I know I have. I should leave before I make things worse."

Weiss was not surprised by this. In her childhood this patient had developed an exquisite capacity to tune into the emotional states of other people. This capacity was a strength in her work as a psychiatric nurse, but it was also an enormous burden. When she entered a room, she felt bombarded by everyone's feelings and wishes. "It's like I'm tossed around by emotional winds from all these people. If the feelings are strong, I almost can't stand up." She was most sensitive to worry and fear in others. When she was a child, her parents' need to act as if her mother's terminal illness did not exist generated a silent, but powerful prohibition against discussing it. Any questions about her mother's deteriorating state, were met with, "Mother's just tired," or "She's had a long day."

Her mother was then hospitalized and died a week later of her advanced cancer. She not only lost her mother, her sense of reality was assaulted. She wondered endlessly about why she had never been told how ill her mother was. She imagined it was because her mother's illness must somehow have been the patient's fault. After her mother's death, her father denied having any feelings about losing his wife, but then suddenly sank into a suicidal depression for which he was hospitalized for months. The patient developed, in response to this, her capacity to be tuned into the slightest hints of physical illness or emotional upset.

"From work we've done before, I know how important it is for you to avoid the shock of suddenly finding someone close to you is ill. You have an eye for the slightest hint of emotional turmoil or physical illness in other people. So today you've tuned into something about me and want to make sure I'm alright."

"Yes, I'm very worried about you. You're sick or something. Sick, I'm sure of it." Weiss would not ordinarily go on to say anything about his own life or health, but this patient, having picked up that there was something wrong, was spiraling into a panic. To reexperience something from the past in milder form can be therapeutic, to go through it with the original panic is not. Weiss knew what he needed to do.

It was so difficult for him to focus on this task, as he was working every moment to ward off his deep worry about his daughter and wife.

"You're accurately sensing that there are problems in my life right now. I'm dealing with them and am confident that I can overcome them. These problems have absolutely nothing to do with you. Nothing whatsoever to do with you. You didn't cause them, and it's not your responsibility to resolve them. Let me say, too, that these problems have nothing to do with my health. I am not ill. Physically or mentally." The patient and Weiss both understood that her concern about her analyst was an incarnation of her unconscious idea that she had made her mother die and her father mentally break down.

"Thank you for telling me this." She reached over and touched Weiss' arm. "I'm still worried about you, real worried . . . but I don't feel that I'm going to fall apart over this." She lay down and spent the rest of the session talking about the terrible pain she felt as a child when her father was hospitalized. When the session was over, she turned back toward Weiss.

"I'm still going to keep an eye out for you."

The patient's picking up that there were problems in Weiss' life was almost too much for him to bear. Weiss had, at times of personal turmoil, even much less serious than this, envied people who could turn to their work as a respite from their problems. But an analyst must use his own mind and his own feelings so fully that the analytic work is no refuge; in fact, it brings up whatever is emotionally raw in the analyst. Weiss was in a constant state of terror over his daughter. Working with his patients was becoming close to impossible, but Weiss worried that if he broke the routine the note had said he must maintain, the kidnapper would never reveal himself.

His next patient, Lawrence Esher, his most emotionally constricted male patient, was tight and closed in every way. He lay on the couch session after session with his arms tightly crossed over his chest, complaining that, "Nothing's coming to mind, I can't get anything out." He would try to force himself to talk, but then would say, "The gates are closed, and someone has thrown away the key."

He and Weiss had worked for many months exploring the extreme anxiety he felt when he came to his sessions. The patient called it his "background anxiety." Through fantasies about Weiss that would occasionally come to the surface, the patient was able to feel more directly his fear that Weiss would reach over from behind him and attack him. In one session he had the thought that Weiss with his bare hands would rip a hole in the patient's abdomen. Just after the patient voiced this thought, he had an anxiety attack and could barely control the urge to run out of the office. He managed to tolerate the feelings and stayed.

Weiss said about the fantasy, "If I ripped you open, that would certainly let things out." This comment was followed by two sessions of absolute silence. When Weiss understood what was happening and said, "I think you're reassuring yourself with your silence that I can't rip you open, that you have the power to remain closed," the silence was broken.

"I never felt I could shut my mother out, she was always trying to dig around inside me, I hated it." The patient then struggled to say the next thing he was thinking. "I'm thinking that if you opened me up, all this shit inside me would spew out and destroy everything, a wide river of crap." This work had helped ease the constriction, but it continued to be the patient's core problem and made producing and playing with fantasies, so necessary in analysis, very difficult for him. As is always the case, the problem that brings the patient to analysis is played out in it.

Weiss appreciated today that this patient not only did not let much out, but also did not let much in. He rarely let himself notice anything about Weiss' office or Weiss himself. Ivan had worked at length on this obstacle, one which made the patient in his relationship with his wife and in many social situations, unobservant and obtuse. While Weiss usually worked arduously to help him observe what was going on around him, to let things in, today he felt relieved that, in contrast to his previous patient, Norma Weinstein, who observed everything, this patient noticed nothing of Weiss' inner turmoil.

Weiss had wondered about the quality and quantity of this patient's rage. When he had talked about him to Jake on one of their runs, Jake had characterized the man as a "walking time bomb." Weiss wondered if it could be possible that the time bomb had gone off, if this patient had kidnapped Sonya. It was, he thought, unlikely, but today everyone who passed through Ivan's life was a suspect. Even this constricted, inhibited, anal retentive man. Everyone.

CHAPTER TWENTY SEVEN

W eiss left his private office just as classes were changing and the streets were filling with students. He bought a cup of coffee at a cafe and drank it as he walked. It was 1:00 p.m. now, the workday half over and no word on what he was supposed to do next, or how much he was supposed to pay, to get his daughter back safe.

He had not until that moment thought about money. How would he get it? How much would he, they, demand. His mind reviewed how he could raise a lot of money fast and how he could get it in cash. The house was almost paid off. Could he remortgage it and ask for cash? But this would take time, and would he need Dana's signature? Do banks give out large amounts of cash without reporting it? To some bank regulatory agency or to the police? His mind raced through the possibilities. He had an old college friend who was a banker in New York. Maybe he could get a mortgage or a loan through him. Again this would all take too long. He began to panic, and his thoughts turned to getting the money from a bank somehow. Maybe robbing it. His panic was broken briefly when he thought of Woody Allen in "Take the Money and Run." Reading the handwritten holdup note, the teller says, slowly and loudly, "'This is a holdup, I have a gub.'" "I have a gun, a gun!" says Allen in a desperate whisper. "No, Sir, you see this is a 'b,' this says 'gub.'" Cross robbing a bank off the list of options. He did have some stocks in a private account, market was down, but he still had about $200,000. He also had a University retirement account, but he was too young to draw from that. And a private retirement account. He could break into this, with penalties of course, maybe another $150,000 there.

But the note had said nothing about money. If the kidnapper wanted money there would be no reason not to say that right off in the note. This may have nothing to do with money. He thought of how impulsively, ragefully, the message had been painted on his door. Some twisted idea of avenging what happened to his stepdaughter by abducting Sonya. For the "Quack" laying his hands on his stepdaughter, he'll lay his on Sonya. Not money, revenge. You abuse my stepdaughter, I'll . . . He thought of Sonya being raped again and then tortured or killed, but he used all the will he could summon to keep these thoughts from overwhelming him. To be a good analyst he worked all the time to facilitate the emergence of thoughts of whatever kind into his mind. Now he was trying to keep them out. He thought of a pilot a colleague had treated in the military who had managed to land a badly disabled plane by keeping from his mind thoughts of the worst outcome. The pilot remained cool and focused on the technical details at hand, weighing his options, never letting his mind run to the possible awful outcomes. But I'm not a pilot, thought Ivan; they are put together differently than I am. He knew that he would have to work against his nature to maintain a calm and focus vital to rescuing his daughter.

As he turned the corner from Liberty to State, he saw her. In her dark coat, with her hair in that familiar wild tangle around her fur collar, there she was, half a block away, crossing the street, his wife, Dana. Weiss dropped his coffee, ran to the curb, stumbled as he stepped off the sidewalk into the slushy street, looked down to regain his balance, then continued his pursuit. A bus, then a truck, blocked his view of her and prevented his crossing. When they passed, he momentarily couldn't find her. Then he spotted her just as she disappeared around the next corner at North University. He ran dangerously among the cars on State, his pant cuffs soaked and heavy from the wet, made it to the other side, continued up to North University, turned, and then spotted her again. He caught up with her and grabbed her shoulder from behind.

"Dana!" he cried.

The woman, a stranger, startled and frightened, spun around.

"Hey, hey! What the hell are you . . . ?"

"Oh, I'm so sorry, very sorry, excuse me. I . . . I thought you were someone else." She shot a nervous glance back at Weiss and darted across the street. He imagined how she saw him, as some kind of demented, crazy man, a disturbed street person, pathetic, or dangerous, or both.

He wanted to tell her what the mistake was, that he was looking for his wife, that he needed to find her, to help him rescue his daughter. He stood frozen to the spot for a while and then walked aimlessly through the streets, scanning the faces of the women, looking for his family. They'll just pass by, he imagined, and I'll grab them away from whoever has taken them. I'll reach out and put one under each arm. Like dolls. And take them home.

He returned to his office. Two messages on his machine. He felt his heart race as he pushed the button. First message was from Kevin.

"Dr. Weiss, hope things are square between us." His voice was quiet and controlled, not surprising considering what had happened. "I'm trying to reach Dana. She was supposed to give a lesson this afternoon, the student's here, but she's not. Maybe the kid got the time wrong, I don't know. I need to talk to her about something else, too. Could you have her give me a call?" What was the something else? Your wife is with me, we're going off together, she doesn't have the nerve to tell you, so I am.

He called Kevin back. He told Ivan that he needed to talk to Dana today. She was supposed to be helping him with a riding clinic at the stable this Sunday. An Olympic level rider was coming in, lots of people had registered, and there were a thousand things that needed to be done. Ivan didn't want to say that he had no idea where she was or when he would see her again, so he said he couldn't reach her right now, but would pass the message along to her. O.K., but tell her it's real important. Right, I'll tell her, Ivan said.

The second message was from the Chairman of the History Department, asking Ivan to call him back. He called back, was put on hold, and then put through.

"Dr. Weiss, the reason I'm calling is that something puzzled me about your query about Professor Streeter."

"What was that?"

"The way you were talking about him, you implied or I inferred," wordy academic, thought Weiss, just get to the point, "that you had seen him recently or had some contact with him. Well, what puzzled me is that Professor Streeter has been away on sabbatical since September. Unlike many of my colleagues, he's using the time to actually do research. His project has taken him, to say the least, way off the beaten track, to Indonesia. He's doing a psychohistorical analysis of Suharto and his cronies. Too current for an old historian like me, smacks of political science or social psychology . . ."

"But doesn't he study the Victorian period, as you said?" Weiss interrupted.

"Oh, yes, of course, that's where he made his reputation."

"Can I ask, is this a senior person?"

"Well, when you get to my age, everyone seems junior to me," the Chairman said, with a formal, pretentious laugh. "As his Chairman I should have simple vital statistics on my faculty at my fingertips . . . if he were a woman I'd say she was of a 'certain age.'" Again the laugh. He was finding himself very entertaining; Weiss was finding him infuriating.

"So, he's mid-career, middle age?"

"Not really mid-career, at least not as far as rank is concerned. He was just promoted to Associate Professor. He did something before his graduate work, oh yes, he was in the military, got a later start in academics than most. I'm remembering now he was in Vietnam and then was stationed for a while with NATO in southern France. Yes, that's right, he was there for some time. I think he's fluent in French."

"Can I ask you one more question?"

"Certainly."

"Does the University publish in advance the names of faculty who are going on sabbaticals?"

"Of course, in the University Record, the faculty newspaper. I think the list appears in June for the following year."

"And where they are going?"

"I believe that's included, too."

"Thank you."

"Why are you so interested in all of this?" Weiss tried to come up with something, but it made no difference to him if the Chairman believed him. He just wanted to end the call.

"As I said the other day, the Psychoanalytic Institute is planning some interdisciplinary activities," which was true, "and with his interest in psychology, Professor Streeter seemed to be someone to include. But I didn't know he was away, so all of this will have to wait."

"Do you want his address in Jakarta?" Though Weiss had, of course, no interest in it, it would have seemed odd not to take the address, so he listened impatiently while the Chairman gave it to him and then hung up. Ivan was reminded why he and Dana had few friends on the faculty outside of psychology and psychoanalysis. Though some of Weiss' colleagues could be stuffy and pedantic, pure academics, like this man, were worse.

So Nicholas Streeter, at least as far as the Chairman knew, had been out of the country for months. Had he come back without the Chairman knowing? Was Sonya with someone posing as Streeter? If he were an impostor, he had obviously done his homework. He found someone who would be away, not just out of town, but out of the country for his sabbatical. He had researched Streeter's area of expertise and talked a good enough game of it to seem genuine to Sonya.

If the man Sonya was working for was an impostor, it intrigued Weiss that he had chosen to impersonate a man with interests so closely aligned with Weiss' own. Why would he do that? Maybe just to find some point of contact with Sonya. He seems to have done his homework on Sonya too. Did he know that her father was a psychoanalyst, and that she would be more interested in him if he told her he had interests similar to her father's?

His next patient was the new one, Adam Stone. He had enjoyed the unfolding of the material in the sessions so far with this man, but he was now so singularly caught up in the upheavals of his personal life, that he had now reached the point where he had no desire to see any patient. Especially a new one, where the analyst is trying to get his bearings, where he must be attuned to everything. He girded himself to do his best under the overwhelming circumstances. By sheer force of will, he tried to review his notes on the previous session with the patient.

> Oedipal themes continue, transference heating up. Competitive efforts hide behind apparent submission and wish to please. The patient felt he needed to be submissive to his Department Chairman by not telling him he had to leave for an appointment, yet during that very meeting with the Chairman, who is Jewish, the patient told him about his interest in Nazi memorabilia. Interweaving of dominance and submission within the oedipal paradigm.

I became aware during the session of a countertransference fantasy of stroking the patient's hair. Was he unconsciously trying to elicit this to fend off the need to fight or vie with me? Why do I feel drawn to him?

Then another rich dream: he's at a lecture where the speaker is at first . . .

Weiss had been barely able to concentrate on the notes. When he heard the waiting room door close, his ability to focus on them was completely lost. He closed the file and paced around his office, trying to clear his head. He then went out to meet Stone.

When Weiss opened the waiting room door, Stone was already on his feet. Though he had been aware before that the patient was at least five inches taller than himself, Weiss was suddenly impressed by the man's height. Weiss felt himself small in his presence. He was uneasy with this patient he had felt so comfortable with, so drawn to. I'm uneasy, he reminded himself, with everyone.

Stone walked into the consulting room differently than before. There was a strength and something more Weiss couldn't find the words for. A confidence? Maybe the work they had done so far had helped Stone feel more at home with himself. But confidence was not quite what he was picking up in the patient. He walked, as usual, to the window, but today with long strides. He looked out, as he had before, toward the horizon.

"I don't see any planes. Guess it's too windy to fly today."

As he stood with his back to Weiss, he raised and lowered his shoulders, stretched his neck, and crossed the room to the couch. What was this difference in him? It wasn't confidence or real self assurance. It contained arrogance. But, not quite that either. Then Weiss found the words: the patient was in control, complete control. With his body he was showing he was totally in command, that he owned the place. Maybe, Weiss thought, he is putting himself in his father's place and making me feel like the small child under the abusive man's control. He's turning the tables and putting his foot on my neck.

Stone sat for a while on the couch, smoothing out with his foot imaginary wrinkles from the oriental rug. Then he lay down and immediately started talking. This time he stayed on the couch.

"Do you want to hear a story?"

"Of course."

"A man takes up the study of psychoanalysis. He reads everything he can get his hands on. Freud, Jung, Klein, the object relations theorists, self psychoanalysts, intersubjectivists, everything. He immerses himself in it – dreams, psychopathology, the psychoanalytic process. All of it. And all of it thoroughly. From this he fabricates a history, a set of problems, a complete false person. He then goes to a psychoanalyst as a pseudopatient, as an impostor." The patient paused and pursed his lips. He cupped his right hand on his forehead for a moment and then slowly, sensuously, drew his hand down over his face, bringing it to rest on his chest.

"What happens next?"

"The psychoanalyst swallows it, hook, line, and sinker. The analyst never doubts he's dealing with a genuine patient."

Weiss was simultaneously stunned and fascinated. He thought of his own dream the night before, the dream of auditioning people for a part in a play, the dream of the curtain covered with live eyes. He thought of actors.

"This man must be a talented actor," Weiss said.

As he said "actor," the patient's body tensed very slightly, but noticeably. It was nothing as dramatic as a spasm, a tic, or a shudder, but a subtle contracting of his muscles, radiating out from his shoulders and chest.

When Weiss began his early psychoanalytic cases, after having practiced face to face psychotherapy, his mentor Norcroft told him, "On the couch the body talks. You will see. It's the magic of the couch." Weiss had seen the body talk many times. When patients are sitting up, the conventions of a face to face conversation force the body into socially accepted, automatic self control. But to talk to someone while lying down, with the other person out of view, all conventions are abandoned. The body is free, as Freud said, to "join in the conversation."

So thought Weiss, this subtle body communication will help me to know if something I say has hit a nerve, even if the patient verbally disagrees.

"Yes, a good actor and not a bad director either," said Stone.

"Who is he directing?"

"Well, the analyst for starters."

"I see," said Weiss. "The impostor plays the part of this patient he has constructed and then directs the analyst to think certain things about this pseudopatient. He's written the script." No response from Stone. "Why would he do this?" More silence.

"It's the only thing left for him to do," Stone finally said.

"Is he getting something out of it?"

"He hopes to thaw himself out."

"So he's frozen?"

"Yes. For a long time." There was a hard determined tone to Stone's voice. This was the voice of someone deeply troubled. How could I have missed this deeper level of hurt, Weiss asked himself. Either he's an incredibly talented actor or I didn't want to see this.

Ivan found himself thinking of something he had learned when he was a lifeguard at a summer camp. A drowning person is a dangerous person. To get air he will push anything or anyone under. Does Stone feel he has been cut off from his air supply? Out of some bizarre, perverted reasoning, would he take my daughter?

"What's frozen in him?"

"Hard to say. Hard to say what's not. Everything."

"So now he's thawing?"

"Starting to, but he freezes again very fast."

Weiss leaned forward in his chair to see the patient's face better. Tense and drawn, but not tired. Chiseled features, thick dark hair. Hollow cheeks that look like they were meant to be fuller. Then the eyes. The eyes that had struck Weiss from his first contact with Stone.

Weiss thought of his own dream again, but now only of the curtain, the curtain covered with eyes. Eyes closing, opening, rolling, blinking, winking, looking this way and that. Weiss craned farther forward to see the patient's face even better. The eyes in the dream, he could see clearly now, were endless duplicates of this patient's eyes. Painted on the curtain. *Painted on.* That's how I described his eyes to myself when I first met him, "painted on eyes."

"So, how would you describe the pseudopatient this man constructed?"

"To put it simply, he had classic oedipal problems. Textbook stuff. Always engaged in battles with men and ruining things for himself. There's a simple beauty to it, a classic neurosis. At least that's how it sounded when he read the psychoanalytic literature."

"And how did the analyst respond to hearing these problems?"

"He just ate it up." And Weiss knew he had.

"Maybe that pleased the impostor that the analyst was so taken with the creation."

"No, he didn't really care about that," said the patient, but his body again subtly tensed. Weiss had touched something. "There was just some thrill that he'd gotten the analyst going, really going. The man played the analyst's game, and he got the analyst, at the same time, to play his." The slightest suggestion of a smile began to play across the patient's face.

"So, tell me more, can you, about how the man arranged this game, and how the analyst was playing, too?" This talking in the third person reminded Weiss of working with child patients in play therapy. A child talks about himself through fantasy play with toys. For many children painful feelings can be tolerated only by staying within the play metaphor, continuing for months to talk about what a boy or animal toy feels about a policeman or father toy. Weiss did not know why this patient was needing to stay within the metaphor, but his instincts told him, at least for now, to stay in it with him. Stone went on.

"The impostor made himself into an anthropologist who can't form any relationships with women, who defeats himself, who is always at war with older men. As I said, oedipal stuff."

"And the impostor created dreams?"

"Of course, dreams about competitive urges and retaliation." Weiss was impressed with how much Stone had devoted himself to the study of psychoanalysis. "In one dream he used the image of climbing, climbing with a group. He goes higher and higher and leaves the others behind. You know, surpassing them."

"The dream where he ends up on the high mesa?" asked Weiss.

"Yes. And then in the next part of the dream there's the menacing man with one arm."

"This is all patterned then on this pseuodpatient's wish to attack and castrate the father who constantly demeaned him. And then his fear of his father's retaliation."

"Exactly. Very smart, Dr. Weiss, very smart." Weiss thought about how "smart" Stone had tried to be by constructing all of this. Though he made it sound like it was easy to create this false person, including problems, dreams, and a life history, carrying all of this out was no small accomplishment. It was a measure of his intelligence, cunning, and diligence, that he could pull this off. Beyond Stone's trying to thaw himself out, Weiss wondered if there were other motives for this elaborate deception.

"And there were more dreams?"

"Yes, next came the dream of the animal with the swastika on its belly." Weiss' stomach tightened, as it had when the patient first presented this dream and his interest in Nazi memorabilia associated with it.

"What was the point of that dream?"

"He made a dream just right for the beginning of psychoanalysis."

"How so?"

"It was all about the patient having a problem, but having trouble telling the psychoanalyst, scared of what might be revealed."

"Scared of the analyst's reaction to the swastika on the creature's belly?" Weiss asked tensely, aware now just how cruel it was for Stone to deliberately create Nazi material and throw it at a Jewish analyst.

"Exactly, excited to have the analyst help him with this obsession with Nazi stuff, but also trying to . . ."

"Trying to find the most sadistic, cruel . . ." said Weiss, boiling inside.

"I guess he achieved his goal," interrupted the patient, "he got the analyst real riled up."

"And the analyst didn't for a minute see that this was all deception," said Weiss, trying to regain his composure. "Why is the impostor doing all of this to the analyst?"

"That's where transference comes in. To be convincing he knew he had to play out his problems with the analyst. He used the dream to provoke the analyst, to get him where he's most vulnerable." For the first time in the session, the patient looked back over his shoulder, now with a smile clearly on his face. Whether in character or not, he was still being challenging and defiant. But maybe, thought Weiss, there is something more in that smile, some pleasure in Weiss knowing what enormous care and effort had gone into constructing this elaborate artifice.

"So he shows the analyst the same competitive, oedipal stuff in the transference as in the dreams," said Weiss.

"Exactly, and in his relationships, too. Let's not forget those oedipal triangles." Weiss, of course, remembered the triangles, the patient twice fighting with another man over a woman. Carol, who the patient had caught in bed with another man and Maria in Mexico, whose husband almost shot the patient. Both fictitious, but convincing to an analyst like me so in love with finding patterns, finding answers, and needing always to find them fast.

"You said the analyst was playing his own game, too. What was that?"

"He was playing the analytic inference game. He's an analyst who loves translating symbolic material. He loves discovering hidden themes. The analyst was living inside his own isolated world. His world of theory. He was trying to stay as hidden as the impostor." "Impostor" reverberated in Weiss' mind. He had wondered, after talking to the Chairman of the History Department, if Sonya's client, Streeter, were an impostor.

Jake had been right about two things. This patient was too good to be true. Themes too clear, too consistent, perfect, seamless. And Jake has also been right about me, that my analytic style can limit my understanding of my patients.

"I'm still puzzled by why the impostor would do all of this. I understand it somehow thaws him out, stimulates him, but is there more?"

"That's for the patient to know and the analyst to find out," the patient said with a lilt and cadence of a child's taunt. What he said next sounded anything but childish. "The stakes on the analyst figuring this out are sky high, Dr. Weiss." There was an unmistakably menacing tone.

"The make-believe patient wants the analyst to understand why he is doing this. He has a message he hopes the analyst will get. Is that it?" asked Weiss. The patient shrugged dismissively.

"What I know is that the analyst getting this right is a matter of life and death. I don't think this analyst has a chance," said the patient. Weiss knew where he needed to go next, but desperately wanted to stay away.

"Does the game this man is playing extend outside the sessions with the analyst? Has he drawn others into his play?"

"Could be."

Stone felt to Weiss like a master chess player, cool and planful.

"I wasn't asking if it could be, I'm telling you I want to know."

"You getting a little angry, Dr. Weiss?"

"No, not a little, I'm furious with you."

"You don't think it was enough of a project to deceive the analyst?"

"I'm sure it was," said Weiss, sensing how important it was for Stone, behind his teasing and manipulation, that Weiss recognize the effort and skill that had gone into the deception.

"Of course the impostor's given parts to other people. He's been hard at work. And he's not been content to create just one false identity for himself. There are others."

"Others?"

"Sure. There was another, this time a professor in the History Department. He's just moved to town, bought a house, and gets interested, or at least acts like he is, in the decorator. You get the drift? Know any decorators?"

Weiss saw himself grab the silver letter opener sitting by his note pad and stab the patient's face, not violently, just one clean, well placed incision through the center.

"Is she alright?"

"For now."

"If you harm her . . ."

"You'll kill me. That's fine. Go ahead. I'm dying anyway. Oh, and if you decide to kill me and it gets bloody, you might want to be careful. I have AIDS. Also, to say the obvious, if you kill me, you'll never find her. I can assure you, I have her where no one will ever find her."

Two vastly different pictures of Stone struggled for dominance in Weiss' mind. He could still see Stone, or whatever his real name was, as he had in the sessions so far. He could easily call up in himself the sense of communicating with him, understanding him, feeling a connection with him. Side by side with this, he could see he was faced with a seemingly conscienceless, sadistic man. Was the person Weiss had felt in touch with all a fabrication, all the pseudoperson? Does the actor not inevitably show through?

Is there, Ivan wondered, in this elaborate drama a wish for contact. If so, can I build on this and invite him to reveal more of the actor behind the part? My only hope is to use my abilities as an analyst to deepen his connection with me so we can explore what has driven him to kidnap my daughter.

Weiss tried to put what the patient was showing him into words. He felt an overwhelming urgency to do something.

"You are clearly in control. I sensed it the moment you walked in, and now I know how true it is. I'm the helpless one. I'm the scared one. Yet a person with such a tremendous need to control must have felt at some point that his own life was completely out of his control." The patient lay in silence for an interminable couple of minutes.

"You think you can analyze me, that you can make interpretations to me and that will save her. You can try, but I don't think so. You see I haven't told you anything true about myself, I've made it all up. You don't know a single real thing about me." He fell silent again.

Weiss thought about what Stone had just said, that everything had been a lie, that he had revealed nothing about himself. Weiss remembered during his training asking a senior psychologist if it was possible to fake a response on a projective test like the Thematic Apperception Test or the Rorschach. The psychologist who was from the Menninger Foundation, where projective test analysis was almost a sacred activity, had said this was impossible. The "fake" responses are still the patient's productions, the patient's creations. They are by him, they are of him. Also, the need to present "fake" material reveals an enormous amount about the patient. The need to fabricate *is* the test response.

Weiss was reminded, too, of another man, reported by Freud, who in his effort to hide a wish revealed it. This man had read Freud's theory that all dreams have hidden in them a wish fulfilled. He approached Freud and told him that he disagreed with his theory, and as proof, told Freud one of his dreams that he claimed fulfilled no wish. Freud responded without hesitation, that the wish in the dream was clear: it was to contradict Freud's theory. Weiss also remembered Freud's observation that a human being is incapable of keeping a secret. And Shakespeare's, "The truth will out." The imaginary person Stone constructed has hidden in it who he is and why he is doing these horrific things.

From behind the couch Weiss looked at the patient's eyes and at that moment realized something surprising in himself: he wanted to reach the patient not only to save Sonya. He felt some tie to him that went beyond what he usually felt with patients. He felt a connection to him, almost a kinship with him that was baffling. He had a deeply personal desire to help him. He is a kidnapper, he has taken my daughter, but I want to help him? Weiss remembered imagining running his fingers through Stone's hair. I am, in spite of everything, drawn to him. Where is this feeling coming from? How can I have anything but rage toward him?

"Everything you've told me you've made up, that's true," said Weiss, "but it was *you* who made it up. Why you chose the persona you did, this was from you, an expression of you. You have presented me your false self, but you're in it somewhere, and I intend to find you."

"Good luck, but I doubt you will. You haven't gotten anywhere so far."

"No, I haven't. And that pleases you, doesn't it?" Stone said nothing, but there was again the confirming tensing of his shoulders.

Weiss worked to put aside his conceptualizations of the patient and to take a fresh look at the archeologist and psychohistorian identities. He tried to infer meaning from the parts the patient had created, hoping that through these pseudoselves he could make some real contact with the man behind them. Ivan worried that if he failed, Stone would leave and never come back.

"You were right when you said I swallowed the act. I completely believed you were who you said you were. Completely. And I saw your problems, just as you planned, as straightforward oedipal ones. I'm struggling now to put all of that aside and find you, know you.

"I'm struck that the pseudopatient you created never gets what he wants. Never. You make the man an archeologist, similar to your choosing to impersonate an historian with my daughter, both study the past. Are you looking for something in your own history?" The patient lay motionless, unresponsive, on the couch. Weiss tried to let his mind hover over what Stone's false patient had said, but he felt his thoughts, and much more importantly his feelings, were constricted and narrowed. His voice sounded to himself dry and wooden. He tried to relax and loosen up.

"I think about the relationships this archeologist you created had with women. Even when I strip away the oedipal, triangular stories of trying to have a woman of your own and being blocked by various father substitutes, even when all of this is removed, there is still some heartfelt effort to find a woman. There is a despair about the elusiveness of the woman. You try and try, but she's never there." This was met with the confirming tensing. The elusive woman. Who?

"I also think about the pseudopatient's relationships with the others on the Hopi dig in Arizona. These are talented people, special people, insiders. He thinks he may become one of them, and for a short while, when he is close to the Director, he is, but then it all ends so disappointingly for him. Do *you* feel on the outside? Was there at some time a feeling that you might be welcomed in?" For an instant the patient saw himself looking up at his mother's face, when she came and took him to Nice. He felt himself pushing this from his mind, but Weiss again saw the tensing.

"Theory, theory, theory, Dr. Weiss. I told you I'm frozen. Theory just rolls off me. And what I know about you, Ivan Weiss, is that you, too, are walled off from yourself. You want to reach me, but you're doing it from inside some tight, little thinking box. You're getting nowhere." And Ivan knew that was true.

The patient suddenly got up off the couch, ready to leave. Ivan wanted to threaten him, to attack him physically, to make interpretations to him, anything to touch the patient enough to get him to stay.

"Adam Stone, or whatever your name is, I want to save my daughter. I don't know why you've taken her. You're not asking for money. It must be for some larger reason connected with this drama you've created. For some reason, even beyond saving my daughter, I want to help you untangle why you're doing this. I should have nothing but hate for you, and I certainly hate you for what you're doing, but for some reason, I want to help you, too." Weiss wanted this to really be heard and so waited before going on. "I want you to come back."

"Of course you do." Stone walked to the window, clasped his hands behind his lower back, pulling his shoulders together. He picked up a bronze statuette of a runner that Dana had given Ivan and tapped it on the window. "Pretty thick glass, but this should do it. You don't know how tempting it is to smash this window and throw myself out. I'd sail down by all those windows, like little picture frames, and then be instantly nowhere."

"And then I'd be nowhere and Sonya would be nowhere, too."

"Right you are, Dr. Weiss." He looked at Ivan and tapped the window again. "Tempting, tempting." Ivan could tell that Stone was seeing the fear of losing Sonya in Ivan's eyes. He could tell, too, that Stone was savoring it.

Then, with surprising gentleness, he put the statuette back on the desk.

"I'll be back. It's part of the game. I have nothing to lose. Even if you call the police and I lose my freedom, I don't have long to enjoy it anyway." Ivan felt enormous relief, but sensed that to show it might lead Stone to change his mind. Ivan did need to ask one more thing.

"Before you leave, I want to ask you, has my wife been given a part in your play?"

"Your wife? How would I know her? See you tomorrow, at, what time would I like, hmm, say ten in the morning, Dr. Weiss." He looked out of the window for a few moments more and then turned to stare at Ivan. Weiss was caught again by Stone's eyes and saw the curtain of eyes from his dream. Then he saw something more.

He saw his daughter looking back at him. He saw her eyes in this man's face. But they were Stone's eyes, too. Ivan wondered if the fatigue and turmoil were causing him to hallucinate, to drift now over the edge into psychosis, but then realized that in fact Stone had eyes just like his daughter's. Neither the color, nor the painted on quality, but the shape – almond eyes, raised just a little at their outer edges, hinting at the eastern, the Asian. Though neither Ivan nor his wife had eyes like that, Dana's mother did.

The patient left, and Ivan heard the outer door close. Sitting in his empty office, the relief he had felt when the patient agreed to return disintegrated into doubt that he would ever see Stone again. He felt impelled to follow him, to keep him within view. He was the only connection to Sonya, and Ivan had to stay with him. He opened his outer door a crack and saw the patient waiting at the elevators. When one elevator came and the patient got in it, Weiss ran out into the hall and pressed the down button. He waited a few seconds, slapped his hand in frustration on the elevator door and then ran down the seventeen flights of stairs. When he reached the lobby, the two elevators stood with their doors open, empty. He quickly described Stone to the security guard and asked him which way the man had gone. The young guard, who was in the middle of chewing an enormous bite of a sandwich, pointed right, and Ivan ran out to the street. Just as he turned right, he saw, a block away, Stone get into a van and pull away from the curb. How can I get to my car in time? Where did I park it? His mind spinning with thoughts of how he could keep Stone in view, he impulsively ran after the van. It was stopped at a red light two blocks away. When Ivan was still a block away, the light turned green. And then the synchronized lights, block after block, cascaded from red to green. Ivan ran faster, but the van was soon out of sight. Walking back to Tower Plaza, he noticed people were staring at him and realized he was out in fifteen degree weather in his shirtsleeves. As Ivan rode the elevator back up to his office, Stone's eyes lingered in his mind.

Weiss was exhausted, more from the session with Stone than chasing after the van. It had been the most grueling session of his life. Making contact with Adam Stone seemed impossible. Maybe, thought Weiss, I should have just stopped on that trestle and let the train smash me into oblivion.

He found himself looking at "Rooms by the Sea," a Hopper print that hung over his desk. He usually was drawn to the deep blue of the water seen through the open door and the sharp angle of the sunlight as it fell on the white wall. Today he was struck instead by the emptiness of the rooms, by their desolation. It was Adam Stone's profound emptiness Weiss realized now he had not wanted to see and that now he had to help the patient, his daughter's kidnapper, to fully face and work out. Some of the ways Stone had revealed this inner emptiness now coalesced in Weiss' mind: the disturbing flatness of his eyes, the far off quality as he gazed off at the horizon, and the bleak empty landscape at the end of his last dream. And the moment of panic when the patient felt so terribly alone when he had first used the couch. These all pointed to some deep absence of attachment, some struggle with loss early in his life. This was Stone's real inner story. And Weiss needed to find some way to get to it.

He knew his only hope was to work on himself, and fast, to free himself up to make his analyzing instrument, his own psyche, much better tuned to hearing this disturbed and dangerous young man. The aim was now clear: help Stone unearth and look at the awful feelings that were driving him and maybe he would release Sonya.

Could Weiss work with himself to break out of the box the patient had accurately perceived he was in, to be a better analyst and reach him? Could he do it in time? He knew it was a very long shot. He knew, too, he had no choice but to try.

He lay down on the couch, still warm from Stone's body. The office was deadly quiet. The eyes on the curtain in his dream now danced before him, some wide open, others shut, yet others creased at the edges by laughter. Familiar eyes, unsettling eyes. He let faint street sounds distract him from listening to his thoughts. He knew he didn't want to look inside. The cracks on the ceiling became erratic rivers seen from a plane. I'm way up, way off, distant. Either distant or locked in my tight, little thinking box. I'm always trying to find connections, meanings in what people say and do, so I can anticipate what they will do next, so I can prevent it. Prevent the next thing.

What is that next thing I must guard against? Someone will fly off into risky, violent action, someone will die. If you put things together slowly, it will be too late. Get that computer of a mind to run fast, superfast. If it's not fast enough, I will miss some subtle sign of mother's unhappiness, some signal of her deep self loathing and she will be dead. Others too. Protect them all.

It all made sense. It was all true. But he felt almost no emotional connection to it. Dry, lifeless thoughts. He saw Sonya in a locked room screaming for help. To ward off my panic, he thought, I'm becoming again the little, thinking boy, child computer, child robot, frozen inside. Just like Stone. Just as Stone would never reach his frozen feelings without help, Ivan recognized that the same was true for himself. So who to turn to?

His own analyst was the obvious choice, but he had years before left Ann Arbor to take a university position in Florida and Weiss had recently heard he was in poor health. Since the end of his analysis fifteen years before, Weiss had flown down several times for "tune ups." Of course with what was going on, he could not do that now, but he could have a session on the phone. In spite of what he had heard about his analyst's health, he called his office at the University of Miami Medical School, where Ernesto Sanchez was an emeritus professor. His secretary told Weiss that Dr. Sanchez had just had bypass surgery, was doing well, but certainly would not be able to talk to anyone for at least a week. Weiss asked the secretary to pass on to Dr. Sanchez Weiss' best wishes for a speedy recovery and hung up. Who else?

Ivan called Jake at his private office two floors below. He got his machine and left a message for Jake to call him. Just as he was about to hang up, he added, "Jake, this is really urgent." Then he lay back down on his couch to try to calm himself, to try to rest, his mind still racing.

As he looked out of his window at a jet soundlessly crossing the sky, he realized the mystery was now solved, he knew who had kidnapped her. He had been assuming that once he found this out everything would be fine. But nothing was fine. One riddle solved, another even harder one, was before him – why was Stone doing this? Weiss had solved nothing and knew the greatest challenge was still ahead of him – to find his way deep into Stone's mind to untangle the wishes and feelings that were driving him.

CHAPTER TWENTY EIGHT

T he sound of the key inserted decisively into the lock awoke her instantly. The door swung open and a burst of light, blinding to her dark adapted eyes, panned back and forth in front of a tall figure.

"I'm sorry the generator died. I thought I'd put enough gas in it to last. I'll be back." It was Nick's voice. She didn't want to believe it, but there was no question.

She heard his footsteps on the floor above her, then the whirring began and the lights came on, first dimly, then a little brighter. The space heater came back to life, almost immediately throwing warm air into the room. The air felt like a caress. She felt enormous gratitude to Nick for giving her light, heat. *He's holding me here, and I'm grateful. This is nuts.* The realization came over her that she was completely in his hands. This, like everything else that had happened so far, certainly scared her, but did not throw her into a panic.

She found herself thinking about the rape in New York and comparing it to what was happening now. She felt for a moment the arms grabbing her from behind, skirt lifted, and then him, like a knife, inside her. She thought of how fast it had all happened, that it had been impossible for her mind to keep up with it. Time was crushed into those few minutes, and she couldn't stop it or him. *Now everything is slower. I can stay with what's happening, awful as it is. That's the difference. Like the unfolding of a story. Or even a play. A catastrophe, but in slow motion. I could be raped again, I could be tortured, or even die at the hands of this maniac, but this time, while it happens, I'm going to be here, right here.* This resolution gave her a focus.

He came back into the room and sat at the card table.

"Nick, why are you doing this? What do you want?"

"You know, this is my game. I don't need to give you any explanation."

"Right, you're in control, no question. I just can't believe you've done this to me. Why! I deserve some explanation, don't you think?" He sat immobile, with the palms of his hands pressed lightly down on the table top. The thought crossed Sonya's mind that *maybe he doesn't even know why himself.*

"Because it's my turn," he said deliberately, the words delivered with an exactly equal accent on each. She felt that there was some puzzle in all this that he was presenting to her to solve. The slow, calculated way he was framing what he said made it all enigmatic and even more frightening. Sonya felt she needed to talk with him in the same slow, spare way.

"Your turn?"

"My turn to be center stage. Things frozen in me will come to life. The death scene will be my scene."

"You're an actor?"

"Of course." He wanted to stop there, but looking at her he couldn't help himself from continuing. "That's all I am."

"All you are?"

"I'm just a shell. I fill myself with the parts I play. Makes me feel sort of alive."

"What does all of this have to do with me? Why me?" she asked.

"You're just an innocent character in the play. Who you are is crucial, but you are innocent."

"Just like you?" He was startled at her understanding.

"Just like me."

"Why not just act in a play, or write one?"

"I could, I have, but what I'm doing is much bigger, a finale to my life. It all makes me feel for a moment, here and there, fleetingly, that there's some center to me, a core. Most of the time I'm just a bundle of guts dragging myself around day after day." He wanted her to get this, to get what was missing in him, what had been taken away. He realized at that moment that he had, earlier in the day, wanted her father, Ivan, to understand this too.

"Here's my life: I'm sitting in a little control booth in my head, and I get messages from my body, they come in like reports. The sensations of heat and cold in my body, the contractions of my muscles, aches, energy, fatigue, sometimes being sexually turned on. It's all just a chaos of stupid, senseless readings on my instrument panel."

"So the engaging, interesting person I've seen was just an act?"

"I'm a very good actor."

"Maybe it was all an act, but something of yourself was in it too. I liked it, I felt in sync with it. It seems nuts, but I still sort of do." The low light and the lingering effects of the drugs made it hard for her to see his face, but she thought she saw a shudder or spasm run through his shoulders and neck.

"You said death scene before. Are you dying, Nick?"

"My name isn't Nick." He wanted her suddenly to know his name.

"What is it?" He hesitated, but then decided it made no difference now if she knew. It really made no difference if anyone knew.

"Paul Matin."

"Paul Matin. Paul Morning," remembering the meaning of *matin* from her high school French. "Who are you Paul Matin?"

"I am . . . part of you, and you are part of me. I'm a mirror image of you, you reversed. I'm the anti-you. I'm you with something missing." And then he added, even more enigmatically, "We came through the same door, Sonya, you and I, and then we went down different roads." She felt confused and teased by what he had said.

"Are you dying, Paul?"

"Not yet."

"Am I going to die, Paul?" she asked, looking straight at him. He tried to maintain eye contact with her, but her stare was unsettling and he looked away.

"I don't know."

He got up quickly from the chair and hurriedly went into the hallway outside the room, where he had stored the food. While he replenished the bread, fruit, and juice on the little table by her futon, she followed him with her eyes. He had planned to stay with her until she ate the drug tainted food, and then go on to the next part of the plan, but her stare was throwing him off balance. He felt an urgent need to get away. It will be easier, he thought, to be with her once she's drugged.

"I'll be back," he said in an anxious voice and rushed out.

She had found her weapon, her eyes.

*   *   *

Ivan was startled from a dream of being on the cruise with Dana by a knocking on his consulting room door. He sat up on his couch, cleared his head and opened the door. It was Jake.

"Thanks for coming, Jake."

"Listen, Ivan, I know why you called. I've been a real jerk lately . . ."

"Jake," Ivan tried to interrupt, "you don't know why . . ."

"Here me out on this. Since you got the Directorship, I've been incredibly envious. And then when you gave that terrific paper on Manson, I got greener yet. With all the problems Eric's had, I've even been envious that you have a daughter who's doing so well." Ivan had never told Jake about the rape. He had yet to hear about the kidnapping. "You've been a real good friend to me, Ivan, and I've not been much of one to you lately. I'm sorry, and I'd like to make it up to you."

"Well, you're gonna get your chance."

Ivan told Jake the whole story, from the disappearance of Sonya and Dana to the vandalism of his office.

"Then I got a note saying Sonya'd been kidnapped."

"Oh my God, Ivan, my God! Have you gone to the police?"

"The note was very clear not to. I probably should have, but I didn't."

"I can't believe it! How much money do they want?"

"There was no money mentioned. That, of course, surprised me."

"No money? Well, why? Do you have any idea who did this?"

"I'll get to that. The 'why' is a complicated question, but I do know now who the kidnapper is. I just found out. Until now, I suspected everyone. Every patient I saw was the kidnapper. The person I most suspected was the stepfather of that young woman who made the scene at the Clinic last week."

"The stepfather of that Generation Y borderline?"

"Right, him. He called me, threatened me, went to the Dean. I know now it wasn't him. Well, not quite. He did paint an outraged message on my door, but I'm certain he's not the kidnapper." Ivan felt ashamed of what he needed to say next. He knew he would need to say it, if were going to be able to open up analytically to Jake. "I suspected everyone, even you." Something passed over Jake's face. Fear or shock, Ivan couldn't tell. He quickly tried to reassure Jake. "I know now, and should have known all along, that it couldn't have been you," Ivan said emphatically.

"That's not what just rattled me," said Jake. "It pains me to think of this, but could it be Eric?"

"No, no, it's not. I thought it might be, too. I even went to his apartment. I'm so sorry, Jake, about how things are going for him. I think he was on something when I got there."

"Probably was."

"But I know, with absolute certainty, that it's not him."

"How can you be so sure?"

"Because the person who kidnapped her just told me he did it. It's that new patient I've told you about, the one you said was too good, too perfect, to be true."

"The guy with all those oedipal problems?"

"Yeah, well, he constructed all of that and carried it out with amazing skill. At least with enough skill for someone like me who's so blinded by a need for quick, neat insight. I believed all the lies. That's what you were trying to tell me. You got that one very right."

"You said there's no demand for money, so why's he doing this?"

"That's far from clear. This game somehow stimulates him, brings him to life. That's at least what he's told me. I'm sure there's more to it. I have to get to what's really driving him. If I can reach him in a deeper way, which I haven't even started to do, then maybe he'll give up the game. Jake, I'm running into my own limits when I try to shake him up and reach him. I'm tight, inhibited, wordy. I'm getting in my own way. If I can clear away in myself whatever's interfering, maybe I can get to him." Ivan then told Jake what happened in the last session with Stone and what he was asking Jake to do.

"Let me get this straight," said Jake. "You want me to be your psychoanalyst so you can open yourself to what this sick guy is saying to you."

"That's right. You see, you've been right about my limitations as an analyst. I've always had to do everything right. Perfect. This impresses a lot of people, but not you. You see that I lead so much with reason that I miss things."

"I don't know, Ivan, I think I may have been just running you down for my own reasons."

"Maybe you were, but you were right just the same. Especially about this patient. He's an impostor, and I fell for it, because it all seemed so clear. You picked up on that and called me on it. You understand this about me and can help me with it."

"So let me make sure I've got this right. You think I can help you be a better analyst by being your analyst."

"I know it sounds crazy. What usually takes years at four or five times a week we have to do at warp speed, tonight. Also, we're friends, you're my best friend, and this may change our relationship forever. I also know this is going to be almost impossible for me to do, worrying constantly about Sonya." Jake fell silent, chewed at his lip, then roughly rubbed the back of one hand with the palm of the other.

"I'm not the guy to do this. This town is full of analysts, good ones. Morty Stein is terrific or that new guy McGrath. I'm frankly not sure I've got it in me to do what you're asking."

"I think, Jake, you're the perfect person. You have the kind of active, let's-get-at-it style that's just right for what I need."

"I don't think so. I can't do this."

"You can, but you won't. You just apologized for being envious, well, you obviously still are. Forget it, Jake, I'll find someone else." Jake got up and began to walk out.

At the door he turned back.

"Ivan, everything goes your way, everything. You get a kind of respect from our colleagues I'll never get, you get the Clinic Directorship, you have a terrific wife, a great daughter. It pisses me off, it royally pisses me off. You're right, I am still filled with envy."

"So the last thing you want to do is help me. You might even want me to slide into this catastrophe that's facing me."

"Yeah, I probably do. I definitely do." Jake took a deep breath and let out a cleansing sigh. "Alright, let's do it." Still standing at the door, Jake said, "what you want me to do is probably the greatest testament I've ever heard of a person's respect for psychoanalysis. You believe you can save your daughter through the power our analytic insight. I hope your belief in our work is well founded, for all our sakes."

Jake had just seen six patients, back to back, and told Ivan he would need a little time to collect himself. They arranged to start their session in an hour and to meet until either one reached the point of exhaustion.

Ivan took Jake's hand in both of his own, like his father and other old world Jewish men do and thanked him. Jake left, as the bell tower rang five o'clock.

Ivan looked down at the Ann Arbor evening. Students streamed out of Angell Hall onto State Street, and cars flowed from the parking structures into the slowly moving traffic heading out of town.

As he stood there, he thought of Stone going to the window at the beginning of their first session and saying the view looked like a picture of the world from a satellite. Was this an announcement of the enormous distance he feels from everything and everyone? Or was that part of the act? Ivan thought about a satellite. Far away from the earth. Orbiting in an airless void, a forbidding emptiness. Yet it is held by the earth, its path determined by the earth's hold on it. Bound by it, but never touching it. Never totally lost in space, yet never really touching mother earth either.

He cranked open the window to check the temperature. Less frigid than in the past few days, but windy. He watched the clouds, arrayed across the sky and moving fast to the east, filled with color from the beginning sunset.

Ivan had always loved being up high, whether in tall buildings, or better yet, in planes. He would often stand so close to his office window that he could generate the illusion that he was not in a building at all, but floating above the world, suspended in space, untethered, looking out into the infinite distance. Just like my patient orbiting in his satellite or searching the horizon for planes. Maybe a plane that will come for him. Or me. I'm more like him than I want to think.

As he stood at the window, the panic he had been trying to ward off surged up in him. He needed to do something, to take action, to race out in the winter night and search again. He knew now that the only way out of this morass would be maddenly indirect, through gaining access to whatever in himself was blocking his best, most therapeutic connection to Stone. But he still had so much energy propelling him into direct, frantic action. He would have to do something with it. If he didn't drain it off somehow, there would be no way he could lie even for a minute on Jake's couch and work on himself. The only way he knew to deal with this pressure to act was to run.

He ran hard, under seven minute miles, with spurts under six. He wanted to go into the session clear and ready.

*   *   *

Sonya's eyes, her fixed stare, stayed with him. Maybe driving will shake it. He drove the van from its hiding place behind the dumpster and headed out of the alley. When he reached the street, he stopped and looked up in the distance at the shimmering building. It was risky and foolish to be sitting in the van at the mouth of the alley, but the reflection of a cloud bending around the building's curved, mirrored surface transfixed him. He saw the sun high over the Mediterranean reflected in the windows of the hotels in Nice. The light in the windows, the light in her eyes. Maybe she will take me away with her today.

When he saw a police car a block away, he quickly pulled out of the alley. He drove toward the river and then took Jefferson Avenue out to Grosse Pointe. He parked the van and walked along Lake St. Claire. He was still trying to get Sonya's eyes out of his mind. A biting wind blew in over the frozen lake and huge blocks of ice jutted up at odd angles near the shore. He saw his mother's face. He felt her arms around him. And then the awful release after her last embrace.

As he walked, he reviewed the status of his body. It was quiet and working better than it had in weeks. From the last visit to the AIDS clinic he knew his T-cell count was low, but the new cocktail was giving him, at least temporarily, more energy. He would need it to carry out the next act in his drama, not to mention the finale.

He returned to the van and took the expressway back to the abandoned building. An accident and rush hour had slowed traffic to a crawl. As he inched along, his mind drifted back to St. Boniface. Brother Anthony was sitting next to him on the small bed, stroking his hand, speaking softly to him. Then excitement began to build within Brother Anthony's body, and as he grabbed the little boy tightly to him, a terrible sense of smallness, helplessness, and most of all fear, filled the child. First the promise of security and then the frenzy of Brother Anthony's ejaculating body. However it was still contact – vital, human contact in an emotional desert. A desert she had left him in. A desert he had fled to other men to escape. And from one he received his only gift, the virus. Now in the decline of his life he would indirectly pass it back.

There was a simple way of doing this. From his heroin days he was very adept with syringes. He had used one to inject the GHB into the fruit he had left her. Just draw his own blood and inject it into her. A certain transmission. A certain death. Yet this very certainty was why this method had no appeal. He needed her to live with the agony of not knowing. He needed to put her through the same misery he had gone through.

The traffic now stopped completely. He looked at a couple in a sports car in the next lane. The man was running his hand up the woman's leg. She squirmed and teasingly pushed it away, then relented and put her own hand over the man's. As he watched, he felt some sexual stirrings in himself. Did I come up with this next part of the plan just to have sex with her?

He had had sex with women, had lived with one for almost a year. His sexual fantasies, though occasionally about men, were mostly about women. In them a woman is catering to his every sexual need. He has no need to control her, because she already somehow knows exactly what he wants the moment he wants it. There is no distance between his desire and its gratification. She is thinking with his mind.

Actually having sex with women was entirely different. The moment during sex he would see any need or desire in her, anything that would distract her from her total concentration on his needs, a tension would build in his arms and hands that could only be relieved by strangling her. He could only restrain his rage if the woman displayed no desire except to please him.

The couple in the car were kissing, and the man's hand disappeared under the woman's skirt. The traffic began to move, interrupting their kiss, but his hand stayed between her legs, as they drove out of sight.

It was dark by the time he returned to the abandoned building. He circled the block several times, waiting for the street to empty, before killing his lights and turning the van into the alleyway.

He found her as he had hoped, groggy from the GHB. Groggy, but conscious. Groggy enough to offer little resistance, conscious enough to know what was being done to her, to know the simple symmetry of what he was doing, the perfect justice of it.

The room had heated up nicely, and she had shed the blankets and coat she was wrapped in when he had left. She lay sprawled out, her arms and legs flopped haphazardly on the futon, her clothes loose and disorganized. She made an effort at raising herself when he came in, looked at him through half closed eyes for a moment, and slumped back on the futon.

He pulled his chair close to her, took her free hand, and as he had before, ran his fingers over each of hers. He studied her hand. It was just like her mother's. Just like his mother's. He squeezed it, and when he felt her respond, he was again the little boy in Nice, looking up at her, the unformed promise in his mind of something good to come. Promise, disappointment, promise again. Emotions once strongly felt, now all unfelt, unknown, locked in the tension of his muscles, the twisting of his gut, all too deep for excavation.

He had taken Viagra, along with his usual regimen of AIDS drugs, to make sure everything worked right. He had also taken some speed to wring whatever energy he could from his deteriorating system.

He released her hand, and it fell like a dead weight over the side of the futon. He ran his hand along her leg, cupping her knee in his palm, and then worked his way along her thigh, then under her skirt, like the man in the car had done. He saw the woman in the car resist, then permit, then respond. Sonya lay unresponsive. He had miscalculated. She was still too drugged. He would need to wait.

He took off his clothes and lay down close to her on the narrow futon. The sound of sirens grew then faded. It was quiet for a while, and then he heard the sound of a low flying plane. He imagined being in a plane that flies so high and so fast that it escapes gravity, sails off free into deep space, and then, as if called back by the earth, returns. He imagined himself in it, the only passenger, safe and secure. He lay, awake and aroused, waiting for her to come to.

CHAPTER TWENTY NINE

Ivan traced a crack on Jake's ceiling. Images of Sonya and Dana, just their faces, crossed his mind. He reminded himself of the "basic rule," the only rule in psychoanalysis, to say anything and everything that comes to mind. He told Jake of the faces.

"You see the people you want to have back," said Jake. Tears gathered behind Ivan's eyes.

"That's right." Ivan then thought about the enormity of the task that lay ahead.

Though Jake was Ivan's closest friend, Ivan realized that some basic things about himself he had never told Jake. He would need to know them now. Jake knew that Ivan's father had been in a concentration camp, but now Ivan told him the core of the story, about his father's deep, wracking guilt and depression connected with having been a barber in the camp. Jake knew that Ivan's mother had died young in an automobile accident, but now learned what was crucial, what Ivan never knew, but always suspected, that she had committed suicide. He told Jake about his obsession, that verged on paranoia, over Dana's infidelity.

"I know you a lot better now, Ivan." Ivan lay silently for a moment. "What's going through your mind?"

"When I came in, you had your sleeves rolled up, and you reminded me of a farmhand ready to do some hard work, like tossing bales of hay or carrying bags of grain."

"You hope that I'll be up to this big job. Maybe if I can lift heavy things, I'll be ready to do some heavy analytic lifting."

"I hope you are. I hope we both are." The crack in the ceiling now looked like a plane. "That crack on your ceiling reminds me of a patient of mine, a cautious, quiet man, who took flying lessons. The first time he went up the instructor was easy going and helpful, but then during the second lesson, the guy had completely changed. My patient felt pushed to do things he wasn't ready for, things he was scared to do. I don't know where that thought came from."

"No? Seems clear to me. You just said you thought this country boy might be ready for some heavy lifting. It sounded hopeful, optimistic. Now you're saying that you're scared I'm going to take you on a dangerous ride."

"I'm sure you're right."

"You're worried about this being a fast, wild ride, but it's got to be fast. I know this scares the shit out of you! You're sure we'll crash and burn." Weiss saw a plane slamming into the ground and bursting into flames. Catastrophe, disaster, and then he thought of Sonya, small, her hair wet with sea water.

"I'm thinking of Sonya."

"Where do you see her?"

"We're on Cape Cod, on a vacation we took when she was four. While she was playing in the surf, a wave hit her and I thought she'd drowned. She was fine. And another time she fell from a jungle gym at school and was again alright. I can see this just means I want everything to turn out alright."

"Of course you do. But, Ivan, speaking of being in a plane, you're still flying high over all of this, miles above it. I can barely see any of these experiences from such a height. And you can't either." Weiss was silent. "What's going on now? What's with the silence?"

Ivan told Jake about Stone's image of himself in the satellite and Ivan's own attraction to being high up, away, distant. Jake listened.

"O.K., so take us out of the sky, down to ground level. What do you see? What do you hear?"

"I see Sonya running into the surf at Nauset Beach. She was fearless. She'd run toward the water as it flowed out and then turn and run ahead of the waves just before they'd crash inches behind her. She loved it. I hear her squeals of delight as the water crashes at her heels. She'd call it, 'racing the waves.' Dana's not there. I think she'd gone up the beach to get snacks."

"Where are you?"

"I'm near our beach umbrella, but I'm not under it."

"Flesh it out. What color is the umbrella? What snacks?"

"Is this important, Jake?"

"Yeah, it is. Bring me along, bring yourself along with all of your senses."

"Alright. I see the umbrella now, it's light blue with a design. White stars. And the snacks were . . . oh yes, we all loved them, these fried clams in a roll. I can taste the waiting for them, feel my stomach churning." Ivan felt his skin warming.

"I feel the sun, I'm hungry for the clams, and I watch her running with the waves. Then a huge wave comes up behind her, she's running, running fast, her little feet sinking into the soft sand, and she trips and disappears under the enormous crash of the wave. I freeze for an instant, waiting for her to come up. Then I start to run down to the water and then . . ."

"What, Ivan?"

"Something weird's happening to my thoughts."

"Go with it."

"What really happened was that after a few long terrible seconds, just as I started running toward her, she came up and ran to me, crying. I comforted her, and she was back racing the waves later that afternoon.

"But what I see now is the sky growing horribly dark, lifeguards pushing past me, running to Sonya, lifting her tiny, limp body out of the wet sand, then running with her up the slope of the beach. I'm turning around now, trying to see if she's alright, but I can't, because there's a circle of people around her. I think they're trying to revive her. My legs are heavy, and my head is light, like I'm going to pass out. Now the circle is opening and . . . she's not there. I'm glad I'm lying down right now, because I'm feeling dizzy and faint, like I'm going to pass out right here.

"This is crazy. I'm out of my mind with worry about Sonya. Dana, too. What are we doing? Maybe we should contact the police."

"I know how overwhelmed you must feel, how almost impossible it is to be doing this work with me. But you also want to get away from some very troubling feelings from your past. So you want to stop, to slam on the brakes." Ivan thought about the brakes his mother never slammed on, but the thought was so difficult that it evaporated before he could say it. Other thoughts quickly poured in.

"I'm on the playground now where Sonya fell from the jungle gym. Sonya's in a little Oshkosh outfit. Her sneakers are pink. She's hanging upside down, her knees hooked over the bar at the top. Now she's swinging. I see her long hair trailing behind her with each swing. She's going higher and higher, arching her back, reaching for another bar with her hands, stretching for it, releasing her legs, and then missing the bar. She gets buffeted around by the lower bars, as she tumbles down. Dana is nearby, rushes to her, and climbs over the bars into the center of the jungle gym.

"Jake, the same thing is happening again. The memory is going wild. People are streaming out of the school onto the playground. They're going to take Sonya somewhere, now all these people are surrounding her, police, medics. A crowd is gathering around her, and I'm pushing my way in, but Sonya's gone." Then Ivan added, in what Jake heard as his dry, abstract voice, "This must express my fear that she's dead."

"Of course, but you're jumping again to insight and your tone just went flat." Jake considered what to do next. "I want you to draw your memories of the playground and the beach."

"Draw them?"

"Yeah, draw them," as he handed a yellow legal pad and pencil over Weiss' shoulder.

Ivan thought for a moment and then quickly sketched with stick figures the two scenes he had imagined. He was ready to hand the pad back to Jake.

"No, no, just hold them up so we can both absorb what you've done, so we can sit with these images."

Weiss held up his drawings. In one he had sketched in the ocean, the umbrella, and the sun in the sky and in the other the jungle gym, the slide, and the school. In both sketches a circle of stick figures were gathered at the center of the picture. A circle with a small break with just enough room for one of them to fit through.

"They're obviously the same, the circles are exactly the same," said Ivan. He was ready to put the drawings down.

"Maybe, Ivan, you could stay with what you've drawn a little longer."

"I see another circle. My heart's racing, and my stomach's twisting. I can't catch my breath." He could barely get the words out. "Circle of people, in the house, the day my mother died." He caught his breath. "I did rescue my daughter those times, but I didn't save my mother."

"I know you didn't. Take me back with you to that day, to the raw experience of the day you lost her. Take us there." Weiss felt an overpowering urge to sleep. It was as if the room was filling with anesthetic gas. Then the past forced its way into the present.

"I feel wind in my face and things passing by pretty fast. My chinos are pulling, constraining somehow. I know – I'm running! I didn't like running then, but I'm running, because I can't wait to tell her about the quiz show in school that day, like the TV 'College Bowl,' that I'd won.

"I wasn't a star student, but she and I had practiced and practiced for this. I see her at the table, piled high with volumes of the encyclopedia, which in our house *was* the Bible. One of the volumes is open, and she's looking up something, quickly turning the pages, her index finger pointing up as she reads and then darting to her mouth and then to the page to turn it. I can hear the sound of the paper. It was printed on very thin paper, I think they called it onion skin paper. Onions and tears, I think just now. Tears. I look at her eyes. They look watery. She's carefully turning the delicate pages, looking for things to quiz me on. Geography, presidents, science facts. It was my idea to work so hard at this. All of the kids participated, but for most of them it was just an amusing diversion from the school routine. For me it became a great challenge. I wanted to be like Van Doren in that glass booth, knowing so much."

"Knowing so much."

"Yes, knowing everything, a theme of my life. But then a few really smart kids started getting into it, and I became discouraged. I became pessimistic. That pessimism, that depressive view was in the air of my home as a child. Whatever good happens, whatever is promising in the future, the holocaust is not far down the road.

"So I got discouraged, but this time, she encouraged me. I wanted to quit and she . . . what was it she promised. She promised something . . ."

"Settle further into the scene, Ivan. What did she promise?"

"I don't know, but I see us going into New York City on the train. This never happened, but I see it."

"Did she promise to take you to New York after the quiz show?"

"Yes, I remember now, that's exactly what happened. I was fascinated by astronomy and had always wanted to go to a planetarium. She promised to take me the day after the contest, just the two of us."

"What a special gift, exclusive time with her. No father to have to share her with."

"Right, she even talked about us going out to lunch and joked that it would be like a date."

"A little special romance with your mother. What a promise."

As Ivan lay looking at the sky beyond his feet, the last of the color faded to black, a few stars appeared, and the wind whistled through a crack in the window. Sonya and Dana are out there, he thought, somewhere in the windy, cold night. He remembered the dome of stars in the planetarium.

"I imagined the planetarium, not as a theater, but as a magical place open to the sky. The contest, the trip to New York, it was lifting her mood, brightening her. The contest was in the morning, and I wanted to call her from school as soon as it was over, as soon as I'd won. There was a pay phone by the cafeteria, I'd brought change for it. I'd planned it all out. But I didn't call.

"The decision not to, my decision to wait, has filled me with guilt, enormous guilt. I didn't call her right away, because I wanted to see her face when she heard I'd won. I wanted this for me, not her. If I'd not been so selfish and called her, maybe she wouldn't have died. Maybe the news would have made her want to live." Ivan began to cry, and Jake offered him the box of tissues.

"I can see how this guilt has plagued you, but take us back to your running home." Just as Ivan dried his eyes, he felt suddenly hot and thirsty and something uncomfortably tight around his head. He described this to Jake.

"Your body is remembering."

"I feel the sweat under my clothes from running. It's a new subdivision with young trees, no shade. The sun is direct and hot. The hat band of my New York Yankees cap is soaked. I smell the freshly cut grass. The retired man around the corner from our house is mowing his lawn. I'm hearing the sound of the power mower receding as I pass him.

"I'm thinking, how will I tell her? Will I tell her right away or make her think I didn't do so well and then surprise her? I'm savoring the possibilities . . . It's all with me now, the sound of my dark leather shoes slapping the pavement, speeding up as I get close to the house, my breathing fast from running and excitement." Weiss fell silent, and his mind kept repeating this same part of the journey home.

"What's getting in the way?"

"I don't know, I just can't turn that corner. When I turn the corner, I'll see our house."

"You want it all to stop right there, before the turn. You must have seen or heard something just as you turned the corner that told you your life would never be the same."

Ivan closed his eyes, forcing himself around that corner.

"The cars. It was the cars. I see them now, my relatives' cars, my uncle's big Pontiac and the others, my father's Chevy. Too early in the day for his car to be there. But her car, the Studebaker, which always looked so odd to me, was missing. They're all parked in a haphazard way, parked by people distracted, people in a state of shock. I see the police cars, two of them, those are carefully parked, one behind the other in the driveway. No panic in how they were parked, just routine. A routine tragedy, maybe not even the first of the day." Weiss felt his heart race and his stomach tighten. "I feel so anxious. I want to stop the clock."

"You can't stop time or kill death. Go up to the house and open the door."

"Don't push me."

"You're angry with me, Ivan?"

"Stop it! Fine, I'll go with it. I'm walking now, and I feel as if my blood is heavy, as if it's thickening and falling down through my body, gathering in my legs and pooling in my feet. My feet are so heavy, I can barely lift them.

"I open the door, and there's the circle, the circle of people. It's like in the fantasies of Sonya I just had. It's the circles I drew. I close the door hard, like I always would, the sound sure to make my mother sing, 'Ivan, Ivan, home again, home again . . .' It was part of some children's song. Slam the door loud, slam it very loud, and she'll call out. Forget the cars, forget the gaping absence of her car, just slam the door loud.

"Instead, the sound unsettled the circle, which now broke open and anxious eyes followed me in. Just like in a dream I had, a curtain of eyes. My nostrils are burning, I feel like I'm choking."

"Was someone smoking?"

"Oh, yeah, my aunt and uncle. My parents called them the chimneys. All the windows are closed. It's very hot. Everyone must have been in too much shock to even think about opening them. The smoke hangs like a cloud over the circle.

"As the circle opens, people are whispering, all different things, but I hear it now as, 'Does he know, does he know?' repeated like a chant, 'Does he know, does he know,' then, 'No, no, does he know, no, no, no, no.' The circle opens, and I see my father in the center, sitting in a chair, leaning way forward, cradling his head like a piece of bruised fruit in his hands. When he looks up, his eyes are so sunken and dark, I think for a second something's happened to him, that everyone's here because he's sick or hurt.

"He motions me to him with some barely perceptible gesture with his body and eyes, but my feet are frozen to the spot. I'm not going to be drawn into that black circle, into that darkness. Just leave me out of this. I'm backing away now. This didn't really happen. The circle closes. Now she's in the circle. I can't see her, but I know she's the hub of all the people."

"She's not, Ivan. You wanted her to be there, but she's not. She's dead. Dead."

"Cut it out, Jake, stop . . ."

"She's dead."

"Shut your fucking mouth, shut it!"

Weiss lay in a seething silence. He could hear Jake sipping his coffee and wanted to turn around, grab the cup, and throw it in his face. He saw in his mind hot coffee scalding his skin. He didn't say this.

"You holding something back?" Ivan reluctantly told him the fantasy. Jake said nothing, sipped some more coffee, and felt they were getting somewhere.

"I think now what I thought then," said Ivan, "that I should have known what was going on with her. I could have seen it coming, I should have helped her."

Weiss continued to feel his stomach boiling with rage at Jake.

"You're still really furious with me, aren't you?" Ivan was silent. "You're backing off again."

"I want to run out of here, just slam the door on all of it."

"I know. This is tough work." Ivan lapsed into silence again. Jake waited.

"I'm walking again toward the circle. It opens, she's not there, only my father. He beckons me over. The top of my head feels odd, like the beginning of a terrible headache, as if there is some unbearable pressure building in my brain, and my skull can't contain it. I'm trying to keep my eyes locked onto his, but areas of my vision are darkening, and then disappearing, as if black clouds are passing in front of me. I take a step, and then all I see is darkness, with just the smallest hole, like a pinhole, through which I see my father's eyes."

"You blacked out what you didn't want to see, that she was gone. Gone."

"I've lost it now, I'm unable to stand up. My knees are starting to buckle, I'm fainting, I'm losing it . . ."

"Losing her, Ivan. She's lost, she's gone, she's the unbearable emptiness in the middle of the circle, of all those circles."

"Then I pass out. I open my eyes at the last moment, as I'm falling, and I see the flower pattern of the carpet coming up at me. The flowers seem right now like open mouths, vicious, ensnaring. Then I slam into the floor."

They were both quiet for a while. A door opened and closed down the hall, the window rattled, and, being dinnertime, cooking smells drifted into the office.

"I know I fainted to escape everything. I just checked out."

"I'm sure, you did just that. No question. But you were not just escaping. You were, as you say, 'checking out.'"

"Like dead, dead myself. I can feel the pain of my head hitting the floor. I'm glad that it hurt, because . . ." Ivan paused, and tears came to his eyes, "because I deserved that. I could have given her something to live for. I wish I had called her that morning. I see her answering the phone and her face brightening. My whole life I've tried to prevent this from happening again. I'll protect the people I love by knowing right away when they're in trouble."

"Next time around you'll be a good boy, the psychological savior, by being the great analyzer."

"Yes."

"And so you developed your talents at psychoanalytic inference to an astounding degree. Everyone who knows you can see this. But it leads you, at the same time, to grab onto an understanding of things too early, to foreclose possibilities. You feel with every patient that a catastrophe is about to happen. At every moment you demand of yourself that you be ready with the perfect, the smartest interpretation to save the patient."

Ivan was face to face with the source of his main limitation as an analyst, what was making it impossible for him to reach the man he knew as Adam Stone. I am operating on my fantasy, he realized, of how I could have rescued my mother – if only I could have known enough, been smart enough, I could have saved her. When this fantasy takes over, I lead with my mind and what I say to patients comes out dry and intellectual. While I'm trying desperately to understand the patient, I'm missing the emotional core. This is my problem with Stone. I'm trying to be smart, no, more than that, omniscient. Only if I can put all of that aside and make contact with his old, frozen feelings, can I get him to reveal why he's kidnapped Sonya and get him to let her go. Jake and Ivan both knew they'd done some important work.

"Ivan, why don't you digest this for a little while, and let's meet in a half an hour."

*   *   *

Sonya is back in her apartment, back in the warm bath, surrounded by scented candles. Her new Enya CD is playing, the singing both restful and sensual. She stands up and steps out of the bath, a cloud of steam rising with her, warm, thick and enveloping. The cloud dissipates, long jet trails dissolving into the air, revealing that she is out in the open. Warm, tropical breezes, heavy with scents of flowers, brush her face. She leans into the gentle wind and tries to breathe it in.

She is startled when she feels a hand touch her shoulder. She turns to see Jerry, and behind him, standing together, her parents. Her father says, "We'll help you through this, Sonya." Through what, she wonders. Jerry backs away and joins her parents, and they all move off to one side, as if they are part of some ceremony she doesn't understand. Suddenly she realizes that she is still naked, and is embarrassed for a moment, but the feeling passes.

The breeze accelerates into a wind. It is still warm, but the rich scents are gone, and the air is thick with sand that pelts her all over. She tries to protect herself, but she doesn't have enough hands to do it. She looks to see if Jerry and her parents are still there. When she looks over, it is now her mother, wearing her riding clothes, who encourages her. "You can manage this, Sonya, you can." Her words somehow make the sand filled wind easier to take. I'll tolerate it, I'll just wait it out. Her body burns, as the sand now comes at her in sheets, like sideways rain in a hurricane. She looks at her father and Jerry standing behind her mother, as if they are all in military formation, backing her up. It is deeply reassuring to see them, and she thinks, I can withstand anything. I will survive this.

The sand and wind now collapse into a tightly spinning spiral, like the bottom of a tornado, which is ready to drive into her. To penetrate her. To rape her. Her legs are wrenched apart, and she hears all of the New York rape sounds and sees all the pictures, his desperate fumbling in the alleyway, her struggle to rip herself free of him, the knife so tight against her throat that she can feel its edge tug against her skin. His hardness ready to drive into her. She looks once more to Jerry and her parents, and everything suddenly slows way down. She can see and feel everything that happened, the grip of his arm, her face pressed against the brick wall, his relentless, presuming part entering her from behind, an anonymous invasion. But she has slowed it down, has wrapped her mind around it now. She is in control. She looks back at Jerry and her parents, and they say with their eyes, you're not done yet. There is something more you'll need to do. And now is the time.

She ascended into consciousness, but her eyes refused to open. She was naked, and he, still clothed, was on top of her, the rough fabric of his jeans scraping her legs. She struggled to open her eyes and move her body, but some connection between her brain and her body was still gone. She could feel what was being done to her, but was powerless to make her body respond. She was paralyzed. She looked around for her parents and Jerry, hoping magically to draw them out of her hallucination. Jerry could just pull him off me and toss him across the room. But they were gone. With absolute and frightening clarity she thought, only I can save myself.

She managed to open her eyes now, the only part of her body she could control. He was off of her, kneeling next to her on the futon, pulling his shirt over his head, then rolling his jeans down his legs and kicking them off. He took his underpants off and loomed over her. He pulled her legs apart and was ready to force himself into her.

Then she found her voice. She saw it like wet clay that she could mold. She formed it into a scream, a wordless scream so loud, she could feel, in the small room, its echo vibrate her skin. This time I'm not going to be that silent, terrified girl, this time I'm a woman in control. The scream was not desperate, last ditch, or panicked. It was calculated and deliberate.

While she screamed, she did something else that she knew was absolutely necessary – she locked her eyes on his, staring straight into their large dark centers.

Shocked, he jumped back. The scene as he had scripted it was expected to include her resistance, her struggle, though he had planned the drug to minimize that. When he had run through the plan in his mind, he had also, of course, heard her scream. What he never imagined was the disturbing combination of the scream and that fixed stare she had trained on him. Her eyes seemed to bind him to her, as if she were gripping his shoulders and forcing the scream into him. Just like he was ready to force himself into her.

He thought of his mother, her mother, their mother, of her letters, of her promises and then of his quiet acquiescence to her final letter, the letter of his ultimate letdown. No scream from him then. Then no feelings at all.

The scream stopped, but her iron stare persisted. In his drama, everything is redressed, what goes around comes around. An eye for an eye. The beautiful symmetry. The scream had unsettled all that. He was still mostly numb, but something had begun to crack inside him, and a distant, faint temptation to care had crept in.

Her legs still paralyzed, she could put up no resistance as he spread them apart. When he felt the warmth of her thighs around him, he felt himself an undeniable presence in her life. I'm here, I won't be ignored. He saw in his mind his poison flow into her. Horrible, intimate, just. His body ached to do it.

Her body was now coming back to life, at least her arms, and she grabbed his head, her hands flattened hard against its sides, and forced him to look at her. You *will* look at me, while you do this, she thought. I will force you to see me, to see a person, a specific person, Sonya, the person you know.

He was ready to force himself into her. Prepared now for another scream, none came. She had his head gripped like a vice between her hands, his ears covered. With sound muffled, his whole experience of her was now through sight. She had locked him with her unrelenting eyes. He pushed toward her, his penis hard through all of this, his fatigue barely noticeable from the effects of the speed.

At the moment of the thrust that would put him, and then the poison, finally inside her, his body recoiled.

He couldn't do it. Beyond the wrongness of rape and the wrongness of kidnapping, it was her eyes that stopped him. Her eyes were his eyes. These shared eyes, these half related eyes, these eyes of the same womb, these eyes that cried out incest at what he was about to do.

At just that moment she saw it too. She couldn't define it to herself, but she recognized what she had sensed before, their sameness. The sameness of their plans to decorate his house, the sameness of their sense of humor, the sameness of their tastes. It was as if they looked out from behind the same eyes.

He slid off her. No matter what happens now, she knew the rape in New York had been put to rest. Even if he kills me, she thought, I have reworked that terrible thing.

He was getting dressed, his back to her, his body hunched forward in what she read as shame. He silently dressed, went upstairs, filled the generator tank to the top, and left without saying a word more to her.

This part of his drama had, for now, failed, but he could always try again. Whatever more might go wrong, he knew with certainty that the last part of the last act would still be his.

CHAPTER THIRTY

Ivan went up to his office. He had a message on his machine. There had been static on the line, but through it he recognized the familiar lilt of his wife's voice.

"Ivan, I know you're worried. I'm alright. I can't tell you more right now, but I wanted to let you know I'm O.K. But I have to ask you not to try to find out where I am or contact me. That would be risky, even dangerous for reasons I can't tell you. Well, I guess I've made you more worried now. I love you."

Ivan breathed deeply. Her message was deeply troubling, and yet it calmed him immensely. The "I love you" most of all.

He took the stairs back down to Jake's office. Jake had shed his tie, and his sleeves were now rolled further up, above his elbows. He was carrying a fresh cup of coffee from the kitchen into the consulting room. The office smelled of coffee and some new cooking smells, along with the acrid odor Weiss knew his own body gave off when he was anxious. He lay down on the couch which was still warm. The message from Dana was, of course, at the center of his mind. As he struggled over talking, he lay in silence.

"What are you holding back?"

"I got a message on my machine from Dana." More silence.

"I can see you don't want to tell me about it. Have any idea why?"

"I'm thinking of Dana . . . thinking of her with another man. With different men, men from years ago, and now with Kevin, her riding coach. She left a message to reassure me, to tell me she's alright, but I still imagine her off with someone else. With every man, any man . . . I even think of her with you."

"So, it's impossible to tell me about her, because maybe I'm making it with her too."

"Crazy as that sounds, that's right, that's exactly what I feel."

Jake now knew this was the time to help Ivan get at some things in himself that Jake had glimpsed, but which were walled off from his friend. In an analysis he would have allowed this to emerge gradually, but there was no time for that. He needed to use his psychoanalytic understanding radically.

"At the worst, darkest times in your obsession about Dana, did you imagine her fucking another man?" Ivan felt frozen. "Did you see him passionately undressing her, first her blouse, then letting her skirt fall, putting his hand . . ." Weiss felt the pressure again in his head.

"Yes, I saw that, I see it now, but stop, stop!" He was almost shouting at Jake.

"Stop what?"

"Stop . . ." The cooking smells now became for Ivan very specific. "I smell pea soup. Really strong. I see my mother making pea soup in a pressure cooker. Something got stuck in the gauge, and the whole thing exploded. I thought a bomb had gone off. She was frightened, and so was I."

"Do you want to blow your top?"

"My head's going to explode." Ivan brought his hands up and cradled his head.

"Looks like what your father did that day, holding his head, just as you said, like bruised fruit."

"He looked so forlorn. His life was dominated by guilt." Ivan told Jake again about his father's private guilt, hidden under a mountain of rationalizations, about being a barber in the concentration camp.

"So your mother kills herself, and you and your father take on a truckload of guilt. And your father loads on even more from what he did in the camp. You become obsessed with thoughts of what you could have done to save her. Maybe to save him, too, from his mental anguish." Jake paused, shifted in his chair, drank some coffee, and gathered his resolve.

"It's all true, Ivan. True, true, true, but at the same time it's all crap. It's true, but it conceals as much as it reveals."

"I feel really nauseous right now."

"What do you see in your mind as you feel this?"

"I'm vomiting all over the place. Everywhere. A huge, disgusting river of vomit."

"You want to barf all over me. If your head doesn't blow off, like the pressure cooker, you'll blow it out your mouth." Weiss swallowed a few times, and the nausea subsided enough for him to keep control.

"You know, your being about to explode all started when you began talking about Dana making it with other men."

"I saw her just as I used to imagine her, off with some dark, old man."

"Hmm, not some young stud like lots of guys worry about, but a dark, old man."

"Even when I think of her with Kevin, he looks a lot older. It was almost always that image of the old, dark, haggard man, sometimes very old. She's stripping seductively in front of him. He's not forcing her, she's the initiator. She wants him." Tears welled in his eyes.

"You see her as a lying, cheating bitch. She seems to be loving, but then goes off with this old, old man. I know Dana very well, she's crazy about you. Always has been. No question. But that means nothing to you. Nothing. Instead you accuse her, malign her, degrade her in your mind into a lying, adulterous bitch."

"I feel like getting up right now and throwing you through that goddamn window."

"Really. Who are you so enraged at? Me? For what? All I'm doing is putting your thoughts into words." Then Jake said, emphasizing each word, "This . . . is . . . your . . . rage."

The muscles in Weiss' body felt like steel bands pulling tight, ready to crush him from the inside. He saw his own face, as it must look now. Sunken eyes, narrow and dark, hollow cheeks. The bones in his face jutting out severely. Then the image began to transform itself.

"I'm seeing my face, and it's turning into something frightening . . . I see my face, and now I see the face of Manson, Charles Manson."

"You see the face of a murderous psychopath. The face of this man who has fascinated you. The man you know from your research is enraged with women. Ivan Weiss, you are a Charles Manson." Jake let that sit for a moment and then told Ivan what he felt it vital for his friend to know about himself.

"All this guilt about your mother is real and true, but it hides something much harder for you to face – *what she did to you*. She promised you she'd be there to celebrate with you on that day. She promised you more – to watch you grow, to love you for what you would become. She promised, and then she checked out. She dropped you. She teased you with a promise of a future with her. You getting this, Ivan? She let *you* down."

The excitement he would have felt to tell her that he'd won burned in him. He felt a welling of something in himself, and then he knew what it was.

"You know, I am furious with her, just so furious."

"Right, but 'furious' doesn't even go far enough. When you want to throw me out of the window or scald me with coffee, or vomit all over me, that's your rage at her. You want to do all this and more to your mother and to Dana, to any woman who is close to you. Your mother was the original lying, cheating woman who went off and had an affair."

"What affair? Affair with who?"

"With that old man. We both know who that is, don't we?"

"Maybe you do, Jake, but I don't know yet. I'm scared to know."

"That's old man death."

"Old man death, I see him now," said Ivan, as a chill ran through him. "I see Dana get into her truck, but the image changes to my mother, and then back again to Dana. It's one then the other, and now it's as if they're combined, like two photo negatives laid on top of each other. This double woman is driving on a bright summer day, and an old man, a hitchhiker, is standing by the side of the road. She can't resist stopping for him. He gets in. They drive, they kiss. They undress each other. This is awful, disgusting. I don't want to go on with it."

"Try, Ivan, try."

"He tells her it will be more exciting if they go faster. She presses the accelerator, and he urges her to push it more. His kiss is so intoxicating to her that she takes her eyes off the road. Legs, arms entwined, her hands off the wheel, her foot pressed hard on the floor, the sound of the wind deafening, as they speed faster and faster . . . I can't take this, I can't go on with it."

"Faster and faster, deafening wind, all entwined . . ."

"I can't stand to imagine this."

"You can't go on with your life if you don't."

"I hear the horrendous slamming of her car into the bridge. I see a twisted tangle of steel. Her body, Dana, my mother, is still. The silence, an empty silence is the worst of all."

"What next?"

"The old man agilely snakes out through a broken window and walks away . . . It's my fault she fell under his seductive spell. I didn't see her pain, her distress. I was just selfishly thinking of seeing her face, seeing her be so proud of me."

"Yes, that's exactly what you wanted. But why not, Ivan, why the hell not? Isn't it the most natural thing in the world for a boy to want his mother to be proud of him? She must have known that. She must have known how much it meant to you."

"You're right, you're right," Ivan said, resigned, disappointed. Then the rage returned. "How could she have done this to me! It was selfish, cruel to take herself from me, at the height of my excitement, at the moment of my success!" Ivan felt his whole body clench and a throbbing pain collect in his temples. A ringing started in his ears that grew progressively louder until it obliterated everything else in the room – he had never felt so angry.

"Blind yourself to your rage at your mother, and you become blind to your patient's rage. His behavior screams rage – he's terrorizing Sonya, you, and maybe Dana, too. If you can own the rage in yourself, you may be able to speak to his."

"I'm back again to the day my mother died. It's later. Everyone has gone. Funeral arrangements are being hurriedly made. Jews are supposed to bury the dead as soon as possible. I'm in my room, staring at the wall paper. It had antique cars on it, with the make and year under each car. I'm going from car to car, trying to memorize the year of each. It's all to stop thinking about what's happening. '55 Buick, '49 Cadillac, an obsessive distraction. I remember now I made a resolution at that moment. I'll just think my way through this myself and anything else that comes up in my life. I remember feeling like crying so badly, sitting on the bed, staring at the wall. By a sheer act of will, I stopped the tears, and decided I'd figure things out. Just like the contest at school, I'll get really smart . . ."

"And?"

"And control the world. Control the people in it. Control it all."

"It can't be done."

"I know. I know," Weiss said in a whisper, his energy draining from him.

"What?"

"I feel I barely have the energy to speak. I feel everything is hopeless, that I'm powerless, impotent."

"You were powerless and impotent with her."

"This is another feeling I numbed myself to."

"Another connection to your patient. You said he numbs himself too."

"Yes, he protects himself just like I do. I don't think I wanted to scratch his seamless surface, that beautifully constructed artifice. There's something there I don't want to find."

"What exactly is that, Ivan?"

"Stone's hate. If I look at it, I have to look at my own old hate toward my mother."

"If you can sit with this hate, with all of your gut reactions, and combine it with your other analytic gifts, you'll get through to your patient."

"I think I can do it."

"Don't think you can do it, Ivan, do it, get to him and get your daughter back."

Weiss got up from the couch, Jake rose, and Ivan put his arm around Jake's big shoulders. He had done some heavy lifting. They both had.

*   *   *

After a two hour delay leaving Detroit and circling LaGuardia for another half hour, Dana Weiss' plane finally landed. As it taxied to the gate, she was reminded of the flight that landed at this same airport long ago, the awful flight with her parents when she was a teenager. She remembered being so exhausted after arguing with them all the way from Paris, in muffled tones, about wanting to change her mind and keep the baby.

She had always known she would hear from him again. She knew, too, that her life had never found a center, because of what she had done to him. Her guilt about abandoning him made her feel that she had no right to a full life. She deserved a life only of aborted efforts, dancing, law, and all the others. And this piece of her past, this secret, had also always cast a shadow on her marriage.

She had never told Ivan about her teenage pregnancy, the birth, giving the baby up for adoption, her vacillations about reclaiming him, none of it. She should have. If she were a stronger person, she had often thought, a person more confident and at home with herself, she would have, but she wasn't.

She worried that if this kind, attractive man found out about what she had done, he would drop her. She thought she had good reason to worry. When they met, Ivan was already deeply involved in his research on the terrible effects on children of abandonment by their mothers. She remembered him talking passionately about how destructive it was to children for their mothers to leave them.

"When a mother abandons a child, Dana, the child loses much more than a mother, the child loses the capacity to trust, to care, to love. The child comes to care only about his own survival, only about himself. No one else really exists for him as a living, breathing human being. When that capacity to love is damaged early, it never gets repaired, never. This makes it possible to kill." It sent chills through her. I am such a mother, Ivan. I, the woman you think you love, I am such a cold hearted mother. So she never said a word about it.

She claimed her bag and took a cab to the Gramercy Park Hotel in Manhattan. He had told her to check in there and wait for him to contact her. If she did what he told her to, he promised to leave her life. If she refused, he promised to ruin it. He never said how. Based on having told him years before, in her last letter, that she was terrified for her husband to know she had a child and given it up, she assumed he was threatening to tell Ivan what she had done. She managed not to let herself think about what more he might be threatening.

How oddly fitting, she thought, that Ivan's research was completely right. This abandoned baby, shuttled from orphanage to foster home to orphanage again, finally adopted far too late, had been so damaged that as an adult he had returned to intimidate her. Has he turned out to be one of Ivan's "Manson men," as he called the murderers he studied?

As she rode through Queens in the late afternoon traffic, looking through the smudged cab windows at the New York skyline, she reviewed what had happened since he had reentered her life.

After she had written her last letter to him almost twenty years before, she had heard absolutely nothing from him or anyone else involved with him, foster parents, adoptive parents, or people at the orphanage. For all she knew he might even have died. There would have been no reason, if he had, for anyone to have contacted her.

Then a month ago, he called her. He never told her how he had found her name or address. "This time I'll keep you guessing," he had said. He told her he wanted to see her. She agreed, and they met at a cafe.

Before she saw him, she thought of all the ways to tell him how sorry she was for what she had done, but the moment she met him and saw the rage seeping through his stony exterior, she knew an apology would be pointless. She knew right off that he was very smart and very good with language. He told her, "I'm Paul Matin, I'm the son you chose, in the turmoil of your troubled youth, to abandon. I have come to strike an arrangement with you, an accord, a balance." He sounded like an actor playing a part, sometimes overdramatic, but mostly well played. It seemed like acting nonetheless.

Then he would call her and tell her where to pick him up and where to drive. They would talk while they drove. He had always chosen where he wanted to go in advance, bringing a map marked with the route. South through farm country in Saline on one occasion, west to the quiet, sleepy towns of Dexter and Chelsea on others. Several times he wanted her to drive slowly through Ives Woods in the City, a heavily wooded neighborhood with large, old, country style homes and unpaved, winding roads. The area had a European feel to her. She wondered if it reminded him of France and the orphanage.

She asked on the first trip when they arrived at the destination if he wanted to stop, to get out, to do something there. "I'll tell you if and when I have such a wish," he had said in his stilted way, but never, on any of the trips, asked her to stop.

Twice they almost crossed paths with Ivan. He told her one day that he wanted to drive through her neighborhood and see her house. She drove slowly down her street when unexpectedly she saw Ivan and Jake, in the middle of the day, through the living room window. She sped up, hoping Ivan had not seen her. Another time, when Ivan was away at a race, Matin had asked her to drive him north to Whitmore Lake. Driving down the main street of the town, she saw a finish line banner strung across the street and realized that this was the race Ivan was running in. In her anxious state, she missed the entrance ramp to the expressway and ended up on the service drive, which she suddenly realized was part of the race course. She passed many runners, didn't see Ivan, but wasn't sure he hadn't seen her. She reassured herself that during races, Ivan was oblivious to everything around him, except the mile markers and the finish line.

Once she had managed to get onto the expressway and collected herself, she asked her son if he had known that Ivan would be in the race. Had he set up this encounter? He responded with silence and an enigmatic smile.

These drives at first seemed peculiar and puzzling to her before she began to understand him. After he got into the pickup and told her where he wanted her to drive, he immediately would make the same vague, but certainly menacing, threat that she do what he demanded or he'd tear her life apart. Dana imagined a little boy smashing a toy. Once he had repeated the threat, often using the same words as he had before, as if it were a speech, another set of actor's lines, he would fall silent or make occasional small talk about what they passed along the way.

What dawned on her was that the real reason for these drives was just to repeatedly confirm to himself that he could control her, that she would come for him whenever he called. That whenever he wanted they would drive away together.

The way he settled in the seat, collapsing his tall frame and pressing it against the door, was just like the posture of the little boy she had picked up at the orphanage and driven to Nice. The little boy who had tried to make himself invisible, while he traced patterns with his fingernail in the seat fabric of the rented car. Both then and now, he said next to nothing.

She realized he also wanted to take her away from others in her life. And he did. His demands to see her interfered with her life with her husband and daughter. The worst time this happened was when Sonya had invited Ivan and Dana out to dinner to meet her new boyfriend Jerry. Earlier in the day Paul had called, insisting she pick him up. She had arrived at the dinner late with the excuse that she'd been delayed at the stable, a lie she was resorting to often these days. She knew Ivan, who was prone to paranoia anyway, was suspicious about her relationship with Kevin.

Her son made it clear to her that he was going to control her life. When she told him that she wanted to know what he wanted from her and when all of this would end, he ignored her. Once she pushed this too far. Feeling exasperated and angry with him, she told him that she wanted to take back control of her life, and that she and Ivan were planning to go soon on a cruise. When she said this, he shot her a look of a teacher rebuking a pupil for raising something absolutely preposterous. "You'd be best advised to put *that* on hold," he said. Keeping these meetings a secret from Ivan required stories and excuses and lies. Lies followed by more lies. She told Ivan she was having misgivings about the cruise because of how involved she was with her riding career. Though she was pleased with how her riding was going, nothing could have been further from the truth. She had looked forward to a trip like this for years. Each lie separated her more from Ivan.

Through all of this she was so torn between her wish to help, to nurture, to love this poor young man in ways she and no one else ever had and her fear of him. The fear made her want him out of her life. She thought that Ivan could understand her son's problems better, but to her mind he just seemed to be a rejected boy, now grown up, emotionless on the surface but down deep still very hurt and angry. She wondered, too, about his health. On some days he moved slowly, and his breathing was labored. Did he have cancer or a heart condition?

He told her he had one "final demand." She was to go to the Gramercy Park and wait. He would meet her there in a day or two, they would talk one more time, and then he would leave her life for good.

She arrived at the modest, old New York hotel, across from an inviting park. The tiny, drab lobby had a slight musty smell and was crammed with Japanese tourists. She checked in and stressed to the distracted young clerk that she be told immediately of any messages. She then took the elevator up to her room, dropped her bag, and collapsed on the bed. She closed her eyes and saw herself on her horse sailing in slow motion over the downed tree in the snowy field. She took herself several times through the scene, savoring the moment when she and the horse were in perfect unison at the peak of the jump. She got up, took a long, hot bath in the old clawfoot tub, dressed, and went out into the busy New York evening.

*   *   *

Weiss felt close to the breaking point. To try to be the best analyst he could be tomorrow with his patient, kidnapper of his daughter, he had opened up old wounds within himself. His three hour analysis with Jake had tuned his analyzing instrument, himself, but it had left him emotionally raw and vulnerable. It had made all of his feelings, past and present, much more intense and immediate.

He saw himself on the narrow ledge of a building, and on the same ledge, five yards or so away, near the corner of the building, were Sonya and Adam Stone. The patient was holding one of her arms just above the elbow, ready to jump, ready to take her with him. Can I manage to overcome my own fears and move closer, talk to him, work with him, before he takes her with him? He's dying and has nothing to lose, and maybe a lot to gain, by plunging with her over the edge. Save her by saving him, that's what it all comes down to. He saw his patient release her and then saw her slip into an open window, to safety. That is what Ivan wanted most, but the fantasy did not stop there. He saw his patient follow her in. Ivan wanted first and foremost to save his daughter, but he recognized that he wanted to save Stone too. For the young man's own sake. For what he has done, I should want nothing more than to push the son of a bitch off the ledge myself. But I don't, I want to help him.

Weiss couldn't go home. The prospect of waiting was intolerable. There was so much waiting in all of this. Waiting with little or nothing under his control. Is this what he wants me to go through?

He drove for hours. He drove to the stable, pulled into the parking lot, turned off the engine, and sat. Light from the indoor riding arena illuminated cracks in the barn, and he could hear the cantor rhythm of a horse, punctuated by instructions from Kevin. He thought about the fight with Kevin and felt ashamed about what he had done and worried that his sense of reality could have gotten so warped by his paranoia that he had attacked Kevin.

He then thought about standing in this lot with Dana, a little over a week before, was it that recently, and how contented and satisfied he had been. The slushy paddocks beside the barn were empty, the horses having been brought in for the night, and the open paddock gate, creaking as it swung in the wind, resonated with Weiss' emptiness and despair. He had hoped stopping here would feel like a connection to Dana, but it was instead reminding him painfully of her absence.

He pulled out of the lot, drove back into town, and found himself passing by all of the places he and Dana had lived, the rented house on Division where the Michigan band, which practiced across the street, would awaken them on Saturday mornings, the first house they owned on the Old West side, and then the modern, quirky bilevel near Virginia Park. He wished he could drive all night, by every place that held memories, immerse himself in them, and get lost in the past. He wanted to distract himself from the burning urgency he felt to work with Stone, to crack open his frozen emotional core.

Weiss went home, lay awake for hours and then slept fitfully until dawn. Good sleep seemed to him now like some kind of old luxury or indulgence for which he no longer had the time or desire.

CHAPTER THIRTY ONE

I van arrived early at his private office and called his three morning patients to cancel their sessions. He reached the answering machines of two and woke the third, Norma Weinstein, the psychologically hypersensitive patient, who was now even more alarmed than usual by "your shaky voice." He tried to reassure her that he was alright, which he knew she didn't believe, and that he would see her tomorrow. With the time freed by these canceled sessions, combined with his usual midday break, he had at least enough time for the work he needed to do.

Paul Matin, who Weiss still knew as Adam Stone, failed to appear at the arranged time. Weiss' mind began to race to what he would do if he didn't show, if he never showed. He'd wait a few hours, if he could stand it that long, and then call the police. He checked his book again to make sure he had the right time. Yes, 10 a.m., no question. I'm waiting again, he thought. That's what he wants me to experience. It's a torturing kind of waiting. Is this a waiting that ends with seeing him again, or is this a waiting that goes on forever? I'm left in the dark, I'm left wondering. Has he already killed her or himself, or just left her and fled? He wants me to consider these possibilities. Listen to what he is provoking me to feel.

Fifteen minutes passed that felt like an hour and then fifteen more that felt like a day. When the outer door and then the waiting room door opened and closed, Weiss jumped from his chair with relief and anticipation. He collected himself before opening the waiting room door.

Leonard Malick, Weiss' surgeon patient, stood up, ready to come into the consulting room for his session. Weiss was thrown by seeing him.

"Dr. Malick, didn't you get my message?"

"No, I didn't. I was on call last night and just came from the operating room, had to get a resident to close for me so I wouldn't be late. I'm not late, am I?" The man was preoccupied with doing the right thing.

"No, no, you're not late. I left a message for you that we can't meet today."

"I'm really, really sorry I didn't check my voicemail, really sorry that . . ."

"That's alright, no problem," said Weiss, cutting him off, wanting to free himself for Stone's arrival. If he came. "I just can't meet with you today."

"O.K. I understand, things come up, happens to me all the time." The patient pulled out his appointment book. "Can we reschedule?"

"Sure, but I'll need to call you this evening or tomorrow on that," said Weiss, now barely containing his wish to throw the patient out of his office.

"O.K., that's fine. I'll talk to you later," and he left.

More waiting.

When he heard the outer door open, Ivan again bolted from his chair and opened the consulting room door.

"A little anxious to see me, Dr. Weiss?" The words carried a provocative edge, but the tone of his voice was dull and dead. Weiss knew that if this session would get anywhere, he needed right now to use himself, to be as emotionally genuine and involved as he could.

"Yes, I am very anxious. I was terribly worried that I'd never see you again." Matin said nothing to this, took off his coat, and walked, as usual, to the window. He stood there for a few minutes, scanning the scene, then raised and straightened his long arms, like rigid wings, and pressed the palms of his bony hands flat against the window. The light of the bright, morning sun illuminated the loose folds of the white shirt that hung large on his shrinking body.

"Flying?" Weiss asked.

Matin said nothing and crossed the room, pulling his pants up as he walked. It struck Weiss that he pulled them up as a small boy would, gripping fistfuls of fabric and yanking them up haphazardly, inefficiently, unselfconsciously. He lay down on the couch and was still and silent. Weiss began to get impatient. You're being made to feel this, too, he reminded himself. Listen to it, use it. Draw on what happened with Jake. Use your feelings, dip deep into your own experience.

"I'm waiting for you to talk to me. I'm waiting with terror that I'll never see my daughter again. I have the most terrible pain in my heart." Silence, but the telling muscular action in Matin's shoulders. More silence. Street sounds, doors down the hall opening and closing, vacuum cleaner on the floor above. More silence.

Finally with a throat dry from nervousness, Weiss began to speak, putting into action his plan for the session. "You told me that you're frozen. You're right. You long ago killed off something in your soul. People who are overwhelmed by unrelenting, awful feelings often numb themselves to everything. They live, as you do, in a kind of weatherless world, and all they have are vague body sensations, where the feelings used to be. People do this who have been through horrendous wartime experiences or been in concentration camps. Or through something terrible in their childhood.

"But you have done something extraordinary with your painful feelings. You've not just numbed yourself to them, you've also put them in me." Weiss paused to let him absorb this. "You've not only been a very convincing actor with me, but as you said yourself, a director, too. An amazing director. You have taken a script from your unconscious and fed it right into mine. You've directed me *to be you,* made me the container of all the terrible feelings you once had. I am your mirror, look into it, and you will see yourself." Matin was still silent, but it was clear to Weiss he was listening.

"You created a person and offered him to me. An anthropologist, someone interested in the past and in his own past. In history and his own history. With interesting, solvable problems. I felt you were such a promising patient. You gave me a story rich with imagery, colorful characters and a suspenseful plot, the Hopi archeologist, the digs in Arizona and Mexico, the love triangles, the jealous husband ready to kill you. Interesting to anyone, but so oedipal, it was especially intriguing to a psychoanalyst.

"So I felt drawn to you, even had the wish to stroke your hair, that's how much I was pulled in. I felt teased and toyed with . . . seduced." The shoulder twitch again.

Matin lay silent, but when the voice behind him said "seduced," it echoed in his mind, and he saw Brother Anthony sitting on the bed beside him. He remembered a familiar tension that radiated out from his neck and down his arms, a tension that was always eased under the firm, but tender, weight of Brother Anthony's large hand cupped around his small shoulder. Seduced. There were now no feelings about this, just a picture of the scene, and a dim memory of the physical feeling, the painful tension, relieved by Brother Anthony's touch.

"Seduced, session after session," Weiss continued, "thinking this would be a rewarding relationship for you. And for me. And then suddenly, unpredictably you slammed the door in my face. You seemed dedicated to reflecting on yourself with intelligence and insight, which drew me in, held out a promise to me. Then by bringing up your interest in the Nazis, you slammed the door. But then more self reflection and insight, and I was drawn to you again. Promise and disappointment. Seduced and let down. And seduced again." The sun caught the edge of a geode on Weiss' desk, and the light broke apart into a spectrum on the wall. The room was warming now, as it did often in midwinter days, when the sun came in low. Ivan cranked open the window by his chair and cool air flowed into the room. Matin felt the air stream into the car as she drove him from the orphanage to Nice.

"Did someone promise something to you? Did someone seduce you with a promise? I'm your mirror. I'm feeling what you went through." Matin saw the nun passing to him, across the pocked surface of the farm table, the stack of letters, bound in the mottled paper, the wide ribbon with its precise, little, self satisfied bow on top. He saw Brother Anthony reading him the letters, letters of promise. Promise. The word seemed to him so tiny for its enormity in his mind. Promise.

"And now I will try to do the hardest part, to tell you what I'm feeling right now. It's the last thing I want to do. You've done terrible things to me, my daughter, and probably my wife. But I'll tell you what's going on inside me and you can look in the mirror.

"I feel fooled, manipulated. You're torturing me. I feel you're trying to break me down, to reduce me to total helplessness. And I'm almost there. I've been lied to, and now you have disappeared into this silence." Ivan's voice began to crack under the emotional strain, and he choked back tears. "I'm trying to find you, to get back my daughter, who I love, and all I get is this stone silence. Stone, you chose a name that fits. I'm looking for you, but you're gone, lost in some inner hardness." Weiss felt exhausted, but went on.

"I'm totally alone. I've lost my daughter and my wife. I don't know where they are, and I'm terrified that I will never see them again. You must have felt all of this. You were promised something, then lied to and let down. You felt as hopeless and alone as I do right now." Weiss thought about his own mother on the day of her death. She, too, had promised. She had promised to share his victory, and more than that, promised a future with him, one filled with her love.

Matin saw himself as a little boy walking into a storybook farm with a large, smiling farm woman, holding up the corners of her broad apron to cradle a mound of freshly baked cookies. Such a stupid, unsophisticated image, he castigated himself, the creation of a foolish child. He could dimly remember, however, wanting it so badly. These fantasies had not just sprouted from his own mind, they were promoted by the people at the orphanage, who said these farm people, *les paysans,* were *merveilleux,* that the children they had already adopted were so happy there, and that his life there would be great. It was all made up, all a trick, all a lie. Yes, Dr. Weiss, I was lied to, I was tricked.

Then the waiting. Right again. The endless waiting. And torture. I'll tell you about torture. The torture of being stuck in that orphanage and at that hellhole of a farm. With no escape.

And then the big promise. "I'm coming for you." Waiting. When will you come? He saw the boy in the early morning in front of the orphanage, praying for her to come down that road. He knew the sun must have filtered through the trees, the wind must have made them sway and rustle, and the morning light must have illuminated the stained glass of the church windows, but the picture in his mind had always been as static, colorless and silent as the waiting itself, as dead as the numbness that had eventually set in.

But now as he listened to Weiss, something shifted inside him, just as it had when Sonya had screamed. Some thin memory gathered within him of being inside the skin of that boy, not just seeing the drab picture in his mind, but looking out from behind the boy's eyes, being the boy. The boy waiting in that deep well of silence, full of longings for her, longings too big for his thin frame.

"I feel you have taken my life away," said Weiss.

"Just like you took mine." Weiss was stunned.

"How did I take your life away?" The patient was more than silent, he was so quiet, so frozen on the couch, so distant emotionally, that Weiss felt there was no one else in the room. Weiss worked to connect with this utterly isolated, emotionally dead state. He knew Matin craved someone to deeply understand this isolation and deadness. The rehearsed self, the fabricated role, had helped Weiss understand more than the patient knew. But now Weiss needed to go much further, to bring up to the patient ways he had shown Weiss this isolated, dead emotional state, to tell the patient that he knew deeply about his inner deadness. Just then the patient reminded Weiss of times when he had revealed this core feeling – he got up off the couch and made one of his regular trips to the window. The bright morning light out of a cloudless sky streamed into the office, throwing Matin's shadow across the room.

"I'm thinking about what you did and said at the very beginning of our first session. The first thing can be the most important. Maybe you didn't even plan it." Long silence.

"What are you talking about? What happened?" He's interested, thought Weiss.

"You walked right to the window and said that from up here it looked like a picture taken from a satellite."

"I remember."

"What's it like in your satellite?"

"I don't know." More silence. Then, "I'm far away, but seeing everything," Matin said, still staring out of the window. "It's safe up here. It's a small, quiet place," his words coming out in a dreamy and monotonic way, as if he were drifting into a trance or hypnotic state.

"Is it all laid out there just for you?"

"Yes, it's all there for me to see. And to have." A feeling of omnipotence, Weiss thought, fends off other feelings, other memories.

"Is it a powerful place to be?"

"Yes. The little peons down there live out their sorry, little, pathetic lives. I have it all. From up here . . . I live . . . everywhere," his voice leveling to an absolute monotone. The autohypnotic quality was deepening.

"Go on," said Weiss.

"Everything is up here. Water, food, controlled temperature . . . I have all I need."

"All you need."

"All I need . . . circling around the earth . . . forever."

"Held to mother earth by the force of her gravity," said Weiss.

"Held by her," said Matin, now resting his head against the glass.

"Held by her, under her power, always influenced by her."

"Yes."

"But you never get to her. You can see her, you feel an enormous attraction to her, but you are so many miles from her, you can never get to her."

"It's safe up here."

"You're safe, but you're lonely. From up here you make believe you are part of everything. In fact," Weiss paused between each word as Jake had done with him, "you . . . are . . . nowhere . . . you are supremely helpless. You have nothing, control nothing, are nothing. You have tried to generate this feeling in me. Making Sonya your prisoner, you're doing the same with her.

"Someone must have left you in a terrible, helpless, hopeless place, and you can't stand to remember an instant of it. You're like a little boy who moves toy soldiers around a pretend battlefield, thinking he's the master of everything, feeling like God. But then the boy realizes these are only toys. His life is completely in someone else's hands, someone who has treated him horribly."

As Paul Matin stood at the window, he felt an unbearable pain across the yoke of his shoulders, as if huge, powerful hands were compressing his body. At the same time a wave of nausea rolled through his body.

Then he remembered the dog.

At St. Boniface, after he had returned there from the farm, a stray dog attached itself to him. He saw it now, thin and wiry, always dirty, a torn ear emblematic of its rough life, running excitedly up to him each morning, as he crossed the courtyard from the dormitory to the classroom building. Not allowed in any of the buildings, the dog waited devotedly outside until he came out in the middle of the day. The other kids thought it was so attached to him because he fed it, but he never did. The dog simply loved him. He saw now in his mind the look of unconditional, unrestrained love for him in the dog's eyes. Helpless, he thought, the animal was helplessly taken with me.

Then the day of her last letter. After he read it, he looked into the dog's eyes, at its love. He tried to fight off the memory of what he had done to the dog.

He had planned a way to get out of the session so that Weiss would not come after him, so he could go on to the last part of the plan, but he didn't need it now. His overpowering nausea gave him a very real reason to leave the office.

"I need to use the bathroom. I feel horribly sick to my stomach." He walked quickly to the bathroom, off the waiting room, grasping his belly. Weiss could hear him retching.

He was on his knees in front of the toilet. He thought of the day he had received her last letter. I've met someone, I can't tell him about you, I'll never see you again. He felt as if his insides, organs and all, were exploding and ready to spew out of his mouth. He retched again. He had looked at the dog, at the love in its eyes, at the blind dependence of this animal on him.

And then he had beaten it. Mercilessly. The dog struggled free, ran cowering off a few yards, laid its ears against its turned away head, trembled, and looked at him out of only one eye. It returned, and he beat it again. And then after a third time, the dog skulked off, and he never saw it again. His hatred of his mother washed over him, as his body convulsed in a final dry heave.

He had not expected or planned the session with Weiss to have affected him. It had. He lay curled up, depleted, on the cold tile of the bathroom floor. He thought of scrapping the rest of the plan. He would tell Weiss where she was and then quietly exit Weiss', Sonya's, and Dana's lives and then exit from his own. He almost did. But he couldn't. The plan, the play, had somehow now a life of its own. It had its own nature, contained its own force. He was in its grip. He had to finish it.

* * *

Weiss heard the toilet flush, and then the water run in the sink. And continue to run. He went out to the bathroom to find, of course, Matin gone. He bolted out of his office into the hall, then back to the window in his consulting room to try to spot him down on the street. He took the elevator to the lobby. He walked and ran the streets surrounding the building. Matin had disappeared. I pushed him too hard, and I've lost him. And that means I've lost Sonya, too.

CHAPTER THIRTY TWO

For two days she walked aimlessly through the city. Matin had called her once to say that he was pleased she had done what he had instructed her to do. She had asked him what she was to do next. His tone superior, all he had said was, "It's your turn, mother, to wait. And to wonder for how long." Then he had hung up.

In spite of all that was going on, the time in New York was a kind of recess from her life. She had managed in some small ways to enjoy the edgy energy and the enormous variety of everything, food, people, sights, that is New York. She had walked for hours through the Metropolitan Museum of Art and then, on an unseasonably mild afternoon, sat with mostly younger people, on its steps overlooking Fifth Avenue. She then walked through Central Park and all the way back to the neighborhood of her hotel, where she ate at a small Korean restaurant. She thought of the pain her disappearance must be causing her husband. Sipping tea after her meal, she hoped that this long unfinished business would somehow soon be put to rest. As she walked back to her hotel, the turmoil over her son pressed in on her. She calmed herself by calling up a feeling of calm and warmth thinking about her other child, Sonya, safe in Ann Arbor.

She slept late the next morning, awaking only when the maid knocked to make up the room. She went to a cafe near her hotel for her regular croissant and cappuccino. Though cappuccino was now commonplace, it still seemed luxurious to her, especially for breakfast. She decided to make it part of her routine at home, whenever she returned to her life there. I'll suggest a cappuccino maker to Ivan for my birthday.

As she looked out onto Gramercy Park, she thought, as she often had in the past few days, what would happen if Ivan learned that she had given up her son. Would it destroy his love for her? The thought plagued her that he would act like he still loved her, go through the motions, but hide from her that he no longer did, until everything else they had together withered and died. This had been her fear all the years she had kept the secret. She wished she had the courage to face him, she wished she had done it long ago.

As she sat watching the people rushing past in their determined New York way and was about to get up to order another coffee, the thought crashed in on her – her son could do much more than reveal her secret to her husband. He might be capable of doing worse things, much worse things. To her husband. Even to their daughter. She couldn't believe she had not thought of this. Though he had begun each car ride with threats, she somehow discounted them because he had seemed so needy and pathetic. She had not wanted to think that she had so severely damaged him that he might be capable of being cruel and destructive.

I wrote off his threats, but he was saying truly menacing things. He was domineering and dictatorial with me, but he always seemed like a two year old trying to get his way. She remembered Ivan once saying of a criminal he had studied, that he operated like a two year old, but that a two year old in an adult body, with the freedoms and license of adult life, is a very scary prospect.

Suddenly Ivan knowing the secret and their living with whatever consequences it might bring seemed to her incredibly minor and unimportant. She had to call him.

*　　*　　*

Weiss' desperation was now making his searching for Matin impulsive and erratic. While at first he had systematically walked all of the streets near his office building and gone into cafes, bookstores, the Union, restaurants, and even the lobby of the Michigan Theater, his search had degenerated into darting up streets he had just walked, running to places on baseless hunches, and even poking around the dusty aisles of several used bookstores. As he was walking again past the entrance to Tower Plaza, the security guard ran up to him.

"Dr. Weiss, I have an emergency call for you." Emergency call usually meant from a patient. His life had become so unpredictable that now it could be from anyone, about anything.

"Who is it?" asked Weiss, as they walked into the lobby.

"It's your wife. She said she has to talk to you right away. She seemed really freaked on the phone."

"She's still on the phone?" asked Weiss, knowing that under pressure, Dana's patience was limited. He could imagine her feeling that she had waited endlessly while the guard was looking for him and hanging up.

"No, she left a number. It's a pay phone. She said she'll wait there for you to call and that you've got to call her right away."

On the way up to his office, he unfolded the message slip with the number. 212 area code. New York City. His hands shaking, he dialed the number once, a child answered, wrong number. He settled himself and dialed again. The phone was picked up on the first ring.

"Ivan?"

"Dana, what's going on? Why are you in New York?"

"Ivan, I have a lot to tell you, but not a lot of time. This is going to be very hard to say, but I know I can say it, if you just listen. Just listen."

"I'm listening."

"When I was young, a teenager, I had a child, his name is Paul Matin . . ."

She told him everything. Jumping from past to present and back again, from facts to her feelings, her fears and regrets, it all tumbled out of her. From her teenage pregnancy and birth, to giving her son up, to the letters and the struggle over what she had done. She told him how bad she felt about promising Paul she would come for him and then breaking her promise.

"I offered something terribly important to this child and then let him down. I promised to bring him into my life and then closed him out of it. How awful I was, how truly awful!" She then moved to the present, to his contacting her, the veiled threats, the car rides.

"I'm thinking right now, Ivan, just before I called you, that he might be much more damaged and dangerous than I wanted to believe." There was a long pause. "Ivan, I'm worried he might do something to you or Sonya."

Ivan was stunned. To have been with Dana for all these years and then to learn she had kept from him something so vital and terrible in her life. He felt betrayed. And then he put himself in her son's place and felt betrayed even more. She had abandoned her child. He wanted to reassure and support her, but his rage at her stood in the way.

"Dana, why didn't you ever tell me about him?"

"I thought you'd stop loving me. You know why. You've been on a damn crusade to condemn women who leave their children. And I was one of those women. You understand?" He tried to speak, but felt his voice was paralyzed.

"Ivan, say something to me, talk to me! My God, this is my worst fear, it's just what I thought, you're pulling away, you hate me for this." He knew he did, side by side with his love for her, he did. He also knew that the rage was not at its core meant for Dana. No, he knew now from his session with Jake where it really came from. He found his voice.

"Dana, I'm making you a scapegoat. I have a lot of confused feelings about what mothers do to their children. I'm beginning to understand that all this hatred of women is meant for my mother, for her dying, or killing herself, or whatever the hell she did."

He heard Dana crying on the other end of the phone. She was in such pain already that he wished he could avoid where he needed to go next. "Can you describe your son to me?"

"Why?"

"Just describe him, Dana."

"Alright. He has thick dark hair like mine. He's tall. How to describe him? He's intelligent, speaks well. At times he talks like he's saying lines he's memorized, like posturing or acting." Dana saw her son's face in her mind and searched for words to describe what was distinctive about it.

"Anything more, Dana, anything at all."

"Wait a second, Ivan, there is something else. Something about the way he looks, about his face. Very pale skin and . . ." and then it came her, "his eyes. Yeah, his eyes are strange. They look like my mother's eyes and Sonya's eyes, but there's something incredibly dark about them, and they don't seem to have any depth, almost like there are pictures of eyes on his face where the eyes should be. That's a really weird way to say it, but that's how he looks. I also think, Ivan, that there's something wrong with him, I mean physically, like he's ill or something."

"He is."

"He is? How do you know, Ivan, what are saying?"

"Dana, you've got to brace yourself for something. Your son has returned not only to your life, but to mine."

"What!"

He told her how a young man, who he now knew was her son, had come to see him as if he were wanting treatment, that Ivan had felt very engaged by him and then learned that he had been acting the part of a patient that he had invented.

Weiss wished he could stop the story right there. If I don't tell her the rest, maybe I can make it untrue. "Whether you say something or not, Dr. Weiss," his analyst had said, "will not make it true or untrue. That's just one of your efforts at magic, word magic."

"There's more, much worse," said Ivan. "He's kidnapped Sonya."

"Oh, my God, my God! Is she alright, Ivan, tell me she's alright!"

"He says she is . . . so far." Ivan told her of her son's AIDS, that he was dying, had nothing to lose, and that one condition for Sonya's release was that Weiss not go to the police. He told her that he felt the only way to get Paul to free Sonya was to reach him analytically, emotionally. Ivan told her that her son had just walked out in the middle of the session, that he had searched for him, but not found him.

"Ivan, you've got to find him! You've got to find her!"

"I'm trying. I sense his drama isn't over yet, and that I'm in the last act."

"Ivan, I'm sure you're right . . . There's something more I need to tell you." He could hear her again sniffling back tears. "He's known about you for a very long time. In my last letter to him, years ago, I told him that I had met you. I didn't tell him your name, of course, but he knows now . . . Ivan, I feel so terrible for screwing up his life."

"Dana, you were young, not much more than a child yourself, you can't hold yourself so responsible," he said, knowing from his own experience how heavy childhood guilt, no matter how irrational, can be.

"I am responsible, I am. But he doesn't just blame me. He blames you, too."

"What?"

"I told him that I couldn't come for him because of you."

"Because of me?"

"Because of you. I should never have told him anything about you, and I should have had the guts years ago to tell you about him. But you were on a mission, and there was no stopping you. I thought I'd lose you." Weiss understood the twisted course of blame that must have formed in Matin's mind.

"You know, Ivan, the funny thing, the awful thing about this, is that you were right. He is damaged, I did damage him by what I did." He wanted to lessen her burden of guilt, but he knew he could not.

"It happened, it's no one's fault." No one's fault. He thought of his own terrible burden of guilt over his mother's death.

"Should I stay here? His last condition was for me to stay here and wait for him."

"Come home. Knowing who he is, I think I understand what he's doing. He never intended to call you or see you again. He wants you to wait, uncalled, uncontacted, forever. He sent you there and promised to call, so he could leave you there, waiting, wondering, anxious, and disappointed. Doing to you what you did to him. Come home, Dana."

"I'm on the next plane. We've got to find her."

"We will, Dana, we will," he said, trying to sound certain, when in fact he was filled with doubt.

He drifted back to when he first met Dana. He now knew that she had been caught up in this secret struggle about her son. I had all my worries about her being involved with another man, about losing her. She was involved with another, but not a man, a boy, her son.

When the tower bell rung the hour, Weiss looked out his window at the students below flowing in and out of buildings in the Diag. He then followed a construction crane turning, stopping, and then lowering its load with impressive gentleness on the roof of a building under construction. A construction worker unhooked the steel beams from the cable and then signaled the operator above to lift the free hook, which swung wildly from a wind that had suddenly come up. Weiss looked up to see the sky now crowded with brilliantly white cumulous clouds, forming and reforming, racing across the sky.

Weiss returned to his desk. Waiting again. Nothing to do but hope he will make contact. From what Dana had told him, he now knew this troubled young man had waited forever. Weiss hoped Matin would not make him do the same.

*   *   *

He mustered enough strength to get his legs under him so he could continue the climb. He estimated that he had climbed a third of the way up the bell tower, when his energy had given out. He had pleaded with his legs to carry him on, but they would not respond. He had slumped to the floor. He had no idea how long he had rested.

He used what he had learned as an actor when he was playing a physically demanding part. Breathe from your diaphragm, slow and even. He made it to his feet, then he slowly lifted his body, stair by stair, up the tower. It struck him as neat and efficient, parsimonious, to be using up the last of his energy just as he would arrive at the point where he would no longer need anymore. The end of his supply of energy would exactly coincide with his exit from this world. Like returning a rental car with the tank empty, he thought, smiling at the absurdity of the comparison.

It was not just body fatigue that was interfering with his effort to get to the top of the tower and finish the plan. Since leaving Weiss' office and vomiting his guts out in the bathroom, his focus had been slipping. He tried to organize his attention around getting them all to play out the final scenes, but he was drawn, in spite of his efforts, back to the session with Weiss.

"I am your mirror . . ." he heard Weiss saying. "I felt teased and toyed with . . . seduced." Seduced by Brother Anthony, seduced by my mother's promises. "You are nowhere," he now heard Weiss saying. Feelings were starting to well up in him. Feelings he tried to swallow down were erupting like the vomit he had been unable to contain.

These feelings were sapping his determination to carry out the last part of the plan, but he managed to suppress them and return to his usual numb state. He knew that this state was now fragile, and that if he lived he would be unable to sustain it much longer. The only way to remain in the deadened state now was to be dead.

When he reached the top of the stairs, through a metal grid floor, he saw the bells. They looked like huge hoop skirts hanging in an enormous closet. He sank to the floor, took out his cell phone, and made the call.

*   *   *

John Farley had just returned to his office after another endless meeting. More meetings than police work, most of them unnecessary exercises in political correctness. These people were more intent on customer relations than on insuring public safety.

Though they had trouble meeting people, Ann Arbor was turning out to be in some ways what John and his wife had been looking for. Last weekend they had heard the blues singer David Bromberg, one of John's favorites, at the Ark, and seen a few days before an impressive production of *Long Day's Journey into Night*. Still John was missing what felt to him to be the real world, or at least a world that had become familiar to him, of drug dealers, thieves, hookers, along with ordinary people punching time clocks, working construction, struggling to make ends meet.

He was ready to call his wife, to tell her he thought moving to Ann Arbor had been a big mistake, when his secretary buzzed him.

"Detective, a Joseph Benedict on the phone." He punched the outside line and picked up the phone.

"John Farley."

"This is Joe Benedict, the guy with the harassment problem, you remember . . ."

"Yeah, I know who you are, so what is it?" said Farley, still impatient from the meeting and with Ann Arbor. He also continued to feel there was something off about this Joe Benedict and didn't want to be jerked around by him again.

"I know now who's been harassing me. He's a psychoanalyst. He said he wants to meet me. I'm going to meet him. I'm calling because I wonder if I should try to tape the conversation. Without him knowing, of course."

"You know, I don't think that's such a great idea. It's not even a good idea to meet him. I take it you know his name."

"Yes, Ivan Weiss." The name was familiar to Farley. As he talked, he pulled the file on the case from the corner of his desk. Ivan Weiss was the man the Psychology Department Chairman had said was doing research on criminal personality, the same area as Benedict. Maybe this guy's on the level, Farley considered, maybe this is a case of an academic turf war going too far.

"Did he say anything about why he's harassing you?"

"He said there's only room for one of us around here, the same stuff he's been saying, you know, like very territorial. He said we're doing research in the same area, studying the criminal mind I guess."

"So why does he want to meet you?"

"He said he could make my leaving the University, as he said, 'very attractive.'"

"Now that you know his name, you'd be better off just to file a complaint. If you're threatened again or followed, we could then get a court order to check phone records, or if it gets even worse, a restraining order. I'm not here to tell you what to do, that's your business, but I don't think it makes sense to meet him."

"Well, I've already agreed to."

"That's up to you, but I'll tell you again, I think it's a very poor idea. Are you meeting him in a public place?"

"Yeah, on Liberty across from Borders."

"I'd still advise you against it, but if you're set on it, make sure you stay in a public . . ."

"O.K, O.K." Matin interrupted, "I'll be careful," then he pressed "end." After he had pressed the numbers for the next call, he closed his eyes for a few minutes before sending it. Once he hit "send" he knew that he would be setting in motion the beginning of the end, the final act, at least for him. The other characters would go on without him to the end of the play.

*   *   *

Ivan had no idea how much time had passed before the phone finally rang.

"I'm at the top of the bell tower." The voice was weak but determined. "Be there. Now."

As Weiss threw on his coat, he thought of several suicides from Burton Tower over the past years, the most recent the wife of a Regent of the University. He rushed to the elevator which seemed to take forever to arrive. When the doors finally slid open, he was met with the round, smiling face of Steve Cernan, a psychiatrist in the building, pleasant man, mediocre therapist, good with medication.

"Ivan, I've been meaning to call you. I saw the notice of your paper on Manson, sounded fascinating, couldn't get there. I heard from Jake Hanson that it was great." All Ivan could think about was how to end the conversation by the time the elevator reached the ground floor. "Could I get a copy of the paper?"

"Sure, Steve."

"I'd like to take a look at it. You know I consult at Jackson Prison, and I've evaluated a few really cold blooded killers out there." The elevator was passing the fifth floor. "I've even tried some psychotherapy with one of them." Leave psychotherapy in the hands of professionals, Steve, thought Weiss, stick to medication. "If you've got a minute, I'd like to tell you about . . ." The elevator settled to a stop on the ground floor.

"Steve, I've got something urgent I've got to do right now. I'll get you a copy of the paper." The doors opened.

"Sure, Ivan, I know how it is. Our lives are dictated by . . ." Ivan bolted out of the elevator before Cernan could finish his sentence.

Once on the street he raced toward the tower. As he ran, a strong wind, thick with snow, flared into sudden gusts that stung his eyes. He pushed into the wind, while he tried to collect his thoughts. What Dana had told him about her son, his patient, his daughter's captor, helped Ivan understand more about Matin's suffering. He felt ready to use what he now knew to get to the long walled off, frozen feelings that were driving this cruel charade.

As he ran, he thought of his attraction to Matin. The fantasy of stroking his hair. The pleasure he had felt seeing him. He now understood why. There were blood ties between Paul and the two people Ivan loved most, his wife and his daughter. And Paul's eyes, like the eyes on the curtain in Ivan's dream, were familiar eyes, they were the eyes of his daughter. There was an echo of his love for his daughter every time he looked into Paul Matin's eyes.

He covered the three blocks from his office to Burton Tower in under three minutes. He entered the building, passed by the ticket office on the ground floor where he had often bought tickets to University events, passed some administrative offices, and found the elevator. He took the elevator to its top floor and found stairs that he climbed until they ran out. He looked up to see the darkness in the domes of the tower's bells. Though the chiming of the bells had for years been familiar time markers in his day, Weiss had never seen the bells and was amazed at their enormous size.

From the landing at the top of the last flight of stairs a narrow ladder continued up, its rungs so thin Weiss felt them through his shoes digging into the arches of his feet. When he had started his climb, he had pictured an observation deck at the top of the tower, like the one his parents had taken him to at the top of the Empire State Building. What he now found was completely different. The ladder that led up to a catwalk seemed makeshift and felt flimsy underfoot, especially in contrast to the massiveness and solidity of the bells. The higher he climbed, the more precarious the structure seemed that was supporting him. A fierce wind blasted through the belfry, the bells answering it with a deep hum. Behind that sound, Weiss could hear the metallic creak and rattle of someone above him. When the ladder ended, he was on a catwalk that spanned the south side of the tower. The belfry was mostly open, and the wind blew viciously now, only slightly tempered by the bells and the granite supports of the tower.

With the low winter sun behind Matin, Weiss saw his thin silhouette on the ledge.

CHAPTER THIRTY THREE

T he space heater was still throwing out a lot of heat, but her thirst, along with the trauma she had been through, had left her terribly fatigued. She still felt pride at how she had handled Paul, especially his attempt to rape her, and she knew that if she ever got through this, she would never feel again that awful powerlessness that had plagued her for the past year. But getting through this, that was the big if. The pipe she was locked to seemed as unnegotiable as gravity itself. She thought of cutting off her hand to escape. The image of blood draining out of her was hideous. She stroked one hand with the other, as if to reassure herself that they were both intact, and remembered the feel of Paul's hands. She was then startled to remember with a vividness she never had before the feel of the New York rapist's hands. Those hands, she was certain, were entirely different from Paul's.

*   *   *

The wind was whipping at the tall, thin man's clothes, and his hair was blown into a wild tangle. Weiss shielded his eyes with his hand to make out that Matin was standing with his back to Weiss, his feet only half on the ledge. Weiss shuffled his feet to announce his presence.

"Quite a view from up here," Weiss said as evenly as he could, hoping at least an illusion of calm might keep the young man from jumping. Matin carefully adjusted his footing to turn toward Weiss.

"Not as good as from a satellite, but not bad."

"Will you come back in?" said Weiss, extending his hand.

"No, I don't think so. This is my launch pad."

"Up into orbit?"

"No, to the next world."

"Are you going to take my daughter with you?"

"I don't know."

"Talk to me a while, you have nothing to lose."

"Nothing to lose is right. I've lost everything already, there's nothing more left." Weiss considered his next move. He wanted Matin to know, to feel, that Weiss deeply understood his feeling of having nothing left. Weiss could do this best by telling him he had talked to Dana. Ivan worried that telling him he had talked to his mother might make the young man feel things had spun out of his control or that his mother had let him down again. He would have another reason to be enraged and might show it by jumping. Weiss decided telling him that he had talked to Dana was worth the risk.

"Nothing more left. I can see how deeply you feel this. I know what happened, who you are. Dana, my wife, your mother, told me some of the story. I know she gave you up."

"That makes it sound so simple. She gave me up."

"It hasn't been simple for you at all, over these many years, to figure out why she did this. I know she held out promises to you and then let you down." Matin saw the last letter from her in his mind. I can't come for you, I've met someone, and I can't tell him about you. Matin with little scissors steps moved down the ledge, away from Weiss, toward the corner of the tower. Weiss thought he might jump, but his instinct was to say nothing. If he feels I'm trying to stop him, he might jump just to disappoint me. Disappointing me, leaving me waiting forever, leaving Sonya wherever he has her, would give him tremendous satisfaction. After a few anxious minutes for Weiss, Matin stepped back from the edge and pressed his back against the tower. Now Weiss felt it was time to speak to him again, but now Matin was too far down the ledge to hear him.

Ivan stepped up onto the ledge himself and eased slowly along it toward Matin. The wind came in such powerful, frigid gusts that he gasped for air. When he was close enough for Matin to hear him, Weiss worked to calm his anxious breathing enough to talk.

"Something is happening in you. In the office just before you left, you were telling me about the dog. When you looked into that stray dog's eyes you were in contact with your own wishes, maybe for the last time in your life. Like you sent the dog with all its needs away, you sent your feelings away. The dog was you. You made the dog feel what was unbearable for you.

"Just like with me. You've made me feel what is intolerable for you. Lost, scared, helpless. You protect yourself that way. Give someone your own terrible experiences. Then you can make believe you've gotten rid of them. Then you try to turn yourself into stone."

As Matin stood on the frigid ledge, with the wind blowing through him, so cold that he had lost all sensation in his hands and feet, he thought again of turning back, back into the tower, telling Weiss where he was holding Sonya and then dying the death meant for him, a slow AIDS death. He saw Weiss extending his hand, welcoming him. He saw himself arrested, then in a cell, but he had no fear of that. There was just something about going back. Undoing all that he had done. Retracing his steps. It felt like a grim, tedious shuffling through old files of a badly lived life. Nausea welled up in him again. Weiss had reached him, had touched him, but he could not go back. Like a gambler who can't bear to miss the next roll of the dice, he needed to see the plan unfold.

He pulled the cell phone from his pocket and made the last call.

Weiss saw Matin's acting ability once more. As soon as he'd punched in the numbers, Weiss saw him clothe himself in another character, breathing fast, a look of terror transforming his face.

"I need to talk to Detective Farley . . . What? You don't know where . . . Just find him, get him!" Matin said, all in a desperate sounding, breathless whisper. "Well just tell him this is Joe Benedict. The guy I went to meet, the one who's been harassing me, Ivan Weiss, is after me. You've got to come fast. He had a gun on me and forced me to go with him to the bell tower on campus. I've gotten away, for now, but he's after me. I told Farley all about it. The guy's crazy." With total conviction he acted the part of a man in the throes of a panic, a man running for his life. "He's coming, I hear him. I'm heading up the stairs of the tower. Help me!" He ended the call and let the phone drop through the snow and fog.

Weiss saw now with total clarity the scene, the tableau, that Matin was constructing.

"I see now what you're doing. It's all about showing what happened, saying to whoever is there to see the play, 'Look, this is the story!' With you it has to be dramatized," said Weiss. "So the police will come, while I'm trying to get you back in, and then you'll jump. You've set it up so they think I'm after you. You've arranged it so they'll think I forced you up here. Right so far?"

"Exactly right."

"When they get here, you'll begin to jump, I'll grab for you, because I need you . . . and want you alive. You'll jump, and it will look like I pushed you. In this last act of your life, you've cast me in the role of your killer."

Weiss tried to feel himself into the scene that Matin had so skillfully arranged. Weiss, Sonya, Dana, and even the police were like toys he was manipulating to tell his story. He was just doing it with real people. Weiss decided to try to read the story back to him. He knew this would be the most dangerous, high stakes, interpretation he would ever make. He also knew the police were on their way, so he had very little time. He steadied himself against the wind. He was so caught up in the importance of what he needed to do, that he blocked completely any awareness of how bitterly cold it was.

"So in the story I'm your killer. And I am. We both know that in a way I am. I never knew it, I never knew anything about you. But the way you see it, I have taken everything from you. Everything. Dana wrote to you that she had met me, couldn't tell me about you, and so dropped you. You think I destroyed your life. So you want to show this, for all to see. See, he pushed me, he killed me. You want me to pay for this. With guilt. With punishment.

"I pulled your mother away from you, and now you are determined to take Sonya, and Dana and me away from each other. You sent Dana to New York, Sonya to wherever you have her, and me, you hope, to jail for killing you. That's the scene. We're all apart, all separate. Feeling what you felt. Suffering the pain of abandonment, of isolation, of rejection. What has been locked up inside you all these years is now ours. In this carefully worked out drama, you're trying to evacuate from yourself, to spit out, the feelings of being a sad, little boy who's enraged with the mother who abandoned him. You are the dog, full of wishes to be mothered, the dog with sad eyes, who was sent away.

"You made me your mirror. I have the feelings you banished a long time ago. But you know what, Paul? You are my mirror, too." Matin, who had been gazing off into the distance, now met Weiss' eyes. "Yes, you are my mirror. I lost my mother, too. She died or killed herself, I don't know, but she was there one minute and then grabbed away from me the next. I see in you all of the longing and hate I still have. I see in you what I could have become. You went off to some remote, distant place. I didn't go that far. I didn't go up into that satellite of yours, into that airless vacuum of space, but I was headed that way. I know you, Paul Matin, I know the world you are living in."

As he said all this, Ivan was seeing another scene. He was running home, exuberant, full of anticipation, running with her love like a wind at his back, wanting to warm her with his success and then be wrapped in her pride. Running with the big news of himself, the big news, not just of *his* success at school, but *their* success. That was the great thing. Hers and his. United.

Around the corner, the wrong cars, scattered in that haphazard way around the house, his father in the middle of that awful mourners circle. Then his eyes sliding out of focus, falling. Slamming into her. Falling for her. Falling dead like her. Joining her.

They heard sirens now, distant at first, but fast approaching. Weiss had almost no time left. He knew where Matin was, because he had been there.

"I see you up here, like in the satellite, forever orbiting around her. Everything that happens to you is determined by her absence from your life. You're held in the grip of your needs for her, but you've felt you can never get to her, never touch her, never hold her." Matin swayed slightly in the wind, his shoes half over the edge. Ivan sensed deep inside himself how the earth below was like a mother drawing Matin down to her. "And now you think you can have her. If you jump, you will fall into her arms, you will smash into that mother earth down there. You will join her, become one with her, and at the same time you will throw yourself ragefully at her."

Matin's vision seemed to him to be blurring, and he realized that his eyes were filling with tears. Though the wind was bitterly cold, something in him was beginning to warm.

The sirens were louder now. They both looked down and saw police cars and fire trucks rounding the corner, passing the Graduate School building, and then jumping the curb on the way to the tower.

"I would lay down with that stray dog," said Matin, "and hug it and pretend it was her. It was so stupid to do that. I hate myself so much for doing that. I hate myself for wanting her. When I got the last letter, 'letter of the big goodbye,' I called it, I beat the dog. I beat it and beat it. It ran off a little way, but it was so stupid, it came back. And I beat it again."

"Like you, it kept having hope."

"But then it just gave up. Just gave up."

"Like you."

"Like me."

"Come back in now," said Weiss, moving with small, careful, sideways steps toward him. Then, when he was close, he extended his hand to the gaunt young man, shivering on the ledge. Matin put his hands down at his sides and shook his head.

"Tell me where she is."

Matin shivered in the wind. He then saw Sonya, cold like him, and scared. He began, for the first time, to feel her pain.

"My plan was when you got here, I would tell you how you might find your daughter . . . before I jumped. I was going to tell you that the location was hidden in the last dream I told you. It wouldn't be easy to figure it out, but you might be able to do it. Might."

"So maybe I'd rescue her, maybe someone would come for her, but maybe not," said Weiss. "I see now. You wanted Dana and me to suffer with a terrible uncertainty about whether we would ever see Sonya again. Sonya would be waiting in that same uncertain, desperate state. Then, we all would finally know the torture you went through."

"That's right," Matin said, fully understanding this himself for the first time.

"But maybe that's all unnecessary now," said Weiss, knowing that he had unlocked something in this poor, lonely, dying man.

Matin saw only the hand extended to him. He struggled to hold onto the sense of whose hand this was. That's Weiss' hand, trying to save me, to rescue me, that's right, it's his. Then it became other hands. Hands that slapped him at the orphanage, then the large callused hands of the farmer. Next the hand transformed itself into Brother Anthony's hand, gentle and soothing, yet dangerous at the same time. And finally her hand, the day she came for him and they drove to Nice, the hand he had first reached for tentatively, but then felt so secure when it wrapped itself around his. His mother's hand that so briefly held his and then forever released it. He reached for this hand.

Ivan saw Matin, first hesitantly, then with certainty, extend his hand for help. Weiss had succeeded.

At that point three things happened at once. A tremendous river of wind blew down from the top of the tower, a wind that seemed not to be made of ordinary air, but of something heavier and thicker. It pried them both away from the wall of the tower. At the same moment Farley and another policeman leaned out through the opening, startling both of the men on the ledge. And then, a split second later, after what sounded like a metallic, ratcheting of gears, from deep in the tower, came an explosion of sound. The huge center bell began to ring the hour.

Weiss felt as if the tower itself was summoning all its forces. It had shaped the wind which was now pouring down on them, had spit people out from its insides, and then had made its explosive sound, all to shake them off its granite body. Weiss managed to brace himself against all that seemed aligned to throw them off, but Matin was faring much worse against these forces. He was beginning to lose his balance, and in a desperate effort to regain it, he twisted his body back toward the tower. One of his feet slipped off the edge and the other began to lose its traction on the icy surface. He opened his arms wide as if he were ready to embrace someone and then grabbed wildly for anything to hold on the tower's sheer face.

*   *   *

It was a dream only of sounds. First the faint sounds from outside the building that had filtered into her sleep. Her dreaming mind transformed them into the louder, closer sounds of cars passing by her on the street, as she walked back to her New York apartment. It was more than totally dark in the dream. It was as if there were no such thing as light or color or the power of sight to sense them. Just sound. Somehow in this world of her dream she knew, as if by some special aural sense, how to make her way to her apartment. She maneuvered around cars as she crossed streets. She heard all of the sounds of the city with a vividness she had never experienced, the sounds of people walking and talking, horns, radios from windows of apartments high above the street, someone behind her coughing, jackhammers, cars starting and stopping. By this magic hearing in the dream, she could not only tell how to get back to her apartment, she knew just where she was along the way. And she could also identify people with this special sense. As she approached her apartment, she knew the old woman who lived next door was coming down the street. She said hello to her, and the woman greeted her back. Hearing was all she needed. She turned the last corner before her apartment house.

Then he grabbed her and wrestled her down the stairs into the entryway of a basement apartment. He forced her against the wall. He tore open her clothes and was about to rape when she said, "I know who you are." She didn't have to see him, she just knew, she could tell this time, by the sounds he made, by the few words he spoke, who he was. I know you, I know you. You're not going to make every man my rapist, because I know now who you are. In this special world where what I hear is all I need, you can force my face against the wall, but I know who you are. Then, as she tried to form her mouth into his name, she woke up.

*   *   *

Weiss could clearly see that Matin had not intended to jump. At least not at that moment. Maybe later, maybe after telling Weiss, which he was about to do, where he had taken Sonya. Weiss released his grip on the wall of the tower and grabbed for the young man's shoulder. He managed to catch a fold of Matin's jacket, but as soon as his fingers began to close around it, the slick wet fabric of the windbreaker slipped through them. Weiss caught the sight one last time of Matin's eyes which still seemed flat, painted on, as he fell soundlessly into a cloud of swirling snow. Weiss looked down, but could see only snow, flying horizontally in sheets, completely obscuring the ground below.

Weiss felt rooted to the spot. He looked to the two cops, leaning out, their mouths moving, but the ferocity of the wind blowing toward them completely blocked their words. The wind seemed more determined than ever to pry him loose. It seemed to be laying claim to the tower, trying to sweep Weiss off it, so it could go on caressing, unobstructed, the contours of the tower's granite skin.

He managed to flatten himself against the wall, facing toward the tower, hugging it, as if to camouflage himself from the relentless wind. He fought it for each small step. The closer he inched toward safety, the harsher the wind seemed to blow. His face was now biting with cold.

So cold now. So hot then. So hot when he ran home into that clot of people, into that terrible vacancy she had left. Hot then, cold now, but the same. Once more he had failed to rescue. The wind is out to punish me, to destroy me for both of my failures.

A mass of pellet-like snow, carried on a powerful gust of wind, lashed his face and stung his eyes. He reflexively closed them. When he opened them, they burned even more, and he closed them again. Robbed of sight, buffeted by the wind, he began to lose his balance. As he had just seen Matin do, he grabbed futilely for the tower.

He knew his balance was completely lost. The terror of the complete certainty that he was going to die shot through him. As he began to fall back, "I deserve this," flashed through his mind. His arms still outstretched, he felt himself giving in, letting go, falling.

Then he felt a pair of hands clamp on his right forearm. And an instant later another pair surrounded his left. His feet then slipped off the ledge, but they had him firmly in their grasp. They pulled him up and in.

He lay on the catwalk and caught his breath as he looked at the two cops, a young uniformed one and an older one in plain clothes with a craggy, weathered face and soft eyes.

"You alright?" asked the younger one.

"Yeah, yeah, I'm O.K . . . Thanks for saving my life."

"It was damn close," said the older, plainclothes one, with some accent Weiss tried to place, maybe southern. "That last step brought you just near enough to grab. Awful close, whew . . . Let's all calm down a minute, then we'll need to ask you some questions."

In a normal state of mind, Weiss would have explained to this cop who seemed calm and reasonable what had happened, how the whole terrible drama had been set up, but he was wracked by guilt over his two failed rescues, of his mother years ago and now Matin. He was terrified that he would fail yet again, this time to rescue Sonya. In his mind he was sure he would never be believed. He felt he was the only one to blame, the one to be punished. And these cops were going to do it. Ivan's father's fear of police was also in the center of his mind. The police are the Gestapo. No cop could be trusted.

He got to his feet.

"Hey, look what's going on down there?" Ivan said, leaning over the ledge and pointing animatedly toward the ground below. "Is that guy still alive?"

"What ya pointing at?" asked the uniformed cop, straining to see what Weiss was trying to show them.

"Over there, there, that's the guy, he's walking away!" As the two cops searched for what Weiss was pointing at, he backed quietly away, jumped down seven or eight feet to a lower catwalk and escaped with the urgency of a fugitive.

CHAPTER THIRTY FOUR

D ana looked down as the plane circled over the ocean and made a big sweeping turn to the west. After talking to Ivan, she had rushed back to her hotel, crammed everything into her carry-on, grabbed a cab to the airport, and managed to get the last standby seat to Detroit. Somewhat rudely, she discouraged conversation with an elderly woman seated next to her. She was not in the state of mind for any idle conversation. She needed to plan what she would do next. She tried to map out what she would do when she landed, how she could help Ivan find Sonya.

Yet, as she tried to think about the future, her thoughts kept returning to the past. She remembered that first romance. The Swiss boy with the penetrating dark eyes and incredibly white skin. He was such a gentle boy and seemed, in contrast to the boys at home, so grown up, so worldly. Like her, he was with his parents at the ski resort. Like her, he was so impatient with being a teenager. More than the pleasure and newness of that first sex, they both believed that in the instant of their intimacy they could traverse their adolescence. And when she felt the tenderness in her breasts and those impossible to describe changes in the rest of her body, she felt it was confirming the arrival of adulthood. That is, before the reality hit her that she was little more than a child, now a pregnant one. As she looked down from the plane at the miniature world below, she wondered for the first time if it had been better for Paul that she had given him up. Being so terribly immature, could she have been any kind of decent mother to him? She didn't know.

*   *   *

Ivan rifled through his file cabinet for the process notes on Matin's sessions. The file was gone. He pulled out all the files under M. Not there. Did I take it home? Or to the Clinic? He was sure he didn't, but where was it?

He was in such a frenzy that it took him a moment to remember that he had just learned Matin's real name and that he had known him as Adam Stone. He looked under S, and there it was. He was so rushed, and his hands were shaking so badly, that he was tearing the sheets as he searched through the file for the crucial process notes, the notes on the last dream, the one that Matin had said contained clues to where he had taken Sonya. He knew the police would be there any minute, but he couldn't leave without being sure he had the notes on that dream. Ivan felt he was the only one who could find her, and knew that Matin's last dream, or pseudodream, was the key.

Just as he found the notes on the dream, he heard the sirens close by. They were growing louder, but had not yet stopped. The police were not there yet. Very soon, he knew, but maybe there was still time. He ran to the elevator, pushed the down button and almost immediately the doors opened. And the elevator was empty. A little luck, finally.

Really the second bit of luck. He had been clever, but also lucky, to have eluded the police when he had fled from the top of the tower. He had jumped to the lower catwalk, while the cops took more time climbing down the ladder, so he gained a few steps on them, but it was just simple luck that when he got to the lobby of the tower, it was filled with people who had been ordered, after Matin fell, to evacuate the building. He had managed to get lost among them and flashed his University ID to a security guard who was not checking names. Just as he had come around the south side of the tower, he had seen in a cordoned off area Matin's body being lifted out of the blood stained snow onto a gurney.

When the elevator door opened on the lobby level, Weiss could see two uniformed cops talking to the doorman. Just as one cop began to turn to look at the elevator, Weiss moved out of view, into the front corner of the elevator, near the buttons. He was less than ten feet from the cops. It might be suspicious, he thought, if the elevator left the moment it arrived at the lobby, so he stayed where he was, hoping the cops were not ready yet to take the elevator up to his office. Luckily again, they were not done with the doorman. Luck, he reminded himself, is just magical thinking. Just probabilities coming out my way. All the same, Ivan was looking for some larger force, for anything, to help him out.

"We're going up to his office in a minute. If he comes in, you let the officer in the car outside know. Got it?"

"I'm not sure I can do that . . ." Weiss tried to place the voice. There were five or six regular doormen, but he couldn't connect this voice with any of them.

"Listen don't screw around with us. You tell the officer when this Dr. Weiss comes in."

"I'm trying to cooperate. I just don't know what Dr. Weiss looks like."

"What?"

"This is my second day. I've learned the names of only a few people in the building." Luck again, a new doorman, I don't know him, he doesn't know me. And he probably doesn't know either about the exit off the utility room that leads into the health food store next door.

Enough time had passed for Ivan to push the button. He went to the second floor, got off, and took the stairs back down to the lobby level. The exit from the stairway was by a door that led to the health food store.

The always talkative owner of the store, who never missed an opportunity to argue with Ivan the relative merits of psychoanalysis and homeopathy, was fortunately engaged with another customer. Ivan poked around the vitamins for a minute and then left the shop by its street entrance. As he came out into the air, he was filled, at least for the moment, with a terrific sense of freedom. Clutching Matin's file, he walked slowly from the building to avoid drawing any attention, and when he was a block away, broke into a run.

Back in his car, Ivan pulled out the notes on Matin's last dream. Just as he began to read, his cell phone rang.

"Ivan, I just landed at Metro. I'm half out of my mind. You must be, too. Anything on Sonya?"

"No, nothing yet."

"Did you find Paul, could you get him to tell you where she is?" Ivan felt paralyzed. How to tell her. Her son was dead. Should he wait or tell her now? He knew he needed to tell her, but he couldn't bring himself to do it.

"No, Dana, I looked everywhere for him, but couldn't find him. I have no idea where he is."

"Ivan, what's going on?" She could hear the strain and stiffness in his voice. "Is there something you're not telling me?" Ivan knew that his wife was so emotionally tuned in to him, that he could never successfully lie to her. He tried to find the words to tell her what had really happened, but there were none. He couldn't bring himself to tell her he had failed to save her son.

"No, Dana, there's nothing more. I wish there were." I wish, Ivan thought, there were less tragic, horrific things that needed to be told. "Dana, I need to go."

"Where are you going, Ivan?"

"I don't know yet. Paul told me," on the ledge, but he let Dana believe it was in his office, "that a dream he made up has in it clues to where he's taken Sonya. I've got to work with it."

"Ivan, what can I do? What should I do?"

"There's nothing for you to do. No, there is one thing – remember that Paul . . ." he almost said "was," " . . . is so disturbed and such a good actor that he has set things up to make me look like the worst kind of man. What you can do, Dana, is to remember who I am."

"Of course, Ivan, of course I will . . . Be careful." They were both silent for a few moments. "I know who you are Ivan. I love you. But I know you're not telling me something."

Just as Ivan finished talking to Dana, a police car drove past. His father's warnings about the police echoed in his mind. "Ivan, Ivan, you have a lot to learn." Weiss knew he would not be able to let his mind do the work it would have to while he was sitting there in his car downtown, distracted by worry about the police. He could not, of course, go home or to the Clinic. He put the car in gear and drove to Gallup park, on the edge of the city, where he often ran. He pulled into a parking area, where he had often seen people sitting in their cars, enjoying the view. Would be nothing unusual to be sitting there in his. He wondered if a bulletin had gone out on him. Probably, he thought, but that's got to take some time. But then again it had not taken the police long to find his private office.

He began reading the notes on Matin's last dream. It was a dream he had talked about in the session before he revealed that he had created the false persona and that he had kidnapped Sonya.

> The patient reported a dream of being at a lecture. An older man, a famous man is giving a talk. The man climbs up on a high platform, but it's more like flimsy scaffolding and could collapse. The patient reports expecting a lot from this speaker, but then as the dream unfolds, he sees the lecturer as very short, with stains on his shirt, mismatched clothes, clown hair. The audience is laughing while the patient listens attentively and feels sorry for the old man.

Weiss ran his hands over his face and felt the tightness of his brow. He took a few deep breaths to relax. He closed his eyes and brought up the image in the dream. The man is put literally on a pedestal and then is made to fall. The patient in the dream is apparently on the lecturer's side, supporting him, regarding what he says as important. He feels sorry for the man, while the audience cruelly, sadistically laughs. He wants it to emerge that he knew about my talk at the Institute. He wants me to discover that the figure in the dream is me.

> I make the interpretation to him that the whole dream is his own creation, to show him that he is representing himself not just as himself in the dream. He's also the audience that mocks me. Patient then tells me how clever my interpretation is. I point out that he's just called me a fool in the dream and now, by telling me how clever I am, is elevating me. Patient seems to have insight into this, sees that he's challenging and provoking me. He recognizes that he did the same thing with the Chairman of his department. Both with the Chairman and with me, he seeks to provoke with antisemitic thoughts, thinking in the session of "kikes in the ghetto."

How is a place, a real location represented in some hidden way in this dream? There are locations in the dream, a lecture hall, the Psychoanalytic Institute, and Farmington Hills, where the Institute is located. There's a view of the lecturer as a clown. Clown, circus. Nothing there. Back to the notes.

> I ask about the setting of the dream. The patient looks surprised, as if
> this was connected with fresher, more emotionally important material. We
> explore the setting of the dream. The lecture takes place outside, on a large
> floating expanse, like a barge. He's at the very back edge, ready to slip off.

Knowing what he had learned from Dana this was now clear. He is the forgotten one, in the last row, ready to fall off, to be dropped. Dropped by his mother, he'll drown. He can't survive without her. Though he had intended this to be a fake dream, it still tells something basic about him. The unconscious always finds a way to express itself.

> He sees on the bank huge silos. New and shiny. Appealing, inviting.
> Beyond them everything looks different, dark and bleak. Deserted streets,
> everyone gone.

Though not included in his notes, Weiss remembered now the physical feeling of emptiness and cold that had run through him when he had first heard this part of the dream. A feeling I should have listened to. I will listen to it now.

At first there is brightness, the shiny silos, but beyond that, after that, is bleakness and loneliness. Everyone's gone. The streets are deserted. He is deserted. From the danger of falling into the water and drowning to the shiny appealing silos to the abandoned streets.

Not an oedipal story at all. The pretense he constructed, made to sound oedipal, was just a thin veneer over the real story. This story seems to be from much earlier in life, the story of a very little boy's early, traumatic loss of his mother and hope for her return. Promise and then stinging loss and loneliness.

Ivan played with his associations to silos. He wished he had the patient's associations, but that was impossible. He would need to rely on what psychoanalysts are usually careful to avoid, using his own associations to the patient's dream images. Silos. The terrible farm where Dana had told him Matin had been placed. Silos filled with endless supplies of food. The vast, cavernous nothingness of an empty silo. Plenty and then emptiness.

The patient at the end of the session announces with a defiant edge in his voice that he has begun seeing a "new woman." He feels that I'll oppose this. I'm seen as a prohibitive father who stands in the way of his relationships with all women. Probably a transference from the father who stood with his foot on the patient's neck. This transference fear leads the patient to tell me about the woman only when he is already on his feet, so he can run from the unconsciously imagined consequences.

More of the oedipal drama. No father stood with his foot on Matin's neck. For all Ivan knew there may never have even been a father in the patient's childhood. But now another chill ran through Weiss. The "new woman" was, of course, Sonya.

Ivan again pulled himself back to the main task, the setting of the dream. The places in the dream. A lecture, the Psychoanalytic Institute, Farmington Hills, the University, Ann Arbor. All possibilities. But considering what kind of person Matin was, and what demons he was struggling with, these places were all too benign. Too standard, too dull. Matin's place needed to be darker.

And then the water. Water, universal unconscious image of the mother, must be a crucial part of this dream. Rough and turbulent water. What water? Michigan is surrounded by water, most of its borders are defined by the various Great Lakes. And much of this water could be at times turbulent. Ships had sunk in rough water in all of the Great Lakes, and the Straights of Mackinac were notorious for dangerous currents and winds so high that cars had been blown off the bridge that spanned them.

And rivers. The river Ivan knew best, the Huron, that winds through Ann Arbor, was always fairly slow and calm, but many others farther north, the Pine, the Rifle, the Au Sable, and the Manistee, which Ivan and Dana had canoed, ran high and powerful in the spring and early summer.

The answer was not going to be found in looking for turbulent waters alone. They were everywhere. Weiss was growing discouraged and frightened. Maybe, he thought, this is a puzzle that was meant for me never to solve. Maybe this is Matin's last legacy. His life finally came to nothing, so Dana's and Sonya's and mine are supposed to come to nothing, too.

Weiss tried to put his pessimism aside and continued on. He thought about his session with Jake. Jake's way of working, he had seen firsthand, was so different from his own. It was closer to direct experience. And something more. Visual. Weiss stepped back from the dream and tried to "see" it, to feel himself into it and look out at the dream scene through the dreamer's, or pseudodreamer's, eyes. What was Matin seeing when he made up this dream?

Weiss descended into Matin's fantasy. Although it was a bleak place to be, he knew he had to settle himself behind the dead man's eyes.

CHAPTER THIRTY FIVE

Dana picked up her truck at airport parking and drove fast on the snowy roads to Ann Arbor. In spite of the bricks in the bed of the truck, she began to skid several times. Finally she eased up and found a speed at which the truck stayed just on the edge of control.

The radio, tuned as always to the University radio station which she usually liked, felt now annoying and irrelevant. She was about to turn it off, when a special news report came on.

> *"An unidentified man died today after he fell from Burton Tower, on the main campus of the University of Michigan. He and an older man were out on a ledge at the top of the tower, which houses the University Carillon. Detective John Farley of the Ann Arbor Police Department said that it is unclear if the man jumped or was pushed to his death by the older man, who fled the scene. Though neither have been identified, Detective Farley said, in a phone interview, that he is fairly sure of the identity of both of the men, but declined to provide that information at this time. The man who fled is being sought. Asked if this case is being investigated as a homicide, and if the man who fled is a suspect, the Detective said nothing has been ruled out."*

Dana tried to tell herself that no names had been mentioned, but she knew in her heart that it was her son who had fallen to his death and her husband who was now fleeing from the police. She knew now what Ivan had been holding back on the phone.

She pulled off at a rest stop in Ypsilanti, turned off the engine, and looked out across a field at the remains of last year's corn, dead broken stalks, poking up through the crust of ice and snow. She lowered her head onto the steering wheel, felt a wave of sadness wash through her, and cried. He had reentered her life, as she somehow always knew he would, just before he exited his. He needed, she thought, to return to deliver me and my family a cruel goodbye.

She saw Paul and Ivan on the ledge. Could Ivan have pushed him? Had he figured out where Sonya was and then become so enraged at what her son had done to their daughter that he pushed him? She tried to imagine it. No. That just isn't Ivan. He is such a loving and nonjudgmental man. He has such amazing tolerance and forgiveness for the criminals he studies, many of whom have committed horrendous crimes. But these people, she reminded herself, had never threatened or harmed anyone Ivan loved. Then she remembered what Ivan had said to her on the phone, to remember who he is. He had been trying to tell her to remember that he is not a murderer, that he could never be.

She knew now what she needed to do. Ivan had one singleminded goal, to find Sonya. He would do whatever was necessary to evade anyone who threatened to stand in his way. That's probably why he ran, she thought. With his suspicious nature, Dana knew he would never trust the police at a time like this. Knowing how clever and manipulative Paul could be, she knew Ivan would have good reason to worry that he would not be believed. He is wasting his time and energy right now trying to avoid being captured, energy that he could be devoting to finding Sonya. They need to know that Ivan could never murder anyone. I need to convince them to call off their pursuit. I must clear away any obstacles that stand in the way of Ivan finding their daughter. She started up the truck, returned to the expressway and drove, now with a focus, to the police station.

*   *   *

The generator was out of fuel. The heater stopped and the room was again plunged into darkness. Sonya felt her body's heat draining from her, and with it, her life. Though there was still food, the water was gone. More importantly, she knew he was gone. From the way he had walked out and never looked back, she felt somehow certain he would never come back. He could now no longer in an active way hurt her. She would never need to summon up from within herself every last bit of mental and physical energy to stop him from forcing himself into her, but at the same time he could now kill her by never coming back, kill her with his abandonment. Why had he done this to her? She knew there was some connection between them, some bond. She thought of him saying they were opposites. And that they had come through the same door.

Though she tried to push aside thoughts of her own death, they kept creeping back into her awareness. She began to think very specifically about how she might die. Hypothermia was most likely. Or she might die of thirst. Her mouth was parched, and she was growing increasingly lightheaded; she knew she was already seriously dehydrated. She remembered a doctor saying when her mother's father was dying of cancer that dehydration was the friend to the dying patient, for it brought on more quickly the final escape from cancer and its pain.

Several times she thought she heard footsteps and called out for help, her shouts answered once by the startled cry of an alley cat and at other times by the chaotic scampering of mice or rats. Though she thought she had managed to put some limits on the fear of her own death, that was all shattered by the morbid thought of these unseen rodents, no longer scared off by her shouting, invading the room and then her decaying body. That was followed by the return of the thought, now less abhorrent to her, of cutting off her hand to free herself. But even if I wanted to, she thought, how would I do it, what would I do it with?

She heard again the helter skelter running in the walls, grabbed some coins from her pocket and flung them at the door. In the dark she heard them bounce off and scatter, before everything was quiet again. After a while, she calmed herself with a sense of her parents and Jerry being there, off to the side, ready to come for her, to take her hand, to lead her out.

*   *   *

When Dana told the desk sergeant why she was there, he picked up the phone, said a few words, then quickly came out from behind the Plexiglas screen and rushed her up to an office on the second floor.

A broad shouldered detective with a weathered face and inviting, playful eyes, was already on his feet, when she was shown in. He reminded her immediately of several horse trainers she had known, men who didn't compete, but who had an instinctive sense of horses. These men, though they had a natural way with the animals, were often however, not particularly good with people. She hoped this man was different.

"I'm John Farley," the detective said, patting a chair near his to suggest she sit down. She ignored this, too agitated to sit, and launched right away into why she was there.

"I'm pretty sure I know the man who just died . . . was killed, falling from the bell tower." She hesitated, seeing in her mind for a moment the little boy, many years before, huddled in the corner of the car, running his fingernail along the grooves of the carseat. "And I think I know the man who was up there with him."

"Maybe the best way to tack this down is for you to describe the man who died." She did.

"Sounds like him. And the other man?" It was much harder to describe the man who was so much a part of herself, difficult to step back and describe him from a stranger's point of view.

"Five ten, dark hair, brown kind of sunken eyes, angular features, medium build, and . . . solid." Solid, yes, thought Dana, that captures him well, solid and not just physically, more than that, a solid, reliable man.

"That sounds like the other man. Two for two." Farley sat down on the corner of his desk, picked up a pad and gestured to her to tell her story. The way he swept his hand out toward her and drew it back to himself, as if he were clearing a space in the air for her words, reminded her of Ivan. It made her more comfortable.

She had rehearsed on the drive from the airport how she would condense this long, sad, complicated story. Most of all she had tried to work out how she could be the most convincing. She needed to be believed. As she looked into the leathery, expectant face of this detective, the outline she had constructed was lost.

"God, how to tell you all this. The man who died was my son, illegitimate son, I had him when I was a teenager, in France. I was just a kid, my father was working there. I never told my husband, Ivan. He was the other man up there on the tower. I'm sorry I keep jumping around." She struggled to organize her story. "So, Paul, Paul Matin, that was my son, came back into my life. I was scared to tell my husband about him. It'd take too long to go into that, but I just couldn't tell him. Paul made veiled threats if I didn't do what he said. All he seemed to want was for me to pick him up and drive him places. I think he just wanted me to be there. Then he told me to meet him in New York and he'd leave my life . . . It was terrible what happened to him, what I did to him. He was moved around a lot when he was young. Not good places. I don't think there was anyone who really loved him. It left him with a lot of pain. And anger. So he forced himself into all of our lives, not just mine. I've just found out about this. He went to my husband posing as a patient. Worst of all he got involved in my daughter's life," she felt herself shaking, "and . . . kidnapped her."

"Kidnapped her!"

"Yeah. And now he's dead, which is terrible enough, but we don't know where she is. Or even if she's still alive." Though she had told the story in a scattered way, she sensed he was following her and hoped he believed her.

"Do you have any idea where he took her?"

"No, but Ivan said that Paul told him a dream that has clues to where she is. He's trying to find her."

"We will too." Farley picked up the phone, reported the kidnapping, and asked for a couple of detectives to be assigned to work with him on it. Then he turned back to Dana. "Your husband would have good reason, wouldn't he, to be plenty fed up with this guy. Did he push him?" He gets right to the point, she thought.

"I asked myself that. That was the first thing I thought. But, I have no doubt about the answer. He's just not that kind of person. I guess anyone could do something like that, but he didn't do it. I just know it."

She couldn't read Farley. Was he believing her? She had thought so before, but now began to doubt it. She needed to convince him. She told him that another reason she was sure Ivan couldn't do this is because more than anyone else, even more than most psychoanalysts, he understood the underlying causes for someone doing what Matin had done. This was her husband's area of study, the effects of early childhood loss on criminal behavior. He has interviewed many criminals with this type of early history and has a great deal of empathy for them.

"He doesn't blame people. Even when he should, he doesn't blame them." She realized that wasn't quite true. "No, he does blame, he blames mothers, he blames me. But he doesn't blame the child." Dana broke into tears. "I feel awful about what I did. When Paul was young I told him I'd come for him and then backed out. I let him down. I have to say this, and I feel terrible about it," she said, turning away, unable to face the detective, "I'm also glad my son's dead."

Her mind wandered back to her parents wanting her to have an abortion. Many years later, she thought, that's just what has happened, his young life has been aborted. "I'm glad to be free of the threats and manipulation. He was a master of dragging us all, Ivan, Sonya, and me, into his awful charade."

"He was good at it. Roped me in, too." Dana looked puzzled, and he told her of Matin's coming in to complain that he was being harassed. First it had been a mystery man and then he called today and said he'd discovered it was a psychoanalyst, Ivan Weiss. He told her Matin's story that her husband was caught up in some crazy vendetta with him.

"He told me that your husband was trying to force him out of town."

"Well, long ago, in a way, Ivan did just that," she said, remembering, of course, writing in her last letter to her son that it was because of Ivan that she would never come for Paul. Now it was Farley who looked puzzled. Dana was too exhausted to explain.

"Let me be blunt with you, Mrs. Weiss. We're considering your husband as a possible suspect. There's a bulletin out to bring him in for questioning. I'd like to believe what you say about him, but we have no choice but to try to pick him up. Is there any way to contact him? Cell phone, pager?"

"He has a pager that he never carries, but he has a cell phone." Though she had reached him earlier on it, she had been surprised, because he rarely remembered to keep it on or charged. She tried it anyway, but there was no answer.

"How about a machine or voicemail?"

"He usually checks his office answering machine every few hours in case of patient emergencies, even his e-mail a couple of times a day, but I don't know if he will with what's going on."

"Sure, but leave messages wherever he might pick them up anyway. Tell him to call you immediately. He's got to come in. Not just because we want to question him, but for his own sake, too."

"What do you mean?"

"What I mean is that whatever he did or didn't do up there on the tower, he's in danger too."

"What kind of danger?"

"He's in a squeeze play, a man pressed from all sides. He's desperate to find your daughter, and he knows we're after him. He's going to do anything he can to stay clear of us, so that nothing gets in the way of his search." Dana knew this was absolutely true of Ivan. "He's apt to do some risky things, some dangerous things. I've seen people caught like this get themselves into big trouble, real fast. I'm also worried about some cop spotting him, trying to apprehend him, him running, the cop overreacting. You get the picture." He saw the fear in her eyes. This fear, he knew, was the real thing. "We need to get through to him. And we need to find that daughter of yours."

"We've just got to," she said.

"We'll do our best," he said, gently resting his hand for a moment on hers.

*   *   *

A large rusted out car pulled into the parking lot near Ivan. He could see through his fogged window an old couple inside it sitting close to each other talking. Then a young woman pulled in, took her little girl from her car seat, wrestled a large sled from the trunk and settled the child on it. She pulled her across the lot, then off onto a path by the river. Then a more troubling car approached, this one ambiguous. Full size, new, with the nondescriptness of an unmarked police car. "One day the police are there to protect," he heard his father say, "the next they are rounding up Jews. You remember this, Ivan." Weiss was taking no chances. He started his car and slowly drove out of the park.

Fearing there would be more police patrolling expressways, he took secondary roads out of town. He drove north and found himself in the small town of South Lyon where he turned onto a snow covered dirt road. He passed a few farms, pulled off to the side of the road, and turned off the engine. He reclined his seat back and set forth, sometimes by just thinking, sometimes by talking out loud, on his last journey into the dead Paul Matin's mind.

I am Paul Matin. I am a frozen man, dead before my real death. I am a mistake of a teenage girl. I have always lived on a rough sea, shifting, unstable. At the center of myself is a huge emptiness. I was desperate as a child to fill it. I turned to anyone who showed interest in me. I became easily filled with promise and hope. I was a promising boy, a good boy. Someone will surely come along and be my good parents.

I'm on the very back of this barge, the legs of my chair teetering over the edge. Will I stay afloat or will I fall off, be left behind, drown? You said, mother, you would come for me, you would save me. You promised to bring me to your calm waters. Promises. Disappointments. The gnawing hope became too much. So I became a frozen boy. I walked etherized through life.

Then I learned a way I could thaw myself out enough to feel something and avoid the pain. I could make other people have the feelings I couldn't bear to have anymore. And then, by looking at them, I could safely look at myself. And feel sort of alive.

This is what I did with Sonya. I am a promising client to her, like I was a promising patient to her father. I even offer her more, a romance. And then I disappoint her. I isolate her from the people she loves and make her wait forever. She's now me.

I did the same with places. Find a place that expresses the essence of my inner world. And so I found just the right place to take her, a place that resonates with what is inside me.

Weiss thought about the final dream and struggled to stay inside Matin's mind. It was a dark and hopeless place, and Weiss wanted to get out. He managed to stay in it. What would make a place just right? He worked to visualize the water, the silos, and the vacant streets. He found again Matin's voice.

Turbulent water, but that's not enough. It needs to be turbulent water near a place of my own despair. Rough water that is near an abandoned, hopeless place. Water near a place of promise aborted. A place teased and tempted by the possibility of rescue and change.

I am back to the water in my dream. The place must have this rough water. Unreliable, hazardous water that threatens my survival. It runs by a place of my shattered hopes, a place defeated. A place waiting, like I waited for you, at the farm, at the orphanage, waiting and waiting.

Then Weiss saw it.

It was the most obvious thing in the world. He saw Dana and himself, late one summer evening, years before, after the Detroit Montrose Jazz Festival in Hart Plaza, walking toward the water, standing at the railing, looking across it at the Seagrams sign on the Canadian shore, a tanker moving against its powerful current.

The Detroit River.

Calm appearing, but cruel underneath. Its surface inviting, promising, its currents treacherous and deadly. Mother river, river that passes me by. Rough, unloving water. An untrustworthy river ready to catch me with its sudden, dangerous currents.

Detroit River, river of Detroit. Detroit. A city worn down by poverty and neglect, ripped apart by riots and then left to decline. A city also struggling to come back, trying to revive itself, waiting to be rescued. The city mirrors Matin's inner world. The shiny silos. The most prominent feature of this dream landscape. The real landscape too. What could they be? The visual has got to be the key. The shape, cylinders, large ones, shiny.

Then he saw them – the towers of the Renaissance Center, the Ren Cen as Detroiters called it, on the Detroit River. A hotel and office complex built in the 70's with the hope that it would be a renaissance for the city. Renaissance, rebirth. Promise. Promise unfulfilled. In the shadow of the Ren Cen are the abandoned streets of a city waiting to be nurtured back to health. Waiting to be loved.

Weiss pulled a map of Detroit from the glove compartment. He unfolded it and laid it on the car seat. He located the Detroit River and the Renaissance Center. He fished around in the console for a pen. He drew a line from a point in the middle of the Detroit River behind the Ren Cen through the complex and beyond. He followed the line, the course of the dreamer in the dream, flying over the Ren Cen into the deserted streets. It crossed Jefferson, which ran along the river, and picked up Randolph. It then ran a short way along Congress. Though Ivan didn't know Detroit well, he knew that so far the line had passed through a thin margin of development by the river, government and office buildings, banks, a few restaurants.

The line continued to Cadillac Square, a once elegant European style plaza, that was showing a few signs of improvement, but was still in very rough shape. It then picked up a major north-south street, a Detroit landmark, once thriving, now the symbol of the city abandoned – Woodward Avenue. The line on the map drawn from the path in the dream ran almost exactly along Woodward. The street captured the essence of Matin's world, neglected and abandoned.

But where along the line? He had no idea where to start once he got there, but he knew he must go there, follow the street, and try somehow to look at it through Matin's eyes.

He started the car, turned it around, and glancing at the map still laid out next to him, planned a route, avoiding expressways, to downtown Detroit. He drove south where he picked up Michigan Avenue, the old route from Detroit to Chicago, and took it east. He turned on the radio to see if there were any reports of Matin's death. He turned to the University public radio station, hoping irrationally to hear the usual uneventful local news. Immediately after the national news the lead local story was, of course, Matin's death.

Weiss began even more vigilantly to watch for the police. As he drove east through Canton, Westland, and Dearborn, he was constantly scanning for them. Several times when he saw a police car in the distance, he turned off the road, twice getting lost.

It was just past five when he finally found his way to Jefferson Avenue in Detroit and followed it the few blocks to the Renaissance Center on the river. It was beginning to get dark, the temperature was dropping, and the wind had picked up again. He pulled into the turnaround in front of the Ren Cen and checked the line on the map. He reviewed the course and began to drive it.

He had no idea what he was looking for, but he reminded himself that in his work with every patient in every hour, he never set out searching for something in particular, rather he tried to put himself in a position where he was ready to let what was important in the patient's narrative strike him. Just like with his patients, he knew he had to let himself be surprised.

He crossed Jefferson, just north of the river, picked up Randolph which passed the Millender Center, a complex of shops and apartments, and the ribbon of development around it. Some promise here. He thought of what a promising patient Matin had seemed to him.

He came to the Wayne County Building, an ornate building with columns and elaborate capitals that reminded him of buildings he had seen in Rome. He turned left on Congress and drove the confused tangle of lanes through Cadillac Square. On the far side of the square, he turned right on Woodward.

As soon as he turned the corner, he was surrounded by the remains of old strife, the '67 riots, and then the neglect that followed. Vacant lots, strewn with litter visible through the snow, some overgrown with leafless errant bushes and scraggly trees, others lacking that and even more lifeless. There were a few struggling businesses.

Most had long since failed, their facades crumbling, boarded up for decades. These buildings and streets are waiting, just like Matin waited, just like Sonya, Dana, and I are waiting.

Gritty snow piled high at the curbs. Here and there Ivan was struck with sights of odd beauty: two surviving walls of what had been a brick apartment house looked to him like the ruins of an ancient city and distant smokestacks against the gray sky reminded him of an image in a Diego Rivera mural. Ivan felt here a past grandeur waiting to be restored.

Though there were other cars on the street, there were so few that he could easily cruise along slowly. A few homeless men, mostly black, walked the streets or were huddled in entranceways out of the wind. How can they tolerate, Weiss wondered, living in this frigid place. Men without homes. Matin, a boy searching for a home.

Having been encouraged by the shortness of the line on the map, he was now faced with the reality of real city blocks, with building after building, each packed solid with rooms. She could be in any of them. Though Matin was dead, Ivan still felt teased and tormented by him. He might be close to his daughter, but never find her. Or find her too late.

CHAPTER THIRTY SIX

D ana failed again to reach Ivan on his cell phone. She had the operator try it, still no answer. She could see the phone in Ivan's pocket or next to him on the car seat. After what Farley had said about desperate people, she had grown even more worried about Ivan and wanted with a fresh sense of urgency to reach him. She had, of course, left messages on his office answering machine, their home machine, at the Clinic, everywhere. She knew he was not going to check any of them. He was on the run and thinking only of finding their daughter. Dana choked back tears. She had lost one of her children today. It filled her with overwhelming sadness to think of losing a second. It was intolerable to think of her husband being in danger too.

"Any luck?" asked Farley, as he walked back in the office.

"No. He never remembers to recharge the damn cell phone. Or he has it turned off, I don't know. I left messages all over the place for him to call me or call here."

"Good. I sent out another bulletin on him saying that we want him for questioning, that he's not armed, not dangerous, and force should not be used."

"Thank you."

"It'll confuse the hell out of those flatfoots out there, but hopefully it'll keep them from trying anything dumb. I also put out a statewide bulletin on your daughter."

"So what do we do now?" she asked.

"Not much. I want you to tell me some more about the kidnapper . . . your son. This is a strange situation. We have a kidnapper, who worked alone, never demanded money, and now is dead. I've worked a few kidnappings. One way they crack is when the kidnappers, there are usually at least two, turn on each other. Another way is through the money, leaving marked money, or by surveillance of the money drop. But here we already know who the kidnapper is, I even met him, he's dead, there's no money involved, and the motive is hard to figure. At least hard for me. This is a whole different ball game." He had gotten so absorbed in thinking out loud, that he had not noticed Dana was barely holding herself together. He realized that each time he said anything to her, he had a way of undermining the little hope she had.

"Mrs. Weiss, look, I think we have a good chance of finding her. Think of it this way, he can't hurt her anymore, can't threaten her, and can't threaten you either. I'll go out on a limb on this, from my contact with him, I don't think he was a murderer. He was warped, he liked to toy with people, but he was not someone who kills. So the good news is she's probably alright, and she's somewhere. We don't have to deal with any kidnapper's threats anymore, we just have to find her. She is, in a way, right now just a missing person."

"It helps," she said, "to think of it that way."

"Good, so I'll get you some coffee, and you'll tell me all you can about this unfortunate young man, and maybe we can get some idea of where he might have taken her. And meanwhile we'll wait either for your husband to call or for someone to spot him. O.K.?"

"O.K."

Farley had managed, at last, to say something reassuring, but he was far from sure what he had said about Matin was true. He remembered enough from his course in forensic psychology to know that if Matin had been a psychopath, anything was possible.

*   *   *

Ivan had driven the line along Woodward Avenue to Grand Circus Park, another expansive plaza similar to ones in London or Paris. Still in rough shape, the renovation of the Detroit Opera House on the edge of the square signaled its rebirth. Just beyond it was the Fox Theater. The beautifully restored 1920's theater and several upscale restaurants near it was another island of urban renewal. Beyond the Fox, the art museum area, with science and history museums and the Detroit Public Library nearby, was yet another of these islands. Like the Ren Cen area, this all looked too good for Matin to have mapped out the terrain of his inner world. Weiss inferred from these surroundings that he had driven too far. He made a U turn and drove back to the beginning of the line.

He decided to drive the route again, but this time to circle the blocks on both sides of Woodward to give himself the best chance of noticing something, of sensing something. As he drove, he saw Sonya's little body pummeled by the waves and then saw himself running to pull her from the aggressive water. Then he saw her disappear forever. The ocean swallows her up, and he never sees her again. This is more of what Matin has managed to get me to experience. This is the hopelessness that he has left me.

It is also my own hopelessness. It is what I felt when my mother died. Reliving with Jake the day of his mother's death had cracked his certainty that he could know everything, control everything. The work with Jake had opened him to his senses, which he had used to reach Stone and was using now in his search for Sonya, but the session had also raised doubts about his own analytic powers. As he felt less the knower of everything, he feared he would never be able to find his daughter.

Weiss realized that even driving at a crawl up the empty streets meant passing too quickly to feel himself into the places along the route. It was bitterly cold now, the late afternoon light was fading, and shadows now carved up the streets. Though the area was dangerous during the day and even more so now as evening was coming on, he decided to walk the route. He had narrowed it down. He knew where the improved area near the river ended and where Grand Circus Park and the nearby gentrified Fox Theater area began. It was only eight blocks between the two. Under a mile. He tried to shorten it in his mind by thinking of how quickly he could run that distance. Under eight minute miles, under seven on a good day, it was nothing.

He parked his car on a side street off Cadillac Square in front of a boarded up drug store. The store's rusted metal sign, curled away from the wall of the building and hung precariously low under the weight of ice and snow. Now walking the frigid, desolate streets, each block seemed endless, each building filled with countless, unknown, unseen rooms. She could be in any of them. He fought to bring himself back to an attitude of openness to the surroundings, but this seemed impossibly passive right now. All he wanted to do was tear into every building and throw open every door. Until he found her.

He knew he needed to narrow down these vast eight blocks. He walked, stopped, tried to listen to what each particular place said to him, and walked again. He then drew on Jake's technique, to use all of his sensations, but especially the visual. He stopped and slowly turned around, taking in the whole 360 degrees. Across the street was a movie theater with *Big*, the Tom Hank's movie from a decade before, still on the marquee. He turned and a dank, putrid smell flowed from the entrance of a long abandoned office building. He turned again and saw two boarded up beauty supply stores covered with graffiti. Turning again, a travel agency, also obviously long since closed, with "Out to lunch, be back in a jiffy," still visible through the grimy glass door.

All abandoned businesses, all dead, all fit Matin's inner life. Weiss felt stymied. Everything from the boarded up stores to the vacant lots, from the homeless people to the burned out shells of buildings, embodied bleakness and neglect that completely fit the topography of Matin's emotional life. So how to narrow down this area that had looked so small and manageable and searchable on the map, but which was turning out to be endless?

As he stood in the frigid late afternoon, he scanned in his mind the sessions with Matin for times that were the most unrehearsed, when he revealed more of his true self. His thoughts kept returning to the beginnings of each session when Matin entered Weiss' office. The young man would enter the sessions and go straight to the window and look off into the distance. There was genuine interest, even some excitement, when he did this, when he looked out toward the horizon, to the airport for planes. People coming, people going. Weiss then thought of Matin in his satellite. Distant, yes, but not completely off in deep space, always looking back toward the earth, toward home.

Then Weiss wondered if he had been missing something important. Maybe Matin's inner world was not only bleak and hopeless. Mostly it was, but could he have in some private recess within himself maintained hope? Off there in the distance, on the horizon. Hope that this time the promise would be fulfilled. Ivan could now assemble in his mind many things that suggested this. Matin's return to Dana's life, while likely motivated by a wish to punish her, might have also expressed a hope for engagement with her. Creating the fake patient had expressed many things, but among them was a hope to be seen, to be known, to be understood. He also wanted to be appreciated by Weiss for his skill in creating his impersonation.

Hope was also expressed, perversely and dangerously, in what he had done with Sonya. He had set it up so she *might* be rescued. She might be reunited with her father and mother. By making up a dream containing clues to where he had taken her and telling it to Weiss, he held out the possibility that Ivan's, Dana's, and Sonya's wishes would all come true. At the heart of Matin's drama was the slim hope, but hope just the same, that everything would turn out alright. So, the place he had taken Sonya could not be completely without hope. It was probably a place from which something better, in the distance, on the horizon, could be seen.

Ivan thought of Matin's love of vistas, of distant scenes. He tried to find some distant view from where he was standing. There was only one. Down Woodward, past the defunct travel agency, past Cadillac Square, he saw what had been the hope for Detroit's renewal – the Renaissance Center, the last of the late afternoon sun glowing orange off its glass skin. The Ren Cen, represented by the shiny silos in Matin's dream, perhaps embodied for him, too, hope. So from this neglected place I can see something better. Ivan thought of the promises Dana had made to her son. The little boy probably could have almost tasted her being with him, yet she was agonizingly unreachable. He could see her on the horizon, like he could always see, but never reach, mother earth from his satellite.

Maybe having a view of a better place, a better life, had to be part of the landscape he had chosen. Weiss began walking the eight blocks, looking back every so often to make sure the Ren Cen was still in sight. At the end of the third block it disappeared behind a building. Weiss realized what a dramatic difference it made to stand on this empty, lifeless street when the Ren Cen was out of view. Wherever he has her must be in view of this symbol of hope.

*   *   *

"Mrs. Weiss," said Farley, putting down the phone, "we're going for a ride." As they made their way down to his police car, he told her that her husband's car had been found parked near Cadillac Square in downtown Detroit. The hood was still warm, so he was probably on foot, not far from the car. The detective explained that he wanted her with him so that if they found Ivan, she could assure him that they were not going to harm him but were there just to talk to him about Matin's death and to help him find their daughter.

*   *   *

While he was still driving the route, he had seen no police. Now on foot, a police cruiser rounded the corner and was heading toward him. He ducked quickly into an entranceway of an abandoned apartment building, tripped on the step, but managed to catch himself before he fell against the door of the building. He could hear the sound of the police car tires crunching on the icy street. The car was slowing, as it neared him. He tried the door. He felt it give so he knew it wasn't locked, but he couldn't open it. He braced his foot on the wall of the entranceway and pulled on the door's rusted handle. The molding around the door cracked, and he was showered with splinters of corroded wood. But the door opened. Just as he closed it behind him, he saw the police car stop and one of the cops in it shine a searchlight into the entranceway. Ivan ran through the abandoned building. He ran down the narrow hallway, its floor a mass of ripped, filthy linoleum, its cinderblock walls covered with grime and graffiti. The building seemed to have been low cost or government subsidized housing. Barely enough light came in through the windows of the small empty apartments for Ivan to see his way. In the low light, there was no color. He saw in his mind black and white films of Jews in ghettos in eastern Europe fleeing the Nazis. He heard again his father's warnings about the police. Ivan was suspected of murder, pursued by the police, a fugitive. My father, he thought, was right.

The hallway ran straight through the building to a back door. This one opened easily, and after checking for police, he ran out into an alley. A few homeless men stood around a fire in a steel barrel. Another, in a wheelchair, his pant legs tucked under his stumps, slowly lifted his eyes toward Ivan. The others continued staring into the fire, oblivious to Ivan and everything else. Ivan ran back to Woodward.

When he reached the street at the end of the alley, he saw police cars in both directions. He ran across the street to another alley and followed it to the next street. Now several blocks off Woodward, he was in another vacant lot. A small dilapidated camper with flat tires and a listing pickup truck stood at its center. In the dirty snow a shopping cart lay on its side with oily engine parts spilling from its basket.

A woman in a torn, stained windbreaker was working at starting a fire in a rusty grill. A teenage girl, who appeared to Weiss to have Down's Syndrome, poked her head cautiously out of the darkened door of the camper. Obviously no electricity, no water here. As bleak and depressing as Woodward was, this was far worse. He looked in the direction of the Ren Cen, but his view was blocked by the burnt out shell of an apartment house. He wouldn't have taken Sonya here, this was a place with nothing better on the horizon, no promise. Ivan's eyes met the retarded girl's. She smiled at him, and when he smiled back, she waved vigorously, letting her hand flap at the end of her arm, like a very young child would. Ivan waved to her and then ran back toward Woodward.

When he had driven through the area, it had seemed almost deserted, but now there were people everywhere. Like the woman and girl and the homeless men, they were not in full view, but as he walked they seemed to appear from nowhere. They were distracting him from his search. Panhandlers approached him on every block, a kid of no more than fifteen offered to sell him crack, and then a tall black man in an oversized Detroit Pistons jacket and wool cap was at Weiss' side.

"Yo, brother, you look like a man who could use some de-version. I got young pussy, black or white, do you right or wrong, your call."

"Whatever," said Weiss.

"Why you so agitated, my man?" said the pimp now walking backwards in front of Weiss. "I got what you need. And I got your price."

"Listen, I'm not interested. Even if it was free, I wouldn't . . ." While Ivan was talking, his eyes had been resting on a building over the pimp's shoulder, a building on the next block, across the street. Like most of the buildings he had passed, it was abandoned, but the exterior of this one was in remarkably good condition. There was something imposing and regal about this particular structure. Along with its size he was impressed with its clean, squared off, almost modern proportions, the deep redness of its brick, and block-like tower at its top. It looked solid and strong. This building didn't happen to be on the street, it presided over it. This clearly had been a grand building and if nurtured could be one again.

Then Weiss recognized the building. Everyone in and around Detroit knew it. And he knew Sonya was in it.

Ivan ran across the street.

"Hey, man, I'm not trying to rip nothin' off ya. Don't go runnin' off."

"Don't take it like that," shouted Weiss over his shoulder as he started to run. He then stopped, ran back across the street, dug some bills from his pocket and, without looking at them, stuffed them hurriedly into the baffled pimp's hand and said, "Hey, you really helped me out."

The building he had seen, that he was now running to, was the long abandoned Hudson's, the department store that had been, during the city's heyday, a landmark in downtown Detroit. Long before shopping malls, Hudson's, like Macy's in New York, was the place to go for everything. It was the hub, the center of the things. Hudson's, Weiss had read in a Detroit magazine, had once even had a fully equipped, small hospital on its top floor. Just as Woodward Avenue stood as the symbol of Detroit's decline, the long abandoned Hudson's building stood as the supreme example of the neglect of the street. There had been several proposals for its renovation into condominiums, shops, and restaurants, but each had fallen through. Proposals extended, proposals withdrawn. There had been very recently an article in the Detroit Free Press about what an amazing spectacle it would be for the building to be leveled with explosives.

The building suited Matin perfectly. An old place, once cared for and valued, which had deteriorated from years of neglect and abandonment. There was a chance for the mother city to rescue this lost child building. I will care for you, Dana had said to her son, I will love you, I will come for you, I will save you. I will reclaim you, and we will be together. Proposals extended, proposals withdrawn. A perfectly nice boy allowed, like this grand building, to decline and die.

*   *   *

"That's him!" exclaimed Dana, still over a block away from a man who had been running in their direction and then darted out of view. Still too far away to see his face, she recognized his run. Though Dana loved her husband's warmth and respected his mind, it was his compact strength, which she saw in his way of running, that had always turned her on. She felt it, too, when they made love. It had to be him.

"Got damn good eyes," said the detective.

"Yes, I guess I do," she said, a little embarrassed to be thinking about her husband's compact strength in bed.

Farley speeded up, got to the corner where the figure had disappeared, and stopped. They got out and looked around, but the only person to be seen was a tall, black man in a Pistons jacket.

A swarm of police cars from the Detroit Police Department slid to a stop on the slick street, surrounding them. Several uniformed cops got out, and Farley identified himself and quickly explained the situation, that the man they were looking for was unarmed and not dangerous, was wanted for questioning, that his daughter had been kidnapped, the kidnapper was dead, and she was very likely being held in this area.

"Listen up, I don't want this man hurt. The program now is just to find him and his daughter. His wife's here to help."

"How do we know his daughter's here?" asked the young sergeant in charge.

"Because her father's here, and we think he knows where to look."

"Got it," the young cop said and ordered four men to begin a search on foot and the others to continue patrolling by car.

Then looking at the cop's name pin, Farley said, "Steve, the most important thing is to find the girl. We don't know what kind of shape she's in, what's been done to her, so we need to find her fast. We have to find her father, too, but we're not doing a manhunt here. Let's try not to make anything worse. Maybe we can start by turning off those damn flashers."

*   *   *

After crossing the street, leaving the confused pimp behind, Weiss saw, coming toward him over a block away, another car, this one with no obvious police markings. First it moved slowly and then as it approached him, he could see from its fishtailing that the driver had suddenly accelerated. As it sped toward him, he saw that there were two people in it. A man driving and . . . was that Dana? He wanted it so much to be her that he was sure he was just imagining that it was. Too dangerous to wait and see. He ducked into an alley, and when the car passed, ran toward the abandoned department store.

Just as he reached the Hudson's block, he saw two police cars round the corner and then drive abreast toward him, no sirens, no lights. On this stretch of street there was nowhere to hide. He stopped running and tried to appear to be calmly walking. Maybe they're just on patrol, he thought. As they drew closer, he could feel, in spite of the cold, sweat pour out of him. He felt his heart pounding in his chest and heard its every beat in his ears. They drew closer. He worked to keep up an illusion of calm. They were so close now that he could see the faces of the cops in both cars. They passed, and he took a deep breath of relief.

The relief lasted only a moment. Now a single police car passed him from behind and drove up to the end of the block. Again no lights or siren. Don't panic, maybe it's following the other two cars, Ivan thought. It made a U turn and slowly approached him. Like a stealthy predator, thought Ivan. It was a half block away and was beginning to drift toward the curb. This one was on to him.

Ivan turned and broke into a run, passed Hudson's, frantically looking for somewhere to hide. He heard the police car's wheels spin on the ice and then grip. The siren screamed. He ran down the first side street he came to and then into an alley too narrow for the car. As he ran, he looked behind him and saw the police cruiser skid to a stop at the mouth of the alley, the police flashers washing the alley walls red and blue. Two cops jumped from the car and came after him. He climbed over a chain link fence halfway down the alley, and then out into a vacant lot, this one scattered with piles of debris from whatever had been demolished there. Just as he heard the running steps of the cops, he picked a pile, frantically dug through the snow at its base, and forced himself into an open space, rough edges of scrap wood and metal cutting into his skin.

He heard the cops just feet away trying to decide if he was hiding in this "shit" or if he had run out of the lot. One poked with his boot at the pile Ivan was hiding in. The other brushed snow off the other side of the pile and cast the beam of his flashlight in. The light panned around the inside of the pile and came to rest on Ivan.

He was completely illuminated. Why the hell did they choose this pile, Weiss cursed to himself. Why doesn't he see me? He knew his only hope was to lie still and try somehow to get lost in the tangle of debris. The light seemed to stay trained on him forever. He held his breath. Why isn't he dragging me out? Is he trying to torture me? Then he felt something crawling on his leg and saw the black mass of a rat beginning to chew on his pants.

"See anything?"

"Nothing except a huge mother of a rat." He's looking right at me, Ivan realized, but he doesn't see me. He's fixed on the rat. Ivan felt a moment of gratitude to the rodent for distracting the cop, at the same time as he felt it almost impossible to continue to lie still, worrying what the rat would chew once it had finished with his pants.

The cop clicked off his flashlight. "Let's move on," he said.

When the voices and footsteps faded, Ivan shook the animal off his leg and quickly clawed himself out. He ran back to the alley to catch his breath and collect his energy.

He was now a block from the department store. He could see its top floor and square tower at the end of the alley. He watched the sun glint off the store's top windows and pigeons alight on its high ledges. He imagined a time when these streets had been bustling with parents and children on outings downtown, coming and going from the store. Parents and children together. Only the pigeons come and go now. It filled him with sadness. The building was waiting to be saved. Above the roof of the store, in the distance, the Ren Cen was in clear view. He knew this would be just the place he would have taken her. He knew, dead or alive, she was still there.

He ran down the alley toward the abandoned building. Just as he poked his head out to check for police, a police car approached. He pulled back into the alley and pressed himself up against its wall. This time the car didn't even slow. He hadn't been seen. He poked his head out again, looked around, and when no police cars appeared, he ran across the street to Hudson's. Just as he got there, a cop on foot down the street spotted him.

"Hold up there!" Weiss took off. He had never run so fast. The cop was running after him. Weiss looked back at him. Young, thin, the guy can probably run. But not as fast as me. He rounded the department store's corner, ran down that street, and rounded another corner. He now saw another cop, this one coming toward him.

He ran into a driveway, all that was left of its pavement a few islands of asphalt sticking up from the dirt and snow. His foot turned, sending a shock of pain through his ankle, and he fell. His hands, which broke his fall, slipped and his face slapped on the gravelly snow.

He saw the little boy faint and fall. He felt the carpet against his cheek. He felt paralyzed, as if there were no connection between his brain that was screaming for him to get up and his unresponsive body. Still on the ground at the mouth of the alley, he looked toward the street and beyond it. The Ren Cen was in clear view. The building more than reflected the darkening sky and clouds, it contained them, it held them.

Then a calm, deliberate voice said to him, "Just get up." He looked around for its source and then realized it was his own voice. He struggled to his feet and ran past a loading dock to a rusty dumpster. A metal door, large coils of peeling paint hanging from it, stood open.

CHAPTER THIRTY SEVEN

I n the beginning of her dream her parents and Jerry were there again, still off at the periphery, still at a distance. She heard them talking but could not make out what they were saying. She thought in the dream how proud they were of her. But now, their pride was not enough. She was impatient with them. She wanted them now to come to her, to congratulate her. Yes, that's what I want. In the dream and out of the dream she rattled the pipe with her handcuff. She rattled it violently until there was a din of cacophonous clanking. She stopped banging and held her shackled hand up as if to say, "Look, do something, come here, right now, and get me out of this!" She stared at each of them and tried to draw them to her with her eyes. She then found her voice, just as she had when Paul had tried to rape her. Using it again, she screamed, "Come here! Come here!"

Her father then walked toward her in the dream. She looked into his dark, warm eyes. Helping eyes. And then she opened hers.

And he was there.

EPILOGUE

F rom the top deck, Weiss looked out at the shores of the Bosporus, as the cruiseship sailed through it. A string quartet played nearby, and the ship's horn sounded from time to time to alert small boats in its path. Dana was still down in the verandah restaurant, lingering over coffee and writing postcards. The cruise had exceeded their expectations. Luxurious cabin, elegant European service, amazing cuisine, tours of archeological sites in Ephesis and Bodrum, all interspersed with making love and long afternoon naps. Ivan was even able to run, either in several of the ports or early in the morning on deck as the ship approached the destination of the day.

Two months later, they were all still recovering. Sonya seemed to be doing the best of all. She was more settled within herself than at any time since returning from New York.

"Somehow, maybe because of what happened, I was able to redo something in myself," was all she said when Ivan commented on how well she seemed to be doing.

As Sonya and Jerry were getting to know each other better, they were discovering they had more in common and were coming to enjoy their differences. She realized that the connection she had felt with Paul, which she had wished for with Jerry, was really a feeling of a sister for a brother. Though Paul had terrorized her, she still felt sorry that his life had ended so tragically. When the last efforts to save the Hudson's building failed, she and Jerry watched its spectacular demolition on television.

Ivan awoke often to Dana crying. Her mourning had deteriorated into depression. She slept little and was so fatigued in the morning that she could barely get out of bed. She was distant from Ivan and Sonya and rarely made it out to the stable. Ivan was very worried about her and suggested she go into therapy. She did and after a few weeks told Ivan she already understood some things about herself. She had always thought she had kept her son a secret because of Ivan's mission to punish neglectful mothers. She had come to realize that she never told Ivan about Paul, because she had wanted to keep her son a secret from herself. To make believe she never had him. And never abandoned him. Also, she told him, her fear of his criticism had been hiding her own self loathing for what she had done. Working out the guilt over this, they both knew, would take time. They both also realized that this secret had always kept them from all they could have together. With the truth revealed, they were enjoying a level of ease and intimacy they never had before.

There had, of course, been an investigation of Matin's death that had been trying for everyone. Matin had done an excellent job setting up the final act in his drama at the bell tower. Farley was soon totally convinced that Matin had engineered it all as a perverse kind of suicide, a suicide, as Weiss had explained, "that held in it an accusation." But one of Farley's supervisors, who had strong town-gown grudges, promoted the theory that Weiss murdered Matin because he had abducted Weiss' daughter. Though never an indicted suspect, Weiss had to get a lawyer and was subjected to some offensive questioning, but fortunately the District Attorney could see there was no basis to pursue the case. Weiss thought, as he was going through this, that Matin would have been delighted at Weiss being questioned and suspected. That was the essence of Matin's drama – see what you have done to me, you have stolen my mother and that destroyed my life. Now you pay. It occurred to Weiss that in some secret way Matin may have also wished everything to turn out alright for Ivan and Dana and Sonya. He may have wanted to see them, against huge odds, survive, to see them have what Paul himself most wanted, the promise of a happy life fulfilled.

In spite of everything that had happened, including Paul's attempted rape of Sonya, which she told the police and her parents about, Weiss still felt sympathy for this troubled young man, who in the end was struggling with psychological wounds not of his own making. Like so many twists and turns in the development of any human being, assigning blame seemed to Ivan futile and arbitrary and to grow from a need in human beings to find a simple moral order. Was Dana, a teenager and later an immature young adult, at fault? Was Matin to blame for the rage he felt at being abandoned, rage that had turned to cruelty? Was Weiss himself to blame for making it so necessary for Dana to keep the secret which prevented her from helping her son? Weiss did not want to excuse every evil just because a psychological source could be found. At the same time, after witnessing the analyses of many people, where individual life histories are relived and examined, assigning ultimate blame had become for him almost impossible. If forced to assign responsibility for the sad end of Paul Matin's life, Ivan placed it at the feet of societies that fail to make adoptions in early infancy by good families a high priority. If such a family had been found for Paul, and found early in his life, he would likely have been one of the many adopted children who grow into satisfied and productive adults.

When Eric Hanson learned of the kidnapping, he left a series of slurred, confused messages offering to help Sonya. She responded to none of them. Soon after, Eric left for California. A few days after he arrived there, he was hospitalized for a drug overdose and remained for a week in serious condition. Jake went right out there. When Eric pulled through, he tearfully told his father that he was really scared. Not angry and demanding this time, scared. Jake saw this as a step forward for his son. Eric accepted his father's offer to come back to Michigan and live with Jake. Jake found a new, intensive drug rehab program for his son, and Eric, for the first time, seemed ready to deal with his problems.

A retired professor from Harvard, who had given several talks about Turkey during the cruise, joined Ivan at the railing. The old man pointed out to Ivan a hillside cemetery overlooking the channel where men fighting for control of the Bosporus were buried. The crosses were all in neat, exact rows, like soldiers still marching in formation. Ivan had during the cruise several good conversations with this man, most beginning with the professor saying to Weiss, "Ivan, you're a scientist of the mind . . ." This one began the same way.

"There are so many reasons why this stretch of water has been fought over for generations, access to the Black Sea and Mediterranean, for trade and military purposes, for dominance by Christian and Islamic peoples, and more. I taught a whole course on this years ago. In a way it explains all of this terrible strife. And in a way all of these explanations leave me unsatisfied." They both stood quietly for a while, listening to a particularly fine violin solo.

"Maybe," said Weiss, "greed, the need for power, and even some pleasure in attacking and killing, are part of all our natures. We find current reasons to explain why we are acting on these desires, but the real truth is that as human beings we get pleasure from them, struggle with them, come to some kind of accord with them, but at times surrender to them. Maybe the solution is to recognize that these urges are right at our very core. We need to be aware of their power and their danger." The professor combed his fingers through his hair, as they both watched the passing shore.

"I think you're right. But I wonder what makes us surrender to this darker side, what brings these aggressive feelings so much to the surface that a people will turn all of its resources, even the lives of its youth, to make war." The quartet came to the end of its piece, and the ship's horn sounded. "I know why," the professor said, answering his own question. "It's always about loss. Yes, that's it, loss. Of territory, pride, prosperity, or an old way of life remembered as better. People will behave in the most heinous and brutal ways to get any of them back. Or to punish those who have taken them away."

"I'm obviously not the only 'scientist of the mind' aboard, that's very insightful," said Ivan, thinking, of course, of the losses in Paul Matin's short life.

As the ship cruised out into the Black Sea and the sunlight flickered through the hilltop trees, Ivan patted the old man on the back, left him, and followed the deck forward where it narrowed at the ship's bow. Behind this small, isolated deck, which Ivan had discovered early in the cruise, were the darkened windows of the ship's bridge. He stood at the front of the deck and watched the ship cut through the water. He looked back at the bridge and could see the suggestion of people moving like shadows behind the smoky glass. Lights blinked on a console inside. He turned to look again at the ship slicing through the water, dividing the sea with such certainty and strength that it seemed hard to believe that moments later the waters would settle and show no sign of the ship's passing.

Ivan lay down on the only chair on the small deck, an old slatted one, the wood weathered black from the wind and sun and salt. He closed his eyes, felt the sun warm his face, and fell immediately into something that lay between a thought and a dream.

As he runs, he is bathed in sunlight, yet he feels cool, his body moving with effortless strength, his clothes loose and sensuous around him. No fatigue, no sweat. He turns the corner and sees the house with his mother's car, neatly parked in the driveway, where it belongs. He slows to a walk, and while he waits for his breathing to calm, he thinks through the various ways he can announce it to her, until he finds just the right one. He sees her see him through the kitchen window, and then, just as he gets there, the front door, like a loving welcome, opens for him. Her eyes fill with delight even before he tells her:

"We won."